YOU WOULDN'T
BE DEAD FOR QUIDS

Also by Robert G Barrett in Pan Books
THE REAL THING

YOU WOULDN'T BE DEAD FOR QUIDS

Robert G. Barrett

Pan Books Sydney and London

First published in 1985 by Waratah Press
This Pan edition published 1986 by Pan Books (Australia) Pty Ltd
68 Moncur Street, Woollahra, Sydney
9 8 7 6 5 4

© Robert G. Barrett

Barrett, Robert G.
You wouldn't be dead for quids.
ISBN 0 330 27074 5 (pbk.).
I. Title.
A823'.3

Printed and bound in Australia by
The Book Printer, Maryborough, Victoria

CONTENTS

ACKNOWLEDGMENTS

I would like to thank Ross and Helen at Coffs Harbour for giving me encouragement. Phil Abraham at *Australian Penthouse* for giving my stories a go. And the English master at Terrigal High, Mr James Tritten, for the invaluable help with my English.

DEDICATION

This is dedicated to the late Paul Turner, one of the best blokes I ever met — sadly only too briefly.

The Publisher would like to acknowledge that the author is giving 10% of his royalty earnings to Greenpeace, an organisation which he deeply respects.

You Wouldn't Be Dead for Quids

You don't have to look hard to find a lot of tough men around Sydney town, especially in the Balmain, Inner City and Eastern Suburbs area. They might be wharfies, truckies, meatworkers, ex-boxers, footballers; they might be anything you like that go towards making up the ranks of what are regarded as hard men. A lot of hard men usually end up working as bouncers somewhere, like a pub or disco, but if they're really good and they've got a bit of brains to go with the brawn there's a good chance they'll finish up on the door of an illegal casino; and while a lot of people say there's nothing too prestigious about being a bouncer, to work on the door of an illegal gambling casino is about as prestigious as you can get in the bouncing rort.

The reason is the huge amounts of money involved. In the 70s when Sydney was a real toddlin' town, the casinos were all run by very rich, very powerful men who had generally been old villains and hard boys themselves in their day. They could soon sort out a sheep from a goat and with millions of dollars in cash going through their hands, cash that had to be minded and collected, they wouldn't employ a lot of cream puffs and would-be's to do it for them. They could afford to pay enormous slings to the police and politicians to keep the casinos' operating, so they got the best protection there was in that department. Being able to pay the best wages for their heavies they only got the best men available in that department also; and the best of these was a big, red-headed ex-Queensland meatworker named Les Norton.

Actually Norton wasn't really all that big. He didn't have a great bull chest and he was just a shade under six feet. But he had good broad shoulders and a wide, powerful trunk that sometimes, especially in a tuxedo, gave him the appearance of being as wide as he was tall. However, he did have exceptionally long, thick sinewy arms covered in bristly red hairs and at the end of them dangled two massive gnarled hands, the fingers literally like Fijian bananas, the knuckles like fifty cent coins. And when he closed those two massive paws to form a fist, they looked like a couple of those Darling Downs hams you see hanging up in butcher shops around Christmas.

As far as looks go Les wasn't ugly, but he was no Robert Redford either. His scrubby red hair topped a pair of dark, brooding eyes set in a wide square face, and with his lantern jaw and the mandatory broken nose of a bouncer Les looked pretty much exactly what he was. His one outstanding feature was a pair of immensely bushy eyebrows, that caused the owner of the casino where Les worked to nickname him Yosemite Sam after a character in the Bugs Bunny show on TV. And whenever Les was about to go into action with his fists those big bushy eyebrows would bristle like the hairs on a dog's back.

As far as fighting went, Les wasn't a really scientific fighter and for all Les knew the Marquis of Queensberry could have been a hotel in Parramatta. Whenever Les went off it was anything goes, and somehow or other, possibly through his huge shoulders and those enormous bony fists, he used to develop this terrifying punching power that could literally fracture skulls and shatter jaws and ribs. It didn't take long for the word to get around the traps that if you wanted a shirt full of broken ribs and you fancied eating your meals through a straw for a few weeks, just go up and put a bit of shit on Les Norton, and Norton was afraid of no one and nothing. Except, funnily enough, dead bodies; even for an ex-meatworker he had an abhorrence of death. Photos in magazines . . . cemeteries . . . he couldn't even walk past a funeral parlour without getting an uneasy feeling in his stomach, but hardly anyone knew this.

Norton drifted into Sydney on his own around 1970, got a job as a meat-carter and settled in Bondi. He came from a little town called Dirranbandi which is on the Narran River about 70 kilometres north of the NSW border. If anyone asked, he told them

10

he'd come down to Sydney to play football but the truth was he'd killed a man in a fight back home and had to leave town and Queensland in a bit of a hurry.

A big German opal miner got full of drink one night and beat up Norton's 60-year-old father in an argument over a game of pub pool. He beat the old boy up pretty bad too — put the boot in and all, then swaggered and snorted around the pub offering on all comers. The locals didn't say much; they just picked the old boy up, wiped the blood off him, had a bit of a chuckle to themselves and took him home. The barmaid didn't say much either; she just cleaned up the mess, looked at the big German still strutting round the bar, shook her head slowly and said, 'Oh dear, oooh dear.'

They found him early the next morning lying in a pool of blood at the bottom of the fire escape outside the hotel he was staying in. His neck was broken, that and a few other things. The local police sergeant put it down to death by accident: he'd got drunk and fallen down the stairs, but he told Les it might be a good idea if he got right out of town and Queensland for a while — out of sight, out of mind.

So Les left the wide open spaces of Queensland, which he loved, and finished in the crowds and smog of Sydney, which he hated. He had a run with Easts and they offered him a contract and it wasn't long before they had him in first grade as an enforcer. He was no ball distributing genius and as raw as a greyhound's dinner but he wouldn't take a backward step and if he had to Les would tackle the grandstand.

Not that Les was all that rapt in playing football. The games themselves he didn't mind. It was all the training and team preparation that gave Les the shits. And after lumping bodies of beef on and off meatwagons all day from five o'clock in the morning, all Les wanted to do when he knocked off was have two schooners, a slice of rump with plenty of vegies and put his head down for about eight hours. The idea of four hours of jogging, sprints, weightlifting and sit-ups four nights a week plus ball work and a team lecture thrown in afterwards didn't wash too well with Norton at all. But the money was all right and it kept his mind off back home, plus the club gave him a couple of good track suits and other training gear and being a man of simple tastes this appealed to him so he put up with it. However,

11

Norton's football career came to an abrupt end at the leagues club one Sunday night after a game against St George.

Saints had brought out this gigantic Maori forward named Henry Outanga. Henry wasn't too bright but he was built like a Russian war memorial and had a head like a bag of cement. He was St George's hit-man, their enforcer, and there wasn't a player in Sydney that wasn't a bit toey of big Henry. Henry knew this and he loved it. He was having a wonderful time belting everyone on and off the field and he was getting away with it. Henry hadn't played against Les yet.

Saints also had this enigmatic coach called Ron Massey who was a genius at psyching players up: he could get an eight stone halfback and convince him he was Muhammed Ali. Just before the Easts game he pulled Henry aside in the dressing room.

'Listen Henry,' he said, his face about two inches away looking Henry directly in the eyes. 'This is what I want you to do and you're the only bloke that can do it.'

'What's that?' Henry's eyebrows knitted and beads of sweat started to form on his forehead as he tried to concentrate.

'I want you to take the ball up and keep hitting them hard, hard all the time okay.'

'Okay.'

'But above all I want you to stop their number ten, a big redheaded bloke with big bushy eyebrows. You can't miss him. He's been saying how he's gonna stick it right up you Henry cause he hates Maoris. In fact I want you to take him right out of the game if you can. You reckon you can do it?'

Henry snorted, spat on the floor and slammed a massive fist into the palm of his other hand. 'Can I do it,' he fumed. 'I'll go over him like a fuckin' lawnmower, the cunt.'

The coach smiled and put his arm around Henry's big shoulders. 'Good on you, Henry,' he said. 'You're gonna have a big year in Sydney.'

They kicked off and the game had been going about 15 minutes when Les made a bit of a break. He turned in a tackle to get the ball away and just as he did Outanga came across and hit him with a stiff arm that was heard all over the ground. It sounded like a falling tree landing and it knocked Les fair on the seat of his pants. As he went to get up Henry stomped on his hand and gave him a knee in the side of his head as well. The referee didn't see who did it but Les did. The Zambuck ran on and cleaned Norton up as the game continued. A few minutes later they formed a scrum which Easts won.

The ball went out to the back line and as the players broke from the scrum to go to their positions Henry felt a tap on the shoulder. He turned slowly around and as he did Norton drove a straight right with every ounce of strength in his body straight into Henry's big, black face. It was horrible. It hit Henry like a wrecking ball, nearly breaking Les's forearm. Even Henry's relations back in Rotorua felt it. As he slumped to his knees Norton slammed a left hook into his jaw and that was the end of big Henry. He went straight to Disneyland. So much for Henry's big year in Sydney. He spent the rest of the season sitting on the sideline with his jaw wired up blowing his nose out the back of his head. Unfortunately the referee saw who did it this time and Les got an early shower.

With their best tackler off the field the rest of the Easts forwards didn't fancy having to do a bit of work for a change so they turned it up and the team lost, by a wide margin. Subsequently Les got the blame.

Up in the gloomy atmosphere of the leagues club that night Les was in the Tricolour Bar having a reluctant drink with his team mates when the club secretary, a drunken fat-bellied old prick at the best of times, decided to make a big man of himself and put Norton on show.

'You bloody big hillbilly,' he yelled at Les. 'We brought you down from shitty Queensland, you didn't even have a pair of shoes on your bloody feet. We pay you big money, big money and what do you do, turn round and cost us the game.' He took another pull on his scotch and dry and turned around to make sure everyone was listening. They were, but with apprehension not amusement.

'You're a mug son, a proper bloody mug, you know that.' Norton looked into his beer, quietly sipping it and trying not to take too much notice. The club secretary slurred on and on and then decided to start poking his fingers into Norton's chest.

'If I had my way,' he slobbered, raising himself up to his full five foot six, 'if I had my way I'd piss you off back to bloody stinken Queensland where you come from. What do you think of that, you goose?' '

He stepped back from Les and glared at him, then glanced round the room. He was putting on a terrific act and getting away with it, half full of free drink and in his glory.

If the club secretary had had any brains he would have let it go at that. He'd made his point and he'd made an undeserved fool out of Les. But no, he had to give Les one more verbal.

'What's the name of that shitpot little town you come from in Queensland?' he asked Les scornfully. 'It starts with a D don't it? Dubbo, yeah that's it. Dubbo. Funny I always thought Dubbo was in NSW but looking at you it seems I was wrong.' He threw back his head and roared with drunken laughter. 'Dubbo must be in bloody Queensland.'

That was enough for Norton. He shook his big head slowly from side to side as he looked into his beer. That was making the cup of tea just a bit too strong for Les. So he let go a short crisp backhander that travelled no more than eighteen inches but sent the top half of the club secretary's false teeth sailing across one side of the room, to land in a skinny-legged blonde football groupie's Bacardi and Coke, and the club secretary sprawling over several chairs and tables on the other side of the room to land at the feet of some Bellevue Hill Jews who were feverishly pumping coins into a 20¢ poker machine. They had a quick look and continued playing.

A couple of blue coats, the club's bouncers, come storm-troopers, heard the commotion and came charging in, hoping it was an old pensioner or a drunk playing up and they could have dragged him into the lift and beat the shit out of him. But when they saw it was Norton they screeched to a halt so quickly their heels burnt a hole in the carpet.

Norton finished his beer in a swallow and placed the glass lightly on the nearest table. He looked at the club secretary lying under the poker machines. 'Fuck you, you old shit,' he said. Then turned and glared at everyone else in the room as well, 'and fuck the rest of you too.' Then taking his car keys out of his pocket he turned and walked defiantly out of the room. The two blue coats finally made a move. They saw Les coming towards them and parted like the Red Sea.

They tore up Les's contract first thing the next morning. They barred him from the club. They barred him from ever playing football for Easts again. They even barred the other players from associating with him or even mentioning his name. If they could have they would have barred Les from jogging along Campbell Parade and having a swim at Bondi. But Les didn't really give a stuff, he'd finished with a few dollars in his kick, he didn't have to go through all that punishing training any more and he still had his track suits and gym gear. What more could a man ask for?

A fortnight or so after Norton's demise from grace at the leagues club he was having a work-out in a gymnasium at Coogee called Gales Baths. The place had been there about 40 years and was famous for it's hot sea water baths and their therapeutic value. It was now run by a gregarious fitness fanatic called Les Morrow and was a gathering place for most of the footballers and sportsmen in the Eastern Suburbs. It was also frequented by members of the racing fraternity, their hangers-on and lots of other blokes who didn't appear to have steady jobs but always managed to have plenty of folding stuff in their 'sky rockets' and liked to drop in for a game of handball and a hot sea water bath every now and again. Consequently quite a bit of the talking at Gales Baths was done in whispers and out the side of the mouth. But it was a big, bright airy place with plenty of atmosphere and since Les Morrow had taken over and done the place up it was arguably the best gym in Sydney.

It was late one Saturday morning. Les was circling a heavy punching bag like a hungry tiger shark and giving it absolutely heaps. He was super fit now from all the football training, his stamina was nothing short of amazing and you could have scrubbed overalls on his stomach. Now that he could train to suit himself Les enjoyed it more and would put plenty into it. Today was no exception. The punching bag weighed over 90 pounds but to watch Les walloping it you would think it was an old pillow case full of duck feathers.

Leaning against the counter at the front of the gym was Les Morrow and a group of punters. It was a bit on the cool side and they were huddled around a radiator, studying the form and listening to Ken Callender's racing show on a small transistor radio. Every now and again Norton would land a combination of punches on the bag that would echo all over the gym. They'd look up from their yellow form guides, absently watch Norton for a moment, then look at each other, smile and shake their heads.

15

Each knew what the other was thinking. How would you like to walk into a couple of those?

Also watching Les from the other side of the room was an ex-boxer named Billy Dunne. Billy had held the Australian middle-weight title and was a pretty good pug in his day, but he'd given prize fighting away for the last six or so years and had worked on the door of the Kelly Club, a well-established gambling casino in Kings Cross. Billy had formed a sort of an acquaintanceship with Norton down at Gales Baths and frequently, if they happened to be in the gym together, they would put the gloves on and have a bit of a move around. He even managed to get Les over to the Coogee Bay Hotel for a couple of quiet beers now and again. Billy realised Les was no Danny Kaye in the personality department but basically he was a pretty good bloke. He was as honest as the day is long and at times did have that dry outback sense of humour. But there were two things about Les, Billy knew for sure: he could punch like dynamite and fight like a bag of cats.

Norton had finished his work-out and was sitting on a bench, sweat dripping everywhere and wisps of steam rising off his big red head when Billy walked over, sat next to him and started up a bit of a conversation. At first he talked about nothing in particular, horses, football, the weather — then he got round to telling Les how his offsider on the door of the Kelly Club was leaving and would Les be interested in the job.

'Ahh, I don't know about this bouncin' caper,' said Les, shaking his head.

'I'm tellin' you Les, it's as easy as shit.'

'Mmmh, how much a week?'

'Eighty-five a night in your hand, four nights a week.'

'Yeah?'

'Yeah, but listen, that's nothing. The boss has got a heap of good race horses and he always gives you the drum when they're goin' and I'll tell you what,' Billy drew a bit closer to Norton and got right into his ear. 'If he has a good win at the punt it's nothing for him to come over and drop five hundred in your kick, and he has plenty of good wins.'

'Mmmh, it sure sounds all right. How come your mate's leavin'?'

'He's bought a motel up the north coast. One of his kids has got asthma so he's goin' up there to live.'

Norton stroked his chin and looked into the pool of sweat forming at his feet. 'It sure sounds all right,' he said thoughtfully.

'Look,' said Billy, 'why don't you come up the club tonight about nine o'clock when it's still a bit quiet and have a yarn to the boss, he's a terrific bloke. You'll like him.'

Norton paused for a moment or two. 'Yeah, righto,' he finally said.

'Beauty,' Billy slapped Norton on the leg and got up all smiles. 'I'll see you tonight then, nine o'clock.'

'Yeah, righto, see you then.' Norton contemplated the pool of sweat at his feet for a while and finally shrugged his shoulders. Oh well, he thought to himself, I don't suppose it can be any worse than lumpin' beef.

The Kelly Club isn't hard to find, it's in Kelly Street, Kings Cross, which is how it got its name. There's a pale blue light out the front with a white neon sign above it saying Kelly Club. Besides that it's just a few hundred yards up from the police station and if you still can't find it just go in and ask the desk sergeant. He'll do everything but draw you a map. Norton was there at nine o'clock sharp. Billy was waiting out the front for him all smiles; he introduced Les to the doorman whose place he'd be taking and took him upstairs to meet the boss.

The Kelly Club was owned and run by a distinguished, silvery haired gentleman in his late 50s by the name of Price Galese and everybody liked him, a lot of people loved him and women absolutely adored him. He was the epitome of a gentleman, dressed superbly and with a string of champion racehorses cut a very dashing figure around the racetracks of Sydney. He contributed heavily to charity and other welfare groups. He also contributed to the welfare of a lot of police and politicians in NSW as well. Consequently in almost ten years the Kelly Club had never been raided once, but then again according to the Commissioner of Police at the time it didn't exist anyway.

Billy led Les through a large room full of green beige tables and pretty girls in evening gowns to a mirror-panelled office with 'Private' written on a door in the front. He knocked lightly and ushered Les in. Price Galese was seated behind a large mahogany desk counting a stack of $50 bills Evel Knievel couldn't have jumped over. He stood up when he saw Les and shook his big hand warmly, told him to sit down and offered him a drink,

17

which he declined, offered him a coffee which he accepted and in about five minutes had a very nervous Les Norton feeling relaxed and completely at ease.

He explained to Les about the job, the money, the hours and what was expected of him. He chatted to him about one or two other things and finally told him that if he could be there by eight next Wednesday there would be a tuxedo waiting for him and he could start. Norton said that was fine by him, so Galese walked him to the office door, shook hands with him once more, reminded him to give Billy his measurements before he went and that was about it. Out the front of the club the two bouncers shook hands with Les once more, the one that was leaving wished him all the best, then they waved a slightly mystified Les Norton off into the gaudy neon Kings Cross night.

Norton started without a hitch bang on time the following Wednesday night and as far as Les was concerned it was without a doubt the easiest money he'd ever earnt in his life. Naturally enough he felt a bit incongruous at first standing around in bow tie and tuxedo.

'Have a look at me, Billy,' he wailed. 'I stick out like a pug nose in Jerusalem.'

'No you don't,' said Billy. 'You just look like a 20 stone penguin.'

But Billy soon introduced him to all the regular clientele and Les soon noticed that apart from being an obviously well-heeled lot there were also a lot of faces he'd seen on TV and in the papers from both sides of the law, and apart from that he began to notice something else. All the people who came there had a certain respect for Billy and before long it seemed to be rubbing off on him. The Kelly Club was an honest, well-run place and it was a good class of people went through the door. They only came there to gamble, have a few drinks, meet their friends and socialise in general. They were always polite and courteous on the way in and out and never treated him like a thug or a moron working on a door: instead they gave him the impression — especially if he would escort someone up to their car if they had a big win — that they were glad Billy and he were there. It was almost a feeling of job satisfaction.

'One thing's for sure,' he thought to himself one night, as he watched one of Sydney's leading barristers escort a beautiful blonde model up the stairs, wearing a tight-fitting black dress with a split up the side that showed enough of a sensational pair of legs to make Billy Dunne try to bite a lump out of the front door, 'this dead set shits on cartin' beef.'

Now and again Norton would go upstairs and move unobtrusively around the tables...a smile here a nod there...and Price Galese would watch him from the other side of the room. He liked Norton's style — quiet, confident and for a big man he moved very lightly. On a crowded night he would weave his way gingerly through the people so they would scarcely know he was there. He was very pleased with Billy Dunne's choice for a new doorman but one thing was on the back of his mind: I wonder if he can fight as well as Billy makes out. He didn't have to wait that long to find out.

The first occasion was late one relatively quiet Thursday night. Les and Billy were standing idly out the front of the club talking about nothing much in particular when the buzzer above their heads, which was installed to sound if there was any trouble inside, started up like it was going to fly off the wall.

Norton put his hand on Billy's shoulder, 'Stay here mate. I'll sort it out,' he said. 'If I need any help I'll give you a yell.' And took off up the stairs.

Inside was complete pandemonium. A gigantic Yugoslav, well over six and a half feet tall and around 18 stone had erupted, and being egged on by a mate almost equally as big, was doing his best to wreck the place. He was about $12,000 down and about 40 bourbon and Cokes up when he started going crazy.

He'd completely overturned the baccarat table and tried to choke the dealer. Two waitresses and another dealer who had tried to pull him off were sent sprawling over the roulette table along with half a dozen patrons, plus all the chips and the roulette wheel. He'd just put his fist through a card table, flattened two people who didn't get out of the way quick enough and now he wanted to take on all comers, the owner in particular. There were cards, plastic chips and money everywhere, women were screaming and a lot of men were starting to look the colour of bad shit when Norton arrived at the top of the stairs like a Harrier jump jet.

He paused for a second to survey the carnage around him. He could see that the bigger bloke doing all the damage was being egged on by his mate so he figured he'd take him out the way first then start on his mate. He caught Galese's eye and shot him a glance as if to say, sorry about what's going to happen but this is what your paying me for, then moved towards the first troublemaker.

As he got to him he bent slightly at the knees and drove his right fist up into his solar plexus smashing every bit of air out of his body in one screaming gasp. He stepped back and drove a devastating left into his face followed by a short wicked right to the temple which sent him crashing to the floor, paralysed and sobbing with pain, blood streaming down one side of his face, the white bone shining like ivory through the gaping slit that had been his eyebrow.

The big Yugoslav who was doing all the damage turned around just in time to see his mate hit the deck and with a roar of rage he charged at Norton like a maddened bull, tackling him round the waist, his sheer weight and power forcing Les backwards, scattering the people behind him like tenpins and smashing Les up against a wall. Only that Les managed to take most of the impact on his arms and legs, it would have broken his neck.

Bracing himself against the wall, Norton raised his right arm and despite the awkward position he was in started pounding the giant Yugoslav's kidneys with his elbow. The big man let out a scream of pain and released his grip from around Norton's waist. Les grabbed him by the front of his jacket, raised him up to eye level and smashed two vicious head butts into his face, the first one squashed his nose like a ripe fig with a sickening crunch that was heard all over the casino, the second one moved it about four inches across his face. Most of the women turned away in horror, the men stood there wide-eyed and slack-jawed. Nobody moved.

The big Yugoslav started to buckle at the knees. Still holding his jacket with his left hand, Norton drew back his massive right fist and said through clenched teeth: 'Bad luck about your front teeth, pal, but you didn't really want 'em all that much, did you?'

Then with an evil gleam in his eye and all his shoulder behind it he drove a murderous short right straight into the big Yugoslav's mouth, mashing his lips to a crimson pulp and shattering his teeth, two or three were torn completely out of the gums and fell plip, plop on the floor.

Completely unconscious now, the big man hit the floor about two seconds after his teeth and landed next to his mate. Norton reached down, grabbed the pair of them by the hair and banged their heads together, once, twice, paused for a moment then gave them a third one for luck. Letting go of their hair he took them both by the scruff of the neck, dragged them over to the top of the stairs and called out to Billy Dunne at the door below. 'Hey Billy, couple of blokes here want to see you,' and flung them bodily down the stairs.

Rubbing his hands together, Norton turned and adjusted his bow tie and as everybody stepped back quickly to let him through, he walked briskly over to Price Galese who was standing there blinking.

'I'm sorry about the ruckus Mr Galese,' he said. 'But I don't think there was any other way I could get those two out of the place. Anyway they're gone and I don't think they'll be back tonight,' he added simply.

Galese took Norton assuredly by the arm. 'That's all right, Les. Don't worry about it, that's the only way to treat mugs like that. Come here for a sec.' Taking a monogrammed pure silk handkerchief out of the top pocket of his $600 suit he led Les over to the office.

'Here,' he said handing the handkerchief to Les, 'best you wipe the blood of your face.'

'Blood.' Norton touched his face and looked surprised. 'That's funny,' he said, 'I don't remember getting hit.'

'Don't worry Les, I'm sure not one drop of it's yours.'

Later that evening a concerned Billy Dunne came upstairs and took Price Galese quietly aside for a moment.

'You know who that was that Les pelted down the stairs earlier don't you?' he said.

'Yeah, that silly big Iron Bar Muljak,' replied Galese.

'There could be a little bit of trouble there.'

'You think so?'

'Maybe.'

'Well, I might just send him a get well card through the week.'

'Good idea.'

A few days later they took Iron Bar Muljak out of intensive care and put him in a public ward. They wired his jaw up and replaced as many teeth as they could; they couldn't do much for

21

his nose, but they put it back as best they could somewhere near the middle of his face. His kidneys would be all right, they told him, in a few weeks and the other good news was that his skull was only slightly fractured, in six places. He was propped up in bed with all his tubes and drips and other odds and ends hanging out of him, still trying to figure out what happened and attempting to get a view out the window through two enormous black eyes when he got a couple of visitors. Only these visitors didn't bring any flowers or chocolates. They brought advice.

They advised Iron Bar that if he knew what was good for him he wouldn't go near the Kelly Club or the Cross for about 20 years, and any ideas he had about a sneak square-up with Norton, he could forget too. Price Galese might have been a wonderful old chap to a lot of people but if you crossed him, you either finished up under about six feet of tarmac watching the planes come in and out of Mascot, or you went swimming, about five miles off Sydney Heads with a couple of car batteries for swim flippers. Nothing eventuated.

The second time Price got to see Norton go off was late on a fairly busy Saturday night. He was parked directly across the street from the Kelly Club talking to a member of State Parliament in the back seat of Price's Rolls-Royce so he got a ringside view of the action.

An American karate champion, Chuck Wallace, was in Australia making a martial arts movie. Chuck was no slouch in the fighting department. He'd been United States champion twice and he was still one of the best in the world, but the booze, the babes, the money and the cocaine had got to Chuck and now that he was a half-baked movie star, he had to have his hangers-on and he loved to show them how good he was.

Chuck's favourite trick was starting fights with bouncers. He would go up to the door of a club or disco or whatever, pretend to be drunk and try to get in, inevitably he'd get knocked back. Then he'd get a bit more boisterous and cheeky until the bouncer would finally put the arm on him and tell his to piss off. The next thing you knew some poor unsuspecting doorman would find himself flying through the air and getting kicked and punched all over the street, and with his stooges egging him on Chuck didn't show much mercy. He'd given out some awful hidings and the more he did it the more he liked it. He'd had a dream run so far but it came to a dismal end the Saturday night Chuck and his hangers-on stumbled across the Kelly Club.

Les and Billy were standing out the front watching a couple of hookers having an argument up the road when Les asked Billy if he was hungry.

'Yeah, to tell you the truth I am a bit,' replied Billy.

'You fancy a couple of George's shasliks?'

'Ohh, mate, I'd kill for one of George's shasliks right now.' George was a Greek who ran a take-away food bar across the road from the Crest Hotel and just round the corner from the Kelly Club. He always looked after the boys, gave them extra-big serves and no matter how busy he was he'd always serve them straight away so they could get back to work.

'How many you want?' asked Les.

'Two, and an orange juice. Here, you want the money?'

'No, I'll get 'em. You get 'em next time. I'll be about five minutes. You be right here?'

'Yeah, sweet. Just keep away from those two molls on the corner.'

Norton smiled and turned quickly off up the street. He'd just got round the corner when up weaved Chuck Wallace putting on his drunk act, his hangers-on about 50 feet down the road.

Chuck looked exactly like what he was, a visiting Californian. He had on blue denim jeans, a blue denim shirt, cowboy boots and enough turquoise and silver to fill a Spanish armada. He lurched drunkenly up to Billy, his thumbs hooked in the front of his jeans.

'Hey, muscles, what's the story? You gonna let me in here or what, baby?'

Billy looked at him and smiled good naturedly. 'Sorry, baby, I can't let you in with jeans on, and I think you've had a few, haven't you?'

'Had a few what, man, a few screws, a few tokes, a few snorts, what?'

'A few too many drinks old son. I'll tell you what. You go home, get a pair of pants and sober up a bit and we'll see about letting you in then eh, fair enough?'

Wallace took a quick look over his shoulder and winked at the hangers-on from the film crew. They were standing there grinning, waiting for the action to start. He started towards Billy.

23

'Man, I'm coming into your goddam place whether you like it or not.'

Billy put his hand out and gently pushed the American back. 'Come on matey,' he said. 'Don't be silly and don't get yourself hurt.'

Wallace dropped the drunken act and stepped back. 'You're the one that's gonna get hurt, cocksucker,' he hissed. And with that he drove a side thrust kick into the unsuspecting Billy Dunne's chest, the heel of his cowboy boot cracking two of Billy's ribs. Billy grunted with pain as Wallace followed up with a right hook kick to the side of his face and a back fist to the other side. Billy was stunned. There was nothing he could so. He clutched his broken ribs with his right hand, tried to ward off the punches and kicks with his left. Wallace had him pinned up against the wall helplessly and was raining kicks all over Billy, laughing sadistically the whole time.

The hangers-on had edged forward a bit for a better view, urging the American on and laughing their heads off at the beating Billy was taking when Norton strolled nonchalantly around the corner gnawing at a shaslik through the open top of a paper bag. As soon as he saw what was going on he dropped the food and drinks and ran towards his helpless mate.

'Hey, what the fuck's goin' on here?' he yelled.

One of the hangers-on saw him coming and screamed out, 'Hey, watch out behind you, Chuck!'

The American left Billy and spun round to face the enraged Norton charging down the street towards him.

'Well what have we got here?' he sneered, 'bad guy number two, come to poppa motherfucker.'

He faced side on to Norton in a typical fighting karate stance and as Les got within range he fired out what was probably the best kick he'd ever thrown in his life. It was a ripper, the side of his foot turned slightly in, the heel out, and it went out in a perfect straight line about a hundred miles an hour, full of power and venom. Perfect.

Unfortunately, they should have warned Chuck about two things when you're street fighting in Australia. Never fight in high-heeled shoes and always watch out for dog shit on the footpath. And that's what brought him undone: as he threw the kick he skidded just slightly in about a medium-sized dog's turd and what should have been the kick of the year just missed Norton's face by about half an inch. Chuck was suddenly in an awful lot of bother.

Norton grabbed the cuff of the American's Rodeo Drive designer jeans and flipped him straight up on his back. It was so quick he never had a chance to break his fall and his head hit the footpath. Stars spun before his eyes. As he scrambled to get up Les crouched slightly and drove a short, powerful right straight into his face. The Yank's nose filled with blood, his eyes filled with water and 20 years of martial arts training went straight out the window. Norton's adrenalin was starting to pump now.

He picked Wallace up by his shirtfront and slammed him backwards into the wall of the Kelly Club. Two left hooks thundered into his face followed by a lethal short right that pulverised his left ear. He started to slide down the wall of the club. As he did Les brought his knee straight up into his balls. Wallace let out a scream of pain and pitched forward on his hands and knees on to the footpath. The only thing that saved him from complete unconsciousness was his physical fitness and the fact that he had all those years of martial arts training behind him. An ordinary man would probably have been in a coma by now.

Norton paused for a moment to look at the blood-spattered, prostrate Wallace lying at his feet, then turned and walked over to Billy Dunne who was still crouched against the wall of the club, holding his ribs. He put his arm under him and helped him gently to his feet.

'You all right?' he asked.

'I've been a lot fuckin' better,' Billy replied painfully.

'What happened anyway? I was only gone five minutes.'

Billy told him briefly what had happened. Norton didn't say anything, he just stood there for a moment stroking his chin thoughtfully, then turned and walked back to the American who was still on his hands and knees making little animal noises, blood still dripping off his face on to the dirty grey cement footpath.

'Y'know,' he said, 'I was watchin' you as I was comin' down the street, you're not real bad with those kicks are you?' Les started to laugh. 'I used to do a bit of kickin' myself once but it was a bit different to that, anyway here's one I used to do. This is called kickin' for touch.'

Saying that, Les stepped back, swung his right leg and punted Wallace straight in the face like a football, flipping him completely over on his back in a shower of blood, teeth and pieces of lip and gums. He landed in among some old metal garbage tins, out like a light. The hangers-on stood there horrified, not moving; they couldn't believe their eyes.

Ignoring them Les walked back to Billy and put his arm round him. 'Come on mate,' he said. 'I'll give you a hand up the stairs.'

'Thanks Les.'

'S'pose you'll duck down to St. Vincent's and get them to take a look at you.'

'Yeah, I think I got a couple of broken ribs.'

'Your mouth don't look too good either.'

'I got a few loose teeth.'

'Then you probably won't want your two shasliks, will you?'

Billy winced and spat a gob of blood on to the footpath. 'If nobody else wants them, Les, they're all yours.'

'Thanks mate.'

From the back seat of the Rolls parked directly opposite Price Galese and the member of State Parliament had silently watched the entire performance, fascinated.

'I say, Price,' the State member finally said, 'he's quite a willing lad, that chap of yours. What's his name?'

'Les, Les Norton,' replied Price smiling. 'Yes, he's a hard man all right, a hard man.'

The headlines in Monday morning's papers said that visiting American actor and martial arts champion, Chuck Wallace, suffered several fractures when he was knocked down by a hit-and-run driver at Kings Cross in the early hours of Sunday morning. All his filming engagements had been cancelled and he would be flying straight back to America as soon as he was released from hospital. The producers and directors were most upset and offered Chuck and all his fans their sympathy, but not everyone was sorry. Actors Equity were quite pleased really. They didn't want the Yank out here in the first place. But that's show biz.

They were the first two of Les's fights that Price Galese saw. There were others, but nothing really worth mentioning: a back-hander here, a left hook there, but it didn't take long for Norton's reputation as 15 stone of red haired, steppin' dynamite, with a very short fuse, to get around. However, Les's reputation as a streetfighter was matched by only one thing, his reputation for his meanness with a dollar bill. When it came to releasing money, Les was tighter than a goldfish's arse. If Norton earnt $400 for the week he'd bank $450, the girls in the Kelly Club said he used to take his money up to the Governor-General every pay day and have it stamped never to be released, and Billy Dunne swore he called round to Les's place one day and found an empty toothpaste tube in a vice in his garage. He also claimed they had a shout in a pub once and when Les pulled a $10 bill out his wallet Henry Lawson started blinking at the light.

But Les's philosophy was simply. Why spend it if you don't have to? It was the same with clothes. Apart from his two tuxedos at the Kelly Club and the track suits he'd got from Easts, Norton's wardrobe was as bare as a Scotchman's knee; when and if Les ever went out he looked like an unmade bed. Despite this Les did have one peculiarity, he once forked out almost $300 for a pair of boots.

Being an old Queensland country boy Les loved his R. M. Williams riding boots, as most country people do. They're comfortable, they go with just about anything and if you're a bouncer, the reinforced toe comes in very handy if you have to do a bit of Balmain folk dancing up and down someone's ribcage. But the boots that cost Les all the money, he had made in Mexico. A Qantas flight steward named Tommy Butterworth used to come down the Kelly Club for a punt now and again and sometimes he used to wear these calf-length iguana lizard-skin boots he had made in Mexico City. As soon as Norton saw them he had to have a pair. So the next time Tommy got a trip to Mexico he took a pair of Les's R. M. Williams with him for the bootmaker to go on and brought Les back his brand new boots. They ended up costing Les $290 and the night Billy Dunne saw Les cheerfully pay Tommy all that money for a pair of what to him were just cowboy boots, he had to have two Bex powders, a cup of tea and lie down in Price's office for a little while.

But they were a beautiful pair of boots. Entirely hand-crafted from the softest, dark green iguana lizard skin, the inside lined with matching silk, a slight high heel balanced perfectly for comfortable walking, zippered for easy removal and with a delicate western pattern stitched into the toes, they were almost a work of art. They fitted like a second skin and were without a doubt the softest, most comfortable pair of boots Les had ever worn in his life, and he loved them. Those boots meant more to Les than the Shroud of Turin and the Crown Jewels rolled into one. He cleaned them, polished them, nursed them and at Les's hands those boots got more care and pampering than a royal baby.

Naturally enough, being on his feet just about everywhere he went, those boots would come in for a fair bit of wear and tear and would have to be half-soled and heeled now and again. Of course Les wouldn't let just any run-of-the-mill bootmaker handle his precious boots: whenever they needed attention he would take them to a Jewish family of shoemakers in Bondi Junction, Solomon Coos and Sons. They specialised in hand-made boots and shoes and catered for all the show-business people, and people in general who didn't care how much they paid for a top quality pair of shoes. Price Galese got his shoes made there and Les got to know the son, who was a bit of a playboy, from when he came down the Kelly Club. The old man got to know Les and being a shoemaker from the old school in Europe he would always admire the leather and craftmanship that had gone into Les's boots. He'd personally repair them and only charge a pittance for the work involved.

Les had left his boots in for repair and had to pick them up one busy Saturday morning. Saturday morning in Bondi Junction is madness, there's people and cars everywhere, and after working late Friday night Norton wasn't in the best of moods when he double parked outside Coos' shoe store in Oxford Street and ran inside to pick up his boots.

Solomon Coos was standing at the counter when Les burst in. As soon as he saw Les his face lit up in a big smile.

'Ah my friend the bouncer,' he said. 'And how is Mister Bouncer this morning?'

'Tired and in a hurry, Sol,' replied Les.

'In a hurry, you young people are always in a hurry.'

'Yeah, well I'm double parked and it's swarming with friggin' brown bombers out there,' Les jerked his head towards Oxford Street. 'Me boots ready?'

'Yes, my friend Les, they're ready.' He reached under the

28

counter and got Les's boots. 'There you go, half-soled and heeled. I did them myself.'

Les inspected his boots carefully and ran his big hands gently over them. 'Yeah, they look all right, what do I owe you?'

'For you Les, how much?' The old shoemaker shrugged his shoulders, smiled and made a magnanimous gesture with his hands: 'Five dollars.'

'Fair enough,' replied Les and fished a crisp $10 bill out of a battered wallet.

'Your son had a big win last night,' he said as he waited for the change.

'My son had a big win, my son doesn't turn up for work this morning, my son is a shit.'

'Oh I dunno,' replied Les as he pocketed the change. 'It is Saturday... maybe he's turned religious. See ya.' He winked and sped out of the shop.

He placed his boots, which Sol had put in a plastic bag, gently next to him on the front seat of the car and joined the smoky, noisy crawl of traffic heading up Oxford Street. He'd got about half a mile when a car pulled out in front of him. Les stopped, threw his old Ford into reverse and quickly backed into the vacant space. Finding a parking in Bondi Junction on Saturday morning is like winning the Lottery. Les had his gas and power bills in the glove box so he thought he may as well get them out of the road and save himself a trip up through the week. It would only take a few minutes.

He took the bills out of the glove box and sped off in the direction of the gas company. He didn't bother to lock the car. He would only be a minute or two.

There was hardly anyone in the gas company office so he was in and out pretty smartly, but in the power company it was a different story, the queue was about a mile long and the cash register was playing up. Oh well, he thought, I'm here now I may as well wait. He suffered in silence, eventually getting to the counter. A team of spaced-out New Zealanders held him up the last few minutes. They couldn't believe that just because they hadn't paid their light bill for two months the company would turn the power off. Another minute and Norton would have booted the lot of them right in the arse, but he finally got his bill paid and darted out the door. He grabbed a 40¢ delicious apple

29

off a barrow out the front, paid the bloke and trotted back to his car.

He jumped in, threw the receipts in the glove box and went to start the engine when he noticed something. His boots weren't on the front seat where he'd left them. Frowning, he ran his hands down the sides and under the front seat; they weren't there. He swivelled round quickly and checked the back seat and floor; nothing.

Norton was starting to feel a little uneasy now. He jumped out of the car and opened the boot. Maybe he'd put them in there and forgot. A wild search revealed nothing. He looked under the car then back inside, thoroughly. They weren't there. He jumped out shaking with rage and had another look in the boot but they were gone, vanished, disappeared, stolen.

Norton's chest was heaving and his dark brown eyes flashed murderously as he slammed the lid of the boot down, buckling the lock.

'You rotten, fuckin' thieving cunts,' he screamed out at the top of his voice and drove his massive fist straight through the rear window of his car, sending a shower of glass splinters all over Oxford Street. He stormed round to the other side of the car and tore the aerial off and flung it down the street. 'You stinkin' thieving Sydney cunts,' he raved. 'My fuckin' good boots, you cunts!'

The air was starting to turn blue now as Norton stormed round to the other side of the car and leant against it, his chest heaving and his hands shaking with fury as he drummed his fingers on the roof watching the people who had started to gather round. He didn't say anything, he just stood there glaring at them, finally he stood back and with a roar of exasperation he gave the driver's side door a kick that shook the whole car.

A stoned-out hippie was standing in the small crowd watching Norton. 'Are you all right, man?' he giggled. He looked like a cross between a Buddhist monk and an Apache Indian.

'Am I all right?' fumed Norton. 'Yeah, I'm all right.' He walked round and took the hippie by the throat, 'I never felt better in my life.' He tore the love beads from round the terrified hippie's neck and stuffed them in his mouth then ground his jaws together. 'You cunts reckon you can live off the universe,' he hissed. 'Try eating these.' The beads crumbled in the hippie's mouth and spilt out over his chin. Les was going to belt him but decided against it and just speared him into the crowd.

Wild-eyed, he stormed back to his car, got in and slammed the door violently behind him. He sat there for a moment or two still shaking with rage and not quite believing this could happen to him. Finally he started the car, revved the engine till it seemed as if the pistons would go through the block, then stormed straight out into the Saturday morning traffic. Every time he changed gears it sounded like somebody trying to run a piece of stainless steel through a circular saw.

Fortunately it was a bit quiet at the Kelly Club that night and just as fortunately there was no trouble. If anyone had of just given Les so much as a dirty look he would have torn their lungs out. Even Billy Dunne, who was used to Les's normally taciturn nature, was slightly puzzled by Les's increased surliness, but apart from Les grunting 'some cunts pinched me boots' early in the night, they were the only words he uttered all evening. Billy, being a bit of wag, was dying to stir Les up or at least get him to release a bit more information, but Les's face was showing about as much kindness as the Sultan of Turkey so he thought it might be best just to let sleeping dogs lie, or in Norton's case sleeping gorillas.

They finished work about three that morning. Les grunted good night, jumped in his battered car with the glass splinters still all over the back seat and headed towards Bondi and home. He hadn't eaten all day and by now his stomach was starting to sound like a concrete mixer, so he decided to duck in and get a couple of steak sandwiches on the way home.

Down the bottom of Bondi Road near the Royal Hotel there's a groups of three take-away food shops, the three are grouped fairly closer together and the locals call it the Devil's Triangle. They're all run by a lot of shifty-looking Lebanese but you can get a decent steak sandwich there and the coffee's always good.

Norton pulled up outside the Devil's Triangle still wearing his tuxedo and bow-tie, went in to the closest food shop and ordered two steak sandwiches, with plenty of onions, to take away.

He leaned casually against the counter, his big hands in his pockets, facing towards the few people seated around the restaurant. It was after three in the morning and fairly quiet, most of the people were just sitting there sipping coffee, a couple of local surfies were laughing and playing a pinball machine near the kitchen at the back, and sitting in a cubicle, opposite where Les was standing, were three soapy bikies and their scruffy frump of a girlfriend. It was very cold and quiet, and it would have stayed that way only Bikie Number One, probably half full of beer and thinking he'd found an easy mark, decided to poke shit at Norton's tuxedo.

He elbowed his way out of the cubicle and sidled up next to Les. He was about six foot three and looked like a sallow, pimply faced version of Clint Eastwood with matted, greasy, long black hair. He had on fairly standard bikie gear, filthy denim jeans tucked into an equally filthy pair of calf-length boots, a battered leather jacket with a Levi jacket, minus the sleeves thrown over the top, and a grease-stained, red scarf tied round his forehead. He probably hadn't had a bath since the Battle of Hastings and when he opened his mouth, it reminded you of an oyster lease at low tide. He eyed Les up and down for a moment then turned to his mates still seated at the cubicle.

'Well, what d'you reckon it is?' he said.

'I dunno,' replied Bikie Number Two. 'Is it a penguin?'

'Nah, it's not a penguin,' said Bikie Number One. 'Penguins are never this ugly.'

'Maybe it's an ugly penguin and it's been kicked out of Taronga Park, for bein' too ugly.'

'Oh, why dontcha leave the poor thing alone,' said the scruffy girlfriend, 'you might get ugly yourself one day and get washed up on Bondi.' She threw back her head and roared laughing. She had a mean, vicious face and her smile revealed a mouthful of crooked yellow teeth, covered in enough blackfish bait to catch a school of niggers.

In the meantime, Bikie Number Two had got up from the cubicle and moved over to Les's left side. He was a bit shorter than his mate but dressed pretty much the same, only he had a mop of curly blond hair that looked like wood shavings, a dirty blue beanie was perched unevenly on his head and through the wood shavings a couple of earrings glinted in each ear. His T-shirt had risen up and an expanse of hairy white stomach flopped out over his filthy jeans.

Norton was still standing there staring quietly at the floor. He hadn't said anything but he'd taken his hands out of his pockets and folded his arms across his chest, and his eyebrows were starting to twitch, noticeably.

'Ow yer goin', penguin?' said Bikie Number Two. 'Haven't seen ya down the south pole lately.'

'Yeah, next time you're down there, give my love to Santa will ya,' chorused Bikie Number One.

'Hey, waddyer reckon that is hangin' round his neck?'

'I dunno, maybe it's a propeller.'

'Well why don't you give it a wind, see if the penguin's head takes off?'

'Yeah, why not?'

Bikie Number One reached over to grab Norton's bow-tie. That was the last thing he remembered doing. After what had happened to Norton that morning this was all he needed and the half inch fuse to the pile of dynamite inside Les had just burnt out.

Like a cobra striking, Norton spun round and let go an awesome left uppercut under Bikie Number One's chin, which lifted him completely up off the floor and flipped him backwards over the counter. He crashed down on the other side in a mess of tabouli, falafal and kebabs, his jaw shattered like a light bulb and a gash running the entire length of his chin, the white bone showing through the blood running over his chest and on to the floor.

In almost the same movement Les hit the second bikie with the back of his massive right fist fair in the face. He followed this with an explosive left hook that sent him spinning into the nearest cubicle, a rivulet of blood splashed over the two people seated there. The bikie threw his hands over his face in a vain attempt to shield himself but Norton simply punched straight into his hands, smashing all his fingers. He screamed with pain. Les slammed a right into his fat stomach which soon silenced him and doubled him up, then took him by his curly blond hair and, spinning him round, kicked him straight up the backside, sending him skidding into the pinball machine near the kitchen. The two surfies stood back as the blond bikie crashed on the floor next to them in a blubbering pain-wracked heap. They were staring at Les like they were sitting out the back at Bondi and he was a 40 foot wave come up out of nowhere.

Meanwhile, the bikie's moll had jumped up, and grabbing a Coke bottle, smashed it against the counter. Norton spun round at the sound of breaking glass just as she tried to jab the broken bottle into his face. He grabbed her right hand with his left and shook the jagged bottle out of her hand. As it hit the floor she lashed out and kicked Les in the shin. He cocked back his huge right fist, looked at her and paused momentarily. Being an old Queensland country boy he'd never hit a woman before, but this was the age of women's lib and equality of the sexes so Les did the right thing, he smacked her straight in the mouth, knocking out most of her rotten green teeth, then gave her another one in the eye for good measure.

Bikie Number Three could see by now he wasn't going to have a great deal of luck with Norton in the fisticuffs department so he decided to bolt. He ducked out behind Les. Les made a swing for him but he was just a shade too quick and ran out the front door, with an enraged Norton in hot pursuit. He had a bit of start on Les as he galloped of down Bondi Road in his bikie boots. Les stopped at the front of the shop, and spying a metal garbage tin wrenched the lid off and flung it down the road after the reatreating bikie. It spun through the air like a gigantic metal frisbee and with a metallic clang hit the bikie in the back of the head, sending him sprawling head first on to the chewing gum encrusted footpath. As he hit the asphalt Norton zoomed up alongside him and kicked him savagely in the stomach, the bikie gave a scream of pain then doubled up and started to vomit.

Les kicked him again then picked up the heavy metal garbage tin lid and started bashing him over the head with it, good and hard. You could have heard the din five blocks away — it sounded like a team of panel beaters on piece work. Finally, when the bikie was nothing more than a bloody, quivering mess, Les gave a grunt of satisfaction, dropped the battered garbage tin lid, with bits of the bikie's scalp still clinging to it, next to him and walked slowly back to the take-away food bar. Two of the owners and a couple of other people were standing at the front, wide-eyed and incredulous. They stepped back quickly to let Norton inside.

Inside, the food bar looked like a cross between a Burt Reynolds movie and a slaughterhouse. Bikie Number One was still sprawled out behind the counter covered in tabouli, a pool of blood forming round his head, the way he lay there it looked as if his neck could have been broken. Bikie Number Two lay slumped under the pinball machine like a broken doll moaning with pain and shock, and the bikie moll was squashed beneath the cubicle, out like a light, one eye looked like a lamb's fry, a gory crimson mess where her mouth and teeth had been.

Norton glanced impassively around the carnage in the food bar then noticed that his two steak sandwiches, with extra onion, were still sitting in their brown paper bag on top of the stainless steel food warmer. He walked casually over to the counter checked the prices carefully, written up on the wall behind, and took some money out of his pocket.

'Two steak sangers with extra onion, three bucks, right?' he said.

The Lebanese behind the counter didn't say anything, he just stood there and nodded his head, a blank expression on his face. Les dropped the three dollars on the counter and picked up his steak sandwiches. He hesistated for a moment then turned and walked down to the two terrified surfies standing next to the pinball machine at the rear of the shop.

'Sorry I tilted your machine, fellahs,' he said. 'Here,' he dropped a few 20¢ coins with a rattle on the glass top of the machine, 'have a couple of games on me.'

Then without so much as another word Les turned and slowly, nonchalantly strolled out of the silent shop towards his car and for the first time that day, since he had his treasured boots stolen, the merest suggestion of a smile creaked slowly, icily across his craggy red face.

Sydney on a clear winter's day is without doubt the prettiest city in Australia and arguably the prettiest in the world. At the back of Bondi Junction, near the microwave tower in Botany Street is the highest point in the city. If you stand up there on a mild clear winter's morning and look west, you can see right over Centennial Park, straight across the monotonous plains of the western suburbs and all the way to the alluring eucalypt sapphire haze of the Blue Mountains. It's this distinct blue haze, caused by the vapour given off by millions of eucalyptus trees, that gave the beautiful Blue Mountains their unique name.

On these clear, cool winter's days, the chilly south-west winds sing their mournful song as they sigh relentlessly down from the Blue Moutains, pushing the few tufts of grey cloud scattered around the sky like pieces of steel wool, over the loveliest harbour in the world and finally scatters them, like a mother bird saying goodbye to her fledgling chicks, through the magnificent Sydney Heads and out into the endless aquamarine of the Tasman Sea.

Norton loved these early winter mornings, they were one of the few things in Sydney he liked; days like this you wouldn't be dead for quids, Norton used to joke to himself.

Though his night job gave him few opportunities to get up early, when he could Les would rise at dawn, drive down to Centennial Park and go for a good long run.

After the noisy, smoky, sometimes hostile atmosphere of the Kelly Club and the neon gaudiness of the Cross and its seedy denizens the uncrowded green beauty of Centennial Park was almost a revelation to him. Sometimes as he'd belt along the edges of the ponds in the early morning mist, scattering the water hens and ducks near the banks, he'd close his eyes and for a few seconds imagine he was back running around the river banks near Dirranbandi, but all too briefly.

It was one of these cool winter mornings in Centennial Park about six or so weeks after Les had had his boots stolen; he still hadn't quite got over getting his good boots pinched but at least he was learning to live with it, and Tommy Butterworth had promised to get him another pair as soon as the opportunity arose.

He'd been running in the park for about half an hour, he'd done two circuits, now he was criss-crossing, just running anywhere, stopping every now and again to do 20 or so push-ups and a few sit-ups then continuing on his way. He would do this for roughly an hour or so. He preferred to run in the more deserted parts of the park, away from the usual running routes and the other people; the less people he saw when he was running the more he liked it. He'd belt along these out-of-the-way trails, brushing any overhanging branches aside with his arms, jumping over logs or stumps; any clearings he came to he'd sprint across, taking in great draughts of cold air and letting it out behind him in huge billowing clouds of steam which would hang in the crisp winter air momentarily till they'd disappear in the wind.

Les was pounding along in this manner, hardly a worry in the world feeling great, the cold air stinging his sweat-stained face.

He was running along a narrow trail and spotting a small sheltered clearing up ahead, decided to take it in one great leap. He picked up speed and as he got to the edge of the clearing threw his hands forward to take off in a mighty leap, but his foot caught on something and instead of arching gracefully through the air, Les sprawled forward to culminate in a noisy, spectacular somersault of dirt, twigs and grass, landing flat on his back near the other side of the clearing. He lay there for a second or two, slightly dazed, then let out a mighty oath.

'Jesus fuckin' Christ,' he roared. 'What the fuckin' hell was that?'

Gingerly he picked himself up, stood there for a moment rubbing his hip and inspected the damage; he'd skinned both knees and his elbow but nothing was broken or sprained. He turned to see what it was he'd tripped over.

Limping back to the other side of the small clearing all he could see was a pile of spread-out newspapers. However, under closer inspection he noticed a scrawny, wizened arm stuck out under the newspapers that seemed to be groping towards an empty wine flagon, and sticking out from under the other end of the newspapers was a pair of skinny white legs clad in a pair of tattered blue pants. But, perched on the end of those skinny white legs was none other than Norton's boots. A bit battered, a bit dirty but unmistakably, unequivocally Norton's $290 iguana lizard skin boots which had mysteriously disappeared in Bondi Junction six weeks earlier.

At first Les just stood there staring, his hands on his hips. With a quick look around the clearing, as if he expected some people to be standing there, he pointed to the boots.

'Hey, they're my fuckin' good boots!' he roared at the top of his voice.

He knelt down and ran his hands over them, then got back up again.

'My fuckin' oath they are. What are you doing with them you old cunt?'

The old wino lay there, sleeping blissfully on, ignoring Norton's raving. Norton didn't know whether to laugh or cry, he was a hotbed of mixed emotions. On one hand he wanted to tell the world he'd got his boots back and on the other hand he wanted to kick the stuffing out of the old wino for stealing them

37

in the first place. Then again, the old bloke might have just found them somewhere so he couldn't really pound the soul-case out of the poor old bugger for that. A few questions were in order; he gave the pile of newspapers a sharp kick.

'Hey you old prick,' he said. 'Where'd you find those boots?' Still no answer. He gave the pile of newspapers another nudge, 'c'mon you old cunt, wake up, I'm talkin' to you. Where'd you get those boots? Don't try and tell me you bought 'em.' Still no answer.

Les stood there glaring down at the sleeping form beneath the newspapers, his chest heaving, steam rising off his face as the sweat dripped of his nose and chin.

'Ah, fuck this,' he said, and gave the newspapers a good hard kick in the general direction of where he thought the old wino's backside would be. Still no answer.

'Jesus, how much piss did you drink last night?' He gave the wine flagon a kick, it disappeared into the bushes, 'Yeah fuckin' empty, I thought so.'

He bent down and tore the newspapers off the old wino's face. 'C'mon you old prick, wake up, I want ...'

Norton's voice trailed away. He gave a little scream of terror and recoiled in horror, as if he'd just uncovered a tiger snake. For one look at the old man's face, with the mouth frozen in a crooked half-smile, the spittle still glistening on the sides and those two opaque eyes, that stared straight through Les and into eternity, told him one certain thing; he could never wear those boots again.

'Oh Jesus,' he said as a shudder ran through his entire body, 'keep the fuckin' things.' Big Les turned and ran for his life.

A Fortnight in Beirut

It was getting on for 11 o'clock on a mild Saturday night in September. The pale blue neon light of the Kelly Club threw an almost translucent glow over the two men in tuxedos standing casually at the entrance; the shorter man was eating an apple, the other was gnawing on a Cherry Ripe bar. The garish neon lights of Kings Cross blending haphazardly in around them added a distinct touch of surrealism to the whole scene.

The shorter man checked his watch for the fifth time in the last hour, a look of mild concern on his face.

'Price is a bit late getting here tonight,' said Billy Dunne.

Les Norton finished his Cherry Ripe bar, screwed the wrapper in a ball and tossed it nonchalantly into the gutter.

'What time is it?' he asked.

'About 11 o'clock.'

'There was a big meeting on at Rosehill today. He's probably still celebrating.'

'Yeah, he had two winners.'

'Good prices?'

'One was 15/1.'

A smile creased the corners of Les Norton's eyes. 'There's your answer,' he said.

They stepped back to let a well-dressed party of four into the club, giving each of them a smile and a nod as they entered. As they did, a light brown Rolls-Royce glided majestically up out the front and stopped about 20 feet down from the club.

'Here he is now,' said Les.

39

Price Galese stepped out from behind the wheel of the Rolls and walked briskly over towards them. He looked a picture of sartorial elegance in an immaculately cut, blue, three-piece suit which was accentuated by his silvery grey hair. A maroon tie and a solid gold tie-bar with large black opal in it added a touch of discreet class to his attire. He had a strange smile on his face.

'Hello boys,' he said lightly. 'How are you?'

'Not too bad Price. How's yourself?'

'All right. Listen,' he took each of them by the arm. 'Come up the office after work. I want to see you about something.'

'There's no trouble is there?' said Billy.

'No, not really. I'll see you when we knock off.' He gave the boys a wink and disappeared up the stairs.

'I wonder what that was all about,' said Billy.

Les shrugged. 'We'll find out after work, I s'pose.'

The night was fairly uneventful. A team of drunken sailors came up to cause a bit of trouble; Les belted the biggest one in the mouth, knocking out several teeth and that was the end of that. Billy banged two bikies' heads together and kicked a cheeky drag-queen in the backside and Les went up and had to eject the drunken wife of a Sydney television news-reader. She was out on the town while her husband was in hospital recovering from a hair transplant. This was done very discreetly and she was out the door and still laughing before she even knew what had happened. Just another Saturday night at the club.

Around 4am they had everyone out so the boys went to the office to see Price; knocking lightly before they entered. Price was seated behind his desk next to the club manager, George Brennan; they were doing their best to count a stack of money an East German gold medallist couldn't have pole-vaulted over. At the end of the money sat a shiny blue-black Colt .45 automatic.

'Come in, boys,' said Price happily. 'Grab yourselves a drink. You know where it is.'

Billy went for the Dimple Haigh and Drambuie, making himself a nice, tall rusty nail, Les settled for one of the cans of Fourex that Price, knowing the ex-Queenslander's taste, always kept in the fridge for him. Billy gave the liquor cabinet a quick wipe and they sat down in front of Price's desk.

Price turned to his manager. 'George, leave me with the boys for a minute will you. I won't be long.'

'Sure,' replied the manager. He picked up the .45, put it in a leather holster under his arm and walked to the door. 'Don't let Norton drink all the Fourex,' he said with a wink and stepped outside.

'Well, what's the story?' asked Billy.

Price eased himself back from the desk. 'The story is, boys,' he said, 'I'm closing up the club for a couple of weeks.'

'Yeah,' said Billy. It didn't come as any real surprise to him. Now and again if there was trouble or pressure on from somewhere they'd close up for a while till it blew over or Price had it sorted out. 'What is it this time?'

'Ahh, there's a shitpot bloody by-election on for this ward and they reckon that whingeing prick from the Festival Of Light's going to throw some rooster in on a law-and-order campaign. You know what he's like.' Price shook his head sadly. 'Also,' he added, 'there hasn't been a decent rape, bank robbery or murder for weeks. Even the kiddy pervs have gone quiet which means the papers will take up the issue.' Price stood up. 'Where's all the rapists and murderers gone for Christ's sake?' he said waving his arms around excitedly. 'What's Sydney coming to?'

'It's enough to give you the shits,' said Billy.

'You better believe it.' Price waved his hand across the huge stack of money on the desk. 'I mean, I'm only trying to make an honest living.'

Les chuckled into his beer.

'Hey, don't laugh,' said Price. 'I'm fair dinkum.'

'Ohh, Price, don't get me wrong,' said Norton, a cheeky grin on his face. 'I know that you're only a small businessman trying to do his best.'

'That's exactly it,' said Price pointing directly at Les. 'A small businessman trying to earn a quid and the bludgers want to crucify me.' He sat back down, a look of abject sorrow on his face. 'Anyway, I'm forced to close for a couple of weeks, so here.' He pulled two stacks of $50 bills out of the drawer and handed one each to Les and Billy. 'There's a grand each there, that ought to keep you going for the next fortnight. Go for a holiday, have a rest for a couple of weeks. Don't worry about me, I'll just have to go back to being a brokey.'

The two doormen picked up the money. Les gave an embarrassed laugh.

41

'That's pretty good of you, Price,' he said awkwardly.

Price dismissed him with a wave of his hand. 'You boys have earnt it, you're the best there is.' He paused for a moment then looked at Billy. 'What do you reckon you'll do anyway?'

'I reckon I'll get my missus and the two young blokes and head down to my brother's farm at Narooma. Might put my arse up and do a bit of fishin'.'

'What about you, Les?'

'Dunno. Wouldn't mind goin' away myself, dunno where though.'

Price looked at Norton for a moment or two before he spoke. 'How would you like a couple of quiet weeks at Terrigal?'

'Terrigal?'

'Yeah, I got a weekender up there, there's no one in it at the moment. I'll tell you what to do.'

The following Wednesday morning Les picked the keys up, along with a map, at Price's Vaucluse mansion and by lunchtime he was through the toll-gates at Mt. Colah and gunning his old Ford-along the freeway heading towards Gosford. He had six dozen cans of Fourex, a box of groceries and a banana chair in the boot and an overnight bag with his meagre possessions on the back seat. An hour and a half later he'd cruised along The Entrance Road, found the Terrigal turn-off at the War Memorial and was sitting outside the Florida Hotel having a cool one and checking his bearings. Ten minutes later he pulled up in the driveway of Price's weekender in Hill Top Road.

Price's idea of a weekender was like something they'd do a ten-page article on in 'Home Beautiful'. A creamy white concrete drive led through an immaculately kept lawn and garden to a four-car garage on the right of the house. The huge house itself was old colonial sandstock brick with enormous plate-glass windows, full of lush velvet curtains facing the street; a massive polished oak door set behind an Italian slate alcove divided the front. A matching brick fence turned into cyclone wire half way down the side of the house. This led to the back where Norton could see the sunlight reflecting off a crystal clear swimming pool roughly the same size as Burrinjuck Dam, only neater. A large, terracotta brick house was about 20 feet away on the left and on the right was just one big open garden, like a small park, that belonged to the other house next door.

42

This'll do me for two weeks, Les said to himself as he rubbed his hands together gleefully while he checked out the front of the house. He went back to the car, got his gear out, placed it near the front door and took the key out to open it. There was no need to, the door wasn't locked. That's funny, he thought as he stepped inside. Oh well, maybe it's a cleaner been here or something.

A short, but high hallway led to a large lounge room which overlooked the pool. To the left was a spacious, modern kitchen and before that a room or study with a louvred wooden door, on the opposite side of the hallway a spiral staircase with a huge chandelier over it meandered downstairs.

Les walked cautiously to the lounge room. Inside it looked as if a tribe of Bedouins had moved in. There was rubbish and junk everywhere. Dirty clothes and wet towels were strewn all over the lounge, magazines were scattered all over the floor. On a large tiled coffee table were two ashtrays, overflowing with cigarette butts. Next to these stood a bamboo bong and alongside this was a bowl, half full of what looked like herb tea. Les picked the bowl up and gave it a sniff. 'Pot,' he said out loud.

The kitchen was the same. Most of the cupboards were open, the stove was covered in grease and the sink was chock full of dirty plates and other cooking and eating utensils. The kitchen tidy was overflowing and an empty grocery carton half full of rubbish sat next to it. They both stank.

Les stood there for a moment contemplating the mess, his hands on his hips. Finally he went downstairs and checked the back door. It had been forced.

'Bloody squatters, I thought so. I'd better ring Price.' He went in search of the phone.

'Throw the dirty, shitty turds out!' Price roared over the phone. 'And when you do, do it a la carte. I want to hear them bounce from down here.'

'No worrys,' replied Les and hung up.

He went outside and moved his car off the drive and down the street a bit then came back in to find a place to stow his gear.

There were three bedrooms upstairs and four below; he opted for one upstairs facing the street. He took two dozen cans and packed them in the fridge. There was some Kentucky Fried chicken in the fridge and a carton of coleslaw. It was fairly fresh so he ate two pieces and all the coleslaw. He washed this down

43

with a carton of milk also in the fridge, gave a belch then picked up a couple of surfing magazines off the lounge room floor and went into the front room to wait for whoever was staying there.

The front room had a window facing the street and the louvred door faced the hallway so he could see both ways without being seen himself. He settled down on the night-and-day to wait.

He was sitting there, half asleep, half awake when the sound of a car pulling up in the drive brought him to full alertness; a quick check of his watch told him he'd been there about two hours. He moved cautiously to the window and peeked through the velvet curtain. It was an old Valiant station-wagon with three surfboards stacked unevenly on the roof. On the windows were decals for every brand of surfboard, wet-suit, leg-rope and radio station in NSW and Queensland. He noticed it had QLD number plates. Three fairly stocky young blokes with blond hair got out, followed by a blonde girl, probably in her teens. He moved to the side of the louvred door and waited while they filed in through the front entrance.

'Wow, those waves were really good.'

'Unreal tubes.'

'Some of those lefts were so hot I couldn't believe them.'

'Feel like a cone?'

'Reckon.'

'You make the mull, I'll pack 'em. Sally, how about makin' some coffee.'

'All right.'

Norton watched through the louvres as the girl went into the kitchen and the boys sat around the coffee table fussing around the bong and the bowl of pot. He waited till one of them lit the bong, sucked the smoke into his lungs and let it out in a great cloud and a croaking 'Wow, that's really good shit man.' Then Les made his move.

He opened the louvre doors, slipped quietly into the lounge room and stood just behind them with his arms folded across his chest and an evil grin on his face. 'Hello surfies,' he said pleasantly. 'Enjoying your stay on the Central Coast?'

They all spun around as one then stood up, their eyes looked like poached eggs. The one holding the bowl dropped it and the mull went all over the floor. The girl came running out of the kitchen. The three boys were all pretty solid from doing plenty of

44

surfing and were all wearing fairly standard surfie garb; multi-coloured board shorts, T-shirts and thongs. The girl had on a Billabong singlet and a wrap round batik dress. She had straggly blonde hair and a good body, but her pimply face had enough holes in it to hold a week's rain.

'Who the fuckin' hell are you man?' said the surfie who had just had the smoke.

'Who am I?' replied Norton sweetly. 'Why I'm Mr. Makeshaw.'

'Mr. Makeshaw. Who the bloody hell's that?'

'I'm here to make sure you cunts are out of the place in about ten minutes.'

The tallest surfie slowly looked Les up and down. 'And just who's gonna put us out man? You?' He turned and smiled at his mates. He was feeling pretty game, there were three of them and they were young, fit and all well built. However, like a lot of young surfies they're world beaters in the water but on dry land they find it's a different ball game altogether.

Their pimply-faced girlfriend decided to put her head in as well.

'We got squatters' rights here anyway, man. There's no one living here and you can't put us out. So why don't you just piss off?'

'Yeah. Sally's right, man.' said another. 'So piss off.'

Norton stood there nodding his head imperceptibly, a sage expression on his face. 'Squatters' rights, eh?' he said slowly. 'I never thought of that.' He stroked his chin and moved over the coffee table. 'Not a bad looking bong. Where'd you get that. Katmandu?'

'Nah, me mum bought it for me,' sneered the tall surfie. The others all laughed.

'Mum bought it for you did she?' Norton picked up the heavy bamboo bong by one end. 'Well, what a nice mummy you've got.'

He brought the bong across in a short vicious arc and smashed the tall surfie across the face with it, sending a splash of evil smelling water across the loungeroom and the surfie cannoning into the wall, his mouth a mess of blood and smashed teeth. He hit the one on his left with a backfist that broke his nose and toppled him over the lounge on to his back. The third one stood there slightly mesmerised looking left and right at his two mates;

45

Les swung his foot back and gave him a Woolloomooloo uppercut straight in the balls. He screamed and doubled up with pain. In almost the same movement Norton jumped over the lounge and gave the second surfie another backfist, just to make sure he got the message.

'Now stompie wompies,' he said, still holding the bong menacingly in his right hand. 'We're going to have a little clean-up party.' He turned to the girl who was standing there shaking, her hands over her face. 'And you're in this too, Sally sea slug.' He took her by her straggly blonde hair, spun her round and kicked her up the backside into the kitchen. She gave another scream. 'And don't come out of there till it looks like the operating theatre at St. Vincent's.'

Norton walked over to an alcove in the hallway, picked up the car keys one of the surfies had thrown there, then walked back into the lounge room, rattling the keys in one hand and slapping the bong menacingly against his thigh with the other.

'Come on girls, liven up,' he said gaily. 'We don't want to be all day now, do we?'

The tall surfie who had copped the bong in the face was propped up against the wall, mopping blood from his mouth with the tail of his T-shirt.

'Think you're pretty bloody tough, don't you?' he said glumly.

Norton strode over to him and stood there almost eyeball to eyeball. 'I don't think I'm tough,' he hissed. 'I am tough. Very tough. Now move your fuckin' arse.' He grabbed him roughly by the scruff of the neck and spun him across the room. 'You too, blondie, let's go.' He picked up the one he'd kicked in the balls and sent him after his mate, propelled by a kick in the backside.

'How are you goin' in there, sea slug?' Les stood ominously at the entrance to the kitchen, but Sally was going at it busier than a one-armed paper hanger with the crabs.

About 40 minutes later they had the house cleaned up enough to pass Les's inspection and their gear was stacked next to the front door. He had another quick check of the kitchen and lounge then walked over, opened the front door and followed them out to watch as they put their belongings in the old white Valiant; still slapping his thigh with the bong.

'Anyway,' said Les, talking to them as if he was farewelling some old friends. 'Don't forget to call in next time you're in

Terrigal, it's always nice to see you. And be careful driving home. Oh,' he added, 'I almost forgot. Your mummy's present.'

He bent slightly at the hip and drove his huge fist straight through the rear panel window of the station-wagon. The girl screamed as splinters of glass showered over her and the bong landed in her lap. Smiling sweetly he walked up to the tall surfie seated behind the steering wheel and handed him the car keys.

'Don't forget to say hello to mum for me, won't you?' he said.

The car started up and they drove slowly off up the street with Les waving to them. 'Ta-taa,' he called out, then went inside and closed the door.

Feeling a bit peckish by now he went straight to the spotlessly clean kitchen, pulled a Fourex out of the fridge and threw a T-bone, roughly the same size as a phone book, under the griller. Three cans of beer later, it was on the kitchen table surrounded by eggs, tomatoes, bread and butter and a big pot of tea. Now that the little drama was over Les settled down and was looking forward to his nice quiet two weeks in Terrigal.

He'd just taken his first bite of steak when there was a knock on the door.

'What the bloody hell?' he grunted. Norton needed a visitor then like Kampuchea needs a year's supply of Metrecal. 'This better not be those fuckin' surfies,' he growled as he stormed to the front door and flung it open.

Standing there was a dumpy little Salvation Army officer; he looked like Peter Lorre wearing a bus conductor's hat. 'Good evening sir,' he said pleasantly. 'I'm collecting for the Red Shield. Would you care to donate?'

At first Norton looked at him like he was going to eat him, but in his heart he always had a bit of a soft spot for the Salvos because of what he'd seen them do round the Cross. He pulled a $20 bill out of his pocket and poked it in the collection box; it was so long since the collection box had seen a 'rock lobster' it nearly spat it straight back out. The little Salvo's knees buckled.

'Thank you sir. Thank you,' he said profusely, raising his cap. 'God bless you.' He God blessed Norton as he backed off all the way down the drive. Norton gave him a wave and went back inside.

A warming feeling of self-righteousness crept over Les as he ate his tea. Yessir, he thought to himself, this is going to be a

47

really nice two weeks. Really nice. He finished his meal, cleaned up, then made his bed and sorted out his clothes. He watched TV for about an hour, finding it boring, so he jumped into bed and went straight to sleep; in the fresh, clean country air and the peace and quiet Les slept like a baby.

Thursday morning dawned warm, bright and clear with the birds chirping and not a cloud in the sky. After a superlative night's sleep Norton was up at six, roaring like a tiger. He had a mug of Ovaltine, put his running shorts on, threw a track-suit over the top and headed for Terrigal Beach.

He parked his old Ford opposite the Florida Hotel and checked out the scene; there was hardly a soul around. The clear, early morning revealed a long golden strip of sand running from Terrigal to the rocks this side of Forresters Beach; Les judged it to be roughly nine kilometres there and back. He wrapped a sweat band round his head, did a few stretches and took off.

The sand at the water's edge was cool and firm under his feet, in no time at all he'd gone two kilometres and when he reached Wamberal surf club he was just starting to clap on the pace. With his lungs full of unpolluted fresh air Norton was going like a machine. An old, yellow labrador dog came down from somewhere and tried to run along with him but threw in the towel after a couple of hundred metres.

He sprinted over the rocks at Bob's Bay and across another short strip of sand till he came to a beautiful, sandy little cove, fronted by a crystal clear lagoon and surrounded by trees and grey, black rocks which he recognised from his local map as Spoon Bay; he stopped there and did a series of push-ups, sit-ups and squats. The sheer beauty of the quiet, secluded little beach got him in so he decided to come back later and do a bit of relaxed sunbaking. He had another quick look around and headed back to Terrigal.

He hit the beach opposite the Florida like a runaway express train, did a few more sit-ups with his feet hooked under a park bench then threw his track-suit on, bought a paper and headed home for a swim, a shower and some breakfast.

After eating enough bacon and eggs to bloat King Kong, Les sat around drinking cups of tea and reading the paper till he decided it was time to go to the beach. He grabbed a few pieces of fruit and a couple of magazines, tossed them in an overnight bag

48

along with a towel and a few other odds and ends, then locked the house up, jumped in his car and headed for Spoon Bay.

It was about 10.30 when he got there. He parked the car in a small parking area, got his banana-chair out of the boot then followed a leafy, narrow path full of frilly-neck lizards taking advantage of the early morning sun, down to the beach, which was complete deserted. He picked a secluded spot near some rocks, opened up the banana-chair and spread a large beach-towel over it. How good's this he thought to himself as he eased his big frame on to it and started to read. Peace and quiet.

He'd been sitting there about half an hour when he noticed a young couple come down the path and on to the beach. They had googoo eyes and were holding on to each other like a couple of limpet mines. They gotta be on their honeymoon, Les thought to himself. They had a little white silky terrier with a pink bow on its head with them. It saw Les, ran over and put its paws on the edge of his banana chair then gave a cute little bark and started licking Les's leg. Les laughed, picked it up and started rubbing it's belly. The girl came running over.

'Oh, I'm sorry about that,' she said, picking up the dog and giving it a little tap on the nose. 'Frosty, you naughty dog.' She was a pretty young thing, big innocent blue eyes and long blonde hair.

'Ah, that's all right,' replied Norton. 'I got an axe in the bag anyway if he'd have got out of control. Bull terrier is it?'

'Frosty? Hardly,' the girl laughed.

'If you don't mind me asking, you wouldn't happen to be on your honeymoon would you?'

The girl blushed slightly, 'Why yes, how did you know.'

'Oh, I don't know. I just guessed. Anyway have a nice day.'

'Same to you. Come on Frosty.'

She ran off with the dog following. Les gave her husband a wave. He waved back then they spread out a blanket and lay there together arm in arm. They looked just like what they were, a couple of nice young suburbanites in love and on their honeymoon. Ain't love grand, thought Norton; then went back to perving on the crumpet in his magazine.

About half an hour or so went by. The soft, warm sunshine was starting to make Les a bit drowsy, he ate an apple, put down his magazine and had just closed his eyes for a couple of minutes when a noise, coming from the path that led to the beach, attracted his attention. Four men carrying two eskys full of beer had walked on to the beach, each one was sucking on a can and they were obviously just out for a day on the piss and see how big a pests they could make of themselves. They each had on Stubbies, thongs, cut-down football jumpers and caps of various descriptions. All had tattoos on their arms and legs and one had a bushy black beard that made him look like he was leaning over a hedge. From his experiences around the Cross Les tipped them to be footballers from somewhere in the western suburbs. Well, I don't give a stuff who or what they are, thought Norton, looking at them disdainfully, as long as they leave me alone. He closed his eyes and drifted off into a pleasant, peaceful sleep.

About two hours later Norton's slumber was abruptly disturbed by the little dog yelping and the girl screaming.

'What the fuck?' he said rising up from the banana chair and rubbing his eyes, he looked over to where the screaming was still coming from.

Two of the yobbos had the yelping dog and were passing it to each other like a football, the other two had hold of the girl. One had her arms pinned behind her back the other had undone the top of her bikini and was fondling her breasts and trying to kiss her; the husband was doubled up on their beach blanket clutching his stomach. One of the yobbos with the dog stopped for a moment to give the husband a vicious kick in the ribs.

Norton looked away for a moment and shook his head. I don't believe this, he thought. It's none of my business but what can you do? But as much as Les hated having his peace and quiet disturbed he also hated bullies. With a vengeance. He got up, threw his sunglasses on the banana chair and walked over.

One of the yobbos with the girl had just started to pull his shorts down when he felt a tap on the shoulder. He turned around to face a not too happy Les Norton.

'Why don't you put the dog down and leave the girl alone?' said Les.

'Why don't you get fucked?' was the drunken reply.

There was obviously no time for niceties. Les slammed a short right straight into his mouth — he gave a loud groan and slumped down on his backside spitting teeth. Two quick, deadly left-hooks dropped his mate next to him, a look of pain and disbelief on his face, his nose spread across it like a squashed tamarillo.

Les turned to face the other two just as one tackled him around the waist from behind, the one with the beard ran up in front of Les and started punching him round the head. Les tucked his chin in, crouched down and picked up a handful of sand and flung it in the beard's face — he gave a curse and started rubbing at his eyes.

The other yobbo still had him gripped firmly round the waist. Les prised his fingers apart, grabbed four and bent them back till they broke with a sound like somebody snapping carrots. Before he could even get a scream out Les spun around and elbowed him across the jaw one way and then back the other. As he started to slump, Les picked him up under the armpits and smashed several bone crunching head-butts into his face. He let out an agonised moan and collapsed on the sand spattered in blood, completely out to it.

'Okay, Whiskers,' said Les, turning to face the last one. 'That just leaves you and me. On your feet, cunt.'

The beard rose slowly and started to shape up but his heart wasn't in it — he was absolutely terrified. He saw the sickening, bloody mess Norton had made of his three mates and his face went as white as a sheet, his eyes bulging out like dog's knackers. Like all bullies, they're keen to bash other people but as soon as the tide turns against them they shit themselves very quickly.

'Give us a go, willya mate?' he pleaded in desperation.

'Sure. I'll give you a go,' sneered Les. 'Just like you gave me and her husband. You dirty weak prick of a thing.'

Two straight lefts zapped into the beard's face, followed by a short right and a left hook. Les was pulling his punches slightly, he didn't want to knock him out. Not yet.

Another two straight lefts and a right to the body, a little harder this time, sent him spinning backwards on to the wet sand. He stood there with his head bowed, trying to cover his face with his hands — he was almost in tears. Blood was pouring out of his nose and mouth into his beard and dripping on to the sand; it looked dreadful.

'Now, Whiskers,' said Les, a vicious, sardonic smile etched on to his face. 'Here's a little trick I learnt off a bloke from Bangkok.' He pivoted on his left foot, swung his right leg and

51

slammed the instep against the beard's right knee, smashing the joint. The beard screamed and fell on the wet sand, writhing in agony. Now he was crying.

Les stood over the top of him. 'Now don't you go away, Whiskers,' he said, 'cause I haven't quite finished with you yet.'

He walked back, picked up one of the eskys and tipped the ice and remaining cans of beer out. 'Have a look at that,' he remarked, 'not one bloody Fourex.' Taking it by the handle he returned to the beard, who was lying on the sand whimpering with pain and fear. He saw Les coming and tried to roll himself up into a ball. Les straddled him and swinging the heavy metal esky like a squash racket started belting him across the back and head with it — you could have heard the din and screaming at Norah Head. When Les was satisfied he'd had enough he took him by his beard and stuffed his head into the empty esky.

'There you go, mate,' said Les happily. 'If you're going to lay on the beach you've got to keep the sun out of your eyes.'

He turned from Whiskers and walked back to the young married couple — they were together on the blanket, she was cradling his head in her arms, tears staining her cheeks. He didn't appear to be hurt too badly but he looked very pale around the gills, like Marcel Marceau had just given him a make-up job. Their little dog was whimpering softly and licking at the husband's hands.

'You two all right?' asked Les.

'Yes I think so, thank you,' replied the girl between sobs. 'I think we're more frightened than anything else. God, those men, they were like animals. I don't know what would have happened if you hadn't been here.'

'You'd have got a bit more than you bargained for on your honeymoon, wouldn't you, love,' replied Norton, a cheeky grin on his face.

The girl started to smile a little through her tears. She was still minus the top half of her bikini; Les picked it up out of the sand and handed it to her.

'Here you are,' he said. 'You want to stick this on?' She had one of the best pair of tits Les had ever seen. They were like two, firm brown grapefruit, with nipples like tiny, succulent pink strawberries. 'There's no hurry of course,' said Les, with the grin still plastered across his face.

Blushing with embarrassment, the girl stood up and with as much dignity as she could, wiggled into the top half of her bikini. Then she turned to Les. 'Would you mind doing me up?' she said coyly.

'Sure.' Norton's big hands were shaking a little but somehow he managed to take the strain and tie a knot. 'I'll — ah, get my gear and give you a hand up to your car,' he said hoarsely.

'Thank you.'

Les returned with his banana-chair. 'If you two can make it to the path I'll be with you in a minute. I just want to check on our friends here.'

'All right.'

The yobbos were all lying in broken, bloody heaps on the sand, still snoring soundly from a combination of drinking in the sun and the horrible battering they'd sustained from Les.

Now Norton wasn't a thief, a bit shifty maybe, but a thief, never. And he never would be. However, living in Bondi and working at the Cross the past year or two had taught him one thing. An earn is an earn and in this world you've got to get it where you can. So while he checked the boys out he relieved them of the contents of their wallets; they were just a team of mugs anyway.

'Four hundred and sixty dollars' said Les, counting the money and putting it in his back pocket. 'Not bad, not bad at all. It's a bone.'

With the husband's arm around his shoulder Les helped the newlyweds up to their car. It turned out she was Diane and he was Colin. They lived in Castlecrag but were spending their honeymoon at Diane's sister Sophia's house at Forresters Beach.

As they were getting into the car Diane turned to her husband, a big smile spreading over her face.

'Darling, I've got a wonderful idea,' she said happily. 'Why don't we invite Les around for dinner tonight? He could meet Sophia, too.'

'Hey, that's a great idea,' replied Colin. 'Come round for dinner and a few drinks, it's the least we can do. And Diane's sister is a marvellous cook, Les.'

Norton shrugged his shoulders. 'Sounds all right to me,' he said.

'Oh good. Look, here's the address.' Diane took a biro and paper out of the glove box, wrote it down and handed it to Les.

'Come round about seven, have a few drinks first and we'll eat about eight. Okay?'

'Sounds all right to me,' replied Norton again.

He shook hands with Colin, Diane gave him a kiss on the cheek and they were off with Diane insisting and Les promising that he'd be there at seven. What have I got to lose? thought Les, I'm very partial to a bit of home cooking and this Sophia might be all right anyway.

There was one other car in the small parking area besides Norton's. An irridescent green, HK Holden with twin exhausts, fatties on the back, tiger-skin seat covers and rev-head decals all over the windows. Not a bad looking old HK mused Les — then let all the tyres down.

It was about four o'clock when Les got back to Terrigal and he was in a fairly good mood considering what had happened. Even though what he had intended to be a day of peace and quiet had been disturbed, the $460 more than compensated for it. And there was still the evening to come.

He had two quick schooners at the Florida then decided he'd better get some drink to take with him that night. He found a bottle shop a short stroll from the hotel, went inside and rang the bell on the counter.

The attendant appeared from out the back. He was wearing the loudest Hawaiian shirt Les had ever seen along with a pair of yellow paisley pattern trousers — he looked like a walking green-house and was obviously gayer than carnival time in Rio.

'Yessss,' he crooned, eyeing Norton up and down. 'What can I do for yoouuu?'

'What can you do for meeee?' replied Les derisively. 'Just give me a couple of bottles of French shampoo, son. Dom Perignon 72. If you ain't got that, Veuve Clicquot will suffice.' What the hell, thought Norton, I got plenty, I may as well bung it on a bit.

'Ooooh, I don't think we've got any of that,' said the attendant. The sight of Les's muscles and hairy chest bulging out under his T-shirt had him starting to gush a bit. 'Would some Moet Chandon do you?'

'Moet bloody Chandon,' sneered Les, really giving it the Leo Schofield treatment. 'You're kidding. I wouldn't give that to my bloody dog. What year is it?' .

'Seventy-two,' replied the attendant meekly. 'Is that all right?' Norton's aggressive macho act had him almost swooning. He was Norton's slave.

'I s'pose it'll have to do, won't it?' replied Les. 'All right, give us three bottles. And toss in a bottle of Tia Maria, too. You'd better bloody well have that.'

'Oh of course we have,' said the attendant, fussing around like an old moll as he got the bottles out of the fridge and started wrapping them up. 'Having a bit of a party, are we?'

'Yeah. I brought me two hairdressers up for a few days,' said Les running his fingers through his thick red hair. 'They're a couple of terrific young blokes, too.' He handed the attendant the money, making a big show of it as he pulled out the wad he'd lifted off the yobs.

'Ooh, you might like to invite me around for a few drinks. Are they from Sydney, are they?' The attendant was gushing like a fountain by now.

'Yeah. But you know the old saying, son,' said Les, pocketing the change. 'Three's company, four's a crowd. I might see you tomorrow, though.' He gave the attendant a wink and left the shop.

As soon as Les walked out the door the attendant slumped down in a chair and started fanning himself with a magazine. He was completely shattered.

Christ, thought Les, chuckling to himself as he put the drink in the car, a man's lucky to get out of there with his cherry. He arranged the bottles securely on the back seat then went to a chemist, bought a bottle of Mennen, some under-arm deodorant and went straight home.

It was almost five o'clock by the time Les had made a cup of tea and put the drink in the fridge, so he decided to lie down for an hour. He wanted to be nice and fresh when he got there; besides this sister Sophia sounded interesting and if she was anything like Diane she'd be all right. A man might be half a chance too, he thought.

He woke up feeling a bit thick-headed just after six. The combination of the two schooners and the day in the sun had dried him out a bit so he had a drink of water, went downstairs and jumped in the pool — the water felt like ice but it freshened him straight up. After splashing around for a few minutes he trotted upstairs and got under a steaming shower.

Fifteen or so minutes later he finished showering and shaving and felt like a million dollars. He threw on a clean pair of jeans, sneakers and a lemon coloured Lacoste pullover he'd bought from one of the thieves at Bondi. Not half a bad sort, son, he thought to himself, checking himself out in the mirror as he slapped the Mennen on to his face and gave his armpits a liberal dousing of deodorant; not half a bad sort at all. All I need is a few gold chains round my neck and I'd look like Barry Gibb. He gave his dense red hair a quick detail with a plastic 'bug rake' and turned out the bathroom light.

Les was whistling softly to himself as he got the chilled champagne out of the fridge and placed it in a carton alongside the Tia Maria. He checked the address Diane had given him in his UBD street directory. It was easy enough to find, so he tucked the carton up under his arm, locked up the house and was on his way; ten minutes later he was almost at Forresters Beach.

Shit, I'm getting nice and hungry, thought Les as he turned off The Entrance Road into Crystal Street for the short run to the beach. I hope they got plenty on.

Diane's sister's place turned out to be a large, purple brick two-storey house in Kalakau Road overlooking the whole of Forresters Beach and then some. A wide sun-deck surrounded by white Roman-style columns stood out the front, with a smaller but identical one underneath at the entrance to the front door. Not a bad digs, mused Les as he pulled up alongside Colin's car which was parked in the double driveway. She must be doin' all right. He got the drink out of the car, stepped through a white wrought-iron gate, trotted up a small flight of steps and rang the door bell. Ding dong, Avon calling, thought Les as he recognised Frosty's tiny bark coming from inside. The door opened and there stood Colin, a warm sincere smile almost glowing on his face.

'Hello Les,' he said warmly, 'good to see you, glad you could come.' He took Les's hand and pumped it vigorously. 'How are you, all right? Hungry I suppose?'

'Yeah, a bit,' replied Les. 'How are you feelin' now anyway?'

Colin patted his ribs lightly. 'Still a little sore but I'm okay. I know I'd be a lot worse only for you,' he said raising his eyebrows.

Frosty ran over and jumped up on Les's leg. Les picked it up under the stomach and let it give him a kiss on the chin. 'You still won't chain this mongrel thing up will you?' he said.

'Can't get a chain big enough,' laughed Colin. 'Anyway, come inside.' He closed the door behind Les and ushered him down a thickly carpeted hallway, through a spacious lounge room full of expensive modern furniture and into a large modern kitchen, that would have suited Bernard King. Diane was fussing over some pots steaming on a stove.

She stopped what she was doing, walked over to Les and took him by the hand. She looked at him for a moment then reached up and kissed him on the cheek. 'We're very, very pleased you could come Les, we really are.'

'Ah, that's all right,' said Les feeling slightly embarrassed, 'I had to anyway, your husband threatened to beat me up if I didn't.'

'That's right,' said Colin, 'and if I hadn't, Diane would.'

Diane gave Les's hand another squeeze and went back to the stove. 'Sophia's just gone to the bathroom, she'll be out in a minute.' She turned to Colin: 'Well, don't just stand there, Colin. Get the man a drink.'

'I sure will,' said Colin, snapping into action. He took the carton from under Les's arm. 'There was no need for you to bring anything Les, there's plenty in the fridge. What have you got here anyway.' He picked up one of the bottles. 'My goodness, French champagne, Moet too, Diane look at this.'

Diane turned and looked at the bottles Colin had taken out of the carton. 'Les, there was no need to do that,' she said. 'It must have cost you a fortune. Tch tch, that's silly. We'll have to give you some money.'

'Ohh that's okay,' replied Les casually, 'I — ah found some money on the beach.'

'Not with a metal detector surely,' said Colin putting the bottles in the fridge.

Les looked at the bruising round the knuckles on his massive right hand. 'No. I didn't use a metal detector,' he replied.

Diane stopped what she was doing. 'Oh Les,' she said. 'This is my sister, Sophia. Sophia this is Les Norton.'

Les turned to face Diane's sister who was standing quietly in the doorway to the kitchen.

Sophia looked nothing like her sister. Where Diane was blonde and petite Sophia was a tall, willowly, olive skinned brunette; almost as tall as Les. She wore hardly any make-up, just a touch of rouge on her high cheek-bones, and just enough

57

eye-liner to accentuate a pair of deep emerald green eyes that seemed to burn into Les like two laser beams. Her hair was combed up on her head in a bun with a few lightly curled strands hanging softly round her ears, an expensive powder blue track suit fitted her snugly enough to emphasise two high, full breasts and a shapely behind. Framed in the doorway with her hands in her pockets she oozed haughty sophistication; several thin gold chains round her slender neck added to the image. Les guessed her to be somewhere in her late 20s, early 30s; and all woman.

'Hello Sophia,' said Les pleasantly. 'Pleased to meet you.' He held out his hand, Sophia's handshake was warm and firm and better than a lot of men's that Les had met.

'So you're the hero of the day,' she said indifferently; the expression on her face didn't change.

'I don't know about hero,' said Les. 'I guess I just happened to be in the right place at the right time.'

'Mmmhh.' Sophia eyed Les up and down then moved into the kitchen. 'Did I hear someone mention Moet?'

'Yes, Les brought some bottles,' said Colin quickly, getting one out of the fridge.

'You brought this?' said Sophia, giving Les a derisive smile.

Les shrugged his shoulders. He could sense Colin and Diane were a bit overawed by Sophia's presence and she obviously wasn't too impressed with him. 'It's a drink,' he said nonchalantly. 'I'd just as soon have a glass of beer myself. But let's knock one off anyway.'

Les took the bottle from Colin and with his powerful grip quickly and easily uncorked it, making a barely audible 'pop'. Colin had four tall champagne glasses ready; Les filled them and handed them around. 'Well,' he said raising his glass 'here's to the newly-weds. May all your troubles be little ones.' He clinked Colin's glass and they all took a sip. All except Sophia; about half of hers went down the hatch in one go.

Les watched her for a moment or two and tried to sum her up. She's a snooty bitch he thought, not my cup of tea at all and I'd just make a dill of myself trying to get on to her. Anyway, I'll have a good feed, a drink and piss off. That'll do me.

He reached over and refilled Sophia's glass, the others declined. 'Diane tells me you're sisters,' he said. 'If you don't mind me saying, you don't look very much alike.'

'We're step-sisters actually,' replied Sophia. 'Same father, different mother.'

'Oh.' Les nodded towards the lounge. 'Nice place you've got.'

'Yes, my husband designed it. He was an architect.'

'Was?'

'He died about a year and a half ago.'

'Oh, I'm sorry.' He looked at her momentarily. 'He must have only been young.'

'Yes he'd just turned 30.'

'Shit, that is young. What happened, if you don't mind me asking?'

Sophia drained the rest of her champagne. 'He had a heart attack,' she said quickly, shooting Diane a frosty look out of the corner of her eye. Diane seemed to blush slightly and looked down at the floor.

Norton was slightly astounded. 'A heart attack at thirty. Christ!'

'It can happen, you know,' sniffed Sophia. She moved over to the wall stove and glanced through the small glass window. 'This should be just about ready soon.'

Les sensed that she wanted to change the subject so he refilled their glasses. 'Well, that bottle went down quicker than a shark shot full of shit, didn't it,' he said turning to Colin. 'I guess I'd better rip the top of another one.' So saying, he did and refilled all the glasses.

'And what sort of work do you do Les,' asked Sophia, taking a healthy pull on her glass of Moet.

'I work in a gambling casino up the Cross,' replied Norton.

'What are you, a croupier?'

'No, I work on the door.'

Sophia gave another derisive little laugh. 'You're a bouncer.'

'Sort of, yeah.'

'And do you get to bounce many people, Les? I suppose you would.'

'I don't bounce people,' replied Norton evenly. 'I just bounce mugs.'

Les then went on to explain a bit about the Kelly Club before they started thinking he was some punch-drunk thug who went around belting people just for the fun of it. He told them about the owner and all the charity work he did and all the people he had to bribe to stay in business and about some of the racehorses he owned. He told them about how his offsider Billy was an ex-champion fighter and some of the sights they'd seen round The Cross. He mentioned a little bit about some of the fights they'd been involved in — not making it too heavy.

Colin and Diane were almost mesmerised at some of Les's stories. Even the haughty Sophia became more than a little astonished when Les told them about the surprising number of rich and respected people who went there. The TV stars, film stars, church dignitaries, judges, barristers, politicians. Rich society women out with young gigolos, prominent Sydney businessmen out with sexy young call-girls.

'So it's not just a sleazy gambling den,' said Les, 'and I don't run around bashing people all the time either.'

'Obviously not,' replied a slightly admonished Sophia.

As she spoke a timer in the wall oven rang. 'Righto,' she said, clapping her hands together, 'if you boys go out into the dining room we'll start serving this up. Les, there are two bottles of wine in the fridge, would you open one and put it on the table.'

'Sure.' Les went to the fridge, took out a bottle of Black Tower, opened it and placed it in the middle of the oblong dining table, then sat down at one end to the right of Colin.

The table had been set tastefully and thoughtfully. Crisp white serviettes in serviette rings, expensive place-mats and a fragrant flower arrangement in the middle. The lack of candles pleased Les, they gave him the shits the way they flickered in your eyes while you tried to eat and the smell almost turned you off your food. Instead, a small crystal chandelier above bathed the table in a soft white light that made a perfect atmosphere for eating.

If the atmosphere was all right, the food was even better — and plenty of it. The entree was curried crab soup with sliced king prawns floating around in it; this arrived with two steaming french loaves of garlic bread and a huge, crisp green salad with a light ginger and herb dressing. Norton had never tasted anything like it. Even though Price had shouted him to some of the best restaurants in Sydney on odd occasions, basically Les was still an old fashioned country boy and loved nothing more than a good home-cooked meal.

Next up was rack of lamb, pink inside and cooked to perfection. This was covered in a sweet prune and avocado sauce and was accompanied by a steaming bowl of lightly cooked vegetables. Baby potatoes, carrots, broccoli, cauli and instead of gravy there was a sauce of chopped zucchini, tomato and onion, sauteed in butter and garlic. Les nearly fainted.

Where Colin was a bit of a picker Norton was going for it like a Canadian pack wolf. The girls could see he was enraptured and were starting to pamper him a bit, filling his glass, scooping more vegetables on to his plate.

'Everything all right, Les?' asked Diane.

'You're kiddin' aren't you. If I'd have known it was gonna be this good I wouldn't have bothered eating those three pies before I came over.'

Sophia looked at Les in astonishment, then when she saw the grin on his face she started to laugh. She was starting to warm up a little towards Les.

They finished the lamb and the second bottle of Black Tower and were sitting there quietly for a moment when Sophia got up.

'Well, are we ready for sweets?' she asked, looking directly at Les.

'Sure, why not?' replied the big red-headed bouncer.

'Sweets was two pears dipped in marsala, rolled in sugar and surrounded by sliced kiwi-fruit and strawberries covered in Cointreau and cream, with scoops of passion-fruit ladled over the top.

Norton took one bite and nearly got a horn. 'Christ,' was all he said.

After finishing his sweets Norton pushed himself back from the table, wiped his face with his serviette and rubbed his stomach. 'Fair dinkum,' he said. 'That's one of, if not the best, feed I've ever had.' He turned to Colin. 'You sure weren't kidding when you said your sister-in-law was a good cook.'

'Enjoy it, did you Les?' asked Sophia, a distinct glow from the champagne, wine and Cointreau starting to appear on her cheeks.

'Enjoy it?' said Les. 'I tell you what Sophia, if you weren't so ugly and broke I'd marry you, myself.'

'Why, thank you Les,' said Sophia, joining in the laughter with the others. 'That's one of the nicest compliments I've ever had.' Norton didn't realise it but with his earthy sense of humour he'd just about won Sophia. Much to his peril.

'Well,' said Sophia, 'why don't we clean up some of the mess and I'll perc some coffee and then we can sit down and relax.'

'Good idea,' said Les rising from the table. 'I'll give you a hand.'

'That's all right,' said Diane. 'We'll do it.'

'Yes, sit down Les,' said Colin. 'You're our guest.'

'Okay, I'll supervise and we can knock that last bottle of Moet off while it's being done. Fair enough?'

'Fair enough,' said Diane.

Between them they had the washing-up done in next to no time with Sophia taking in plenty of Moet and managing to bump into Norton or at least rub herself up against him quite a number of times during the proceedings.

'You certainly like your food, Les, don't you?' she said.

'He has to,' said Colin. 'Look at all those muscles and you want to see him fight. Phew.'

'Yes, you look as if you'd be quite strong,' said Sophia. 'Do a lot of training do you?'

'Yeah, a fair bit,' replied Norton. 'We have to because of the job. In fact I'm not trying to skite, but me and Billy are probably the two fittest blokes down at the gym where we work out.'

'Mmmhh,' purred Sophia sweetly, 'that's very good, isn't it?'

The coffee had percolated, so they all moved back out to the dining room. Norton grabbed the bottle of Tia Maria from the kitchen and opened it.

'Why don't we have a few nice Jamaican coffees?' he said, pouring four large serves into the coffee mugs; they all nodded in agreement.

They sat around talking and drinking coffee till the bottle of Tia Maria was almost gone and so was everybody else. Les glanced at his watch; it was nearly 11 o'clock.

Colin stretched back in his chair and stifled a yawn. 'Ohh, excuse me,' he said, 'but I'm just about on the nod.'

Norton noticed that for the last half an hour he'd been giving Diane the same sort of looks Wily Coyote gives the Roadrunner.

Can't say I blame you, he thought, a trifle enviously.

'Yes, it's been a fairly traumatic day for both of us,' said Diane. 'I'm rather tired myself.'

'Well go and get a good night's sleep,' said Sophia. 'It'll do you the world of good.'

They rose from the table. Colin shook Les's hand, Diane gave him a squeeze and a big, wet tender kiss on the cheek and made him promise he would come round again before he went back to Sydney. Les said he would. Then they were gone, leaving just him and Sophia. Oh well, thought Les, it hasn't been a bad sort of night. They're nice people, I've had a top feed, a good drink and I'll have one more cup of coffee and piss off.

He poured two more Jamaican coffees, picked his up and moved out on to the balcony. 'Jesus, Sophia,' he called out to her, 'you sure got a grouse view from out here.'

Below him the full moon had turned the water into liquid silver, broken only by the odd gentle wave wrapping quietly around the island that divides Forresters Beach. The reefs and the high rocky headland at the northern end reminded him of photos he'd seen of Honolulu.

'This looks like something out of Hawaii Five O,' he said to Sophia who had come out on the balcony to join him.

'It's lovely isn't it?' said Sophia, 'Especially on nights like this.'

'I'll tell you what,' said Les tugging at his pullover, 'I don't know whether it's all those Jamaican coffees I had or what but struth it seems hot for this time of the year.'

'Yes, I'd love a swim right now,' said Sophia. 'But I had the pool drained yesterday, I'm getting some tiles re-grouted.' She looked at Les for a moment. 'Did you say there was a pool back at your place?'

'Yeah, a big one, but the water in it's like bloody ice.'

'That's just how I like it. Why don't we go back to your place and have a swim, I'd like to see this Price Galese's house anyway.'

'All right, please yourself. Just grab your costume. There's plenty of towels back there.'

Sophia gave Les a strange smile, then disappeared into one of the bedrooms returning with a large handbag. 'Let's go,' she said.

He followed her downstairs while she got her car, a white BMW, out of the garage and told her to follow him.

Funny sheila, thought Les as they turned off The Entrance Road and headed towards Terrigal, fancy wanting a swim at this time of night. He looked at her headlights in his rear vision mirror and stroked his chin. I wonder if she's after a root? Nah, she's just a cockteaser, I reckon, put a hand on her and she'd probably scream rape. Oh well, who gives a stuff? Let her have a swim and she can piss off.

They pulled up in the drive about five minutes later, Les opened the door and followed Sophia in; he'd left the hall light on, so he walked straight over and switched on the lounge room light.

'Ooh this is nice,' said Sophia admiring the expensive furniture and fittings. 'Where's the pool?'

'Out here.' Les hit two switches on the wall and the electric curtains hissed back to reveal a large kidney-shaped pool and spa with underwater lights glowing translucently in the huge sculptured backyard below.

'That's for me,' said Sophia.

'You can get changed in one of the rooms downstairs if you like,' said Les. 'I'll get some towels.'

'All right. Are you going to come in?'

'Yeah, I suppose so.'

'Good.'

Norton went into the bedroom where he had his clothes, got changed out of his jeans and into a pair of Speedos, taking two large fluffy beach towels out of one of the wardrobes, he stopped at the door on the way out. Shit, he thought, I'm a moral to get a horn splashing around in the pool with this sheila and I don't want to be running around with a great fat stickin' out all over the place. He put a pair of Stubbies on over the top of the Speedos.

With the keys jangling in one hand and the beach towels in the other Norton trotted downstairs and opened the back door.

'Everything all right?' he called out as he fiddled around trying to find the right key.

'Sure is,' came the reply.

Norton got the door open and turned around just as Sophia came out of the bedroom and walked just a little unsteadily towards him. She'd decided to leave her costume at home too. Instead she had on a tiny white tank-top and a pair of lime-green silk knickers; the tightness of the tank-top revealed her large firm breasts to their fullest and her skimpy little green knickers barely covered the bulge of her crutch and the bristle of her pubic hairs. Fuckin' hell, thought Norton, feeling like someone had just run a blow-torch across his balls, thank Christ I put these Stubbies on. He handed her one of the towels and followed her out to the pool on three legs.

Sophia dropped the towel by the edge of the pool and tested the water with her toes. 'No good mucking around,' she said and dived in, hardly making a splash. She surfaced a few metres down the pool.

'What's it like?' Les called out to her.

'Beautiful.'

Yeah, I'll bet, he thought. Oh well here goes nothing, and with a great splash he dived in. The chill of the water as he dived down deep into the pool nearly took his breath away at first but feeling a bit heady from all the Tia Maria and champagne he found that when he surfaced he was instantly freshened up; he let go a yell and dived down again. After splashing around for a while he paddled over to the side of the pool and stood there treading water.

'I told you it was nice,' Sophia called from the other end of the pool.

'Yeah, it's not that bad,' replied Les.

He watched as she glided effortlessly up and down the pool, she had a lazy, easy style about her and her knickers had crept far enough up her backside to reveal a beautiful white bottom that almost made Norton break out into a sweat even in the cold water.

After a while she drifted over and stopped in front of Les, resting her hands on his shoulders. She didn't say anything but her emerald green eyes had turned into two smouldering pools of onyx that burnt deep inside him. He ran his hands up under her armpits and drew her gently into him, paused for a moment then kissed her. Her tongue was hard, sweet and hot and struck inside Norton's mouth like a cobra. He slid his hands up along her ribcage lifting the tiny tank-top at the same time and cupped her warm firm breasts in his hands, they were too big even for Norton's huge hands to go around. He ran his thumbs over the nipples, they firmed up even more and stuck out like bullets. Sophia gave a moan, threw her arms around Les's neck and crushed her mouth hungrily on to his, at the same time wrapping her long legs around his waist. By now Norton had a fat so hard you could've cracked fleas on it.

They bobbed up and down against the wall of the pool for what seemed like hours till Les finally said. 'Come on, let's go inside.' They swam to the other side of the pool and he helped her out. Sophia slipped her tank-top off and dropped it on the ground. As she stood there in her knickers, the soft lights from the pool surrounding her, Les realised what a stunning body she had; he couldn't believe it. Is this really happening to me, he thought.

He handed her a towel and took his Stubbies off. What Sophia sees now is what she's gonna get, he thought.

'I'd better get these off,' he said. 'I don't want to be dripping water all over Price's good carpet.'

They hurriedly dried off, then almost ran inside. Les took her straight up to the main bedroom where he had his clothes and there was a queen-size bed; he didn't bother to close the door and the light from the hall was just enough to let them see what they were doing.

He eased her on to the bed and started running his tongue over her neck, around her ears and down across her breasts and nipples, removing her knickers at the same time. Sophia gave a groan and put her hand down the front of Norton's Speedos, she gave a louder grown when she felt the thickness and hardness of Norton's cock. He ran his tongue down over her navel and around her crutch, the hairs were black, bristly and thick enough to lose golf balls in. Norton was like a Viking in Valhalla. He plunged his tongue deep inside her ted and Sophia kicked and shook like she'd stuck her toe in a power point. Norton tore off his Speedos, got between her legs and started to enter her.

Sophia hadn't had any sex for a while and the cold water in the pool had contracted her vaginal muscles, so Les had to push hard to get in. He gave a solid shove and Sophia let out a scream you could've heard six blocks away. Norton started with a steady stroke but it was too good and within five minutes his arse was going up and down like a sewing machine needle — Sophia was screaming and moaning with ecstasy and delight. She flung her arms around Les's neck and with her mouth wide open crushed her tongue into his mouth and ears.

Norton couldn't believe it, it had to be the best sex he'd ever had in his life, stars and comets spun in front of his eyes and he felt as if his balls were going to explode. Les wanted to go on for ages and though he tried his hardest to control himself the pure sensation and the delightful agony of Sophia's beautiful warm tight ted drawing on his cock got to him.

He hooked the crooks of his elbows behind Sophia's knees and lifting her legs up over her head, drove himself deeper inside her. Sophia let out one long high pitched scream as Les arched his back and with a moan of lust and a shudder that shook every muscle of his huge frame poured himself into her, nearly driving her through the end of the bed.

After a minute or two he removed himself and slumped down on the bed alongside her, his chest rising and falling and his heart thumping like it was going to burst through his rib cage. He reached under the bed, got one of the towels, gave himself a wipe and put it between Sophia's legs.

'Are you all right?' he panted, looking over at her. Sophia just nodded her head slowly, saliva was trickling down the sides of her mouth and her eyes were still spinning round like the end reels on a 10¢ poker machine. Well, that's fixed her up, the snooty bitch, thought Les; he lay back on the bed and closed his eyes a smug, half grin on his face. He'd just got his breath back when Sophia came to life.

'Righto Les, you gorgeous big hunk of man,' she hissed, slipping her tongue wickedly into his mouth. 'Let's do it again.'

She gently took hold of Norton's cock and started stroking it. Norton's old boy wasn't real keen on the idea at first but after a few minutes of kissing, cuddling and squeezing Sophia's big tits it rose to the occasion and before the big red-headed bouncer knew what was going on he was well and truly on the nest again.

This time they went non stop for about half an hour with Sophia screaming and moaning through each second of it. Every time Les would plunge down Sophia would thrust herself up at him; she wanted everything Les had to give and then some. About every five minutes she'd gasp and shudder, wrap her long legs around Norton, scratch his back, bite into his neck and have an orgasm. Les couldn't believe it. He was expecting just a bit of quiet love-making with her the first time around. Instead Sophia was going off like a box of rusty detonators.

Finally, with a great moan and a groan Les climaxed and slumped down next to her on the bed. Sophia waited a moment or two then reached across him and got the towel off the floor.

'Mmhh Les,' she crooned as she wiped the sweat off his face and chest. 'You're my idea of a man.'

'Thanks,' muttered Norton closing his eyes.

'But don't you go to sleep on me now.'

'Aw come on, let me have a rest for a minute, willya?'

'Nooo, no way.' She reached down and started stroking Norton's cock again but it was just flopping around like a broken arm.

'See I told you, it's gone.'

Sophia gave a chuckle that sent a shiver up Les's spine. 'I'll soon fix that,' she said.

She slid down the bed and started running her tongue around his cock and across his balls, finally putting as much as she could in her mouth. Stay down you bastard, thought Les, but no, Les's dick had a mind of it's own and soon rose to the occasion once more. Before he knew it, Sophia had slipped underneath him and they were into it again. Christ, thought Les looking at his watch, three o'clock in the morning and I'm being raped.

Number three went for about 45 minutes with Sophia still giving it everything she had. She was blowing like a southerly and snarling like a Bengal tiger; to Les it was just getting to be plain hard work. He finally emptied out, rolled off her and crashed face down on to the pillows in a lather of sweat, a completely shot bird. After a couple of minutes Sophia got a towel and started wiping the sweat off his back.

'Mmmhh, how are you feeling, lover?' she crooned in his ear, giving it a little nibble.

'I'm buggered.'

'You're not tired are you?'

'Sophia it's nearly 4 am.'

She gave him a push. 'Come on don't go to sleep.'

'I don't want to sleep,' muttered Norton. 'I want to die.'

'Ohh.'

'G'night Sophia.'

'Oh, all right then.' She pulled the sheets up and turned her back on him. 'Good night.'

Bloody hell thought Les. In five seconds he was dead to the world.

Dreams of his home town in Queensland were swirling round in his mind. Fishing on the riverbank. The tall gum trees. The trees were full of kookaburras. They were all laughing at him. Two of his sisters came out from behind the trees. They pinned him down. He tried but he couldn't move. One had a thermos full of hot coffee, it was Jamaican coffee. She started pouring it all over his loins. He couldn't move. Fear. Panic. He could feel the hot coffee on his loins.

He woke up and noticed daylight was just starting to filter through the curtains. His eyes were puffy and he had a slight headache but something else felt strange. He raised his head slightly off the pillow.

Sophia was crouched over him half way down the bed with her mouth around his dick — her long, dark hair was now billowing loosely around her shoulders as her head moved from side to side. He could hear her moaning gently. Ohh no, thought Les looking at his watch, it was five to six. Not a chance, not now. But it was too late — Norton's old boy rose to the occasion once more. It no sooner had than Sophia straddled him and sat on it with a great shuddering moan. Christ thought Les, does this sheila ever stop?

She started slowly at first but it wasn't long before her backside was going up and down like a fiddler's elbow, almost driving Norton through the Sealy Posturepedic mattress. Les's stomach was churning and his head was banging like a dinner-gong but after about 30 minutes he gave a great groan of relief and emptied out. Sophia let out a high pitched scream of ecstasy and tried to keep going but Norton's dick was just slapping around inside her like a loose piston so she climbed off.

Les lay on his back exhausted; Sophia crawled up on his chest and started kissing and nuzzling him.

'And how's my gorgeous little bouncer this morning?' she asked. Her emerald green eyes were swimming as she looked into Les's face.

'Knackered.'

'I feel absolutely marvellous.'

'I'm sure you do,' replied Norton groggily. 'Listen, don't you think it's about time you went home.'

Sophia's eyes narrowed slightly. 'Are you trying to get rid of me?' she said.

'Ohh shit no. It's just that Diane and Colin might be a bit worried. That's all.'

'All right. Come on, darling, let's have a shower.'

Hello, thought Les, as Sophia dragged his weary body off the bed and into the shower, now she's calling me darling. What next?

They frolicked around in the shower for about ten minutes; Les didn't feel that much better when they got out but Sophia was almost radiating; her cheeks were glowing and her eyes were sparkling like French champagne. They went into the bedroom and Sophia started towelling them off. Halfway through she got that look in her eye again, dropped the towels on the floor and started to ease Norton back on to the bed.

'Come on darling,' she said sweetly, 'one for the road.'

One for the road finished a little before nine o'clock. Sophia finally put her clothes back on and with the last ounce of strength left in his body Les dragged himself up off the bed and walked her to the door; he looked like the portrait of Dorian Gray, Sophia was grinning like a rat with a gold tooth.

'Bye bye darling,' she said as Les walked her out to her car. 'I'll see you at lunchtime.'

Les squinted his eyes painfully at the bright sunlight. 'Lunchtime?'

'Of course. You don't think I'm going to leave you in this big house all by yourself all day do you?'

'No, that's — real nice of you. Well, I might be asleep inside so I'll leave the key in the door.'

'Yes get some sleep, darling,' she gave him a wink. 'You're going to need it.'

She threw her arms round his neck and kissed him, her tongue darting quickly into his mouth. 'Till lunchtime,' she said, then drove off bipping the horn happily.

Les gave her a wave then went back inside, leaving the key in the door as he closed it. He went straight back to the bedroom, pausing to check himself out in the mirror before he lay down. Apart from his eyes being all puffed up like a cane toad his face looked all right, but his neck was covered in bites and his back looked like he'd been given 50 lashes with a cat-o'-nine-tails.

Norton reflected on his two weeks of peace and quiet in Terrigal. He hadn't even been there three days and already he'd been in two fights and beaten up seven blokes. A red hot poof had tried to get on to him in a bottle shop and now some girl who he'd met over what was supposed to be a quiet dinner had turned out to be a mad raving case and was trying to root him into an early grave; and she was coming back in three hours.

'Christ,' he said as he fell on the sheets and crashed out.

'Les, Les, come on, wake up. I've brought you something to eat.' Norton raised his head groggily to see Sophia sitting on the edge of the bed. He blinked his eyes and shook his head.

'I thought — you were goin' home,' he mumbled still half asleep.

'I have been, it's after one o'clock. Come on, get up. I've brought you some lunch.'

He rose wearily from the bed and followed her out into the kitchen. On the table was a roast stuffed chicken, some coleslaw, a tub of home-made potato salad and a thermos full of hot beef broth.

'What, are you trying to fatten me up for the kill?' he said.

Sophia just smiled and started serving out the food. As she walked around the table Norton noticed what she was wearing; she couldn't have looked much sexier if she'd tried. She had on a red see-through tank top that finished about two inches above her navel, making her tits seem even bigger than they were and a pair of pink, crutch-hugging shorts, that looked as if she'd put them on with a spray gun. Norton had a fair idea what was in store for him so he tore into the food like a ravenous polar bear; he realised he was starving hungry anyway.

After he'd finished eating, Sophia put the dishes away and with a lascivious smile on her face led him into the lounge room.

'Enjoy the meal darling?' she asked, putting her arms around his neck and kissing him on the lips.

'Yeah, it was beautiful,' replied Les.

'Good.' She stepped back, took off her top, slipped out of her shorts and stood there wearing nothing but a pair of tiny black lace knickers. 'Now how about some dessert.'

She screwed Les in the lounge, she screwed him in the kitchen. She screwed him in every bedroom in the house and in the master bedroom she did her best to rewrite the Karma Sutra. She screwed him up and down the pool and in the kabana, she even made him give her one in the laundry. She gave Norton absolutely no mercy. Whenever he looked like flagging she'd mouth his dick till it came up and scream all sorts of obscenities at him then beat him till he got going again. She made him tie her up and beat her up. Norton couldn't stop her no matter what he did. She took everything Les had to offer and wanted more; she was like a battalion of Chinese soldiers, she just kept coming on and coming on.

By about seven in the evening Norton didn't know what had hit him. He lay on the bed completely drained, one arm hanging over the side, sweat was trickling down it and dripping off his hand on to the floor; Sophia was lying next to him on one elbow wiping his back with a towel.

'Isn't it wonderful darling?' she crooned.

'Whassat?' mumbled Les sleepily.

'You and I, and the way we've met.'

'Yeah, t'riffic.'

'And to think, I've got you for another two weeks.'

Christ, thought Les, another two weeks of you and I'll be able to walk through a harp.

'You know, I've been thinking, Les,' Sophia went on. 'It's silly you being in this big house on your own. I might bring some things over and stay with you while you're up here.'

Norton opened one eye. 'You what?' he said.

'I'll move in with you. Keep you company, then you'll have me for almost two weeks.' She ran her tongue down Les's spine and back up again. 'Mmmhh, wouldn't that be lovely,' she purred.

A slight shudder went through Norton's body; he could feel the brustle of Sophia's ted pushed up against his thigh. Christ, he thought to himself, another two weeks of that and I'll look like a Chinese lantern.

'What about Colin and Diane?' he said, raising himself slightly up on one elbow. 'What about work?'

'Colin and Diane are on their honeymoon. They'd be glad to have me out of the place so they can run around and play chasings. And as for work. When my husband died he left me almost two million dollars so I don't actually spend my week checking the boards at the CES. Anyway that's it,' she said getting up off the bed. 'It's no good arguing, I'll move in tomorrow. I'm going for a drink of water. Do you want one?'

Norton nodded his face into the pillow. 'Yeah,' he grunted.

Jesus, thought Les while Sophia was in the kitchen. What bloody next? He was almost at the point of exhaustion, his back was a welter of scratches and bruises and his loins felt as if

72

someone had run a blow-torch over them. If she moves in I'll have to move out. But deep down Les fancied himself as a fair sort of a tooler and there was a bit of pride involved. The idea of having some sheila get over the top of him in bed was complete anathema to Norton; he'd rather let some bloke beat him in a fight. Shit, he thought, as a few drops of cold sweat started to form on his brow, how am I going to get myself out of this? I can't admit defeat. Norton was starting to get a bit worried.

Sophia came back, handed Les a glass of water and started getting dressed. 'There's no food left,' she said, 'and there's not a drop of anything in the fridge. I'll go down and get some Chinese take-away; and I'll get you a case of beer too.' She sat on the bed and kissed Norton's back. 'Nothing's too good for you,' she whispered in his ear.

'Thanks Sophia,' mumbled Les. 'There's some momey on the dressing table.'

'That's all right, I'll get it. I've still got a couple of million left, you know.' She stopped in the doorway. 'Les,' she said.

Norton lifted his big red head slowly up off the pillow. 'Yeah?'

'How would you like to marry a rich widow?' She blew him a kiss and ran out the front door.

Les closed his eyes and dropped his face into the pillow. She's half-pie fair dinkum too, he said to himself, more worried now than ever.

In about half an hour Sophia was back with the Chinese food and the beer. She dragged Les out of bed, watched him as he gingerly climbed into a pair of Stubbies then ushered him out in the kitchen. Les went straight to the fridge. Inside was a two-dozen carton of Fosters Lager, not Norton's favourite beer by any means; who does she think I am, Barry bloody McKenzie, he thought to himself. But Les was so thirsty he would have drunk a gallon of gorilla's piss through a bus driver's sock. By the time Sophia had the food laid out he'd knocked over four cans.

They sat down at the table and started spooning large helpings of sate-chicken, garlic-prawns, fried-rice and other tasty dishes into their mouths. Norton was going at it like a school of piranhas but Sophia was almost matching him bite for bite. All the time she had this tigerish gleam in her eyes. When they finished there wasn't a grain of rice, a skerrick of meat or a drop of soy sauce left. Sophia rose from the table and started to clean up, Les sat there and polished off another four cans.

'I might — ah stick the TV on,' he said tentatively.

'Good idea.'

Hello, she's gonna have a rest, thought Les. He made a bee-line for the TV, switched it on and lay back on the large ottoman lounge with a cushion under his head. Bill Collins had hardly introduced an old Humphrey Bogart movie, which Norton fancied watching, when Sophia zeroed in alongside him; the tigerish gleam was well and truly in her eyes now.

'Take off your shorts,' she said.

'What?'

'Take off your shorts. Come on.' Before Les had a chance to argue Sophia had dragged his Stubbies off and flung them across the room. From out of her handbag she produced a large jar of Vaseline. 'Just lie back and relax, she said. She took a scoop of Vaseline from the jar and started massaging it into Norton's burning loins. This is all right, he thought as he lay back and relaxed, letting Sophia do her thing.

Under her gentle touch the pain was almost starting to go away. However it wasn't long before the constant massaging caused a definite stirring in his loins. Oh no, thought Les, stay down you bastard. But Norton's old boy, like a punch-drunk fighter that can't tell when he's had enough, started to rise to the occasion again. It no sooner had than Sophia had her clothes off and was straddling him with a vengeance. Norton didn't even get a chance to see a commercial, let alone any of the old Humphrey Bogart movie.

Whether it was the spices in the Chinese food that did it or what, Les couldn't tell. But somehow or other Sophia just seemed to come on stronger than ever. By stopping every hour or so to massage Les with Vaseline she managed to keep him going all night, almost grinding him through the ottoman lounge, then just before midnight she switched the TV off and dragged Les into the bedroom for what he hoped and prayed was going to be the grand finale. Although his pride wouldn't let him admit it to Sophia, deep inside Norton felt that he was almost gone and by now he knew that he needed another root like Custer needed more Indians. But Sophia would show no mercy.

Around 1am Les was lying on the bed in a state of semi-shock, he was dog tired but in too much pain to go to sleep. His loins were throbbing and the sweat on his back was running into all the scratches, making them sting like a thousand sandfly bites. He was dying to use the bathroom but by some strange quirk of fate Sophia had fallen asleep next to him and Les was terrified that if he moved she would wake up and start attacking him again. Eventually he could hold out no longer.

Slowly, cautiously he eased himself up painfully from the bed and tip-toed quietly to the bathroom, closing the door gently behind him before he turned on the light. After he'd finished he examined himself closely in the full-length mirror. What he saw scared shit out of him.

His old boy was dangling there like a skinned whiting fillet, just to look at it made it hurt; it was that red and chaffed it glowed in the dark. His bloodshot eyes had ugly dark circles under them and were sunken deep into his head, the skin seemed to be drawn across his face like a ghastly mask. It reminded him of photos he'd seen of some prisoners in a Russian labour camp. His back was a welter of bruises and criss-cross scratches that were starting to weep openly; noticing how his ribs appeared to be sticking out he stepped on to a set of bathroom scales.

'Jesus Christ,' he said out loud. 'I've lost nearly ten kilos in three days.'

As he stared in horror at the face reflected in the mirror it suddenly dawned on him why Sophia's husband died of a heart attack at thirty. The poor bastard, he thought, she's shagged him to death and now she wants to do the same to me. Christ, what am I gonna do? A sudden knock at the bathroom door nearly made his heart jump straight up into his mouth.

'Are you all right in there?'

'Yeah, yeah. I just feel a bit sick.'

'What's the matter?'

'I — ah — think one of those prawns must have been a bit off. I'll be out in a second.'

He flushed the toilet, gargled a bit of water then stepped out of the bathroom clutching his stomach and moaning. Sophia was standing there, a concerned look on her face.

'Oh Les, are you all right?' she said.

'Ooohh,' replied Norton. 'Oohh, I don't feel real good at all. Must've been those bloody prawns.'

'I had some and I'm all right.'

'I must've cracked it for a dud one. Give us a hand into bed will you.'

Sophia helped Norton on to the bed where he lay moaning softly and clutching his stomach.

'I'll get something,' said Sophia. She returned with a wet face cloth and started mopping his face. 'You do look a bit pale.'

'I'll be okay,' said Les. 'Just let me lay here for a while.' He lay there with his eyes closed for about ten minutes, then started to snore softly, pretending he was asleep. He could feel Sophia staring at him but after a while she gave a sigh, turned out the bed-lamp and went to sleep herself. Before long Norton relaxed, then slipped into unconsciousness himself.

Saturday morning was a carbon copy of Friday. Norton's sleep was broken by Sophia's moaning as she prepared him for her morning glory; a groggy check of his watch revealed it was 6am. Oh God, here we go again, he thought and braced himself for the onslaught.

Sophia savaged him till about 8.30am. Till finally she gave one last scream of exhilaration then fell on the bed next to Les gasping with satisfied bewilderment. 'Ohh! How good was that?' she cried and threw her arms across Les's chest.

Norton lay there shuddering like a pole-axed bullock; for the last hour tears had been streaming down his face. He was in so much pain he thought he was going to go mad and he knew that if Sophia had gone another ten minutes, with his last ounce of strength he would have punched her fair on the jaw.

'Yeah. Bloody unreal,' he groaned.

They lay on the bed in silence for a while till eventually Sophia got up and started getting dressed. 'I suppose I'd better get going,' she said. 'It's almost nine o'clock.' She bent down and gave Les a big wet kiss. 'But I'll be back darling. About three.'

'Beauty,' groaned Les.

She gave her hair a quick tidy in the mirror and picked up her handbag from the dressing table. 'You stay here,' she said smiling over at Les. 'I'll bring back everything we need. I'll get some meat and make you a nice big carpet bag steak for tea. Plenty of oysters.'

'Thanks.'

'And I'll get you another case of beer.' She paused for a moment. 'You — don't like stout at all, do you Les?'

'Not particularly.'

'Mmhh. Oh well, never mind.' She blew him a kiss from the door. 'See you at three.'

'See you then.'

Les lay there with his face in the pillow listening while she got in her car and drove off down the street, giving the horn a couple of beeps as she went. Oh shit, he thought, how am I going to get out of this? He worried about it for a while but tiredness overcame him and he dozed off.

Three kookaburras in a tree next to the bedroom, arguing fiercely over an unfortunate little grass snake one of them had caught, woke him just after midday.

'What was that?' he said, raising his head off the pillow. For a moment he thought he was back in Dirranbandi. He glanced at his watch; it's after lunch, he thought, I'd better get up and have a shower. He swung his legs off the bed and sat there staring numbly at the floor for a moment then headed slowly towards the bathroom.

The hot water stung all the cuts and abrasions on his body, the soap made it worse; but after a lengthy burst of cold water he felt noticeably better. Almost wide awake. He checked himself in the mirror, shuddered at what he saw, then went out to the kitchen to make himself a cup of coffee; towelling himself as gently as possible. With a steaming mug of brew in his hands he sat in the lounge sipping it slowly and staring glumly into space. His eyes had narrowed and worry lines an inch deep were forming on his craggy forehead, adding menace to the darkness that was spreading across his face.

How the hell am I going to get out of this? he thought. If I stay here with her I'll be dead by Monday, or that close to it it doesn't make any difference. If she keeps it up I'll finish up doin' me block and hitting her on the chin, then I'll be on an assault charge and she'll probably say I tried to rape her. Hah. Or I can turn tail and piss off, like a dingo, and know some sheila's held the wood over me; I'd never be able to look myself in the eye again. Neither of the three options appealed to him. He glowered into the empty mug for a few minutes his anger steadily increasing then got up to make some more coffee.

'Fuck it!' he cursed out loud. 'I only came here for a bit of peace and bloody quiet, there's been nothing but trouble then that bitch has to turn up.' He flung the coffee mug into the sink, breaking the handle. 'Why me?' he roared through gritted teeth waving his arms around the kitchen in frustration. 'Why bloody me?' He was just about to put his massive fist through one of the redwood teak cabinets when unexpectedly the phone rang.

A feeling of extreme trepidation swept over him. It's got to be bloody her, he thought; she's ringing to say she's coming over early. He stood in the kitchen staring at the phone, transfixed with fear and hate as it kept ringing for almost three minutes. I suppose I'd better bloody answer it. Reluctantly he walked to the lounge and picked up the receiver.

'Hello.'

'Hello Les. It's Price, how are you son?'

A great sigh of relief oozed out of Norton's body. 'Oh Price, how are you? It's good to hear from you.'

'Yeah. Listen Les, I've got some horrible rotten news for you, mate.'

'What's that?'

'Mate. I'm going to have to cut short your holiday.'

'YOU WHAT?'

'Ohh, Les, I can understand you blowing up. I know I promised you two weeks up there but all the trouble's blown over and I'm opening the club tonight. I need you back here.'

Norton stared into the mouthpiece. 'You want me back tonight?'

'Yes mate. Sorry.'

Norton was speechless, he kept staring at the mouthpiece. 'No, no that's all right Price,' he said quickly. 'I'll be there, don't worry.'

'Ohh good on you, Les. I know how you must feel and I hate having to do this to you but don't worry, I'll make it up to you. I'll see you tonight then?'

'Yeah, no worries, I'll be there for sure. Goodbye.'

Norton stared at the phone for a moment then a grin like a split in a watermelon spread across his face and he sprang into action.

Within 30 minutes Les had the house tidied up, the broken mug fixed, his clothes packed and thrown with the remaining beer and groceries on the back seat of his car. He scribbled a quick note to Sophia explaining briefly what had happened and telling her he'd ring her from work. Don't know how though, he thought as he slipped it under the large brass knocker on the front door, I don't even know your phone number. And I don't want to. He gave it and the house a last look and sprinted for his car. The next thing he was belting his old Ford along The Entrance Road, looking in the rear vision mirror for speed cops or possibly a white BMW and heading for the freeway back to Sydney.

The pale blue neon light of the Kelly Club threw an almost translucent glow over the two men in tuxedos standing casually at the entrance. The shorter man was peeling an orange, the taller one was leaning against the wall not doing very much at all.

'Well,' said Billy Dunne tossing the orange peel into the gutter. 'Wasn't much of a holiday was it?'

'No. Not really,' replied Les Norton.

'I suppose you must have the shits having to come back so soon.' He offered Les a piece of orange, Les shook his head. 'I had a prick of a time myself.'

'Yeah?'

'Yeah. Never stopped bluein' with me missus the whole bloody time, smashed the windscreen of the car half way down, one of the kids has trod on a broken bottle and got eight stitches in his foot. I've had an argument with me brother in a pub over nothing and ended up flattenin' two of his mates. Fair dinkum, Les, I was glad to get back to tell you the truth.'

'Go on, eh?' replied Norton.

'Yeah. Not like you, you lucky bludger. That nice big house, the pool, all on your own. At least you got a few days of peace and quiet.'

'Yeah, it was just great.'

'Anyway you can always go back up again I suppose if we get another break.'

'What was that?'

'I said, I suppose you'll be heading straight back up again if we ever get another break.'

'Billy,' replied Les slowly. 'If Price ever offers me two weeks of peace and quiet in Terrigal again, you know what I'm gonna do?'

'What?'

'I'm going straight to the nearest travel agent and book a fortnight in Beirut.'

The garish neon lights blending in around them as Kings Cross started to come to life on Saturday night added a distinct touch of surrealism to the whole scene.

Grungle

When Les Norton first came to Sydney and settled in Bondi, he lived in the usual variety of places new settlers to the Eastern Suburbs generally live in. Boarding houses, hotels, sharing flats and houses with other people, flats on his own, etc, till finally after working a year at the Kelly Club he bought an old semi-cottage in Cox Avenue, Bondi. Though Norton didn't actually buy the house out of shrewd judgment or a masterly plunge in real estate; it was almost given to him on a plate.

A couple of Painters and Dockers, hit men, came up from Melbourne to do a job on a night club owner at the Cross, and not being the two brightest hit men in the business they got Price Glaese mixed up with the bloke they were supposed to neck. Naturally enough it was the last job they ever did; or in this case tried to do. About a week after botching their contract they finished up wired to a couple of Holden gearboxes, feeding the snappers at the bottom of Port Phillip Bay; their heads and torsos well and truly ventilated with rather large holes. Which a .38 calibre revolver at close range is apt to make.

Their bungled attempt was made outside the Kelly Club early on a Thursday night as Price was walking back to his car. Norton, being born and bred in the bush and the son of a spiritually minded mother, had this uncanny sixth sense that always seemed to tell him whenever something wasn't quite right. So even though it was early and still relatively quiet he decided to walk Price up to his car.

'You're a bit of an old sheila at times Les, aren't you?' said

Price to his big doorman as they sauntered slowly along the footpath in Kelly Street.

'Ah, I just felt like stretching me legs to tell you the truth,' replied Norton laconically. His narrowed eyes darting all over the street.

As they got to Price's Rolls, Norton noticed the unusual way a dark blue Valiant seemed to cruise directly towards them. Saw the glint of a gun barrel reflected in the neon lights around them and flung himself in front of Price; badly bruising him but undoubtedly saving his life as a fusillade of automatic weapon fire slammed into the Rolls, shattering two windows and blowing away the outside rear vision mirror.

Norton stopped two bullets, one through the shoulder another through his thigh. They were only superficial and luckily he wasn't hurt very badly at all, but as far as Price was concerned he owed the big red-headed Queenslander his life and did everything he could to make it up to him.

However, Norton stubbornly refused to accept a thing. He offered him half a million in cash. Norton refused to take it. He offered to buy him a new home. Norton still said no. A trip overseas, his wages doubled and a share in the casino. But nothing could break Norton's pertinacious resolve. All he'd say was, 'That's what you're payin' me for, ain't it?' shrug his big, broad shoulders and smile.

This annoyed the absolute shit out of Price. He owed Norton his life and wanted desperately to repay him; so he cooked up a scheme with his brother, one of Sydney's leading barristers, to sell Les a house. Price knew Les only lived in an old flat in Bondi and he was always saying that if he ever got enough money together he'd like to buy a house of his own. So Price bought the old semi, nothing too flash of course as he didn't want Norton smelling a rat, and got the message back to him through his brother that there was a deceased estate up for sale and if he got in lively he'd pick it up for around $10,000. Price would guarantee him the finance.

Now Norton might not like to accept charity but when it came to the chance for an earn or a bargain there was none smarter, and having a reputation for being so mean he wouldn't lead a blind grasshopper to a lawn Norton had no qualms whatsoever at making a hustle because some poor old pensioner had kicked the bucket. As far as Les was now concerned Price's favour had been returned, Price felt a lot better and Les was absolutely jubilant. He finally had a home of his own; and he'd got it under his own steam.

It took about six weeks for the contracts to be finalised then Les moved in, after brassing his Jewish landlord for exactly that amount of rent. Norton didn't do this out of malice or prejudice; he did it simply to save money and knowing that if you live in Bondi and have a Jew for a landlord it's more or less compulsory for the 'goyen' to have a go and try to get their own back. Norton always reckoned it was worth ten years of his life just to see the look on Benny Rabinsky's face when he found he'd been taken to the cleaners for around five hundred bucks.

The team at the Kelly Club all contributed a little something towards helping Les move into his new home. Some cutlery, a few gadgets for the kitchen, the girls ran him up a few curtains, the boys all shot in and bought him a washing machine. Price Galese insisted that Les let him shout him a good ottoman lounge and Billy Dunne lined up a couple of willing thieves to have the place carpeted at the right price. In about a week Norton had the old semi looking pretty schmick, it was all nice and comfortable inside and he was just starting to get to know some of his neighbours.

They were a fairly mixed bunch. A few old pensioners lived in the houses opposite. Alongside these were some wharfies, an old SP bookie who still wore a hat everywhere he went and a sleepy looking fireman who did a lot of Yoga. His side of the street appeared to be mainly Jewish migrants of all nationalities and in the houses directly alongside him, a family of Greeks owned one and a mob of noisy New Zealanders rented the other. Naturally enough Norton sorted the Kiwis out first.

Actually the Kiwis weren't a real bad bunch. There were four of them sharing the house, three guys and a chick. The were all working and they were a happy enough, easy-going lot but like all New Zealanders, as soon as they arrive in Australia and get their first flat or house they're not happy unless they're partying 24 hours a day, seven days a week. This didn't worry Norton that much because he didn't get home from work till after 4am, so he'd miss the worst of it. But he did find it a bit punishing when he'd just off to sleep and they'd start up again about 7.30am. Not that Norton was a nark when it came to music, he was very partial to a bit of Cold Chisel and he used to love training to AC/DC and Rose Tattoo. Nor was he the kind of bloke who wanted to lie around in bed all day; as long as he got his six hours sleep in the morning and an hour before he went to work he was happy, but this particular lot and their friends didn't even want to let him have that.

He copped it sweet for almost three weeks till finally he arrived home absolutely buggered above five one Sunday morning to find about a dozen drunks sitting on their front verandah sucking on cans of Fosters and banging away tunelessly on a couple of guitars with a Dragon album still blaring on the stereo back in the house. Some empty beer cans in his front yard and several pools of urine where some one had pissed up against his fence didn't cheer him up that much either.

He ignored them as best he could as he went inside, had a mug of Ovaltine and went to bed, but try as he may he just couldn't get to sleep. The noise was right under his bedroom window and they more he tossed and turned, even with his face under the blankets and the pillow over his head, the louder the noise seemed to get. Finally, about 6.30am, he got up, put on a pair of Stubbies and a sweat shirt and decided to go and have a word with them. They didn't even notice Norton come through the gate and stand scowling alongside them, his eyebrows bristling over a pair of bloodshot eyes all puffed up like two cane toads from lack of sleep.

'Excuse me matey,' he said to the nearest Kiwi banging away on his guitar. 'Do you think you could quieten down a little so's I can get some sleep? It is getting late you know.'

If the Kiwis had noticed him they chose to ignore him and just kept singing along, sucking on their tinnies.

'Mate,' repeated Norton through clenched teeth, 'it's half past six. Do you think you could ease up a bit, I just want to get some sleep.'

'What's the matter, fellah?' the first Kiwi with a guitar finally said. 'You don't look very happy. Here, have a beer.' He giggled drunkenly and offered Norton a sip from his can.

'I don't want a beer, mate. I just want some sleep.'

'Don't want a beer, mate,' echoed one of the other Kiwis apeing Norton's Australian accent. 'What sort of an Aussie are you if you don't drink beer, mate?' The others all laughed uproariously.

Norton could see he wasn't going to get anywhere; they were all too pissed and just a bunch of smart-arses anyway.

'All right then,' he said ominously. 'If you're going to play your guitars, the least you could do is get them tuned properly. And I know the quickest way to tune a guitar. Fellah.'

He tore the guitar out of the first Kiwi's hands and smashed it over his head with a hollow splintering of wood and a twanging of breaking guitar strings, leaving it sitting on his head like a big wooden hat. It happened so fast the others still sat there blinking.

'Now, as for this other one,' said Les reaching over and grabbing the second guitar. 'It's too big. You could make this into two ukuleles.' He leaned it up against the pillar supporting the roof of the verandah and gave it a forearm jolt, smashing into noisily into two crumpled halves. 'There you go,' he said brightly. 'That's much better, isn't it?'

'Hey. What do you think your doing, fellah?' said one of the Kiwis, starting to rise drunkenly to his feet. Norton gave him a backhander that split his mouth open and dumped him straight back down on his arse. 'Shut up while you're in front. Fellah,' he said evenly.

'Oh. One more thing,' said Norton looking at them for a moment. 'I almost forgot to mention it.' He went inside and walked quickly down the hallway which was littered with empty cans, glasses and wine flagons and stank of stale beer, stepped into the lounge room, over some people crashed out on the floor, pulled the leads out of the speakers and tore the Dragon album off the turntable. 'As far as I'm concerned,' he said returning to the others out the front, 'Marc Hunter couldn't carry a note if it had handles. Jimmy Barnes'd play him off a break.' With a few twists of his huge hands he broke the album up like an arrowroot biscuit and dropped the jagged pieces of black vinyl noisily on to the guitar still wedged firmly on the first Kiwi's head. 'Get into some Cold Chisel. It's much better than this.' For a moment he looked at them sitting there with their mouths open, then rubbed his hands together. 'Now I'm going to beddy byes,' he said. 'I suggest you all do the same. Goodnight.' Norton left, closing the gate gently behind him. In five minutes he was in bed and dead to the world.

The Kiwis quietened down considerably after that, though Norton sensed there was something in the wind; but he didn't lose any sleep over it. However it came to a head the following Sunday morning, exactly one week later.

Norton got home knackered about 4.30am, had a mug of Ovaltine and hit the sack. His head was no sooner on the pillow and he was snoring his head off revelling in the new found peace and quiet. About 7.30am his sleep was shattered by some loud reggae music and this other horrible sound which he couldn't identify. All he knew was that it was coming from the Kiwi's house.

'What the bloody hell's goin' on?' he mumbled angrily, swinging his legs over the bed and rubbing his eyes as he stared numbly at the floor. He stumbled sleepily over to his bedroom window, pulled back the curtain and stared into the Kiwis' front yard.

Sitting on the steps of their verandah, playing an electric guitar and singing at the top of his voice next to a ghetto blaster about the same size as a large suitcase, on full bore, was the biggest Astra bat Norton had ever seen in his life. Whether he was a Maori or a Cook Islander Les couldn't tell, but he was well over six feet tall and at least 17 stone, with arms like tractor tyres and a big ugly scarred head with a mouth like a Murray cod sitting on a neck as thick as a tree stump. Behind him sat the three Kiwis and the girl, sipping on cups of coffee and trying not to laugh. They spotted Les looking through the curtains and went into a huddle.

'I wonder what our friend next door will do now,' said the girl.

'I don't think he'll do too much when he sees Big Tiki,' replied one of the boys.

'Big Tiki'll murder him.'

'Play it a bit louder, Big Tiki.'

Big Tiki was only too willing to oblige. He turned the tape up another two notches on the ghetto blaster and accompanied it on the electric guitar with his own horrendous version of Bob Marley's 'Coming in From the Cold'. You could have heard it back in Jamaica.

'Just as I thought,' growled Norton, letting the curtains fall back into place. 'A bloody set-up. Oh well.'

He stood there stroking his chin, thinking for a few moments then put on a sweat shirt and a pair of old Stubbies, went to the bathroom, cleaned his teeth and splashed some cold water on his face and neck. Feeling half awake he sauntered into the kitchen and put the electric kettle on. While it was boiling he started limbering up with a few push-ups, sit-ups and stretches; he wasn't worried about fighting the big mug next door but he could see that he was built like an ox and he didn't expect it to be any pushover, so there was no use in going off half cocked. After the exercises and gulping down a large mug of scalding hot coffee and honey Norton felt almost wide awake; he also felt extremely mean. He finished his coffee, did another 20 sit-ups, then slipped his mouth guard in his pocket and went out to confront the giant Astra bat.

The Kiwis in the meantime were chuckling amongst themselves at Norton's non-appearance, it had been over 15 minutes since they saw his face at the window and they were convinced he had dogged it. They were congratulating Big Tiki and laughing out loud when Norton suddenly seemed to materialise out of nowhere at their front gate. His eyebrows were bristling like two red scrubbing brushes and the look on his face would have frightened a bulldog out of a butcher's shop. Their laughter immediately stopped. He glared at the now silent Kiwis on the steps then strode straight up to Big Tiki and turned off the portable stereo; in the abrupt silence Norton's voice sounded like far away thunder.

'Listen, soul brother,' he snarled right into Big Tiki's face. 'If you don't stop playing that fuckin' guitar, I'm gonna shove it right up your big smelly black arse and use you for a fuckin' licorice paddle-pop. And I'll shove that fuckin' Third World briefcase up there as well. You understand? You fat heap of shit.'

Big Tiki was slightly taken back by Les's direct approach but he had about three stone and four inches on Norton.

'We'll soon see about that, fellah,' he snorted, unhitching the guitar and rising to his feet.

Norton stepped back to give himself room and as the monstrous black lumbered to his feet he bent at the knees and drove a ferocious right rip straight up into his solar plexus. The big Maori's eyes bulged out like two boiled eggs as every breath of air was torn violently out of his body. He was instantly paralysed. Norton followed this up with two savage left hooks that mashed Big Tiki's mouth into a nauseating crimson mess, spraying blood and teeth all across the front yard. Before he had time to blink, a knee thumped viciously into his groin, making his eyes roll with pain and slamming him up against the wooden pillar supporting the front of the house. He would have collapsed on the spot but unfortunately his belt caught on a hook imbedded in the wooden pole to support pot plants. Not being able to fall forward and still paralysed from the first deadly blow to his solar plexus, he just had to stand there and suffer Norton's pitiless rain of punches. And the big red-head wasn't pulling any either.

A short right broke most of his ribs, another opened up a cut above his eye almost half the length of his forehead; a left closed the other one. Christ, thought Norton, as Big Tiki still stood there, what have I got to do to drop this big goose? He unleashed another barrage of hellish punches that almost tore the big Maori's face apart and crumpled his ribs up like balsa-wood. Finally, the weight of Norton's punches wrenched the hook out of the pole and Big Tiki started to totter forward. As he fell towards him Les stepped back and brought his knee up into his face with a deep crunch that moved what was left of his nose six inches across his face. Big Tiki's torture was finally over and he slumped face down on the path unconscious; blowing bubbles in the widening pool of blood oozing out of his face.

'Now. You cheeky team of Kiwi pricks,' Norton snarled fiercely at the terrified New Zealanders still sitting ashen faced on the steps. 'You're next.'

He strode over and grabbed the closest two by the hair, banging their heads together violently; a hefty back-hander sorted the other one out.

'As for you, you poxy looking moll,' he said. Reaching across the others and taking the screaming girl firmly by the hair also. 'I'm just gonna rape you on the spot.' He held the sobbing, trembling girl in front of him for a moment. 'Then again you've probably been stuffed by half the Astra Hotel and I'll end up with the jack.' He spun her around and kicked her up the backside. 'We'll forget about that,' he said. A look of extreme distaste on his face.

'Now listen, you team of wombats,' he said evenly, walking over to the terrified New Zealanders. 'All I want is a bit of sleep in the morning. No more. No less. You understand?' They all nodded their heads nervously.

Norton picked up the portable stereo and turned it back on at a moderate volume. 'There you go. That's heaps loud enough,' he said, placing the huge ghetto blaster down in the pool of blood next to Big Tiki's battered and broken head. 'See, even your big mate agrees. Don'tcha son?' He gave Big Tiki a nudge in the ribs with his foot but he didn't budge. 'Oh well. I hope so anyway,' said Norton with a grin. 'He's too big to argue with.'

Bob Marley was cruising into 'Oh Woman don't Cry' as the others picked Big Tiki up and Norton hosed the blood off himself in his front yard and soaked his sweatshirt. Five minutes later he was back in bed; the barely audible sound of Bob Marley singing 'Is This Love' was drifting pleasantly through his bedroom window as he dozed off.

Strangely enough, Norton finished up fairly good mates with the Kiwis after that. They realised they'd been a little out of order and apologised to Norton and Les not being the sort of person to harbour grudges accepted this with a laugh over a few cans out the front one afternoon. In fact it wasn't long after that they invited Les in for a barbecue one Sunday afternoon and he ended up pulling this young Air New Zealand hostess, a really spunking little blonde, and throwing her up in the air. As for Big Tiki, he wasn't quite his old self when he eventually got out of hospital so he went back to Auckland and joined a religious movement.

On the other side of Norton lived the Greek family. Stavros Poltavaris, his wife Despina, their two sons, Nick and Steve, and Stavros's mother; she used to get around dressed in black with a black scarf over her head all the time. Norton nicknamed her Johnny Cash.

Les got to be the best of neighbours with the Poltavaris family and as far as Les was concerned Stavros was a pretty good bloke. He came out to Australia in the early 60s with a spare pair of pants and about two dollars in his pocket. But by sheer hard work he'd managed, after marrying Despina, to own his own home, get a new Valiant every year, send his kids to Waverley College and bring his mother out to Australia; where he was able to keep them all well-fed and comfortable with the excellent wages he earnt as head foreman in a big smallgoods factory out near Botany. He was overweight and over proud of his family and always rabbiting on to Les about how smart his sons were and how many goals they'd kicked that weekend for Hakoah Juniors. But Norton copped this sweet because if there was one thing Stavros could do, he could organise a barbecue and his wife and mother were two of the best exponents of Greek cooking Les had ever seen. They were always calling out over the fence to him and offering him a plate of souvlakia, or moussaka. Some stuffed eggplants, honey cakes or spicy little meat dishes rolled up in vine or cabbage leaves.

Every Sunday afternoon Norton would wait till Stavros got his barbecue going, give him about half an hour, then casually stroll down the backyard with a rake and kid to be tidying up the garden. Before long Stavros would call out over the fence.

'Les, my good friend. Have you eaten yet?'

'Oh, I had a bit of breakfast this morning thanks, Stav,' Norton would nonchalantly reply. His mouth welling up with saliva at the tantalising aromas coming off the Poltavaris barbecue.

'Hah. This morning. That is hours ago,' Stavros would exclaim. 'A big man like you, you must have food. Some meat. Here my friend, try some of this.'

'Well if you insist, Stav, I suppose I could fit a little something in,' Norton would modestly reply.

The next thing, over would come beautiful shasliks, grilled lamb with lemon, continental sausages, some fetta cheese salad full of big, plump, black olives. For a bloke who wasn't hungry Norton would eat enough for six people.

Stavros never twigged to Norton's subterfuge, or if he did neither he nor any of the family ever let on; but Les always did his best to reciprocate Stavros's genuine hospitality. Some of the fishermen in the boat-sheds at Ben Buckler owed Norton a few favours, so they were always laying a snapper or a few red bream on him, which invariably ended up going over the fence to Stavros and if ever the thieves, where Norton used to drink, ever hoisted any ouzo or zambuka Les would get it at the right price and lay that on the Poltavaris family too. There was no way Les would take an unfair advantage of Stavros's honesty and warmhearted generosity. He was too good a bloke.

Stavros, however, for all his good points had one glaring fault. A great fat, over-fed, savage, hulking german shepherd dog he owned called King. King was without a doubt the greatest prick of a dog God ever put breath into; a big dumb bully, but also as cunning as a shithouse rat. It had everybody in Cox Avenue, from the old pensioners across the road and their silky terriers to the postman, terrified. Everybody except Norton that is. It would growl, snap, bark and do its best to try to bite anybody who came within 100 metres of the house. It was spoilt rotten. It had its own carpeted kennel with an electric blanket in winter and a fan in summer, its own monogrammed dish and jacket and it only got the best cuts of beef and the juiciest bones available from the smallgoods factory where Stavros worked. So King, knowing where its bread was buttered, would naturally put most of this snarling, bitting act and show of canine devotion on for Stavros's benefit. And Stavros thought the sun shone out of its big, fat hairy arse.

'By golly Les,' he'd say to Norton over the fence. 'I've got a champion watch-dog here, you know.' He'd pat King's dopey big head and King would sit at his feet like a good, faithful, loyal companion. In the back of its mind though, it was just waiting for another hand-out of juicy, lean gravy beef.

'Yeah. I can see that,' Norton would reply derisively. 'He's a beauty all right.'

'And he's savage too, Les, you know. Absolutely scared of nothing. Nothing.'

'Yeah. He's a gem all right Stav. You're lucky there.'

'Ohh, don't ever come over the fence Les, my friend. I'd hate for anything to happen. I'd never forgive myself. Never.'

'Yeah. It'd be awful, wouldn't it?'

'My word yes. But then again the big fellow seems to get on all right with you. It's amazing.'

'Yeah. Probably cause I come from the bush, Stav. We sort of got a way with animals. Especially dogs.'

'Yes it's amazing. He's a killer with everybody else you know. But he seems to leave you alone. Amazing.'

'Yeah. It just goes to show, eh? He must know I'm a good bloke.'

'Yes, that's what it is.' Stavros's eyes lit up and he gave King's big boof head another pat as it sat at his feet wagging its huge tail and playing the part of man's best friend to the fullest. 'He's intelligent, see. He knows you are a good man.'

Norton winked and nodded his head. 'That's what it is Stav,

he's got heaps of brains, see. Just like his owner. He might even have a bit of Greek in him do you reckon? Can he play one of them bazoukis?'

Stavros threw back his head and roared laughing. 'Ahh, Les you have the sense of humour. You know what, my friend? I think this calls for a drink.' Stavros was still laughing as he went into the house to get two beers. King followed him inside.

King tried its barking, snarling, biting act on Norton when he first moved in. If it spotted Les in his backyard it would throw itself at the fence as if it wanted to smash through the palings in an effort to get at Norton's throat and poor Stavros would have to grab it by the collar, screaming. 'Down boy, down King. Easy boy.' And King would sit there behind Stavros, snarling at Les, its mouth drawn back to reveal a row of huge gleaming fangs like a crocodile.

Norton appeared to ignore this. Then about three weeks after he moved in he waited for a while, after Stavros took the family shopping one Saturday afternoon, went down the back yard and as King went into his act he jumped over the fence with a cricket stump and gave the big german shepherd the greatest serve it ever had in its life, nearly turning King's head into mashed potatoes. Before it managed to crawl up under the house and hide, he added several solid kicks in the stomach that had it pissing blood for a fortnight. King tried a bit of long distance barking after that but Norton kept a pile of half house bricks stacked near the back fence and a steady barrage into its ribs soon made it knock that idea on the head also.

So it switched its act back to the people next door till the woman there finally threw a pot of boiling tea over its head one day. King left its immediate neighbours alone after that and settled on terrorising everybody else in the street instead.

Not that Norton had anything against dogs, he had two champion blue heelers of his own back on his father's property in Dirranbandi, and he missed them constantly. But he'd never bring them down to Sydney; dogs stuck in backyards in the city both bewildered and annoyed him, he couldn't see the point in it, but he tolerated them. Though he was standing outside the Flying Pieman one afternoon, getting into a nice fresh 'depth charge' next to this massive Jewish woman with one of those oversized french poodles. The poodle kept jumping up and trying to eat Norton's steak and mushroom pie. The woman, instead of pulling her dog into gear, thought this was quite amusing. Finally Norton said to her. 'All right if I throw your dog a bit?' The woman replied. 'Yes, certainly.' So Norton picked it up and threw it half way across Campbell Parade, under a bus.

But he'd watch with amusement as Stavros would proudly put King on a lead and walk it snapping and straining around Bondi and up and down Cox Avenue where you had to queue up to hate it. Even Stavros's family didn't like King, especially his mother who invariably had to clean up the giant turds the stupid thing used to leave all over the backyard, and by the animosity he could feel around him Stavros knew deep inside it would probably be only a matter of time before King either got baited, stolen or something happened to it.

After sorting out the Kiwis Norton settled into Cox Avenue cosier than a baby beaver in a toothpick factory. He always stopped and had a bit of a mag to everybody, especially the old birds across the street with their silky terriers, who used to sling him a sponge cake now and again, and everybody seeing him come and go in his tuxedo thought he played in a swing band. Everybody except the old SP bookie in the hat: he woke to Norton's profession in about five minutes.

The big ex-Queenslander always kept in touch with his family and about six months after he'd been there the phone rang one Sunday night. It was his brother Murray ringing from Dirranbandi.

'Hello,' said Norton as the phone rang. He could hear the STD pips on the line.

'Izzat you Les?' came the voice on the other end.

'Yeah.'

'It's Murray. How are you, mate?'

'Muzza. Jesus it's good to hear from you. How's things, son?'

'Pretty good. Listen I'll be down to see you next week.'

'Fair dinkum?' Norton was ecstatic. 'You gonna bring the old man?'

'No, I'll be comin' on me own. I'll only be stayin' a day or two at the most.'

'Oh. Oh well don't matter. What's the story anyway?'

'I got a couple of opals I want to flog.'

'Fair dinkum? They any good?'

'Yeah. I showed one to a buyer up here, some reffo from Sydney, and he offered me seven grand for it.'

Norton whistled over the phone. 'And you got two of them?'

'Yeah. But I don't want to say too much over the phone, so I wrote you a letter to explain things a bit better. You should get it early this week.'

'All right then. So when do you reckon you'll be down?'

'Next weekend. I'm drivin' down so I should be there about lunchtime Sunday. All right?'

'Good as gold, Muzz.'

They chatted for a minute or two about different things before saying goodbye and hanging up. After he put the phone down Norton got a Fourex out of the fridge and sat there with a quiet smile on his face, reflecting on his brother and thinking how good it would be to see one of the family again.

A lot of people thought Les was a hillbilly when he first came to Sydney with his awful clothes, his slow way of talking and his rough bush mannerisms. But they'd never met Murray; Murray was a hillbilly. He wore hillbilly clothes, listened to hillbilly records and lived on a hillbilly type of property about 20 km out of Dirranbandi. Out of a family of six he was two years older than Les and didn't look unlike him except he was about two inches shorter than Les and where Les was more bulky and solid Murray was lean, tough and wiry. As hard as a cricket ball and built like he was made out of iron rods. He had deep mahogany colored eyes topped by a pair of bushy brown eyebrows, poked back under a wide, almost receding forehead plastered with thick, untidy brown hair.

He worked for the Queensland Dingo Control Board, shooting and trapping dingos. He also took tourists pig shooting and did a bit of opal gouging on the side, with varying degrees of success. He had a wife almost as tough as him and five of the wildest kids ever born in Australia. He had two horses, three goats and a pet wedge-tailed eagle. He also had a dog. A cross bull-terrier cattledog, called Grungle.

Grungle was the toughest, hardest dog in Dirranbandi, probably Queensland, and as far as dogs go Grungle was something else. He was jet black with a blue blaze on the front, about four feet long and about three feet wide with a neck as thick as a man's waist and teeth and jaws like a white pointer shark. He had those typical, pink, piggy eyes of a bull terrier and was absolutely fearless. He'd been bitten, gouged, gored, shot, blown up with dynamite and still came back for more. He loved nothing better than to go pig shooting with Murray and was never happier than when he was charging into battle against some huge, wild black boar, taking his chances against its slashing, razor sharp tusks. He'd get underneath the hate maddened, monstrous black pigs, bite their legs off then rip their chests open and tear their hearts out with his massive jaws. And if he had to take on more than one at a time, so much the better. A fight wasn't a fight for Grungle unless he got gored a few times and Murray had to sew him up with a darning needle and fishing line. But he got on okay with most other dogs, unless they were silly enough to start anything. And he loved people, especially the mob at home; and even though the kids used to kick, punch and annoy shit out of him he guarded that family like it was the Crown Jewels. Consequently Murray and Grungle were inseparable.

Murray's letter arrived on Tuesday. It conveyed greetings from everyone at home and a little bit of news, though not in great detail as Murray was flat out reading and writing at the best of times. But he did his best to describe his two opals and how he found them. From what Les could gather Murray had gone to Lightning Ridge with his son Wayne to show him how opal mining was done. They were fossicking around looking for floaters and decided to have a dig around down this old abandoned mine with a couple of hurricane lamps. They were chipping along when they came to a bit of toe dirt, finally digging through this into a biscuit band. Wayne got sick of being hit in the face with salt and shin cracker so he went back up top. Murray kept plodding along when suddenly instead of hearing 'chip, chip, chip,' as he dug along the clay face, he heard 'clunk, clunk, clunk,'. He dug along carefully and pulled out what he first thought were a couple of nobbies. But after giving them a bit of a tap with his pick the colour burst out like an explosion. Even in the soft glow of the hurricane lamp he could see he was on to something.

He climbed back out of the dig and later that evening took them to an old miner who dopped them up for him. A good rub with some pumice powder showed he'd found good opal and a final going over with cerium oxide revealed an unbelievable red flash of colour on a black background. Murray knew he had something for sure. He took one to a buyer the next morning who weighed it in at 85 carats and offered him $7000 on the spot. Murray took his card and said he'd see him in Sydney. He left with the buyer chasing him all the way to his car. The letter finished with love from Elaine and the kids and everybody else and to expect him down there Sunday. Norton read the letter again, stroking his chin thoughtfully, and decided to show it to Price the following night at work and see what he thought.

The following night Les and Billy Dunne were standing outside the Kelly Club talking about nothing much in particular when Price glided up in his beige Rolls about 10.30pm. He looked suave and debonair, as always, in an immaculately tailored oyster grey three-piece suit, black Italian calf skin casuals and a narrow, green checked tie with a matching green silk handkerchief tucked neatly into the top pocket of his suit.

'Hello lads,' he said, rubbing his hands together happily as he approached his two favourite employees. 'How's things?'

'Real good Price,' chorused the two doormen.

'What's this? St. Patrick's Day,' said Billy, pointing to Price's green tie and hanky.

'What's up?' said Price, holding his arms out by his side. 'I look all right don't I?'

'To tell you the truth Price, that outfit makes you look half an hour younger. Fair dinkum.' Price laughed and gave Billy a slap on the shoulder.

'Hey Price,' said Norton. 'All right if I see you about something after work.'

'Sure,' replied the casino owner. 'Why, what's up? You're not in any trouble are you?' He looked at Norton for a moment, a stern look creeping over his face. 'You're not after a bloody raise are you?'

Norton laughed. 'No, nothin' like that. It's just that one of my brothers is coming down Sunday and he's got a couple of opals he wants to sell. Evidently they're pretty good. And seeing as you're an opal perv, Price, I thought I might have a word with you about them. All right?'

Price stroked his chin, looked at Les and contemplated for a moment. 'Opals, eh?' he said quietly. He reached over and rapped Norton on the chest with his knuckles. 'Come up and see me in the office after work. Okay?' He disappeared up the stairs.

They had the last punter out of the club about 3.45am and at 4am Les and Billy were settled in the plush office with a couple of drinks quietly discussing the evening's events while they watched Price and the club manager, George Brennan, count the money and put it in the safe. It had been a fairly uneventful night. One or two arguments with some drunks out the front and a bit of a skirmish with some big gangling goose trying to impress his girlfriend. He was dressed more like he was going to change the gearbox in his car but he told his equally grubby girlfriend he was going into the Kelly Club by hook or by crook and no pair of dopey bouncers would stop him. Billy decked him with a light left hook and he ended up sitting on his arse in Kelly Street minus most of his front teeth, crying. Apart from that the boys had earnt their money easy.

'Right. That's that,' said Price, as he crammed the last stack of 50s in the safe and gave the tumbler a spin. George Brennan handed him a Dimple Haigh on the rocks. Price thanked him, took a sip and turned to Norton. 'Now what's all this about opals, Les?'

Norton took Murray's letter out of his inside pocket and read the relevant parts to Price. When he'd finished, the casino owner sat there quietly sipping his drink for a moment, idly running his index finger around the rim of the glass. Billy and George had interested looks on their faces also.

'I'll tell you what,' Price finally said. 'Your brother could have something there. Eighty-five carats with a red flame on a black background. He could've fluked a fair dinkum black opal, it could be worth anything. It could be another Red Admiral or a Flame Queen.'

'What are they?' asked Billy.

'Two famous opals found at Lightning Ridge in the early part of the century, Billy. They're absolutely beautiful, worth a fortune. The bloody Yanks bought them of course.'

Norton looked back at the letter. 'Murray says he's got to see some buyer in Bellevue Hill, Sunday night.'

Price rose from his desk and dismissed Les's last statement with a contemptuous wave of his hand. 'Oh you can forget about that. He'll only be some shifty reffo out to rip him off. I'll tell you what to do.' He poured himself another drink before he spoke. 'Have him call round to my place with the opals on Monday. It's no good coming over Sunday, I've got the Police Commissioner and some other bludgers coming over for a barbecue. I'll arrange it through the week to have the owner of Consolidated Diamonds there. If I don't buy them he will and at least that way we'll make sure he doesn't get touched.'

'Thanks a lot, Price,' said Norton. 'I appreciate that.'

'That's all right, Les,' said Price. 'There might even be a bit of an earn in it for me yet.' He flashed the boys a cheeky grin. 'Christ knows I could do with it,' he added.

They had a couple more drinks and a bit of a mag and about 4.30am Les and Billy saw Price to his car and they all went home.

The rest of the week went fairly quickly. Price had made all the arrangements for Murray to meet the gem expert at his house on Monday and most of Les's thoughts were preoccupied with the arrival of his brother on the weekend.

The following Sunday afternoon, about 3.30, Les was sitting in his lounge room watching 'Wide World of Sport' on TV. It wasn't much of a day outside, cloudy but no rain, so he decided to stay home, soak his right hand in an ice bucket and wait for Murray's arrival. They'd had a bit of a stink at work the previous night with a bunch of yobbos from the Western Suburbs out on a bucks' night just looking for trouble, which they found in ample quantities outside the Kelly Club. Les decked five, Billy got three, however in the melee of flying fists and feet Norton threw this wicked right at one mug's face but accidently caught another in the back of the head. He fractured the poor goose's skull but bruised a couple of knuckles in the process. It was more an annoyance than anything else and the ice treatment had just about got it fixed. He was sitting there soaking his hand and thinking how much he'd like to get into one of the young Russian women gymnasts on TV when he heard a loud 'shave and a haircut, two bits' banged on his front door. He strode rapidly up the hall, threw the door open and there stood Murray, a grin from ear to ear and looking as tanned, fit and wiry as ever.

'Muzza,' exclaimed Les, 'by Jesus it's good to see you.'

'G'day Les. How are you, son?'

They shook hands with enough bone crunching enthusiasm to crush a billiard ball then threw their arms around each other in a warm brotherly embrace, finally standing there for a moment shaking hands, just looking at each other. Each brother more than just a little misty eyed.

'Murray. You're looking well, son. Life sure must be treating you okay. That's good.'

'You don't look too bad yourself old fellah,' said Murray, giving Les a solid thump in the stomach. He nodded his rough head at Les's house. 'So this is your new digs, eh?'

'Yeah, this is it mate. Maison Norton.' He noticed Murray's dust-caked Holden panel-van standing out the front. 'Did you have any trouble finding it?'

'No, I got meself one of those Gregorys. Only trouble was the traffic. Jesus I don't like these cities Les.'

'Yeah, they're not much are they. But you get used to them. Well come on inside son and we'll have a beer. I suppose you could do with one. I got the fridge crammed with Fourex too. None of that NSW shit.'

'Good on yer, Ginge. To tell you the truth I'm drier than a dead dingo's derrick.'

Les was about to usher Murray inside when a movement at the bottom of the front steps caught his eye. 'Holy bloody shit,' he cried out. 'Grungle.'

Sitting patiently at the bottom of the steps, wagging his tail and looking mean and ugly enough to make a bottle of medicine sick was Grungle. As soon as he heard Norton call his name he bounded up the stairs and threw himself at Les with a great squeal of delight, almost knocking him through the front door. Les picked him up under his front legs and laughed like mad as the ecstatic bull terrier started licking his face with affection, obviously delighted at seeing him again. Norton dropped him on the floor then rolled him over on his back and started rubbing his stomach. Grungle started kicking his legs and twisting his head and body from side to side as he howled with delight.

'Jesus, what made you bring this ugly looking little prick with you?' said Les happily. 'I'm glad you did though.'

'Couldn't leave him up there without me. Anyway, your two blues are looking after the place while I'm away.'

'Ohh, how are Shemp and Larry? They all right?'

'Yeah, good as gold. Took 'em pig shootin' last week. They went well.'

'That's good. Real good,' said Norton softly. A look of sadness crept into his eyes as he slowly patted Grungle. 'Well, come on, let's have a beer anyway,' he said rising to his feet.

Murray picked up his overnight bag and clomped down the hall after Les, with Grungle following. In his R. M. Williams riding boots, moleskin trousers, tattered check Millers shirt and an old brown bushman's hat with its sweat-stained band and the brim turned up at the sides he looked like he'd just stepped out of a Marlboro cigarette commercial. You could almost smell gum trees and hear flies buzzing.

'You can throw your swag in there, cowboy,' said Les, indicating a room running off the hall. 'We'll stick Grungle out on the back verandah. There's an old lounge out there; he can doss on that. I'll go down the road later and get him a couple of tins of Beef Chunks.'

'Nah, I wouldn't feet him that shit. I got his tucker here,' replied Murray. He threw his overnight bag on the bed, unzipped it and took out two parcels wrapped in blood-stained newspaper. 'I got a couple of kangaroo legs. I'll give him one now and whack the other in the fridge. He only eats raw meat anyway.'

'Oh, fair enough,' said Les. He took the other leg off Murray and they went to the kitchen where Les put it in the fridge and took out several cans of Fourex. 'Come on outside,' he said nodding his head towards the back door.

They walked down a small set of stairs leading off the enclosed verandah. Les tugged the ring-pulls off two cans and handed one to his brother. 'Cheers Muzz,' he said.

'Yeah. All the best,' replied Murray.

They sat there on the steps drinking and watching as Grungle happily tore the kangaroo leg apart, his massive jaws noisily crunching through flesh, fur and bone like it was a piece of sponge cake.

'He sure is an ugly looking prick of a thing,' said Les laughing. 'But you can't help but like him.'

Murray grinned and nodded his head. 'Yep,' he drawled, 'and I wouldn't swap for anything in Australia.'

'I wouldn't blame you, mate,' said Les with a smile, reaching over and patting Grungle's scarred head.

They sat there in the cloudy afternoon sunlight, talking about old times and steadily knocking over the tinnies, when the aroma from Stavros's Sunday afternoon barbecue started to drift over the fence and cause a bit of a rumble in Norton's stomach. 'Are you hungry?' he asked his brother.

'Oh, a bit,' replied Murray.

'Well come down and I'll introduce you to my neighbour. He's a Werris, but he's not a bad bloke.' They got up and walked over to the fence. 'How you goin' there, Stav?' called out Les.

Stavros looked up from his chops and steaks sizzling on the hotplate and smiled. 'Hello there Les, my friend. How are you?'

'All right. Stavros, this is my brother, Murray. He's down from Queensland for a couple of days.'

'Hello there my friend,' said Stavros, reaching over the fence and offering his hand.

'G'day Stavros. Pleased to meet you,' replied Murray. Unconsciously almost crushing the Greek's hand to a pulp. Stavros winced and introduced Murray to the rest of the family. Murray shook hands a little gentler this time and there were smiles all round. Stavros was just about to offer the boys some food when the sound of Murray's strange voice attracted King's attention. He was lying over by his kennel, not taking a great deal of notice, being more interested in what he could scrounge from the barbecue. He looked up at Murray and as he did he suddenly spotted Grungle through a crack in the fence palings. His ears pricked up and he drew back his mouth revealing a row of gleaming white fangs. A horrible deep growl came from his throat. In an instant he flung his huge frame at the fence in a barking, snarling frenzy of rage and frustration as he tried to get at Grungle; flecks of foam and saliva flew round the yard. The sudden noise was horrifying.

Grungle looked up from his kangaroo leg and his pink, piggy eyes narrowed, a ridge of black fur started to rise along the middle of his short powerful back. He looked up at Murray as if to say, what do you want me to do? Go over the fence or straight through it.

Quickly Murray put his hand on Grungle's nose. 'Stay there mate,' he said. 'It's all right.' Grungle ignored King and went back to his meal.

Thinking he had Grungle bluffed, this only annoyed King more, he jumped up at the fence barking and snarling, almost

101

screaming with rage. Stavros ran over from his barbecue and took him by the collar.

'Easy boy,' he said. 'Down big fellow. It's all right. Come on now King, take it easy.' With a considerable amount of effort Stavros managed to calm King down a little and drag him snarling and snapping viciously back to his kennel where he was just able to slip the chain on him; almost dislocating his shoulder in the process as the huge german shepherd kept lunging back towards the fence. After finally getting him chained up he returned to Murray, who was leaning against the fence, a look of utter disbelief on his face as he watched King straining on his chain snarling at Grungle. He looked over at Les who winked back impassively.

'Oh boy. I'm sorry about that,' said a puffing Stavros. 'It's just that the big fellow goes mad when he sees other dogs. He's a killer you know.'

'Go on, eh?' replied Murray slowly.

Les caught the look in his brother's eye and winked again. 'That's Stavros's guard dog, King. He's a real terror Murray. You got to watch him.'

'Fair dinkum?' replied Murray, slowly again.

'Oh ho, you better believe it,' said Stavros. 'Fod God's sake don't let your dog come in here. King would tear him apart.'

'You want to put money on it?' said Murray quietly. Slowly pushing his hat down over his eyes.

'What was that?' said Stavros.

'He said, you could bet money on it,' cut in Les quickly.

'Oh of course,' said Stavros lightly. 'I mean look at the size of your one compared to mine. King is a giant. A killer as well. It would be a ... a slaughter.'

'We got an old saying in Queensland, mate,' drawled Murray 'it's not the size of ...'

'What Stavros is trying to say, Murray,' interjected Les, 'is that King's too big and he wouldn't like to see your dog get hurt. That right Stav?'

'Of course,' said Stavros, making an open-handed gesture. He looked down at Grungle still quietly sitting there chewing on the last of the kangaroo. 'He seems a nice little fellow, funny looking though. I've never seen one like that before. What is it?'

'Fox terrier,' replied Les.

'A fox terrier.' Stavros threw back his head and laughed. 'A fox terrier against The King. Tch, tch, tch. I'd hate to see the result.'

'I'm bloody sure you would,' Murray muttered under his breath. His dark brown eyes flashing.

'What's he eating there?' said Stavros. 'It looks like a leg of lamb.'

'Yeah, Murray feeds him baby lamb,' said Les. 'It's easy for him to chew.'

'Lamb. Hah. You should feed him beef my friend,' said Stavros looking at Murray. 'This is what I give King. Raw beef. That is why he has such strength.'

'I wouldn't want him to get too savage,' said Murray, patting Grungle's horrible scarred head as the last piece of bone got ground up and disappeared down his throat like some potato peelings going down a disposal unit.

'Anyway, my friends,' said Stavros. 'Talking of meat, are you hungry? Let me make up for King's terrible behaviour with some food. There's plenty here. Plenty. Despina, bring another two plates.'

'Well. Only if you insist, Stav, me old mate,' said Les, winking at his brother once more.

Stavros insisted so Les and Murray got into it. Murray was an old pie and peas man from Queensland and he had to admit the food was a little bit spicier than what he was used to and Les reckoned he wasn't that hungry anyway. However, between the two of them they managed to chomp their way through almost a side of lamb and two scotch fillets.

Stavros was giving the beer a bit of a nudge as he was taking Monday off from work to go to some Greek wedding. He was also giving Les and Murray's ears a bit of a nudge about how good his kids were and how good a house, car and job he had and about how he'd killed them in general since he came to Australia. But the boys didn't mind, as the food was going down it was all going in one ear and out the other.

After about an hour or so Stavros well and truly had his wobble boots on and was suffering very badly from verbal diarrhoea. Les could feel that Despina and the kids were starting to get more than a little embarrassed, so he and Murray thanked Stavros for his hospitality, told Despina how much they enjoyed her cooking and went inside, leaving Grungle in the backyard; much to King's intense aggravation.

'Christ that Werris can talk, can't he?' said Murray, sitting back on the lounge with his leathery hand wrapped round a steaming mug of coffee. 'And what about that silly big bloody dog of his?'

'King?'

'Yeah, bloody King. I'd like to give it King, right in the nuts. I felt like gettin' Grungle and tossin' him over the fence. You wouldn't want to be wearin' a white shirt if I did. My dog's a killer.' Murray snorted contemptuously into his coffee. 'I'd like to take it back home and see it put it's act on down The Royal one Friday arvo. It'd last about five seconds. Bloody German shepherds.' He snorted into his coffee again. 'They're not worth two bloody bob.'

'Yeah I know, they're useless,' replied Les. 'But apart from that he's not a bad bloke, so let him have himself on.'

'Yeah, I s'pose.'

'And I got to live next door so for Christ's sake don't let Grungle near King. Okay?'

'Yeah, fair enough.'

'Anyway, what about giving me a look at these opals.'

'Yeah. I haven't showed you yet, have I?' Murray stood up and from a pocket deep down inside his moleskin trousers produced a small leather pouch containing the two precious stones wrapped in tissue paper. With great care he spread them out on the coffee table in front of them. 'Well, what do you reckon?' he said.

Sitting on the coffee table with the lounge room light reflecting in them from above, the two opals looked like a pair of small boiling red suns, tinged with blue, yellow, green and every colour imaginable. As he moved them around, the colours appeared to explode out of the stones one minute, then dance and roll in waves the next with an almost hypnotic effect. Les thought they were the most fascinatingly beautiful things he had ever seen, yet with a beauty that was eerie, almost unearthly at the same time.

'Jesus, they are something, aren't they Murray?' he said sublimely. 'I've never seen anything like that.'

'Neither have I, to tell you the truth,' replied Murray slowly.

Les then told his brother about the conversation he'd had with Price Galese earlier in the week and to forget about seeing the rip-off merchant in Bellevue Hill that night as there would be a

104

driver round to pick him up tomorrow and he'd be getting the right money for the gems at Price's house tomorrow no matter what. Murray was rapt.

'Les, I appreciate what you've done for me,' said Murray reflecting into his mug of coffee. 'But as soon as I do this deal tomorrow I'm heading straight back home. I'd like to stay a while but I can't stand cities, mate. I'm sorry.'

'That's all right Muzz, I understand. I'm a bit the same way myself. But you know how it is with me,' said Les sadly.

'Yeah. But that'll blow over eventually.'

'I hope you're right. I'd love to come back home and see everyone.'

'Anyhow look,' Murray reached over and slapped Les on the leg. 'What about letting me take you down the pub and shout you a couple of beers. I just feel like having a few over the bar and then I might hit the sack. What do you reckon?'

'All right. You can shout me a middy or two down the Bondi. We take your car or mine?'

'Let's walk down. I just been in a car for 17 hours and I wouldn't mind stretching me legs.'

'Righto. I'll just throw a pair of jeans on.'

While Les got changed, Murray pocketed the opals and checked on Grungle in the backyard, giving him a big pot of water from the kitchen. He was all right and Murray could see King was still chained to his kennel so there was no chance of him getting at Grungle and getting torn to pieces for his trouble. King saw Murray and started growling again. The wiry bushman walked over to the fence, cleared his throat and spat a big gob right on to Kings face. 'Shut up, you prick of a thing,' he snarled. King didn't know what to do but he quietened down immediately expecting a couple of house bricks to come sailing over the fence into his rib cage.

'Everything sweet out there?' said Les when Murray came back inside.

'Good as gold.'

'Right. Well let's go and throw a few pig's ears down our motor boats.' Les locked up the house and they walked leisurely off up Cox Avenue and down Hall Street in the direction of the Bondi Hotel.

There was quite a mob at the hotel when they got there, more than Les expected for a Sunday night. He recognised a few people in the crowded bar he knew from round and about and nodded his head, but he didn't bother to introduce his brother as he didn't really know them all that well; more casual acquaintances than anything else. Murray got a couple of beers and they found a spot near the end of the bar and stood back to watch the passing parade. Les could sense the stares his country brother was getting in his big bush hat and boots and could hear some of the derisive remarks. But he didn't let on. Murray was equally fascinated by all the different types of people as well.

There were bushy-headed, overweight Maoris; all covered in tattoos, both the men and the women. Beefy pommies were drinking schooners with red-headed Scotsmen, rosy-cheeked Irishmen were arguing at the top of their voices with swarthy, dark-haired Europeans. Around the pool tables drunken Aussies were clumsily banging balls around with equally drunken New Zealanders, and leaning against the bar several off-duty coppers were checking the crowd out and tipping schooners down their throats like they were expecting a brewery strike. Standing across from them, around a small, circular raised table, a team of shifty-eyed men dressed in T-shirts, shorts and white shoes were talking quietly over their drinks and checking out the coppers. Scattered amongst the various drinkers, wearing cheap dresses and faded jeans, were a number of seedy looking women, looking bored and wishing they were somewhere else. The general atmosphere was very smoky and very noisy.

'Strewth. What a nice mob of strays this is,' said Murray, pushing his hat forward and scratching the back of his head. 'Where've they all drifted in from?'

'It sure ain't the Royal at Dirranbandi is it?' said Les with a grin. Some one in the crowd caught his eye. 'Hey wait here a minute will you Muzz?' he said to his brother. 'I just want to see a bloke for a sec.' He drifted over and got into what looked like a serious conversation for a couple of minutes with a nuggety little bloke in his late 30s, wearing a pair of dirty, blue overalls.

'What was that all about?' asked Murray a little anxiously when Les returned.

'He's a wharfie I know. Got a couple of hot VCRs. I might get one off him through the week.'

'Oh.' Murray ordered another two beers. 'Hey Les. You feel like a game of pool?'

106

'Oh yeah, if you want.'

There was a row of coins on the side of one of the pool tables, Murray put his 60¢ at the end of the line and waited for his game to come up. They finished another two beers then it was their turn. Just as Murray started to walk over to the pool table someone else shoved his 60¢ in the slot, the balls rattled down and he and his mate started placing them on the green felt table.

'Hey, just a minute old fellah,' said Murray, 'it's my turn.'

The bloke who'd put his money in the slot looked up at Murray. He was a thick-set Pommy with straggly black hair and tattoos on his arms; he looked like a shorter, barrel chested version of Joe Cocker. 'What's up with you?' he said in a heavy Yorkshire accent.

'That was my 60¢ you just pushed in.'

'Leave it out Tex,' said the other Pommy, racking the balls. He was a little taller than his mate, with curly blond hair and about the same amount of tattoos. A noticeable scar ran across his cheek and finished under his broken nose. 'You've been on the farm too long. You've got the coins mixed up.'

'No I haven't,' said Murray a little heatedly as his hackles started to rise. 'It's my turn.'

'What's up with Tex? Has he been at the sheep dip again?' A third Pommy put his head in. He was the biggest of the three, over six feet tall with dark greasy hair and a sullen, jaundiced appearance. Like the others he was tattooed and a bit overweight.

'Hang on,' said Murray, placing a hand on top of the triangular placed balls. 'I'm not coppin' this shit. It's my turn.'

'Get your hands off the pills Tex. Or you might find your hat out in the street with your head in it.'

'You reckon,' said Murray. His voice starting to rise.

Just then Les came over. 'What's up?' he asked looking round the table then back at his brother.

'These kippers have jumped the gun,' said Murray angrily. 'Now they want to get smart about it.'

'Come here,' said Les, taking Murray by the arm and leading him away from the pool table. He'd seen that many fights in pubs over games of pool he knew the futility of it. 'Look, don't be starting a fight in here, I've got to come here all the time and sometimes I do a bit of business through the joint. So I don't want to be shitting in my own nest.'

'Well how about I just take a couple of the bludgers outside,' replied Murray.

'You'll only end up getting pinched. There's a bunch of coppers over there,' he nodded towards the bar, 'and they're going up and down the front all the time Sunday night. Give it a miss.'

'Ahh, it's enough to give you the shits though.'

'I know.'

'Why don't you take Tex back to the farm, Blue,' said the blond haired Pommy, 'and get his hat blocked? While he's got his head in it.' The others all laughed.

'Don't push your luck too far pal,' said Les, stony faced.

'We wouldn't dream of it. Would we lads?' said the biggest pommy, looking directly at Norton.

Murray was still seething when they got back to the bar and ordered another two middies. 'Fair dinkum, Les,' he said, taking a giant pull on his beer. 'I'd like to go over and shove that pool cue fair up that Pommy's fat kyber.'

'Anywhere else I'd give you a hand. I wouldn't mind snottin' the big goose myself. But I don't want to get barred from here and it's no use getting pinched.'

Murray took a deep breath and snorted it out through his nose. 'Yeah, I s'pose your right,' he said through clenched teeth. He glared over at the Pommies, who just ignored him and continued with their game.

They had another couple of beers, Murray cooled down a bit then he began to yawn. 'We might get goin' soon anyway, eh?' he said. 'I'm startin' to get a bit tired.'

'One more and we'll stall. I'll get 'em.'

They finished their drinks and quietly left the hotel. They walked along casually with their hands in their pockets, talking idly as they slowly strolled along grimy, narrow Gould Street.

'You know one thing I notice when I come to the city, Les?' said Murray glancing round at the shops and dilapidated old blocks of flats. 'Apart from all the mugs you have to put up with.'

'What's that?'

'All the rubbish in the streets.' He shook his head sadly. 'It always amazes me.'

'Yeah. You wonder where it's all coming to at times.'

They meandered along down the dingy, garbage-strewn street, talking quietly, just taking their time. The milky, yellow street lights threw sickly, crooked shadows around them and gave their brown faces a bleached, ghostlike appearance.

As they crossed Hall Street and were walking past the Post Office an old, blue Leyland P76, with a coathanger for an aerial and a Tottenham Hotspurs decal on the rear window drew up alongside them.

'Hey Tex,' a voice called out. 'Enjoy your game of pool?'

'Well I'll be buggered,' Murray said quietly, turning to Les. 'It's your Pommy mates back. Hey Les, we're not shittin' in your nest here. And I don't see any coppers about.'

'Go for your life, Muzz,' said Les evenly, slipping his watch off and putting it in his back pocket.

'Oh it's you back,' Murray called out to the Pommies in the old Leyland. 'I thought I could smell something. For a moment I was sure I'd trodden in dog shit.'

'Why don't you throw a cake of soap in the car?' said Les.

'No good doin' that,' said Murray. 'They'd only eat it. Think it was green chocolate.'

'You're a right funny geezer, ain't you Tex?' came a voice from the car.

'Not half as funny as you smell, arseole,' replied Murray.

'Hey Murray,' said Les. 'How do you tell a Pommy's age?'

'I dunno. How?'

'Give him a bath and count the rings.'

As they roared laughing, Les heard the crunch of a handbrake being jammed on. The next thing the blond haired Pommy with the broken nose jumped out of the front passenger side. 'Well we might just see how good you are, Tex,' he said savagely, walking straight over to Murray and squaring up.

He shaped up like a boxer and fired two straight lefts and a short right into Murray's face, knocking his hat off. Unfortunately, Murray was pretty much like his brother and you have to run him over with a double-decker bus just to bruise him. He just laughed.

'Bit of a boxer are you mate?' he said.

Murray shaped up with his hands down by his side, outback style, and threw a big overhand right; it looped a bit but it was lightning fast with a lot of weight behind it. It caught the Pommy flush on the jaw, shattering several teeth and knocking him up against the wall of the Post Office. In an instant two deadly lefts slammed into his face followed by another looping right. The Pommy saw stars and covered up as he felt himself being battered unconscious. Blood was starting to pour out of his mouth, nose and an awful cut in his ear.

Les was more interested in watching his brother's style and he didn't notice the Pommy who looked like Joe Cocker jump from the car, run over and king hit Murray in the side of the head, almost knocking him off balance. The big redhead quickly stepped in with a neat left hook that squashed Joe Cocker's ear flatter than a trodden-on potato chip. As he started to buckle at the knees a thundering uppercut split his bony chin open and shattered his jaw.

A movement to Les's right caught his eye. He moved fractionally just as the third and biggest Pommy came charging over and threw a big bowling left at the back of his head, He let it slide past, then, grabbing the big Pommy's left arm at the wrist, slammed a solid, right, back fist into his side; just under his floating rib. The big Pommy was a bit short of a gallop and hadn't been doing too many sit-ups; most of his training had obviously been on yorkshire pudding and beer. He sucked in his breath and gasped with pain. Les drew him slightly forward by the arm and slammed two stunning elbow shots into his temple. The big Pommy grunted with more pain and comets started to spin before his eyes as his brain was slammed violently from one side of his skull to the other. He started to sag like a wet sack. As he did, Les, still holding his left arm, stepped over it and drew it backwards into his crutch, squatting at the same time. The big Pommy let out a final scream of agony as his arm was snapped at the elbow joint, like a carrot. Just to make sure he was finished Les took him by the hair and slammed his face into the footpath several times, leaving patches of blood all over the dirty grey asphalt.

'How're you goin' there Muzz? Everything under control?' he called out to his brother.

'Good as gold, son.' Murray had the first Pommy lying on his side, his hands over his head, moaning with pain as Murray kept doing a bit of Balmain folk dancing up and down his ribcage with his R. M. Williams riding boots.

110

'That's not very nice is it Murray? Kicking a man while he's down.'

'They're not very nice blokes, Les.'

'True,' replied Les laconically.

'Well, that should do it,' said Murray giving the whimpering Pommy a last solid kick in the ribs. 'Let's piss off.'

'Yeah, come on. I think they've had enough.'

Murray reached down to pick up his hat. 'Hey wait a minute,' he said looking at the dark haired Pommy that Les had flattened. He took hold of his wrist. 'Isn't that one of those grouse Seiko quartz diver's watches?' He undid it, looked at it for a moment then slipped it into his pocket. 'Young Wayne's always wanted one of those to wear down the river. He'll be rapt when I give it to him.'

'I didn't know you were such a caring father, Muzz.'

'Nothin's too good for my kids, Les.'

Murray walked over, opened the front door of the P76 and looked inside. 'Hello. What have we got in here?' he said brightly. He reached inside and came up with two dozen cans of beer. 'Victorian Bitter. That'll do, it's not a bad drop.' He took two cans out and tucked the carton up under his arm. 'Here y'are,' he said slinging one over to Les.

They whipped the ring-pulls off and started drinking from the cans, walking slowly and quietly up the street, the same as before. After a while Les spoke.

'Been much rain up home lately?' he said taking a decent sort of a swallow from his can of beer.

'Nah,' said Murray, finishing his and tossing the empty can in the gutter. 'It's been that hot and dry even the goannas are gettin' round with zinc cream on their noses.'

'Go on, eh?'

They strolled leisurely along, talking and drinking a few more cans. They had another couple when they got home and called it a night.

Monday dawned cloudy with a little bit of rain around that looked like it could increase later on. One of those typical, unsettled days Sydney always seems to get in mid spring. Not cold enough to wear a jumper but too lousy to go to the beach; the sort of day you're better off being at work. Or in a pub.

Murray woke up to find Les standing at the bedroom door dressed in a pair of football shorts, running shoes and an old sweat shirt with the sleeves cut off at the shoulders. A sweat band made from an old T-shirt was wrapped around his head. 'G'day Muzz,' he said brightly, 'how did you sleep?'

'Mate, I never moved,' said Murray blinking his eyes several times while he got his bearings. 'What time is it?'

'About half past eight.'

'Shit, is it?' Murray was a bit surprised, being the sort of bloke that's normally up at the crack of dawn.

'There's a pot of tea in the kitchen. I'm just going down to Centennial Park for a run, why don't you get Grungle and come down, give him a bit of exercise.

'Yeah, I might do that,' said Murray rubbing his eyes. 'Just give me five minutes to have a snake's and put me strides on.'

'Take your time. There's no real hurry.'

An hour and a half later, Les had finished a 12 km run, sprints included, 150 sit-ups, the same amount of push-ups and a fairly solid spar and wrestle with his rock hard brother; which was a work-out in itself. Grungle had chased all the water hens, swans and everything else to his heart's content, while Murray had a good mag, bush style, to the park ranger and two young mounted policemen. Country boys themselves. They were fascinated by the strange, wild looking bushman and his equally strange, wild looking dog.

It started to rain again when they got back home, a little harder this time, so they had to sprint from Les's car to the house. After a quick shower Les changed into a track-suit and fresh sneakers then cooked them both up a big feed of breakfast sausages and plenty of scrambled eggs with chopped up shallots; plus a pot of tea and huge stack of Vogel's toast. Grungle was wet, so instead of having him lie around stinking up the lounge or the verandah Les put him out the back with the other kangaroo leg, which the dog immediately started crunching up with terrifying efficiency. King put his usual act on when he saw Grungle, who snarled a little at first then simply ignored him.

Over breakfast the boys watched Grungle through the back door, chewing on the leg. Across the fence they could see King's big head sticking out of his carpeted kennel in Grungle's direction. Every now and again he'd snarl bitterly at him.

'Go on Les,' said Murray between mouthfuls of sausages and egg. 'Let me toss him over the fence. Just for a couple of minutes.'

'Turn it up,' replied Les shaking his head. He took a great slurp of tea from his mug and looked at his watch. 'The bloke should be here soon to take you to Price's place.'

'Good. To tell you the truth I'm looking forward to meeting this boss of yours.'

'You'll love him Muzz. He's a terrific bloke. And wait'll you see his home, it looks like Buckingham Palace.'

'Yeah. Has he got a swimmin' pool? I might take me cossies.'

'Turn it up. You'd leave a ring around it a foot wide.'

They finished the first pot of tea, Les made a fresh one so they sat there talking and polished off the rest of the toast. They started to put the dishes away when Les heard a car horn bip a couple of times out the front. 'That'll be him now,' he said walking out and opening the front door. He recognised the driver and waved; the driver waved back from Price's brown Rolls-Royce.

'You right, Muzz?' he called out.

'Yeah. Wait'll I have a quick leak.'

It had stopped raining so Les walked down to the car to talk to the driver. 'G'day, Eddie,' he said as the driver's side window slid quietly down. 'How're you goin'?'

'Not bad, Les. How's y'self?' The driver was Eddie Salita, a short wiry Calabrian, who wore glasses and smiled a lot with flashing white teeth. There wasn't a real lot of Eddie, but he was a tough little rooster and Price's number one hit-man. It was Eddie who went down to Melbourne and shot the two Painters and Dockers who shot Les in their attempt to kill Price. 'Hey what's goin' on here, Les?' he asked. 'Price told me to guard this brother of yours with my life. Christ, I've got enough guns in the car to start a shooting gallery.'

Les smiled as he noticed the .38 police special sitting snugly under Eddie's shoulder and the butt of a sawn-off police riot gun sticking up between the front seats. An unopened box of shells was lying on the floor.

'Here he comes now,' he said. 'He'll tell you all about it on the way over.'

As Murray got into the front passenger's seat Les introduced him to Eddie. 'Listen Muzz,' said Les, 'it's half past twelve. I reckon you should be back half past two or so. I'll wait here for you anyway.'

'All right.'

'So I'll see you then. Good luck.'

'No worries. See you.'

'See you later, Eddie.'

'See you, Les.' Eddie gave the horn a toot as he drove off. Murray had a grin from ear to ear.

As the Rolls slowly cruised off down the street Les noticed Stavros herd his family, all arguing in Greek, out of the house and bundle them noisily into the Valiant; Despina got in the front, Johnny Cash sat in the back between the two boys. Despina looked quite nice in a sleeveless white dress with a floppy light blue hat, the boys were brushed up also in their dark blue Waverley College suits; all freshly dry-cleaned. Stavros was wearing the most ostentatious, black, chalk striped suit imaginable with a red tie about a yard wide. He looked like a heavy in a spaghetti western.

'Off to the big wedding, Stav?' Les called out as Stavros was getting into the car. Despina and the kids turned around inside, smiled and waved; Johnny Cash flashed a toothless grin from the back seat.

'Yes. Yes, off to the wedding,' replied Stavros. 'But I tell you something Les, my friend.' He put his hands on either side of his head and closed his eyes. 'I do not feel very much like it. Yesterday, too much. Ooh.'

Les couldn't help but laugh. 'You'll be right, mate,' he said.

He stood there for a moment as they drove off, idly kicking some rubbish into the still lightly flowing gutter. The rain had eased and out towards the ocean he could see a couple of small blue patches among the pastel greys of the sky. He was about to go in his gate when he spotted one of the old pensioners across the road, Mrs. Beatty, trying to manoeuvre a large, potted rubber tree plant from her front verandah down the front stairs.

'Hey, hang on Mrs. Beatty,' he called out. 'I'll give you a hand.' He trotted across the road and effortlessly picked up the heavy, black concrete pot. 'Whereabouts do you want it?' he asked.

'Just in the corner near the oleander thanks, Les.' Mrs. Beatty straightened up, dusted her hands on the apron she was wearing and tucked a loose strand of blue-grey hair back up under an old yellow scarf she had tied over her head. 'Oh, you're a pet Les, for doing that,' she said.

'That's all right,' said Les, nudging the heavy pot finally into place with his foot. 'If ever you need a lift with anything and I'm around, give us a yell. No good you bustin' a poofle valve.'

'Well, I generally get Mrs. Curtin next door to give me a hand, but she's in bed lying down. She's not very well today, poor thing.'

'Yeah. What's up? Bit off-colour is she?'

'Oh no, she took a dreadful turn yesterday evening. Didn't you hear what happened?'

'No, I was out. What happened?'

Mrs. Beatty produced a crumpled tissue from her apron, took off her glasses and polished them vigorously. Les could sense she was winding up for a bit of good gossip.

'Oh it was something shocking,' she said, placing her glasses back on her face. 'We were standing out the front having a bit of a talk ... we'd just put the garbage tins out. Mrs. Curtin had Sally with her.'

'Her little sydney silky?'

'Yes. Anyway, Mr Poltavaris has come out of his front gate with that great big alsatian of his, King, on a lead.'

Les's eyebrows knitted and he looked at her quizzingly. 'Go on,' he said slowly.

'Well, the next thing, King's torn itself off the lead, ran across the road and started savaging Sally.'

'Her little silky?' Les was incredulous. 'It's no bigger than a powder puff.'

'Yes I know. Luckily I had a broom handy and I gave it a crack across the face and he dropped her, otherwise he'd probably have killed the poor little thing.'

Les stood there po-faced, silently shaking his head.

'Anyway, poor Mrs. Curtin has picked up Sally, who had terrible gashes in her back, and King's gone her. She's fallen over and hurt all her back. By this time Mr. Poltavaris has ran over and managed to get hold of King and he's shouting at it to get down, but the blessed thing hardly takes any notice of him, you know. So I gave the rotten thing another crack with the broom. That made it shut up a bit.'

Les thought back to his episode with King and the cricket stump. 'Yeah, it would,' he said. 'So what happened then?'

'Oh Mr. Poltavaris was all apologies of course, but we had to take Sally to the vet and get its back stitched. Honestly, Les you should see some of the gashes. They're something dreadful.'

'I could imagine.'

'And we had to get the doctor for Mrs. Curtin. She took a very nasty turn, you know, when she fell down and hurt her back.'

'That's understandable.'

'Like I said. Mr. Poltavaris was all apologies and he's offered to pay any costs involved, he's quite a lovely person really. But that's not the point Les. It's that darn dog of his. Honestly, it's a bloody menace if you ask me.'

'Yeah, it's a pain in the arse all right.'

'Really Les, something should be done about it, you know.'

Les nodded his big head slowly. 'You're right there,' he said. As they were standing there it started to rain again. 'Look at that,' he said. 'Just as I thought it was going to clear up. Well, I'd better get inside.' He made a move for the front gate.

'Are you sure you wouldn't like a cup of tea?' said Mrs. Beatty as she went up the front steps.

'No thanks,' replied Les. 'I've got a few things I've got to do. When you see Mrs. Curtin say hello for me.' He started to head across the road. 'I'll see you later Mrs. Beatty.'

'Bye Les. Thanks for the lift.'

'That's all right.' He sprinted for his front gate as the rain increased. His front door was still open so he ran straight inside.

He went to the kitchen, put the kettle on and began cleaning up the dishes. While he was doing this he started thinking. He was still thinking 15 minutes later while he stood at the back door with a mug of coffee in his hand watching Grungle bulldoze an empty wine flagon around the backyard with his nose. Across the fence he could see King's sour face sticking out of its kennel. Every now and again it would snarl and bare its teeth towards Grungle, still spoiling for a fight and obviously still flushed with its victory over Sally.

Finally Les called Grungle over. 'Grungle, come here mate,' he gave a soft whistle and slapped his hand against his thigh, Grungle dropped what it was doing and ambled happily over. As it walked towards him, it reminded Les of a small train engine with a cow catcher on the front the way it seemed to push its big head in front of it in the bull terrier style; unlike other dogs that carry their heads up in a straight line.

It climbed up the stairs and flopped on its backside, resting on its paws next to Les's feet. Les patted its scarred head and gave its stomach a rub. Grungle gave a grunt of satisfaction and licked Les's hand. Looking up at Les, the happy smile on its face and the laughing effect of its pink piggy eyes almost hid the awesome, destructive power of those razor sharp teeth and massive jaws propelled by its short, unbelievably strong neck. Sitting there wagging its tail peacefully, it looked just like a family pet. Except that when you got up close it looked like at some time the family pet's face had caught on fire and someone tried to put it out with a pick axe.

As Les patted Grungle's unlovely head, he reflected back to how he used to watch his brother help it to develop those crushing jaws by taking a piece of thick branch at either end and with Grungle clamped on to it in the middle he'd lift the dog clean off the ground and swing it around for up to 15 minutes at a time. The dog would grip the wooden log like it was riveted to it till finally Murray would let go, then Grungle would crunch through the solid piece of wood like it was a scotch finger biscuit.

Les looked at Grungle, looked across the fence at the snarling King, thought about Sally across the road and looked back at Grungle again, scratching his chin thoughtfully. Finally he finished his mug of coffee and put it down on an old table on the verandah.

'Come on Grungle,' he said slapping his hand against his thigh again, a strange look on his face. 'Let's go for a walk, mate.' With Grungle at his feet he walked down the back yard towards the narrow lane that ran behind the houses. He slipped the bolt on the shoulder high wooden gate, set in the wood paling fence the same height, then he and a very happy but very curious Grungle stepped out into the lane. The skies were still leaden and overcast but it had stopped raining; there didn't appear to be a soul around.

Stavros's back gate was the same as Les's; wooden palings closed by a metal bolt with a hole like half circle to put your hand through. Les had another quick but cautious glance up and down the lane, still no one around, so he opened Stavros's gate, put his foot behind Grungle's solid backside and pushed him through, closing the gate quietly behind him.

His adrenalin pumping steadily and a wild look on his face, he dashed back into his place, propped an empty wooden box up against the fence and with his mind a whirl of avid and excited anticipation, climbed up on it to watch the proceedings. Les couldn't have been any more delighted if he'd been a black ghetto brother sitting ringside at an Ali-Frazier fight at Caesar's Palace in Las Vegas.

Squinty-eyed, Grungle still stood there quietly panting at the back gate, his sloppy pink tongue hanging over those gleaming white teeth, dripping saliva on to the lawn; he still wasn't quite certain what was going on. For some strange reason King still hadn't noticed him. Les hissed at him over the fence. He scowled up at him, then a movement at the back fence caught his eye; he couldn't quite believe what he was seeing. A dog, the cowardly wretch from next door, in his, King's, backyard and half his size too. There would be no mercy, the miserable cur would die for this act of audacious insolence. That was certain.

A deep ominous growl rumbled from King's throat and the thick brindle hairs stood up all over his back as he slithered treacherously out of his kennel, and with his tail tucked firmly between his legs and his stomach almost dragging on the ground he advanced slowly and deadly, like a maleficent great snake, towards the still smiling Grungle.

Grungle spotted King coming towards him and the smile on his face quickly vanished. A ridge of bristly, black hair stood up along his spine but oddly enough he still stood there, slowly wagging his tail. King quickened his advance till he was about two or three metres away, then with one great hideous snarl he raised himself up on his huge hind legs and like some maddened jungle beast leapt on to Grungle in a snapping, biting whirlwind of unbridled ferocity.

King's first strike was straight at Grungle's throat, the sheer weight of the monstrous german shepherd knocking him clean off his feet; only the thick, studded collar he was wearing probably saved him from King gouging half his throat out. Grungle rolled with King's onslaught and came back up about a metre or so behind him. However, instead of taking the fight back to King he seemed to start smiling again and just stood there, slowly moving his head from side to side and wagging his tail. Watching from the fence, Les couldn't believe his eyes, it seemed as if Grungle just wanted to play. But King certainly did not.

He pounced on Grungle again, snapping and snarling in a wild, blood-lusting, maddened frenzy; white flecks of froth and foam flew from his mouth as he repeatedly tried to savage Grungle's throat. Grungle went down under King's fearsome charge, rolled over and came back up behind him again. King immediately spun around and with amazing speed for his size leapt furiously on to Grungle once more; frustration was mixing with his anger at not being able to pin the cross-bull terrier down. From the fence Les still couldn't figure out why Grungle hadn't made some sort of a move. Is he playing, he thought? Well if he is, he'd better forget about it or King will end up making him into dim sims.

This time King's bruising charge was a little more effective and as he knocked Grungle over he managed to rip a piece out of his ear, sending a small spray of blood spattering across the back fence to soak into the rain-dampened palings. Grungle gave a slight, but strange, yelp of both pain and delight and rolled up behind King again. However this time, as he stood there, his tail had stopped wagging and his stubby, black ears were flattened down on either side of his head. His pink, piggy eyes had narrowed into two barely discernable slits, noticeable only by a fierce, sinister gleam, glowing from within.

King charged furiously into Grungle once more but this time, instead of rolling over, Grungle ducked under King's rush, got his jaws around one of the german shepherd's front legs, and bit it straight off. As neat and quick as someone snapping a carrot. King let out an agonised howl of pain and shock, he crashed forward and the jagged stump of white bone dug into the lawn; pink arteries and blue nerve ends dangled loosely as a torrent of blood spurted out on to the wet grass.

Before the horrified King knew what had hit him, Grungle spun around and with one mighty crunch of his massive jaws ripped about two kilograms of flesh from one of King's back legs, but instead of spitting it out, he gave the huge bloody lump of leg a quick chew and swallowed it, fur and all. Grungle gave a strange, primeval howl of excited delight and with another awesome snap of his jaws bit through the remainder of King's rear leg. It flopped on to the lawn not far from the front one.

King was now screaming with terror and agony as thick, dark red, almost black blood spurted from his torn arteries and shredded tendons, soaking the grass on Stavros's lawn in a sickly fusion of red and green. The huge german shepherd was now down to two legs and losing blood rapidly. In the betting he had just blown out from even money favourite to 500/1. In fact as the race callers would say 'you could write your own ticket'.

Howling with pain and fear, King rolled over on his back and tried frantically to kick away from Grungle's relentless attack with his remaining rear leg. His screams were cut off into a stomach-churning gurgle as the smaller black dog sank his gleaming fangs deep into his throat, biting straight through his collar. Rising up on his stocky hind-legs, Grungle lifted the huge german shepherd bodily off the ground and twisting his head viciously flung him over his shoulder, tearing half his neck out. King crashed to the ground and lay there writhing in agony, almost paralysed with fear, watching in terror as the huge piece of his flesh was chewed up to disappear quickly down Grungle's throat also.

Watching from the fence, Les's eyes were sticking out like two soft boiled eggs, he could hardly believe what he was seeing. Grungle wasn't content with just destroying King. He was eating him alive. There was blood and fur everywhere, the noises emitting from King's tortured body were dreadful; even for a man who had spent years working in a meatworks Les found the spectacle quite horrendous. He was going to jump over the fence and stop it but he thought; oh well, Grungle only gets a chance to come to the city now and again, so why not let him enjoy himself.

The wretched King lay there in a state of shock, pain and confusion; he still couldn't believe this was really happening to him. His life's blood was pumping out of him and as Grungle kept savaging him he could see it being splattered all over the backyard, even landing in his kennel. He put his remaining front leg up in a pathetic attempt to protect himself and the wild eyed Grungle bit it straight off. He tried to scream but his scream turned into a rasping, bloody gargle as Grungle sunk his fangs deep into his throat once more. Blood gushed out of King's nose and mouth. Grungle then switched his merciless attack to King's body, crunching noisily through his ribs like someone crushing up a wicker basket. King's tongue lolled loosely to one side of his mouth and the whites started to show as his eyes rolled piteously back in his head. The big german shepherd knew it was only a matter of time now and death would be the only thing that would relieve him of his terrible agony. The last thing he saw was Grungle's head rip through his breast and tear his still beating heart from his body, chew it and swallow it. King twitched a couple of times, then a hideous rattle came from his throat and he lay still.

The big german shepherd's agony was finally over.

Grungle still continued to savage King's mangled remains, chewing his body in half, then ripping his head off. Les watched as King's liver and kidneys went down Grungle's throat, plus a large portion of rear leg and decided it was time to put a stop to Grungle's gory afternoon tea.

'Righto, Grungle,' he said, leaping over the fence. 'That's enough, mate. Come on.' Grungle chose to ignore Les and kept chewing on King's decapitated head. Les took hold of the head and tried to prise it from Grungle's jaws. Grungle set his jaws like a vice and refused to budge. 'Come on,' said Les 'give me the fuckin' thing will you.' Grungle kept his jaws clamped around King's head, defying Les to take it off him.

'All right Grungle,' said Les indifferently, seeing he wasn't going to get anywhere in the tug-o-war with his brother's dog. 'That's the way you want it, is it.' He stepped behind Grungle, drew back his foot and kicked him solidly fair in his promiment balls. Grungle yelped with pain, let go of the head and ran to one end of the yard where he sat licking his throbbing scrotum and looking at Les in bewilderment.

'Come on, inside,' said Les, taking Grungle by the collar and leading him back into his own backyard. He locked the gate and dashed into the kitchen, returning with two large, green plastic garbage bags. He vaulted over the fence and started to clean up the carnage Grungle had left behind, hoping he could get it finished before Stavros returned from the wedding. If Stavros asked him where King was he'd just have to lie to him and let him think it had got over the fence and been picked up or run over or something.

Stavros's backyard looked like Homebush abattoirs. There were blood, bones, fur and pieces of dog meat and intestines scattered everywhere. Blood was splashed all over the lawn, the fence, Stavros's barbecue and the late King's kennel; next to the remains of his torso lay his leather collar, bitten cleanly through.

121

Les felt like he was taking part in some sort of cheap horror movie as he started hurriedly picking up the pieces and stuffing them into one of the plastic bags. Part of King's smashed ribcage tore the side of the bag; he pushed it down with his hand, blood smeared the sleeve of his track-suit and got in his watchband. Finally he had the remains of the german shepherd in the plastic garbage bag, he sealed it with a small plastic tie, dropped it into the other bag and sealed that too.

'Don't you bloody go near that,' he said to Grungle as he dropped the sodden, squashy bundle over the fence. At the sound of Les's voice Grungle retreated to the other side of the yard and sat there rather apprehensively. He wasn't in any hurry for another one of Les's Woolloomooloo uppercuts.

Les uncoiled Stavros's garden hose, turned the tap on full and started hosing away the blood; fortunately it had been raining most of the day so it washed away easily without leaving any trace. He had it all done in less than ten minutes. A quick check around revealed a few spots of blood inside King's kennel, he wiped them off with the sleeve of his track-suit. He had another check around, while he replaced Stavros's hose exactly as he'd found it. Everything was in order so he jumped back over the fence. He looked up and down the other backyards, there still wasn't a soul around so despite all the noise nobody had seen or heard a thing; luckily the rain must have kept everyone inside also. Thank God for that, he thought.

'Righto Grungle,' said Les. 'You're next.' He unhooked his own hose, took Grungle by the collar and started to hose the blood off him, giving him a final wipe over with a wettex. When he'd finished Grungle shook the remaining water off and sat there staring at Les, a rather flummoxed look on his face. He still couldn't figure it out. He's beaten up the neighbourhood bully and his own master's brother turns around and kicks him in the nuts. It's all very confusing, especially if you're only a bloke down from the country for a couple of days.

Les could read the look on Grungle's face. 'All right mate,' he said, reaching over and patting Grungle's horrible but sad big head. 'I suppose I shouldn't have reefed you in the Niagras like that. Here you are.' He opened the plastic bags, took out one of King's front legs and tossed it to Grungle, who caught it in his mouth, wagged his tail and trotted over to the other side of the yard to sit there crunching it up noisily. He was quite happy now.

Les resealed the garbage bags, picked the bundle up and took it out the front, putting it in the back of his brother's panel-van. I'll get him to drop it in a river somewhere on the way home he thought. Back inside the house he changed out of his rain-dampened, blood-smeared track-suit into a pair of jeans and a long-sleeved sweat shirt, then settled back on the lounge with a can of Fourex to have a think about what had just happened and wait for Murray to return.

Poor Stavros, he's going to be broken hearted for a while he imagined, but, what he don't know won't hurt him. Besides, King had a good run, he had every dog and just about everybody in the street terrified, especially those just across the road.

But like they say, all good things to an end must come and King, your end was a rather sticky one. Picking a fight with Grungle is like bleeding in front of a shark. So here's to you sucker wherever you are. Les raised his can of Fourex in silent toast to the late, but unlamented King, and drained it in one go. He was on his third can and really starting to see the funny side of it when the phone rang.

'Hello,' he said, picking up the receiver.

'Hello Les. It's Price, how are you?'

'Hello Price. I'm good mate. How's yourself?'

'Couldn't be better.'

'That's good. How did that business with Murray go?'

Price chuckled into the phone. 'That's what I rang to talk to you about.'

Les felt a little apprehensive at the tone of Price's voice. 'Something wrong is there? Those stones no good? Murray make a bit of a blue did he?'

'No good?' Price exploded into the phone. 'You're kidding. They're worth a bloody fortune.'

Les paused for a moment before he answered. 'Fair dinkum?'

'Fair dinkum. Look, I know a fair bit about opals and as soon as he showed them to me I bloody near fainted. I've got Brenton Richards here from Consolidated Diamonds, he's had one look at them and just about shit himself. He reckons they're two of the best matching fire opals he's seen in over 20 years.'

'They're that good, eh?'

123

'That good? They're incredible. They're absolutely unique.'

Les didn't answer for a few seconds. 'So — what happened? Your mate from Consolidated Diamonds bought them did he?'

'Yeah. Pig's arse he did.' Price snorted into the phone. 'I bought the bloody things myself. I made your brother one offer and he took it.'

'How much, Price? If you don't mind me asking.'

'One hundred and fifty thousand dollars.'

Les nearly choked on his mouthful of beer, coughing and spraying it all over the lounge room. 'How much did you say?' he spluttered into the phone.

'A hundred and fifty grand. But don't worry, I still got them cheap, which I've explained to your brother. I've told him that with my contacts I could probably sell them in New York in six months for over a quarter of a million so he knows the whole story. Anyway he's more than happy, he was only expecting about ten grand or so.'

'I'll bet he is,' replied Les, still shocked.

'But there's no way I'll be selling them, Les. Bugger the Yanks and the Arabs. They go straight into my collection. And guess what I'm going to call them?'

'What?'

'The Kelly Twins. I'm going to name them after the club. How's that sound?'

'Sounds good,' replied Les. 'It's certainly original.'

Price roared laughing into the phone. 'Ironic isn't it, to think that what will be two of Australia's most famous opals are named after an illegal gambling casino. In Kings Cross, too, of all places.' Price burst out laughing again.

'I reckon it's beautiful,' said Les.

'So do I. Anyway listen, your brother's out by the pool having a cuppa, and talking to my missus, but he reckons he wants to drive straight back to Queensland tonight. Do you reckon he'll be all right with all that money? I paid him cash.'

Les smiled into the phone. 'I'd hate to see anyone try and get it off him,' he said dryly.

'Yes. Well being a blood relation of yours I can understand that. One could say you Nortons are extremely careful when it comes to a dollar bill.'

'One certainly could, Price,' replied Les evenly.

'Okay. Well that's all settled. I'll have Eddie drop him off, he should be back at your place in less than half an hour.'

'All right Price. Well, thanks for doing that for Murray, I appreciate it. And that's a bloody lot of money too.'

'Turn it up, Les. It's only money. It's not an arm or a leg is it? If anything it's another one I owe you. I couldn't be happier.'

'Oh well. Whatever.'

'Anyway, I'll get going and I'll see you up the club on Wednesday night. We'll have a yarn about it then. All right?'

'Righto. See you Wednesday. Goodbye Price.'

'Goodbye Les. Thanks again.'

Les sat there for a few moments slowly shaking his head and staring vacantly at the phone. Finally he got up, took another beer from the fridge and still slightly mesmerised stood at the back door watching through the lightly falling rain as Grungle chomped away contentedly on King's front leg.

'Well, what do you think of that Grungle, you ugly little bludger?' he said half laughing to the dog. 'Your loving master, my so called hillbilly brother, has just picked himself up a cool hundred and fifty thousand bucks.'

Grungle looked up at the sound of Les's voice, squinted his little piggy eyes, wagged his tail enthusiastically a few times, then went back to crunching up the last of the leg.

'You're right, Grungle,' continued Les nodding his head slowly. 'It is something isn't it? It's a bone all right.'

Les was still shaking his head a half an hour later when Murray burst through the door like Elliot Ness and came clomping down the hallway at a hundred miles an hour. He stood at the loungeroom door staring down at Les; there was a wild grin spread across his face and his eyes were bulging out like two tennis balls. Suddenly he tore off his hat, threw back his head and let out a piercing yell you could have heard down in Tasmania. He screamed again then ran at Les and started belting him over the head with his hat.

'Well what do you think of that, old fellah?' he said excitedly. 'Did your boss tell you what happened over the phone?'

Les stood up, grinned broadly at his brother and shook his hand.

'Good on you Muzz,' he said warmly and sincerely. 'I reckon that's great. You and the family are set for life now.'

Murray pulled a white canvas bag stuffed with money out from under his shirt and handed it to Les. 'Look at that,' he said, 'a hundred a fifty grand. I can't bloody believe it.'

'I told you Price would look after you,' said Les, dropping the bag of money on to the coffee table.

'Look after me? Christ, that is putting it mildly,' said Murray, picking up the bag of money and dropping it down again. 'I still can't friggin' believe it.' He looked at Les and shook his head. 'Christ I gotta get a beer.'

Les waited till Murray came back from the kitchen before he spoke. 'I got another little surprise for you too. I took Grungle for a little walk while you were away.'

'What do you mean you took him for a walk?' said Murray, looking at his brother quizzingly while he took several healthy pulls on his can of Fourex. 'He got a ton of walking down in that park this morning.'

'Oh I didn't take him far,' said Les casually. 'Just into my Greek mate next door's backyard. While he was out.'

Murray laughed and drained his can of beer. 'You didn't put him in with that big savage german shepherd did you? Not the killer. What happened?'

'Oh, what do you think happened? It was the most horrible thing I ever seen in my life.'

Les went on to tell Murray about the slaughter next door, not leaving out any details. By the time he'd finished Murray was doubled up on the lounge with laughter, tears were pouring down his cheeks.

'So what did you do with the killer's remains?' said Murray trying to sit up and spilling a fresh can of beer Les had brought him all over himself in the process. 'I'll bet there wasn't too much left.' He roared laughing and thumped his leg. 'Knowin' old Grungle, you'd be lucky to find a drop of blood.'

'They're in garbage bags in the back of your panel-van. You can dump them somewhere on the way home.'

'Heh, heh, heh, my dog's a killer.' Murray threw back his head and let go a great bellow of laughter again. 'I near pissed meself when your wog mate said that. That german shepherd was about as much use as tits on a bull. Jesus, Grungle took on a ten foot crocodile six months ago and flogged it.'

'He what?' said Les, staring open mouthed at his brother.

'He stuck it up a croc. There was a flash flood. The Narran overflowed and I was down the caravan park with Sergeant Austin pullin' out a few vans with his Land-Rover. We're down by the river bank when all of a sudden this bloody great crocodile slithers out of the river and heads for one of the kids. Grungle's jumped straight on to it, ripped off its front leg and started tearing its guts out.'

'Christ,' said Les.

'The poor bloody crocodile didn't know what hit it. It's jumped back in the water and went for its life. Grungle's dived in and started swimming after it. He couldn't catch it in the water though, Grungle's not a very good swimmer. They found the croc about ten miles downstream a couple of days later. Dead as a mackerel. So you can imagine how much chance that big dopey lookin' thing next door had. Buckley's. I'd have given half that money there to have seen the stink, though.'

'Yeah. It was something else, I can tell you,' said Les.

They both sat on the lounge laughing for a while then as the laughing subsided there was an uneasy period of silence; each knew what the other was thinking. Finally Murray spoke.

'Well Les,' he said awkwardly, 'I hate to sort of, get up and just be runnin' straight out the door, but, I reckon I might get going.'

'That's all right Muzz,' replied Les easily. 'I understand. I don't blame you wanting to get back home to the family. Cities have never been your go.'

'You're not wrong.' Murray looked at Les for a moment and slowly stroked his chin, a smile flickered round his eyes. 'But before I go, there's a bit of squarin' up to be done I think.'

'What do you mean?'

'Board and lodgings for me and Grungle. Me 'n the dog pay our way.'

'Oh don't give me the shits. I don't want any friggin' money.'

'You'll either take it or have it shoved up your big red arse.'

Les sat back on the lounge, looked up and shook his head as Murray reached towards the canvas bag sitting on the coffee table and started rifling through the wads of notes. He paused for a moment, looked at Les with one eye closed, then flicked through some more money finally pulling out a wad of $50 bills which he tossed into Les's lap.

'There you are,' he said. 'There's twenty-five grand there. I reckon that's fair enough for two days board.'

Les looked at the pile of money sitting in his lap. 'Come on, turn it up Murray,' he said. 'I can't take this.'

'Pig's arse. If it hadn't been for you and your boss I'd of got ripped off by that reffo in Bellevue Hill, so I owe you that at least. Besides, don't you come your shitpot benevolence act with me. You've been as tight as a tom-cat's quoit since the day you were born. It's a wonder you don't want half.'

'Yeah, I suppose you're right.' Les leaned back on the lounge and grinned. 'Why don't you toss in another five, make it an even thirty?'

'Fair enough.' Murray counted out another five thousand and tossed it to his brother. 'Now I might get going,' he said, 'while I still got a hundred and twenty left.'

'You're sure you don't want to leave it with me and I'll send it up to you. Be safer that way.'

'Go and get rooted.'

'I was only trying to help.'

While Murray collected his few clothes and tossed them loosely into his overnight bag Les went to his bedroom, slipped a thousand dollars out of the stack of money Murray had given him, put it in his pocket, then wrapped the rest in an old T-shirt and stuffed it down the bottom of his dirty clothes basket. Murray had finished packing when he returned to the other bedroom.

'I'll get you to drop me off at the Bondi on your way. I might have a couple of beers and get one of those VCRs off that wharfie.'

'Righto. Don't forget to say hello to those Poms for me if you see them.'

'Yeah. I'll tell them Tex sends his love. I'd better go and get Grungle.'

Les went to the back door and called the dog, he was relieved to notice Stavros hadn't arrived home yet. Murray was waiting in the hall and the three of them walked slowly and silently to the front door.

When they got outside the rain had stopped and the sun was just starting to go down behind Bellevue Hill, tinting the sadness of the grey, white clouds spread out over the Tasman with delicate shades of orange, yellow and red. It was quiet and still after the rain and the hissing of the passing cars tyres on the still wet road seemed gentle and soothing as somewhere in the distance the raucous cries and shrill whistle of a passing paper boy echoed about, beckoning people to come out for their evening Sun or Mirror.

'Well, looks like it's stopped raining anyway,' said Murray, tilting his leathery face to the sky as he opened the back of the panel-van to let Grungle in, tossing his bag in after him. He noticed the green garbage bag with its grisly contents sitting towards the front.

'Is that the killer's remains, is it?' he said with an evil grin on his face.

'That's them. Just give them a decent Christian burial somewhere on the way, will you?'

Murray just looked at Les and laughed as he closed the back of the panel-van. They climbed in the front, Les placed a dozen tinnies, in a carton, on the floor for Murray to drink on the way and his brother started the motor, letting it warm up for a while before he took off.

'You just going to drive straight home are you, Muzz?' said Les, sitting there listening as the motor idled gently.

'Yep. Might stop for a bit of petrol, that's about all.'

'What about tucker? I suppose you'll find a few truck-stops along the way. There's a good one just out of Glen Innes.'

'No, I won't even stop for food. We'll eat that dog if we get hungry.'

Les looked at his brother curiously for a few seconds. 'What do you mean you'll eat the dog?'

'Me 'n Grungle. If we get hungry we'll eat that german shepherd. No worse than eatin' dingo.'

'Are you fair dinkum?'

'Course I'm fair dinkum.' Murray looked at Les sceptically. 'Jesus, you've been in the city too long, son. What do you think I eat when I'm out trapping dingo and I run out of tucker? And what do you think I do when it's raining and I can't light a fire. Look, I'll show you.'

He reached into the back, opened the plastic bags, put his hands in and tore off a large piece of still-warm flesh. He took a huge bite from the purplish, red piece of meat, still covered in fur, and tossed the rest to Grungle, who gave it a quick chew then swallowed the lot in one gulp and wagged his tail for more.

'Not too bad,' said Murray, chewing it slowly in front of Les. 'Nowhere near as stringy as dingo. It's a bit fat actually. Here, you want a bit?' He reached for the bag in the back.

'No thanks,' said Les quickly.

'Suit yourself,' shrugged Murray, wiping the grease from his mouth with the back of his hand as he chewed away on the piece of german shepherd.

'Christ,' said Les, looking at his brother in disbelief. 'I'd hate to be around your place during a full moon.'

'Full moons.' Murray threw back his head and roared with laughter. 'Full moons don't worry me mate,' he said as his eyes narrowed evilly. 'What about yooou? Awooo. Ow ow owoooo.'

Murray started howling fiendishly out the window of the car and from the back Grungle joined in, in a ghastly, bone chilling, unholy unison with his master.

Les looked at the pair of them and slowly shook his head. 'Just drop me off down the Bondi will you?' he said.

Bowen Lager

'Well, that's the last of them.' Billy Dunne turned to Les and nodded his head as the remaining few gamblers shuffled out the door of the Kelly Club and drifted slowly off into what was left of the night. He slammed the heavy steel door, slipped the bolts and turned the two deadlocks. 'Not too bad,' he said checking his watch. 'Just on ten to four. Let's go up and have a couple of drinks.'

'Reckon,' said Norton as they started walking back up the stairs.

'It's your week off next week too,' said Billy giving Les a friendly punch in the back.

'My oath.'

'S'pose you're lookin' forward to it.'

'Wouldn't you be?'

'Yeah, you're right.'

The two doormen had worked it with Price Galese for one of them to have every second week off for the next four weeks. A friend of theirs, Big Danny McCormack, a wharfie who used to do a bit of part-time door work, had got into a bit of trouble and needed some money to square things off with the coppers and pay a lawyer to avoid going away for a little holiday courtesy of Her Majesty. He'd managed to find that but just as he did one of his five kids got heart trouble and needed an operation urgently, so he had to find some more money. Les and Billy found out and knowing how Big Danny hated having to accept charity offered him the extra work at the Kelly Club. Price was agreeable, provided the boys didn't go too far away and it was or.ly four

131

weeks, as he liked to have his ace men around all the time. At the same time it suited them down to the ground. Between tips, their wages, the money they didn't spend by not going out and the slings and racing tips Price kept giving them they had enough money to take every week off for the next 50 years. But the job was that good and Price was such a gem of a bloke they rarely took any nights off, so naturally enough they were looking forward to the chance for a bit of a break.

They were still talking when they got to the top of the stairs and started walking across the quiet blue cigarette haze of the casino towards Price's office. Les called out to a group of waitresses and croupiers who were still seated around a table talking, laughing and having a few staffies. 'Let us know when you want to leave and I'll come down and let you out. All right?'

'Righto Les,' several of them called back as the two doormen knocked lightly and entered the office.

Les and Billy sat around inside drinking and talking quietly while Price and George Brennan got the money counted and nearly gave themselves a hernia each trying to jam it in the safe.

'Why can't they open the bloody banks on Sunday?' cursed Price Galese as he finally got the safe door closed and gave the combination tumbler a spin. 'Lazy pen-pushin' bastards, they don't want to do any work at all.'

'You can't work on the Sabbath,' said Les. 'You're a Catholic Price, you should know that.'

Price stood up and gave Norton a filthy look. 'You've got an answer for everything, Les, haven't you? You bloody big Queensland hillbilly.' He winked at George then got them all another drink. 'Good health lads,' he said raising his glass.

They sat around drinking and cracking jokes till about 4.30am, then they all filed out. Les and Billy waited out the front while Price locked up. When he was satisfied it was all secure both got either side of him and walked him carefully to his car where they all said goodnight. Saturday night at the Kelly Club was over for another week.

The following Monday morning Les was relaxing in the backyard of his house in Bondi. Although he wasn't short of a dollar he shared the house for next to nothing with a bloke he'd met through work, Warren Edwards. Working such unorthodox hours, Norton liked to have someone there to keep an eye on things. Also Warren, who looked like and had the personality of a young, fair haired David Niven, worked in an advertising agency where he seemed to know more good sorts than Hugh Hefner, so every now and again he'd throw Les a bone; and though Warren was a diminutive sort of bloke with a bubbling personality, whereas Norton could sometimes be classed as a taciturn 15 stone brute, paradoxically they got on quite well together.

The warming rays of the mid-morning sun were just starting to fill Norton's backyard as he sat there on his banana chair reading the paper and sipping his third mug of tea. How good's this, he thought, no work till Thursday week. What a ripper. Unexpectedly the phone rang, disturbing his relaxation. Who the bloody hell's this? he thought as he reluctantly heaved himself off the banana chair and walked into the lounge.

'Hello,' he barked gruffly into the receiver.

'Hullo Les. It's Warren. What are you doing?'

'Well, I was sitting in the backyard relaxing. Why?'

'Listen, you got next weekend off, haven't you?'

'Yeah,' replied Norton cautiously.

'How would you like to do a TV commercial?'

'A TV commercial? Oh don't give me the shits.'

'It's a hundred percenter.'

'A what?'

'You've got to talk in it. You've only got to say half a dozen words. Jesus, even a Queensland hillbilly like you could string six words together.'

'Keep that sort of talk up and I might string six of your vertabrae together, you skinny little prick.'

Warren laughed on the end of the line. 'It's a beer commercial.'

'Yeah! What sort of beer?'

'Bowen Lager.'

'Bowen Lager? Never heard of it.'

'No, it's a new one they're putting on the market. Listen, it's worth three thousand bucks if you get it.'

'Three grand!' The cash register inside Norton's always-keen-for-an-extra-dollar mind suddenly rang up that amount. 'What do I — ah, have to do?'

Warren started laughing on the other end of the line. He could read Norton like a book. 'Listen, it's simple.'

He explained to Les how his agency was looking for a big, red-headed Aussie looking bloke to play the part of Bluey Riley, a Queensland cane cutter. All Bluey had to do was walk into the pub with his mates looking thirsty and mean, say a few words about Bowen Lager and drink a few beers. The ad was being shot in Brisbane, they'd fly him up and back first class, put him up in a top hotel and give him an expense account. He'd leave late Saturday afternoon, shoot the ad Sunday and be back in Sydney Monday morning. The cheque would arrive about a week later.

The idea certainly appealed to Les. Three grand, free piss and a chance to stand on beautiful Queensland soil and breathe beautiful Queensland air again. 'All right. I'll have a go,' he said. 'What do I do?'

'Grab a pen and paper. I'll tell you.' Warren gave Les the address of the agency and told him to be there no later than 1.30pm for the casting. 'You got that?'

'Yeah. No worries.'

'Right, good luck. I should be home about six, I'll tell you how you went.'

'Okay, thanks Woz. I'll see you tonight.'

Norton made himself a fresh mug of tea and returned to his banana chair, a half smile on his big rough face. Funny if I got the thing, he thought, the folks back home'll get a laugh. But the $3000 interested him more. He lay there for another hour or so then decided to get changed.

He put on a clean T-shirt, jeans and sneakers. There was no need to shave, he thought, but he did run a plastic 'bug rake' through his scrubby red hair. He gave himself a quick check in the bathroom mirror then drove to Bondi Junction and caught a train to Martin Place; a few minutes later he was standing among the passing shoppers outside the advertising agency in George Street. Yeah, this is it all right, he thought to himself as he checked the address Warren had given him over the phone. Dudley, Dunk, Fenwick, Scrartinvitch and Crutchsnack Advertising Consultants. Another quick check of the directory in the foyer said castings and inquiries, third floor. He got behind some other people and filed into the lift.

The lift doors swished open and he walked out into a large, cool, green carpeted room with a small marble fountain gurgling in the middle around which he could see several other people seated haphazardly against the walls. A long narrow corridor seemed to run off into nowhere and next to this a bored looking peroxide blonde, wearing about six coats of make-up sat tapping away at a typewriter.

'G'day,' said Les approaching her carefully. 'My name's Les Norton, I'm here about some booze ad in Queensland.'

She looked up unsmiling and checked a piece of paper behind the desk. 'Mr. Edwards sent you. Is that right?'

Les nodded his head. 'Yeah.'

'Just take a seat. They'll call you shortly.'

He sat down next to a thin, sophisticated looking blonde in a leather mini-dress reading a Vogue magazine. Next to her were two other blondes who could have been her sisters, and across the room were three of the best looking, best dressed blokes Les had ever seen outside of the Kelly Club. Nobody was saying anything but every now and again one would look up, check the others out intensely and look away again.

Christ, thought Les, if these blokes are going for the same ad they're walk-up starts. They make me look like something you see when you're drunk. Can't say much for the sheilas though, they all look like a good fuck and a green apple would kill the lot of them.

He reached over, picked up a magazine off a large tiled coffee table and smiled at the blonde next to him. 'Just like waiting to see the doctor, ain't it?' he said.

She gave him a bored smile then looked at him like he was something left over from last month's garbage strike. In your arse you skinny turd, thought Les, and started thumbing idly through his magazine.

Before long an overweight, happy faced but obviously gay guy wearing a polka dot bow tie stepped out of the corridor with a clip-board in his hand. 'Les Norton,' he lisped, glancing round the room.

'Yeah, mate.'

'Follow me please.'

'For a minute I thought you were gonna say walk this way,' said Norton. 'Be a bit hard in these jeans I can tell you.'

He ignored Les's remark and led him down the long narrow corridor. 'You're here for the Bowen Lager commercial?'

'Yeah, something like that,' replied Norton.

'Mmmh, useful type,' he said looking Les up and down. 'Should be able to do something there.'

'Thanks. I'm rapt.'

They stopped outside an already open door. 'Just go straight in,' said Bow Tie and swished off up the corridor.

Norton stepped into a bright, windowless room with posters all over the walls. Seated around a long velvet ottoman lounge next to a television set with a video recorder on top were three middle aged men and a middle aged woman. The men all wore trendy clothes, trendy hair styles and trendy glasses; the woman looked like a barracuda in an expensive pants suit. Les hadn't got in the door and already she was giving him the same sort of looks Zeke Wolf gives the three little pigs.

The trendy on the end of the lounge closest to Les introduced himself as Maurice McMichaels the director, on his right was Mitchell Buchannan the writer; the other two remained silent.

'All right Les,' said Maurice McMichaels as Norton sat down in the chair opposite. 'This is the story. We are promoting an exciting new brand of beer. Bowen Lager. And basically what we want you to do is this.' He stared intensely at Norton, emphasising every word with his hands and spoke slowly and deeply as if he was delivering the Sermon on the Mount.

'Imagine Les, you're in a hotel bar drinking with all the boys. You've got a beer in your hand.' He handed Norton an empty middy glass. 'Now. How would you say, "Bowen Lager, it's the beer my friends and I enjoy the most"?'

Norton looked at him incredulously. He could just imagine himself standing in a Queensland bar full of meatworkers, shearers and cane cutters and coming out with a line like that.

He lifted up the empty glass with a cheeky grin on his face. 'Bowen Lager,' he said. 'It's the beer me 'n me mates love to drink.' What a load of shit, he thought, I've wasted my time coming here. These dills wouldn't have a clue.

There was complete silence for a moment, then as one they all sat up on the lounge.

'Would you say that again?' said the director.

'Bowen Lager. It's the beer me 'n me mates love to drink.'

There was another silence then they all started jumping up and down on the one spot, waving their arms around like a lot of excited school kids.

136

'Great, fantastic,' said the director.

'Absolutely amazing,' said the writer. 'We'll change the concept of the whole campaign.'

'Incredible,' shrilled the third trendy. 'It's just so, so Oz.'

The barracuda was speechless. She just fell back on the lounge and coughed in her rompers.

'Stand up, Les, and hold the glass near your face,' said the writer. 'I want to take a polaroid.'

Les got up bewildered but still grinning. The next thing a flash went off, temporarily blinding him.

'All right Les, thanks for coming,' said the director as he and the writer escorted him to the door. 'We'll be in touch with your agent.'

'Yeah righto,' said Norton. They shook hands once more and Les left the building still absolutely mystified as to what was going on.

He was still mystified but had just about put the whole silly episode out of his mind by late that afternoon. He was at home sucking on a can of Fourex and reading the paper when the phone rang.

'Hello,' he said into the phone.

'Hello Les. It's Warren.'

'How are you?'

'I'm all right. But how are you? You little film star you.'

'What do you mean?'

'You got the ad.'

'Fair dinkum?'

'Fair dinkum. They loved you.'

'Well that's good. See, I keep telling you Woz, I'm not just a pretty face.'

'No, you're a fuckin' ugly one. But don't ever forget one thing.'

'What's that?'

'I discovered you baby. I'll be home in an hour, I'll tell you all about it then.'

'Righto. See you when you get home.'

Well I'll be fucked, thought Norton as he stared absently at the phone. That director's got to have a pumpkin for a head grabbing me instead of those other blokes out the front. He shook his head and went back to his can of beer and the paper.

'Now for Christ's sake, Les, behave yourself up there,' said Warren as he drove Norton out to the airport the following

Saturday afternoon. 'Don't get too pissed and for God's sake don't go belting anyone.'

'Piss off will you,' said Norton, grinning from ear to ear. 'I'm a movie star. Movie stars don't go around beltin' people.'

'No, but you do.' Warren was still lecturing Les after he'd parked his Celica and they walked into the domestic flight terminal at Mascot aerodrome. Mitchell Buchannan was waiting there to greet them.

'Hello Les, hello Warren,' he said shaking hands warmly with Norton. The writer's thinning sandy hair was plastered untidily across his head and he had noticeable dark circles around the puffiness under his eyes. He looked like he could do with about 24 hours' solid sleep. 'Looking forward to the weekend in Brisbane, Les? The ad should work really well.'

'Yeah I am,' replied Norton with a grin. 'My agent drove me to the airport.' He nodded towards Warren. 'He's been giving me some excellent advice to help me at this tender stage of my career.'

'Just remember what I said, Les,' said Warren evenly.

They had time for a chat and one quick drink at the bar before the announcement came over that Flight 602 for Brisbane was now ready to depart. All aboard the aircraft please.

'Like it says on the garbage tins Les,' said Warren, shaking Nortons hand as they left through the departure gate. 'Do the right thing.'

'Jesus, you're a worry, Woz,' said Norton slapping him on the shoulder. 'What could go wrong? I'll see you when I get back. The next thing they were winging their way to Brisbane.

About 15 minutes into the flight the stewardess stopped in the aisle next to their seat. 'Can I get you a drink at all, Sir?' she said pleasantly.

'Yeah. I wouldn't mind a can of Fourex myself,' replied Norton. 'What about you, Mitchell?'

'Just a brandy and soda for me,' he said tiredly.

When the stewardess brought the drinks back Norton went to pay her. 'That's all right sir,' she said. 'There's no charge for drinks first class.'

'Oh. Is that right?' replied Norton casually.

Les and Mitchell didn't say a great deal on the flight up, but when they landed at Eagle Farm there wasn't a drop of Fourex left on the plane and Norton was in a pretty good mood.

138

As soon as they stepped out of the hatch and the realisation that he was back in Queensland hit Les, about four gallons of adrenalin surged through his body like a miniature tidal wave. 'Ah, smell that Queensland air, Mitchell,' he said stopping half-way down the gangplank. 'You can bloody near taste it.' The writer smiled back briefly. 'If you like,' said Les, 'I'll grab our swags and you can get us a cab.'

'There'll be a car waiting for us,' replied Mitchell.

They picked up their bags and went to the front of the airport where a shiny black Mercedes and driver was waiting for them. He took their bags and placed them in the boot.

'Crest Hotel. Is that right, Mr. Buchannan?' said the driver. 'That's right.'

As they left Eagle Farm and cruised quietly through the darkened suburbs towards downtown Brisbane signs flashed past the windows of the car that engulfed Norton with pangs of nostalgia. Cairns Draught. Fourex on Tap. The Courier Mail Sold Here. 4BK Number One On Your Dial. When they pulled up at The Crest Norton was misty eyed. He was true to the old saying. You can get the boy out of Queensland but you can't get the Queensland out of the boy.

They booked into the hotel and while taking the lift to their adjoining rooms Mitchell told Les that he would be eating in his room as he had some phone calls to make and a few things to organise; he suggested Les do likewise. He wasn't keen on Norton's suggestion that they go out for a few drinks later, but he agreed to meet Les in his room and maybe go for a few; he'd see him then.

This is all right, thought Les, as he threw his bag on the bed of his $100 a night room and stepped out on to the balcony to view the Brisbane skyline and gaze fondly at the coloured lights reflecting on the Brisbane River as it wound a long silver snake through the heart of the city. Not too bad at all.

He unpacked his clothes then picked up the phone. 'Hello room service? This is Mr. Norton in 704, could I have two mud crabs, chips and a large side salad please. And a bowl of straw-berries and cream.' A small bar fridge with an electric jug on top caught his eye. 'You'd better send up a bottle of Taylors White Burgundy and a dozen cans of Fourex too. Thank you.' He smiled to himself; James Bond, eat your heart out.

By the time Les had finished a shave and a shower the food arrived. He gave the room waiter $2 then tore into the two muddies; the first bite nearly brought tears to his eyes. By a quarter to ten all that remained was the gleaming shells, the Taylors was gone and Norton was in a terrific mood and starting on his second can of Fourex. He finished that and went to collect Buchannan.

'Where do you fancy going Les?' asked Mitchell wearily as he stepped into his jeans.

'Dunno. I just feel like a few drinks, I'm not used to going to bed early on Saturday night,' replied Les.

'And if there's a bit of crumpet available you'll be in that too, eh?'

'Oh yeah. Why not?'

Acting on one of the room waiter's advice they went to a bar about 10 minutes walk from the hotel. There wasn't much happening, a few frumpy looking beer bandits were propped up on stools round the bar and on the dance floor several couples were shuffling around listlessly to a hackneyed band murdering some old Beatles songs in the corner.

'Not much doin' here is there?' said Les checking his watch. It was 11.30.

'Do you want to go up the Brisbane Underground?' asked Mitchell.

'It couldn't be any worse than this,' replied Les. They finished their drinks then walked out the front and caught a cab.

The Bianca Jagger look-alike on the door of the Underground nearly had a stroke when she saw Les. 'I'm sorry,' she sniffed 'but it's members only.' Being a trendy on the door of a half baked exclusive nite-spot she was determined to let only trendy types in and her idea of a non trendy was anyone over five feet six, that didn't look like John Travolta and dress like Roger Moore. However, like all would-be glamours, as soon as Mitchell told her who he was and mentioned the names of an advertising agency and a film company she started gushing, batting her eyelids and had them escorted to one of the best tables in the place. Norton hardly had his bum on the seat when some money changed hands and a waiter returned with an ice bucket and two chilled bottles of Veuve Clicquot.

'This is a bit more like it,' said Les.

'It's all right,' shrugged Mitchell.

After a couple of quick glasses of shampoo, Norton settled back and let his gaze wander around the night club. The place was fairly crowded with punters of both sex all decked out in their Saturday night 'kill 'em' gear. On the packed dance floor serious faced couples were pivoting and gyrating under a spinning mirrored ball and doing their best to imitate all the latest dance steps they'd seen on TV. A few disconsolate waiters and waitresses glided among the tables and everybody seemed to have a look of bored indifference, appearing to be out for a pose more than just a good time.

Les ordered another two bottles of shampoo. He glugged one down almost straight away when he noticed Mitchell seemed to be staring behind him, a look of apprehension on his face. Norton was about to say something when he felt himself grabbed under the armpits and hauled roughly to his feet; champagne spilling down the front of his shirt. 'Righto, on your feet cunt,' he heard someone bark.

Norton's eyebrows were bristling on his darkened face as he spun angrily around, fists clenched ready to fill the Brisbane Underground with left hooks and uppercuts. When he saw who it was he dropped his hands and let out a roar of laughter that shook the glasses on the surrounding tables.

'Well I'll be fucked,' he bellowed. 'You pair of dills. What are you up to?' It was two of his old mates from Dirranbandi, Lawrie Walters and Joey Lynch. 'Christ it's good to see you,' he grabbed the two men's extended hands and started pumping them vigorously. 'You're the last blokes I expected to see, especially in this joint.'

'Listen blood nut, don't be worryin' about us,' said Joey shaping up to Les. 'What the fuck are you doin' in Brizzie?'

Norton threw back his head and roared laughing again. 'I'm a bloody movie star.'

'Ah bullshit.' The two men grabbed Norton and started pummeling him again. Finally Les sat them down, introduced them to Mitchell and told them what was going on, smiling smugly as they sat there laughing with amazement.

'So what are you pair doin' here anyway?' asked Les.

'Well, you know that magnificent thoroughbred horse of ours?' said Lawrie.

'You don't mean that refugee from a glue factory, Flash Dirrin do you?' said Les. 'Christ, that thing should've gone into a carton of Pal years ago.'

'Hey don't knock it. We got him up today.'

'It didn't win a race, did it?'

'My oath,' said Joey. '66/1.'

'Fair dinkum?' Norton was astounded.

'And how much do you think these two little old country boys had on it?'

Norton shook his head.

'Ten thousand.'

Norton stared at them both. 'You've won over half a million.'

His two friends just nodded their heads and grinned back at Les.

Norton let out another great bellow of laughter. 'By Jesus, I always said old Flash was a good horse now, didn't I?'

'You lyin' red headed bastard,' roared Lawrie.

'Anyway Les old son,' said Joey. 'We brought old Flash down for the meeting, we've left all the bookies at Doomben with faces longer than a milk run and now we're out celebratin'. Why don't you get your mate here and join us. We got a couple of sheilas at our table and we can soon get some more.'

Mitchell looked at the three of them and realised there was going to be a bit of a night on so it was as good a cue as any for him to leave. He stifled a yawn and turned to Norton.

'Les, I don't want to sound like a wet blanket but I might leave you and your mates to it. I'm just about knackered and I've got a fair bit on tomorrow, so ...'

'All right Mitchell, if you want to hit the toe fair enough.' Les stood up as Mitchell rose to leave. 'Listen, we'll probably kick on so will you give me a yell at say 10 o'clock. We don't start till 12.'

'No worries.' Mitchell turned to the others. 'See you again fellahs. Nice meeting you.'

'See you, Mitchell.'

'Righto blood nut, over to our table,' said Joey as Mitchell left the club.

Norton picked up the remaining bottle of champagne plus the ice bucket and followed the boys over to a large table where two attractive but street-wise blondes were sitting surrounded by more ice buckets full of champagne.

'Hello,' said Norton to Joey. 'Where'd you find the two lovelys?'

'Escort agency. They're not bad scouts either, you want us to get you one?'

'Fuckin' oath. Why not?'

They sat down and Lawrie introduced Les. 'Terri, Jill, this is a mate of ours, Les.'

'Hello Les.'

'Hello girls. How are you?'

The two blondes were in their mid-20s and fairly much alike except Terri was a little taller than Jill and wore her hair long and straight whereas Jill's was done up in a bun. They still had their good looks and figures though the hard life and the sands of time had etched a few small lines on their faces that make-up couldn't quite conceal. But there was no hardness in their eyes tonight. The two country racehorse owners were good blokes and obviously looking after them, so as far as the girls were concerned they were out to have a good time and get paid for it. Handsomely.

'Old Les here reckons you're two of the best sorts he's ever seen in his life,' said Joey. 'And he wants to know if you can get a girlfriend for him.'

'Sure Les,' said Terri smiling at him. 'Anything in particular you'd like?'

'Yeah. A redhead with big tits,' replied Norton, a cheeky grin plastered across his face.

'Sounds like Renee,' Jill said to Terri without changing the expression on her face. 'Is she available tonight?'

Lawrie pulled out his wallet which was thick enough to choke a hippopotamus and rifled it a couple of times like a deck of cards.

'She's available,' said Terri shortly. 'I'll go and ring her.' Five minutes later she was back. 'She'll be here in 20 minutes.' She turned to Norton and smiled. 'You're going to love Renee, Les.'

'If she's just half as nice as you Terri, she'll do me,' said Norton raising his glass.

They sat there drinking, laughing and carrying on, stopping only to let an ubiquitous waiter with the scent of a rather large tip set firmly in his nostrils take away the empties and refill the ice buckets. Suddenly Jill looked up and started waving across the room; Norton glanced over in that direction and his jaw nearly hit the floor. Walking towards them, wearing a light blue, backless, almost frontless dress with a huge split up the side was a tall, leggy redhead with the biggest pair of tits Norton had ever seen. Every eye in the place was on her and escort or not she was the biggest spunk to walk through the door that night.

'Christ Les,' said Lawrie. 'How would you like them for speakers in your house. You'd have to have them 50 feet apart.'

She arrived at their table with a big smile and confidence written all over her face; she'd knocked everyone out and she knew it. Les rose from the table and got her a seat. As she sat down next to him Jill introduced her around.

'Much doing tonight is there?' Jill asked her.

'No, it's been pretty quiet actually,' replied Renee. She had a slow, deep voice that both fascinated and appealed to Les.

'Well, there's plenty doin' here,' said Terri, her eyes spinning from all the French champagne. 'So hold on to your girdle, love, cause I think it's gonna be a big one.'

She wasn't far wrong. They gave the shampoo an awful nudge, with the girls nearly wetting themselves at some of the stories the boys were coming out with. Anything they wanted they could have and they were just having a ball and getting paid for it. Norton couldn't believe it either. Coming to Brisbane to do the ad was a buzz in itself and he bumps into two of his best mates and they're half a million dollars in front; they were equally as rapt in seeing Les after all these years. The only sour note on the night for Norton was the fact that he had an expense account and the boys wouldn't let him go near his pocket. Then they hit the dance floor.

In no time at all they had their section of it all to themselves as they tore into the boogaloo, the bump, the Dirranbandi shuffle and other crazy moves no one had ever seen before. Renee was a pretty hot mover on the dance floor and before long she had Norton doing steps that made Michael Jackson look like a water buffalo with a club foot.

'Well this ain't too bad,' said Lawrie as they took a breather and tore into some more champagne while a photographer hovered over them taking photos. 'But we got a little something better back at the hotel. Haven't we Joey?'

Joey gave a sly grin. 'We sure have,' he said.

Norton looked at them, stroked his chin thoughtfully and

smiled. He had a bit of an idea what they were on about.

'Well, what do you reckon girls?' said Lawrie. 'You want to take the party back to our hotel. We might just have a little surprise for you.'

'Whatever suits you suits us,' said Renee, her hand on Norton's knee.

'Okay. We'll finish these and Harold Holt.'

They knocked over the remaining three bottles and got the waiter to have a cab waiting for them out the front, then after tipping him admirably they all trooped out of the Underground. Norton couldn't help himself and dated the snooty receptionist on the door; she screamed and immediately called the bouncers but they took one look at Norton, winked and opened the cab door for them. They climbed in noisily, sitting all over each other and headed for the Hilton.

When they pulled up outside they were making more noise than a horde of marauding English soccer fans but the doorman welcomed them with open arms. His palm had obviously be well greased beforehand.

'Mr Walters, Mr Lynch. Have an enjoyable evening, did you?' he beamed.

'Reckon,' said Lawrie. He pulled the doorman aside and a fifty changed hands. 'We might be having a little drink in our room, see that we're not disturbed and tell room service we'll probably be needing them. Okay?'

'Certainly sir. No problems at all.' He tipped his hat to the girls. 'Evening, ladies.'

The girls smiled drunkenly back, then they all bundled into the lift and went to their room.

'Not a bad digs you got here,' said Norton. The suite was about three times as big as Les's, beautifully appointed, with it's own bar and stereo.

'Three hundred a night. You'd want something,' said Joey.

Lawrie rummaged around looking for some glasses and Les knocked the tops off two bottles of bubbly. As they were doing this Terri produced a small, thin package wrapped in alfoil and a packet of cigarette papers from her handbag. 'Anybody fancy a smoke?' she asked looking around the room.

'You can put your pot away love,' said Joey, groping under the bed for his suitcase. 'I've got something a bit better than that.'

Norton threw back his big red head and laughed. 'You haven't got what I think you've got have you?'

'Some nose candy?' said Jill, her eyes lighting up with expectation.

Joey ignored her and stood up holding two bottles full of a clear, pinkish purple liquid. 'Here you are girls,' he said, a triumphant grin on his face. 'All the way from downtown Dirranbandi. Prickly pear wine.'

'Prickly pear wine?' chorused the girls.

'My fuckin' oath,' said Joey. 'Dirranbandi Drambuie.'

Norton looked at him, a suspicious smile on his face. 'You didn't give any of that to the horse, did you?'

Joey flashed Norton a villainous grin. 'Only gave him two cups and old Flash thought he was Phar Lap. Won by 10 lengths.'

Norton threw back his head, slapped his thigh and roared laughing as his thoughts drifted back to the first time he drank prickly pear wine.

He was about 20. Two mates of his father's, a couple of old opal miners from Lightning Ridge, brought a flagon up when they stayed with the family one weekend. They were a couple of funny old dudes about 70 with long hair and earrings and he remembered them and his father laughing their heads off as they poured Les and his brothers a large glass each. Nothing happened at first but about 20 minutes later Les didn't know what hit him. He went out the front of their property and the moon looked like a huge shimmering silver plate that seemed to take up the whole sky. Stars and comets were literally dancing through the heavens and the night was so clear and velvety soft he felt as if he'd dissolved into it. Strange thoughts raced through his mind as the trees changed into the shapes of animals and he could distinctly hear them talking to each other. Music, coming from a radio on the verandah, seemed to envelope him in a vibrating silver fog and he could see the notes as they left the radio. The trip only lasted a couple of hours and though it was a little frightening at first Norton thought it was one of the most beautiful experiences of his life and backed up for more.

He couldn't figure out what did it but a couple of weeks later one of his brothers handed him a copy of the National Geographic with an article in it about Mexico and how these natives in the hills extracted mescalin from the peyote cactus for religious ceremonies. They put two and two together and after asking a mate of theirs, a chemist with the Department of Agriculture, it turned out that prickly pear is full of mescalin and that's what caused the trip.

Norton was still laughing as he watched Lawrie fill six glasses with the almost honey thick liquid; strands of wine wisped between the bottle and the glasses like glistening purple cobwebs. 'Okay girls,' said Lawrie. 'Bottoms up.'

'Ooh, it's funny stuff,' said Renee, wrinkling her nose as she drained her glass. 'It's almost tasteless. What's it supposed to do?'

'You'll find out soon enough,' said Les. 'Here, wash the bitterness away with some more shampoo.' He reached round and topped up everybody's glass.

They sat there talking and laughing amongst themselves. After about 15 minutes the first tingle went up Norton's spine. He looked at Renee and she was sitting there wide eyed just staring at her hand. She caught his eye and started to laugh, then Les started to laugh and as he looked around he noticed all six of them were starting to crack up with Jill on the floor in a collapsed state of the giggles.

Lawrie struggled to his feet, turned up the stereo and killed the main lights, leaving just the soft glow from the bed lamps. The next thing they were all down to their underwear.

'What do you think of the old Dirranbandi Drambuie, Renee?' said Les, hooking his thumb under her bra strap.

'Mmmhh. You can't get it in 44 gallon drums can you?' she replied slipping her hot moist tongue in his ear.

Les took her gently by the hand and led her into the closest bedroom, where he eased her softly on to the bed, removing her knickers at the same time. Renee lay her head back on the pillow, closed her eyes and smiled as the music coming from the other room seemed to engulf her in a floating melodic fog. She couldn't believe her luck. Here she was full of the best French champagne, tripping off her head and although really he was just a customer she genuinely liked Les and his mates and already they'd dropped a thousand dollars in her bag. And now she was going to get what was promising to be a nice enjoyable fuck thrown in. She threw her arms around Norton's neck, wrapped her gorgeous long legs around his waist and got into it with him.

147

There's got to be worse ways than this of earning a dollar, she thought.

The first rays of sunrise stabbing painfully into his eyes like streaks of horizontal lightning coming through the curtains, woke Norton about 6am, filling his mind with confusion. But when he saw Renee's head on the pillow next to him and heard Lawrie's snoring coming from the next room the realisation of where he was and the memories of the previous night's events flooded into his fog-bound brain. Christ, he thought, looking at his watch, I'd better get moving. Mitchell will be banging on my door at 10 o'clock.

He rose gingerly from the bed and dressed as quietly as possible, picking out his clothes from amongst all the others strewn untidily around the suite. His head ached considerably and his mouth tasted like an Iranian tank driver's jock strap. The last thing he remembered was them all running around naked, drinking champagne from the bottle and singing the Mickey Mouse Club song with the girl's bras over their heads. He clicked the door softly behind him and caught the lift to the foyer.

The night porter was still on duty. 'Good morning, sir,' he said pleasantly. 'Looks like being a beautiful day.'

'You ought to see it from my side, mate,' replied Norton groggily.

He caught a taxi drifting idly past the front and went straight to his hotel, stopping once at a newsagency for a packet of Vincents powders and a large bottle of soda water.

Back in his room he dumped three APCs in a large glass and topped it up with soda water, then closing his eyes he downed the whole bubbling, frothy pink mess in one go. After gagging for a few seconds he let go a belch that rattled the chandelier in his room and made his eyes water profusely, then crashed out on the bed.

Right on 10am the phone next to his head started ringing. 'Hello Les. How are you feeling?'

'G'day, Mitchell,' he croaked into the receiver. 'How are you?'

'Real good. Listen, I've got to go now but a driver will call for you at 11.30. Can you be ready then?'

'Yeah, sweet.'

'Okay. I'll see you at the pub. Goodbye.'

'Righto, see you.'

Norton lay there for a moment rubbing his eyes and debating whether to get up or prop a while longer. His head still ached a bit but he'd felt worse, though when he couldn't remember right off. He decided to get up.

He rang room service and ordered scrambled eggs, bacon and toast, a large pot of coffee and a litre of orange juice with plenty of ice then got under the shower. Fifteen minutes of intermittent hot and cold water had him feeling almost alive so he tore into his breakfast.

After the last of the coffee he felt considerably better. His headache was bearable and the nausea had disappeared, he just felt awfully seedy and the last thing he wanted was a beer but he knew what was in front of him, so he braced himself for the event. At 11.30am sharp, the phone rang to tell him the driver from the film company was waiting out the front; two minutes later he was in the front seat of the Fairlane heading for the Ipswich Arms Hotel.

The hotel was a typical Queensland pub, built up off the ground with a green corrugated iron roof. A verandah ran around the entire building, facing on to a large, neat beer garden full of native trees and plants out the front. The driver whisked him straight round the back where the make-up lady was waiting for him in a storeroom she had converted for the occasion.

She was a blue-eyed English blonde and very petite with a lovely personality and a typical dry English sense of humour.

'Hello,' she said pleasantly, guiding Norton into a chair and draping a nylon cape around his shoulders. 'You must be Les. My name's Annabelle.'

'G'day Annabelle. How's things?'

'Pretty good. Looking forward to the ad are you?'

'Dunno. I've never done one before.'

She laughed. 'Well you're going to love this one, there's about 200 people in there to keep you company.'

'Two hundred? Shit, they must have hired some blokes.'

'They didn't hire anyone. These are all locals, you and two girls are the only ones getting paid. The rest are just here for the free piss.' She started trimming the hair around Norton's neck. 'And they've been into it for two hours,' she added.

Christ, thought Norton, I've got to do this fuckin' thing with 200 drunks. This is going to be nice.

149

Annabelle finished his hair and started daubing softening make-up on his face with a large soft brush. 'I'll tell you what, Les,' she said. 'You reckon you've got a rough head. Wait till you see some of these geezers inside. They make you look like Rock Hudson.'

'Fair dinkum, they're that bad, are they?'

'Bad? Some of these blokes wouldn't get a ride on a ghost train.'

'Dead set.'

'Dead set, Les. They remind me of a lot of inbred wart hogs.' She daubed more make-up on his face and started putting gel in his hair.

'Hey, how come I got to wear so much make-up?' Norton protested.

'For the camera, love. Can't have your big ugly dial shining around in there like the Portsmouth Lighthouse.'

'Oh.'

'Yes Les, all those rough heads inside, I'm glad you're doing the ad not me. Still you can always look on the bright side of it.'

'What's that?'

'You'll probably be the best sort in the place. Come on, handsome, you're done.'

She pulled the cape from round his shoulders and Les stood up and checked himself in the mirror. He nearly died. She'd slicked his hair down with pink gel and he had pale brown pancake make-up plastered all over his face; he knew what he could expect from the locals when he went inside. The butterflies in his stomach suddenly turned into screaming wedge-tailed eagles as he reluctantly let Annabelle lead him into the bar. Inside was pandemonium.

Annabelle said there were 200 in there; it looked like at least twice that number to Les and they were of every race, creed, colour, denomination, shape and size imaginable. There were teams of stoned-out hippies, a big bunch of bushy-headed Thursday Islanders, mobs of Chinese, a sullen gang of bikies, the Marauders, and their mammas were crammed up against the bar screaming for more beer and itching for trouble. Around them was a pushing, heaving mob of sweating, barrel-chested, big-bellied blue collar workers, mainly wearing shorts, singlets and thongs all wallowing in the free beer and all well on the way to getting blind drunk.

Annabelle led him straight up to the film crew who had laid out some tracks on the floor and were just finishing some wide shots. Les recognised Mitchell and the director Maurice McMichaels. They introduced him to the publican and the rest of the film crew but their names just went in one ear and out the other. The mob quietened for a moment when they realised the star of the show, Bluey Riley, had arrived and, standing there in his hair gel and make-up, Norton could sense that every eye in the place was on him, he knew that one thought was flashing through all their minds as soon as they saw him. Poofter.

'Okay Les,' said the director, taking him by the arm. 'We'd better get straight into this before the mob gets too out of hand. Here's what I want you to do.'

He then started taking shots of Les walking towards the bar with a big of a swagger, walking through the crowd pretending to acknowledge some old friends and stopping to have a few words. He picked out half a dozen of the roughest but most semi-intelligent locals and made them Bluey's offsiders and Les had to burst through the door with his mob behind him, look mean, hit the bar and order beers all round for the boys. Then when they all had a beer in their hands Les had to look into the camera, smile, wink and come out with his line 'Bowen Lager, it's the beer me 'n me mates love to drink.'

Still a bit on the seedy side, Norton didn't really feel like drinking at all and being a Fourex man from way back he wasn't too keen on the taste of Bowen Lager. It was too sweet. But after about ten pots, which he had to drink, even though he wasn't too happy, he started to get a bit of a glow and it started to taste at least drinkable.

After getting off to an uneasy start Norton began to handle the film star rort all right. Some of the director's terms he found a bit strange like 'cut', 'action', 'this is a rehearsal', 'final rehearsal', 'this is a take'. A guy would run in with a diagonally striped clapper board, bang it under Les's nose and say something like. 'Scene 27, take 6.' Then. 'All right, check the gate.' And someone would reply. 'Okay, the gate's clear.' Then someone else would say. 'Okay everyone. Let's wrap for lunch,' or 'let's wrap for coffee.'

This was all going over his head but he was steadily bumbling his way through and they'd got most of it done before Norton started to get too pissed. They still needed some wide shots and the director wasn't totally satisfied with Norton's delivery of his line about Bowen Lager.

But they had plenty of time and everything seemed to be going well. The mob had accepted Les for the ad's sake even though they were convinced he was a poofter and were copping it sweet. All except the bikies still jammed up against the bar.

'This fuckin' Bluey Riley, the so-called cane cutter's startin' to give me the shits, ay?' The leader of the Marauders, a tall, heavily built, morose faced bikie with a Pancho Villa moustache and several earrings in his dirt-caked ears, sneered to his lieutenant.

'This whole thing's startin' to give me shits,' replied his lieutenant. He was equally as big, ugly and dirty except he had straggly blond hair and a big, bushy beard which he'd tinged with green dye.

'I reckon I might go over and liven the big poofter and his artsy-fartsy mates up. What d'yer reckon, ay?'

'Why not, ay? I'll tell the boys.'

The head bikie sauntered over to where Les was standing amongst his offsiders near the bar, rehearsing a scene and stood next to him. As Les turned around he gave him an elbow in the ribs and spilt his beer on him.

'Ooh, take it easy old mate,' said Norton giving a small grunt of discomfort.

The bikie scowled and looked Les up and down. 'You're a big, tough cane cutter, aren't you?' he sneered. 'You should be able to take it.'

Norton's eyebrows bristled slightly as he gave the bikie a bleak smile. 'Yeah,' he grunted through clenched teeth and turned away. As he did the bikie gave him another elbow in the ribs. A little harder this time.

Norton's nerves were on edge as it was, he was strung up and tense from doing the ad and nowhere near in the mood for being stuffed around. The Bowen Lager wasn't going down all that well, he still had some of his hangover and he was starting to get a bit pissed.

He turned around slowly to face the leering bikie, a half smile on his face. Reaching across, he took the leader of the Marauders by his greasy shirt front, pulled him forward and head butted him across the bridge of his nose, not hard enough to knock him out but enough to give him the drum to drop off, then pushed him aside and turned back to his 'offsiders'.

The enraged bikie's eyes watered and he snorted out a thin trickle of blood on to the back of his tattooed hand. If he'd had any brains he would have let it go at that, but instead he let out a roar of anger and punched Les viciously in the back of the head, propelling him into the bar. The two acting barmaids let out a little scream of terror. As he spun around the big bikie hit him with a round-house left and right, catching him on the eye and mouth.

Norton's face twisted into a scowl and all the gallons of keyed-up adrenalin in him surged into his veins like a dam burst. He bunched his massive right fist, set his feet and belted the bikie under the chin with an uppercut that lifted him almost a foot off the floor, smashing every tooth in his head and completely shattering his jaw. He crashed into the 'offsiders', then slumped forward, straight into a left hook that squashed his nose like an over-ripe fig. He hit the floor oozing blood, completely comatose.

Norton was hoping that might have been the end of it but as it is with bikie gangs, you fight one you have to fight the lot. Like sharks in a feeding frenzy the rest of the Marauders charged through the crowd to get at Les.

Norton dropped the first two pretty smartly but the rest pinned him up against the bar, crawling over each other in an effort to get a shot at him. Norton started butting, punching, kneeing, elbowing, gouging and biting like a well oiled machine and was giving the surprised bikies almost as good as he was getting. But the odds were stacked heavily against him. However, just as Les was starting to go down under the sheer weight of numbers the cavalry arrived in the form of 'Bluey Riley's offsiders' who started pulling the bikies off Les.

He got back to his feet just as one of the Marauders whipped off his bike chain belt and went to wrap it round his head. Norton grabbed the chain from his hand, picked up a beer bottle off the bar and smashed it straight into the bikie's face, opening him up like a tin of strawberry jam, then smashed what was left of his face into the bar several times.

'If you want to start gettin' fair dinkum, that's okay with me,' he snarled as he dropped his body on the floor.

Now that he could get a fair go at them there was no stopping Norton. All the pent-up rage and tension poured out of him and he started snotting bikies left, right and centre. And loving every minute of it.

However, in the melee one of the Thursday Islanders got a smack in the mouth so he belted the nearest whitey. Some drunk yelled out. 'Come on boys, let's give it to the spooks.' The next thing all the Thursday Islanders were going at it hammer and tongs as part of the mob turned on them. The rest of the drunken horde spotted the Chinese. 'Yay boys. Let's get the dingbats.' Up went the cry and in an instant the drunken Australians charged into the Chinese, to be met with a barrage of kung-fu kicks and karate chops. A lot went down but they were too big, too many and too drunk to feel anything and before long there were terrified Chinamen getting speared all over the place as what started out to be a slightly humorous beer commercial turned into a gigantic, riotous brawl that looked more like a scene from a Mel Brooks movie. And standing in the middle, a wild grin on his face, was a blood-spattered Norton trying to turn every bikie into minute steak.

As soon as they could see that things were getting completely out of hand the film crew picked up what gear they could and hurriedly retreated to the corner and the end of the bar. The director tried vainly to break it up at first. He was running around shrieking, 'Stop it you idiots. Stop. You stupid bastards, you're ruining my beautiful commercial.' Not one of the drunks took a scrap of notice and when someone tore his megaphone from his hands and smashed it over a bikie's head he quickly got behind the others and stood there staring in horror at an equally shocked Mitchell Buchannan. Both were trying not to cry as they watched an entire days filming and about $300,000 go down the drain in a welter of punches, kicks, blood and torn clothing. And as far as they were concerned the cause of it all was the new modelling discovery that had been sent to them. Les Norton.

'Some bastard's going to pay for this back in Sydney.' The director screamed at Mitchell, as through the mass of heaving bodies they watched Les punch and kick three bikies from one side of the bar to the other. 'Someone is going to pay. I swear to God.'

154

The soundman kept recording at first but as soon as he realised it was turning into a riot he switched everything off, grabbed most of his equipment and got down behind the bar. The cameraman was fairly safe perched up on the bar with his camera resting on a big pile of sand-filled, canvas weight bags, like a soldier in a gun emplacement. And being half full of drink and a bit of a wag, contrary to the seething director's screams to cut he filmed the lot. Laughing like a hyena the whole time.

Leaning on the bar next to the director was the bleary-eyed publican. He was so drunk he could hardly stand up. He put his hand on Maurice's shoulder, as much to steady himself as to attract his attention. 'I suppose I'd better do something,' he hiccuped. 'I'll call the cops.' Just as he said that eight of the biggest Queensland wallopers you'd ever wish to see burst through the doors. 'Jesus, that was quick,' he said blinking his eyes in amazement.

They were all members of The Brisbane Policemens' Rugby League Team. Each one built like a council dump truck and each with the disposition of a trapdoor spider guarding its eggs. They happened to be in the area after training, and hearing about the commercial being filmed thought they might drop in and see what was going on. And maybe, just maybe, have a free drink.

As soon as they saw what was happening they charged straight in, belting and collaring everyone they could get their hands on. At the sight of the police uniforms an immediate change came over the fight and within seconds there was a stampede for the door, with the Thursday Islanders leading the way. They knew that if there were going to be any arrests they'd be the first to go.

Once the fighting stopped and the police were doing their best to round up as many drunks as possible, from out of the destruction Norton walked slowly towards the film crew. His clothing was in tatters, he had pieces of scalp missing and blood all over him but across his face was a wry grin. Behind him was utter carnage.

Body upon unconscious body, mostly bikies, lay stacked haphazardly across the floor in a writhing, moaning heap of drunken, blood-spattered pain. The beer sodden floor was a sea of shattered chairs, upturned tables, broken bottles, smashed glasses and other debris. Every window was broken and two wrecked air conditioners were dumped on what was left of the tracks the film crew had layed down, which looked like a bombed railway line. Every now and again one of the bodies would try to rise then give a little moan of pain and collapse again.

'Well. What do you reckon, Maurice old fellah?' said Les, standing in front of the astonished, irate director. 'Was that scene convincing enough or did it look a little too rehearsed?' He threw back his head and roared laughing; somehow the director failed to see the joke.

Norton stood there for a moment picking his teeth to get rid of some hair and pieces of flesh that had become imbedded when he had to chew his way out of a couple of headlocks, when he noticed the grinning cameraman up on the bar with the soundman standing next to him. A strange look came over Norton's face.

'Hey, is that stuff still working?' he said to the two of them.

The cameraman looked to see if there was any film left then nodded. The soundman checked the boom mike, put his headphones on, twiddled a couple of dials on his Nagra-Kudelski and nodded his head also.

'All right then,' said Les. 'We won't fart-arse around. We'll make this a — what do you call it? — a take.' He turned to one of the girls behind the bar. 'Righto, give me a beer.'

With the beer in his hand he turned back to the cameraman. 'Righto. Roll camera,' he said.

'Camera rolling,' was the reply.

Norton clutched his beer firmly, looked directly into the lens and with a big cheesy grin on his blood spattered face said 'Bowen Lager. It's the beer worth fightin' for.' Then, with a wink from his one good eye threw the lot down in one go.

'Better do another one for safety,' chuckled the half-pissed cameraman. Norton got another beer and repeated the performance.

A ripple of laughter ran through the film crew; even Mitchell Buchannan couldn't help but raise a bit of a smile. The director just stood there looking at him. 'Get the fucking idiot out of here,' was all he said. Then covered his face with his hands.

When the driver dropped Les off at the Crest there were gasps of horror and amazement when he walked through the foyer and collected his keys from the front desk.

'How did the day's filming go, sir?' said the desk clerk. 'That's an excellent make-up job.'

'Yeah. Great,' grunted Norton through swollen lips. He looked like the lone survivor of a nuclear holocaust.

Back in his room he got cleaned up then over a can of Fourex checked out the damage to himself in front of the bathroom mirror. It looked a lot worse than it was.

He had a lot of bark and a few pieces of scalp missing but nothing appeared to be broken. His lips were split and swollen, several teeth were chipped and his left eye was completely closed and so black you could have written on it with chalk. By probing around with his fingers he figured he had a few torn rib cartilages but no fractures and there were plenty of boot marks round his torso and kidneys. But apart from that and some swollen knuckles he was okay. So he rang room service and ordered a big feed of mud crabs, a bottle of nice white wine and another half a dozen Fourex; then settled back in front of the TV.

However, as Les was enjoying his meal, in a casualty ward on the other side of town a team of doctors and nurses working overtime patching up what was left of the Marauders. Wiring jaws and removing smashed teeth mainly. Their leader was still in intensive care, where the mammas were keeping a vigil out the front and hoping the interns were right when they said he should be out of a coma in the next few days.

After a good night's sleep, Norton rose about eight the following morning. He noticed he was a lot stiffer and sorer when he bent down to pick up a note pushed under the door. It was from Mitchell Buchannan. Get a taxi to the airport and charge the film company, was all it said. There was no driver to take him there this time and no one rang to see if he was all right so he figured they weren't too happy with him and he doubted if his modelling career held much future.

Oh well, he thought, watching the houses go past in the cab on the way out to Eagle Farm. It hadn't been that bad a weekend. At least he'd seen his two old mates and had a terrific root.

The only thing that really annoyed him, apart from the stares of the other passengers on the plane back to Sydney, was the thought that he'd probably done the $3000. 'Fuck it!' he cursed out aloud.

He didn't have much trouble getting a taxi after they landed at Kingsford Smith and by 12.30pm he was back in his banana chair in the backyard having a mug of tea and catching up on sports results in the paper. He was in an indifferent sort of mood when the phone rang.

'Hello Les. It's Warren.' He didn't sound very happy.

'G'day Woz. How are you?'

'Jesus Christ, Les. What the fuckin' hell happened up there?'

'Nothin' much. There was a bit of a stink, that's all.'

'A bit of a fuckin' stink. The pub got wrecked. The whole shoot was ruined. The agency is absolutely screaming and I look like losing my bloody job.'

'Yeah?'

'Yeah. Fuckin' yeah. Jesus Christ Les I told you before you left not to get into any trouble.'

'It wasn't my fault.'

'No. It never fuckin' is. Is it?'

'Look. It's no good talking over the phone. I'll see you when you get home. All right?'

'Yeah great. See you then.'

He's kidding, thought Les, as he got his mug of tea and returned to his banana chair. All he's worrying about is his lousy job. What about my bloody head.

When Warren got home about six that evening his David Nivenish face looked more like Jedd Clampett's dog. When he saw the condition of Les's melon his jaw dropped even further.

'All right Les,' he said, shaking his head with bewildered annoyance. 'What happened?'

Les eased himself back from the kitchen table and folded his arms across his chest. 'Like I said Warren. There was a bit of a stink, that's all.' He went on to explain how everything was going along famously till the Marauders started the fight. How it got a bit out of hand and finally the police arrived. 'And that's fair dinkum, Woz. Everything would have been sweet only for this big mug belting me.'

'Yes but they reckon you just carried on and on. Trying to massacre these blokes.'

'Well fuck it!' Les's voice was starting to rise. 'What would you do if a dozen, dirty big galahs in leather jackets started kickin' the shit out of you? You'd want a bit of a square-up too wouldn't you? Jesus Christ.'

'All right. But there's no need to near kill half of them and get the pub wrecked and ruin an expensive commercial Now the

158

agency's looking for a scapegoat and that's me for sending you round there. So now I lose my job.'

'Oh fuck your agency.' Norton rose angrily from the table. 'What do they call themselves. Doodlebop, Deadshit and Dudfuck. They're a bunch of wombats anyway if you ask me. All I know is that I was getting the shit bashed out of me and if it hadn't of been for a few good Queensland boys jumping in they'd be still scraping bits of me off the floor of that stinkin' pub. So tell your agency that next time you see them. Anyway what about my head. What about my three thousand bucks.'

Warren just stood there looking at him blankly. 'Yeah I suppose you're right,' he sighed.

'Anyway what are you worrying about? You'll get another job.'

'Oh yeah. They'll give me a great reference, won't they?'

'Yeah, well I can't help that. Look I'm going down for a couple of steak sandwiches. Do you want one?'

'No I'm not real hungry, thanks Les.'

'All right. I'll see you when I get back.'

Warren stood there for a while in gloomy silence as Les went out the front door, then stripped off and got under the shower reflecting sadly on what had happened. He'd tried to do the right thing by everyone and it had all fallen on his head. He felt dreadful.

There was a pall of gloom throughout the house all that week with hardly a word passing between either of them. Warren hinted once that he would probably be moving out. Les just shrugged his shoulders when Warren told him. Fuck him. Let him go, he thought. But deep down he liked Warren a lot and he knew it would sadden him to see the little bloke go. Not to mention all the choice crumpet that used to come through the door.

By the end of the week Norton was just about at the end of his tether. He was sick of Warren's silence, sick to the teeth of every second mug asking him what happened and his black eye wouldn't go away no matter what he put on it; everything from leeches to scotch fillet steak. Also he heard there was a rumour going round that just one bloke had given him a serve and he was too knocked up to go to work and that's why Danny McCormack was on the door at the Kelly Club. Not to mention the frightful bagging Billy Dunne had given him when he called round for a drink.

Early on Friday afternoon Norton was in the kitchen sipping a can of Fourex and making an Irish stew. He'd just put the carrots and onions in and was about to add some potatoes when he heard the front door open. Hello, he thought, here's happy Warren home early from work. They've probably just given him the arse. As he heard him come down the hall he turned slowly around to grunt hello, expecting to see Warren's unhappy face in the kitchen door. Instead, Warren was standing there holding a bottle of French champagne, a grin on his face like a split in a watermelon. He looked as if he'd had a few sherbets too.

'Hey Les, my old mate,' he cried. Then ran across the kitchen and started punching Les around the arms and chest. Norton had been kicked harder by butterflies.

'What's the matter with you?' he said frowning. More than a little bewildered.

'What's the matter with me?' said Warren. His eyes were a bit glassy and he was obviously in a state of great excitement. 'Nothing's the matter with me. It's you that's the matter. You fuckin' star you.'

Norton looked at him and shook his head. 'What are you talking about you fuckin' idiot?' he said.

'What am I talking about? The ad's what I'm talking about.'

'What. That Bowen Lager thing?'

'Yeah. That. They love it.'

'Who? What? I don't understand you.' He took another suck on his Fourex and gave the stew a stir.

'The advertising manager for the brewery loves it. The film company dudded up the ad. They picked out parts of the fight, put in some honky tonk piano music and made it around a big pub brawl. They've changed the whole concept of the ad to coincide with that line you used. "Bowen Lager. It's the beer worth fighting for."' Warren was laughing fit to bust.

'Are you fair dinkum?' said Norton incredulously.

'Yes, of course I'm fair dinkum. The film company showed the brewery the rushes on Wednesday and they were knocked out. They said it was the best make-up job and special effects they'd ever seen. The ad went to air Thursday night and viewer reaction has been unbelievable. All the advertising heavies are convinced Bowen Lager's going to be the biggest selling beer in Australia. It'll make Fosters Lager and Fourex look like tom-cat's piss.'

160

'Yeah?'

'Yeah. The brewery's already booked another half million dollars worth of advertising. I've got a raise. And here. This is for you.' Warren grinned and handed Les a cheque.

'Four thousand bucks,' said Norton. Looking at it with raised eyebrows. 'Well I'll be fucked.'

'So there you go. Everything's worked out for the best. And Les, I'm sorry I've been a bit moody all week, but Jesus I was worried, you know.'

'Oh that's all right Woz,' said Les pocketing the cheque. 'I understand, mate.'

'So all's well that ends well.'

'Yeah. Something like that.'

Warren threw back his head and roared laughing. He was ecstatic and obviously relieved that everything had worked out fine. Better than he could have expected. Les was still standing there impassively sipping his can of beer and giving the stew a stir now and again.

Warren let out another roar of laughter, looked at Les and shaped up as if to fight him. 'Bowen Lager eh,' he said 'it's the beer worth fighting for.' He dropped his hands and fell up against the fridge almost doubled up with laughter.

'Oh I don't know,' said Norton draining his can of Fourex and nonchalantly tossing the empty in the kitchen tidy. 'It's a cunt of a drop if you ask me.'

Definitely Not a Drop Kick

A thin mist of spring rain hung in the air like a dirty lace curtain, giving the garish neon lights of Kings Cross the appearance of a badly painted watercolour as they blended into each other and threw sickly crooked shadows around the shabby buildings and the people in Kelly Street hurrying to get inside from the clinging dampness.

It was about 11.45 on a Saturday night. The two solid men in tuxedos huddled under the awning outside the Kelly Club seemed oblivious to the inclemency of the weather and despite the dismalness of the night were smiling as they carried on with the conversation. Saturday night was the end of the working week for them.

'Looks like being a quiet one,' said Billy Dunne, taking a quick look up and down the almost deserted street, then casting an eye up towards the blackened sky.

'Yeah,' replied Norton, as the enveloping mist turned into light rain, making a rhythmic drumming on the canvas awning above his head. 'Looks like being a prick of a day tomorrow too,' he added.

'What do you reckon you'll do?'

'Dunno for sure,' said Les thoughtfully. 'If it's not raining too hard I might go out the Sports Ground and watch Easts play Balmain. Should be a good game.'

'You've still got a bit of a soft spot for the Roosters, haven't you mate?' said Billy, a hint of a smile creasing the corners of his eyes. 'Despite them dumping you like that.'

Norton shrugged his big, broad shoulders, put his hands in his pockets and leant up against a pole supporting the awning. 'The players are all right,' he said. 'They're a bunch of good blokes. It's just the officials running the club I can't cop. They're a bunch of old pricks.'

A taxi hissed to a stop out the front and they stepped back to let two well dressed couples into the club, giving them a smile and a nod and a light comment about the weather as they entered the premises. After pausing for a moment to check out the legs and backside of one of the girls going up the stairs, Billy turned to Les.

'I told you my missus has gone away for the weekend, didn't I?' he said.

'Yeah,' replied Norton. 'Gone to see her sister up at Swansea or something. Is that right?'

'Yeah. Her sister's married to a builder up there. The two young blokes went with her, took their surfboards. They reckon some place called Catherine Hill Bay's got unreal tubes, or lefts, or rights or something.' Billy shook his head and smiled. 'Fair dinkum, I don't know what they're talking about half the time.'

Norton laughed. 'Yeah, they're funny all right. They love goin' away but, don't they?'

'Reckon.' Billy paused again for a moment, stroked his chin thoughtfully and looked at Les. 'You fancy going for a drink after work?'

'What's wrong with having a drink upstairs?' replied Norton, his eyes slightly narrowed, a subtle smile on his face — he had half an idea what Billy was hinting at.

'No, I mean like somewhere with a bit of music and a few people around. Just for a bit of a change.'

'And a bit of crumpet.'

'Not necessarily.'

'Like where?'

'What about the Mandrake Room?'

'THE MANDRAKE ROOM!' said Les raising his voice. 'Christ Billy, it's that dark and dingy in there even the kitchen rats put Murine in their eyes.'

'Turn it up. It's not that bad.'

'Yeah. It's not that bloody good either.'

The Mandrake Room was a nightclub in a narrow lane off Macleay Street, Kings Cross, about half a kilometre from the Kelly Club. It was for late-niters only and they called it the Drake for short. The place itself wasn't all that bad, just some of the people who went there were a bit off. It had a disco as well as live entertainment and although they closed the doors around 4am, they didn't close the bar until the last punter got swept out with the butts and used drink coasters — generally around 8am. A good rock band always played there and the place was a haunt for musicians and entertainers finishing gigs and needing a late-night drink and a bit of a 'yahoo' to wind down. There was no drug dealing on the premises but it was a pretty sure bet that the vast majority of the patrons in there had a lot more coursing through their bloodstream and minds than red corpuscles and brain tissue. But although it was a bit smoky and dingy, and the patrons a trifle seedy, it was very popular and not quite as bad as Norton made out.

'Jesus, you're a nark Les,' said Billy. 'You wouldn't wrap a Christmas present. The joint's not all that bad.'

'Mmmhhh.'

'Come up and have two drinks. It won't kill you. We'll be out of here by 3.30am, you can have a couple up there and you'll still be home with your mug of Ovaltine and tucked into beddy-byes by five, you big sheila.' Billy threw a straight left at Norton's chin then quickly stepped back grinning. 'Come on, don't be an old tart. Just have two drinks.'

Norton turned away and shot Billy a derisive look out the side of his eye. 'I can't figure it out,' he said. 'A bloke with a missus as good looking as yours and you want to go out chasing those cane toads hangin' round the Drake.' He shook his head. 'You'll probably pull some slag out of there, throw her up in the air and finish up with the jack. Don't make no sense to me.'

Dunne's wife was an ex-model and a country girl from Grafton, in northern NSW. They'd been married almost ten years and although they had two sons, Louise still had her looks and shape and in photos for some modelling assignments which she still occasionally did, she didn't look a day over 18. A lot of guys around Sydney town would have given anything to get into Louise's pants but no one would touch her with a 40 foot barge pole. They knew if Billy ever found out they'd spend the rest of

165

their lives in a wheel-chair. But Louise would never play up, she was too much in love with Billy and although Billy was a little reluctant to admit it, the feeling was very, very mutual.

Unfortunately, however, Billy was a ladykiller. He didn't really mean to be; it just happened that way and being married to a beautiful ex-model it just seemed to spur the girls on all the more. He had a ton of personality and rugged, tanned good looks, a sort of a Burt Reynolds without the moustache, in fact Billy's legacy from years of professional boxing, a broken nose and a bit of scar tissue around his eyes, only seemed to add to his masculine charm. In a town full of increasing numbers of boring posers, gays and pretty boys with streaks through their hair, Billy attracted women like a prawn trawler attracts seagulls. There wasn't a girl working at the Kelly Club wouldn't let Billy slip his shoes under her bed for the night.

But there was no doubt Billy was a happily married man and for all the sex he could have got on the side he very rarely played up behind Louise's back. However, Billy was still a bit of a rogue and having to watch all those beautiful women coming and going at the Kelly Club and being offered a bit more than just a cup of tea and an Arrowroot biscuit with a bit of butter on it if he'd like to go back to their place with them, there were times when Billy would weaken and not be able to help himself. Tonight was one of those nights.

'Hey just a minute, Les,' said Billy. 'Who said anything about me going up there just for the sake of doing a bit of stray tooling?'

'Well, you're not going up there just to listen to the band.'

'I might. I like music.'

'Oh arseoles.'

'Look, mate. I just feel like having a little drink after work. Besides, it's going to be awful when I go home tonight, Louise and the kids not being there. I'll be lonely in that big house all by myself.'

'Ohh Jesus Christ,' Norton spat in the gutter. 'I've never heard so much bullshit in all my life.'

'And another thing,' continued Billy, ignoring Norton's last remark. 'That's not very nice to refer to the ladies that patronise the Mandrake Room as cane toads.'

'Well what are they?' snorted Norton contemptuously. 'What about the last time you dragged me up there and you tipped me into that blonde. I got her back to my place and she had "Harley Davidson Motorbikes" tattooed across her arse in inch-high letters. They filled me that full of penicillin a week later all my clothes went mouldy.' Norton spat in the gutter again as Billy's face broke into a grin. 'Yeah, you can laugh, you clown but I'll tell you what, if I pull anything out of there tonight back to my place it'll be gettin' a Dettol bath first.'

'That means you're coming,' said Billy quickly.

'I'll think about it.'

'You'll be there.'

'I'll think about it.'

By 1.30am the rain hadn't eased up and although there had been a fairly steady stream of punters going into the club they were only arriving in ones and twos and it was nowhere near crowded; Billy was right in his prediction that it was going to be a quiet one.

Just before 2am, Pattie Cameron, one of the female croupiers, came down the stairs with a thermos full of hot coffee for the boys. Pattie was one of the best sorts that worked in the Kelly Club, a well stacked blonde with a wide, sexy, crimson slash of a mouth. She looked a bit like Hotlips Hoolihan out of M*A*S*H on TV, but with a ten times bigger pair of boobs.

'Here you are boys,' she said, handing the thermos and cups to Les. 'Price said to get stuck into it, it's got some Jack Daniels in it. He also said it's pretty quiet upstairs so you can slam the bag about 3am. All right?'

Billy winked at Les. 'See, I told you.'

Pattie took a quick glance up and down the still almost deserted Kelly Street, noticing the milky lights from the buildings and passing cars being reflected in the inky blackness of the wet road. The wind had picked up slightly, putting a chill in the air as it bowled the wispy rain before it and scattered the vaporous haze across the flowing gutters and into the darkened buildings like a movement of grey ghosts.

'Ooh,' she said, rubbing her arms and shivering as a chill ran up her back. 'Isn't it an awful night.' She moved over to Billy and linked her arm in his. 'I hear your wife's gone away for the weekend, Billy,' she purred.

'Yeah. Be back Monday.'

'My flatmate's on a stopover in Perth and I'm all on my own too, in a great big unit.' She tightened her grip on Billy's arm.

'Would you like to come back for a cup of coffee and tuck me into bed. I get scared on my own.'

'Nah. I'd better go straight home, I think. You'll be all right.'

'Well anyway,' Pattie smiled, kissed her index finger and placed it gently on Billy's lips. 'If you change your mind you know where to find me.' Billy slapped her on the backside and she laughed and ran up the stairs.

'I can't figure you out,' said Norton, handing Billy a steaming cup of coffee. 'You've got the best sort in the joint hangin' off you and you'd rather go up the Drake. Are you sure you're all right?'

'Listen mate,' said Billy, taking a large sip of coffee. 'There's one thing you've got to learn. Never shit in your own nest. All those sheilas upstairs and my missus, all get their hair done in the one salon in Double Bay. Stylish Coiffure. And the way they gossip, it'd take about five minutes before Louise found out something had been going on and my nuts'd finish up in the dog's bowl.' Billy shook his head and took another sip of coffee. 'I wouldn't even be game to kiss one of those sheilas upstairs if it was her 21st birthday, let alone have a root.'

'Fair enough,' replied Norton. 'Jesus, this coffee's all right ain't it?' Les could feel the flush from the Jack Daniels in his cheeks.

A few more people entered the club while they finished their coffee but just as many left, disappearing into the darkness of Kelly Street. Billy checked his watch and turned to Les.

'Well, it's after two. I'd say it's all over bar the shouting now. Not even an hour to go.' He stepped out from under the awning. 'The rain seems to have eased up a bit too. It's been an easy one tonight, Les.'

'Yeah, but it's always nights like this when you least expect it something happens,' replied Norton sagaciously.

'Christ, what could happen? Have a look, there's hardly a soul around.'

'I'll relax when we've got the last one out of the club.'

Billy shook his head and smiled. 'Jesus, you're an old sheila at times Les.'

It hadn't been five minutes since Billy spoke when around the corner into Kelly Street came four blond headed German seamen — all very big, all very mean and all very drunk.

They were off a Danish freighter berthed at Walsh Bay to pick up a cargo of wool and canned fruit. They were sailing with the tide on Sunday afternoon and as this was the last night out in Sydney they were keen for a bit of action — and the more active the better. They spotted the blue light and the awning outside the Kelly Club and figuring it to be a disco sauntered up to Billy and Les.

Norton noticed them coming up the street first. 'You wouldn't believe it,' he said to Billy. 'Not a soul around and have a go at this coming up the street.' Norton might have been a bit of a slow-talking Queensland country boy at times but he could smell trouble a mile away.

'She'll be sweet,' replied Billy. Billy was game at the best of times but with Norton backing him up he wouldn't have cared if a truck load of gorillas armed with baseball bats had pulled up out the front.

The four Germans ambled up to the boys like they owned Kings Cross. The biggest one spoke. He was a monster. Well over six and a half feet tall with a huge bull chest, a bit of a paunch and a big surly blond head, about the same size and shape as an Otto bin. He was dressed in faded denim jeans and a heavy flannelette shirt, much like the others. He spoke reasonable English and being the biggest he was obviously the spokesman for the group. Not that the others were much smaller.

He just about stood on top of Norton when he spoke. 'This is disco, yes?' He nodded his big head in the direction of the club then back to his mates. 'We come in, yes?' The others shuffled forward as Les stepped back and put his hand up in front of him. Billy moved round a few paces to the group's left.

'Sorry boys,' said Norton slightly apologetically. 'It's not a disco, it's a gambling casino.'

'Gambling casino?' Ridges like in a piece of corrugated iron appeared on the big German's forehead as he tried to fathom out what Les had just said.

'Yeah. You know, roulette, baccarat, cards.'

The big, slow-thinking seaman turned to his mates and they had a brief conversation in German. Then he turned back to Les.

'So we come in. Gamble. Maybe play some cards.'

Norton shook his head. 'Sorry boys, but it's a private club. Members only.' He could just imagine what it would be like inside once the horny Germans got full of free drink then spotted Pattie Cameron and the rest of the girls walking around in their low cut, backless evening gowns. Pandemonium.

'Members only?' repeated the big German.

'That's right, old mate,' said Les.

Just as he spoke, two regulars came up behind him, nodded to him and Billy and stepped smartly inside. The big German noticed this and a heavy scowl darkened his already brutish face. He jabbed a finger about the same size as a banana towards the door.

'You say members to us. They going straight in.'

'I know 'em,' said Les. 'They're regulars.'

'Fucking shit. Liar bastard,' snapped the huge German. Behind him his almost equally as big mates were starting to shuffle their feet — they looked as if they were starting to get a bit restless too.

'Look mate,' said Norton, slowly and deliberately. 'It's a private club. There's no women in there, just gambling. And we close in less than half an hour. You and your mates are better off going down to the Arizona Tavern. It's open till six and there's heaps of girls in there. There's none in here.'

The big German turned to his mates again and they had another quick conversation in their own language. One of them put his hands in his pockets and shrugged his shoulders. They were starting to see reason and with Norton emphasising that there were no women inside it was starting to get through to them and they were starting to lose interest. All would have been sweet only Billy, who had been conspicuous by his silence, decided to put his head in. He was starting to get a glow from the Jack Daniels laced coffee and with his wife being away and knowing he was going out on the run after work he was obviously in one of his cheeky moods.

'Hey,' he said to the nearest German, who turned towards him unsmiling. 'Is that right it takes four barbers to give one of you Germans a haircut?'

'What do you mean?' said the blond seaman slowly.

'One for each side of your head.'

Norton undid his jacket, quickly slipped his watch off and shot Billy a look as if to say. 'You stupid prick.'

The German took his hands out of his pocket and moved towards the smiling Billy. 'Smart Australian bastard,' he said, and threw a big bowling right at Billy's jaw. Billy moved easily inside it and smashed a crisp left hook into the German's nose. He gave a grunt of pain as it broke all over his face. A short right opened up his cheek bone and another left hook squashed what was left of his nose and dumped him on his backside, blood pouring all over his face. Then it was on.

The biggest German moved towards Norton, his massive right fist cocked ready to throw a punch he expected would just about take Les's head off. Norton stepped back, drew the monstrous, ox-like seaman in and as he was just about to throw his big king-hit, stopped flat on his feet and slammed a shattering right straight into the big German's jaw. It hit him like a sledge hammer. His mouth went slack and several teeth fell straight out as his hands dropped and he careened backwards across the footpath and crashed into a parked car. He made a futile grab at thin air then his legs gave way and he crashed down on his elbow on to the pavement and lay there almost unconscious with shock and pain — blood bubbling out of his mouth. He couldn't believe anything human could hit so hard.

His mate next to him fired two quick punches at Norton's head. Les heard the ringing noise as they landed but he didn't feel it. He whacked two quick lefts into the nose of the seaman, whose face contorted with pain. He closed his eyes and went to grab Les in a bear-hug. Norton pushed the back of his head down then brought his knee thudding up into the German's face two or three times. As the seaman fell to the ground, Les stepped back and kicked him viciously in the mouth. Blood and teeth showered everywhere and he lay still.

The big German was trying to get to his feet but he was floundering around like an inexperienced skater trying to get up on an ice rink; Norton casually walked over and drove the toe of his boot almost up to his ankle in his solar plexus then let him have several solid kicks in the ribs as well. The monstrous blond seaman clutched feebly at his stomach, gave a gasping moan of pain and lay there motionless.

Billy, meantime, was making fairly heavy going of it with the remaining seaman. They were standing there almost toe to toe, Billy was landing six punches to one and easily riding all those the big German was throwing at him, but he was twice Billy's size and although Billy had torn his face to ribbons he had such a thick, bony head Billy was having a bit of trouble knocking him out. He shot a quick glance over at Norton who was standing there nonchalantly adjusting his watch.

'Hey Les,' he called out between punches. 'If you've got a spare minute, you wouldn't care to give me a bit of a hand here would you?' He ducked under a wild swinging right and slammed two left hooks into what was left of the huge German's face. 'Fair dinkum, this box-head's got a melon on him like a retaining wall.'

Norton finished adjusting his watch, fixed his bow-tie, put his hands in his pockets and leant up against one of the poles supporting the canvas awning grinning at Billy. 'You started it smart arse,' he said. 'You finish it.'

'Thanks, cunt.'

Billy fired another left and right into the German's already mangled face then stepped back, swung his leg and kicked him solidly in the balls — the big seaman screamed and grabbed at his throbbing groin. Now that he was crouched over down to Billy's shoulder level, Billy set himself squarely on his feet and drove a devastating right straight into the German's temple, knocking him almost senseless; he gave a little sigh and slumped to the footpath. Billy stepped back again and kicked him several times in the face but his head just wobbled from side to side like a sock full of wet marbles — he was completely out to it now.

A few patrons who had been leaving the club stopped to watch Billy and Les's brutal demolition job on the four German seamen. They stood there slack-jawed and slightly horrified as Billy delivered the final bit of 'Balmain folk dancing' on the last German's head. When he'd finished he walked slowly over to Les, shaking his head.

'Christ,' he said. 'I didn't think I was ever going to finish that big mug. Fair dinkum, his head's almost as hard as yours. It's as big, I know that, I couldn't miss it.' He gritted his teeth and started to wave his right hand around in the air. 'I think I've popped a bloody knuckle too, wouldn't it root you?'

'Ten years in the ring,' said Norton, 'and you have to go and kick a poor drunk in the balls to beat him.' He shook his head sadly. 'You'd better hand in your tuxedo. It's a good thing Price didn't see this or he'd have you upstairs picking up glasses or helping the sheilas in the kitchen.' He reached out and took hold of Billy's arm. 'Give us a look at your hand anyway.' He examined Billy's hand thoroughly, then took a firm grip on his wrist and an equally firm grip on three of his fingers. 'Yeah, you've popped a couple of knuckles all right,' he said. 'Hold on.' With a grunt and powerful movement of his huge sinewy hands Norton callously wrenched the two knuckles back into place.

Billy grimaced at the sudden rush of pain and started waving his hand around again. 'Ow, you prick!' he shouted at Norton who was standing there with half a smile on his face. The few patrons who had been standing around watching the evening's events decided it was time to leave and drifted off into the night. Billy was still muttering under his breath with pain but after opening and closing his hand a few times he found it was just about all right and the knuckles were back in place.

'Thanks mate,' he said with a smile. 'You ever thought about being a doctor?'

'A doctor,' replied Norton. 'You don't need a doctor, you need a bloody psychiatrist, you wombat. Nothing would have happened if you hadn't of started mouthing off.'

'Ah fuck 'em,' said Billy. 'Box-heads shit me at the best of times. You'd think they'd won the friggin' war, not lost it.'

'Yeah. They don't do much for me either,' said Les absently reflecting back on the German opal miner he'd killed back in Dirranbandi for his father. 'If it hadn't of been for one of these bludgers I wouldn't be down here in the first bloody place.'

'What was that?' said Billy quizzingly.

'Nothing,' said Norton quickly. 'Come on, we'd better dump Sergeant Schultz and his mates up in the lane.'

Running off Kelly Street, about 25 metres up from the club, was a narrow, malodorous lane full of rusty garbage tins and the evilest, scrawniest tom-cats in Australia. Whenever Les and Billy had to flatten any mugs out the front of the club and their opponents were either unconscious or too battered to walk away under their own steam the boys would drag them up to the lane and leave them there till they'd come to and either make their way home or down to St. Vincent's hospital. None of them ever came back for a second helping.

Unceremoniously Billy and Les took the unconscious Germans by their shirt-collars and taking two each, dragged them off to the lane and dumped them there, stacking a few garbage bins in front of them just in case some concerned citizens should happen to pass by and start hollering for the cops. By the time the four seamen came to, the club would be closed and Les and Billy would be long gone.

'Thirsty work son,' said Billy, as they hauled the huge Germans along the footpath. 'You'll have to come for a drink now.'

'S'pose so,' growled Norton.

'What about all this blood?' said Billy, when they returned to the front of the club. Even though the footpath was still wet, the rain had eased and the large dollops of congealed blood were quite noticeable as they glistened on the dirty grey asphalt. Several chipped teeth were quite noticeable too, which Billy deftly flicked into the gutter with the side of his shoe.

'I'll duck upstairs and get a bucket of water,' said Norton. He vanished up the stairs and returned a few minutes later with a stainless steel ice bucket full of water which he poured over the bloodstains, washing most of it into the gutter.

'I had to tell Price more or less what happened,' he said.

'What'd he say?'

'Nothing. He said we may as well close the doors and come up and start getting them out anyway.'

'Beauty.' Billy had a quick look at his watch. 'It's just on ten to three.'

By twenty past three they had everyone out of the club and by half past three Price had the money counted and in the safe, the boys had been paid and were having their customary after-work drink. Billy didn't mention anything to Price about them going up to the Mandrake Room for although Price might have run an illegal gambling casino and been involved in the odd bashing and gangland killing every now and again he was still a strict Catholic and had a fairly stringent sense of moral values; if he'd known Billy intended playing up behind his wife's back he would have blown up a treat. He also had a touch of the flu and was keen to get home early, so after just a couple of quick drinks the boys escorted him down to his car.

'Eddie should be waiting for me out the front,' said Price as they walked down the stairs, then locked the doors behind them.

Outside, Price's Rolls-Royce was double-parked in front of the club with the engine quietly ticking over. Behind the wheel was

174

Eddie Salita. Under his arm was a .38 Smith and Wesson police special and between the front seats with a newspaper over it was a sawn-off M.1 Carbine with a 40-shot banana clip fully loaded and attached. There was a little bit of trouble in the air. A team of ex-Painters and Dockers from Melbourne were in Sydney sussing out the possibility of getting an illegal gambling casino going and the rumour was that with Price out of the road it would make things a lot easier for them. It was nothing definite but Price's favourite saying was 'an ounce of prevention is worth a pound of cure'. And Eddie Salita with his sawn-off M.1 was about the best prevention available. Eddie spent a year in Vietnam with the 2nd Battalion, loving every minute of it and was filthy when Whitlam brought the troops back. If anyone had even looked twice at Price that night there would have been more lead in Kelly Street than Broken Hill.

'G'day Eddie,' said the boys as they opened the car door for Price, carefully checking out the street at the same time.

'Hello fellahs. What's doing?' replied Eddie cheerfully, flashing his big white grin.

'Not much.'

'Listen,' said Price from the window of the car. 'Are you two training down at Gales Baths on Monday?'

'Sure are,' chorused Les and Billy.

'Well I'll probably see you down there. I'm going to play a bit of handball then I'm having a few hands of euchre with some bookies from City Tatts. And there's a barbecue on at Clovelly Surf Club in the afternoon. The Eskimos are trying to raise some money for the club to get a new surf boat.' Price smiled and shook his head. 'They'll probably get me half full of piss and I'll end up buying the bloody thing for them, I suppose. But do you want to come down for a steak and a few beers? Probably be a good day.'

'Yeah, for sure. We'll see you down Gales anyway.'

'All right boys, see you Monday. Goodnight fellahs. Thanks.'

'See you Price. See you Eddie.'

The window hissed up, Eddie tooted the horn and the big beige Rolls-Royce cruised regally off along Kelly Street; the rear, amber blinker seemed to be winking a jaunty goodnight to them as it melded in with the other traffic.

As it drew out of sight Billy slapped Norton on the back. 'Righto mate,' he said happily. 'Let's hit the Drake.'

175

'Yeah. Let's get up there and get it over with,' replied Les a little reluctantly. 'Who wants to go home to a nice warm bed anyway?' With Billy leading the way, like a dog straining on a leash, they headed for the Mandrake Room.

After the relative quietness of Kelly Street Norton was slightly surprised to find that although it was almost 4am on a rotten wet night, when they turned into Macleay Street the sleazy, pitiless black heart of Kings Cross was still beating strongly.

Packs of trouble-seeking yobbos from the Western Suburbs swarmed contemptuously along the footpaths past scruffy, leather-clad bikie gangs standing idly in doorways, watching the passers-by but mainly keeping an eye on their chrome drenched motor bikes parked neatly at the side of the road. Huge Maori pimps would drive past in equally huge American cars, looking morosely out the windows and keeping an eye on their main sources of income. Heroin addicted hookers wearing crutch-tight shorts, high-heeled shoes and skimpy tank tops were propped up in doorways like so many broken dolls — their faces the same texture as sheets of wet newspaper, their eyes cold and lifeless like sharks. By the time they reached McDonalds Billy and Les had been approached at least a dozen or more times with the slurred words. 'Hello mister. Looking for a girl?' The boys would smile as kindly as they could and shake their heads.

The touts-cum-bouncers standing in the doorways of the strip-clubs would break off their raucous spiel when they spotted the boys, wave, give a big hello and watch with admiration as they walked past, wondering what the two hardest men in the Cross were doing walking down Macleay Street at such an odd hour.

As they crossed Macleay Street they had to walk around six young drunks who were savagely kicking at the doors of a taxi because the driver had refused to pick them up. A paddy-wagon driven by three trepidatious but hard-faced policemen cruised past ignoring the whole thing.

The tawdry neon lights, the car fumes, the noise, the prurient looks on the faces of the late-night voyeurs, had Norton feeling slightly disgusted and decidedly ill at ease and wishing he'd gone home to bed. Billy on the other hand was keener than a greyhound that had just been given a kill.

The solid wooden door of the Mandrake Room was closed when they got there. A small group of exotically dressed people were standing outside and to the left; four were handing around a joint about the same size as a corn-cob, the other two were sniffing something from a piece of aluminium foil through a rolled up $20 bill.

Billy was about to knock on the door when it flew open inwardly and out on to the footpath, scattering the group standing there enjoying their smoke and snort, burst big Danny McCormack, the bouncer, holding some bloke firmly in a headlock. The bloke's three mates were behind him, all arguing violently with Danny. Once outside he let the bloke in the headlock go and they all stood there in a seething, pushing, aggressive mob; all abusing each other at the top of their voices. Les and Billy leant unobtrusively against the wall near the half-open door and silently watched the proceedings — bemused smiles starting to appear on their faces.

'Think you're pretty fuckin' tough don't you? You big prick,' roared the bloke Danny had released from the headlock. He stood there rubbing his neck and glaring murderously at Big Danny.

'What do you expect, you flip?' replied the big, amiable bouncer. 'The waitress won't serve you cause you're pissed so you throw a drink over her. You're lucky I don't break your neck.'

'You break my neck, you fat turd,' bellowed the drunk Danny had just thrown out. 'That'll be the fuckin' day.' He was out of the headlock now, his mates were with him, Danny was on his own and he was all fired up with drink and dutch courage so he decided to have a go at the bouncer. 'I might just break yours, you arse.'

He lurched towards Danny and threw a big slow right and a left. Danny blocked them fairly easily and was just about to tap him on the chin when one of the drunk's mates jumped on his back pinning his arms, the first drunk moved in to throw another punch as Danny tried frantically to dislodge the one on his back; the other two moved in a bit closer for the kill also. With his arms pinned and faced by four belligerent drunks Big Danny McCormack suddenly found himself in quite a bit of hot water. Seeing this, Les and Billy moved away from the wall.

'Hey Danny,' called out Billy. 'The door's open, all right if we go in for a drink?'

Big Danny quickly looked up at the sound of Billy's voice. When he saw the pair of them standing there it was like the cavalry arriving just in the nick of time for Danny and a look of relief shone across his face brighter than the sun coming up over the ocean.

'Ohh, Billy am I ever glad to see you?' he grunted. 'And you too Les.'

'Yeah, nice to see you too, Danny,' said Norton casually as if nothing was going on. 'We're only going to have a couple,' said Norton as he and Billy moved slowly towards the door. 'We won't be staying long. Okay?'

Big Danny pulled his chin in as the first drunk threw another couple of punches which bounced off the top of his skull, hurting his assailant's hands more than it hurt Danny's big head.

'Yeah, sweet Les. But do you reckon you could do us a bit of a favour?' Danny pulled his chin in again as another flurry of punches bounced off the top of his skull and grunted audibly as one of the other drunks punched him in the ribs.

'Yeah sure Danny,' said Les turning back from the door. 'What is it mate?'

'Do you reckon you could just get this prick off my back?'

Norton turned to Billy and winked. 'What do you reckon. We give him a hand?'

'I don't know,' said Billy shaking his head slowly. 'You do it once and they expect it all the bloody time.'

'Well I wish youse'd make up your fuckin' minds,' wailed Danny, grunting again as another assortment of punches landed on his head and ribs. 'Cause I'm startin' to get in a bit of trouble over here.'

'Oh all right,' said Norton. 'But only because you're an old mate.'

Casually, effortlessly Norton strolled over to the unsuspecting drunk clinging to Danny's back and slammed a short but crushing right up under his floating rib. The drunk gasped with pain as he felt several of his ribs crack and his kidneys were squashed violently against his spine. He quickly slid down Danny's back and lay on the footpath holding his ribs, trying desperately to get some air into his ruptured lungs. He had a look on his face like someone had just given him a large spoonful of strychnine.

At the same time Billy crossed round behind Les and smacked the drunk that was pummelling Danny's ribs with a crisp left

178

hook that split his mouth open from just under his nose to almost half way down his chin. He gave a yelp and fell on to the footpath next to his mate, blood bubbling out of his lips and through his fingers as he tried to hold together what was left of his mouth.

Now that his arms were free Danny was able to get a decent punch into the bloke he'd thrown out of the Mandrake Room in the first place and with a big smile on his face he did just that — a big loping straight right with all 16 stone of overweight wharf labourer-cum-part time bouncer behind it. 'Headlock' was standing there blinking and wondering what to do now that the odds had just been evened up dramatically when it bulldozed him right between the eyes, pulverising his nose and slamming him up against a parked car where he went down like the Titanic. Most blokes who had just been four-outed would probably start putting the boot in for a bit of a square-up once they got on top but Big Danny wasn't like that. He just did his jacket up, adjusted his bow-tie and left the bloke lying there, bleeding steadily between the gutter and a parked car.

This left the last drunk, a skinny, fair-haired young bloke wearing glasses and his older brother's brown leather jacket, standing there on his own facing three very tough, very mean bouncers who weren't at all rapt in the idea of having their night's work made any harder for them. The young bloke's eyes were bulging out under his glasses like two hard boiled eggs and understandably enough he was shitting blue lights.

'Ohh, C-C-Christ,' he stammered. 'I'm n-not looking for any t-t-trouble. I was t-t-trying to b-break it up. F-f-fair dinkum.'

Which was fairly true. The poor young bloke wasn't much over five feet tall and about as wide across the chest as a sparrow is between the eyes. He hadn't throw a punch and did make a half-hearted attempt to stop the fight.

Billy winked at Les and with his fists held up in front of him in a professional fighter's stance and an absolutely diabolical look on his face he advanced towards the visibly trembling young bloke. 'Pig's fuckin' arse you tried to stop it,' he snarled 'you're the ringleader, you're an animal and I'm gonna whup you boy and stomp all over your head.' Billy was doing his best not to crack up laughing as he moved malevolently towards the by now almost petrified young bloke.

'Oh, J-J-Jesus mister, d-d-don't hit me,' wailed the ashen faced kid vainly holding his trembling hands in front of his face. 'I'm an ast-ast-asthmatic.'

'You'll be more than an asthmatic when he's through with you,' thundered Big Danny. 'You'll be a bloody paraplegic.'

'Ohh, God, don't c-c-cripple me. I'm c-c-crook enough as it is.'

It was this last anguished plea that finally cracked Billy up. With tears in his eyes he spun around and put his hand on Norton's shoulder for support. 'Les, take over for me will you,' he croaked. 'I can't go on with this.'

Looking as serious as he could Norton took the terrified young bloke by the collar. 'Listen soupbones,' he said. 'Where are you from?'

'P-P-Pennant Hills.'

'Well pick up your fuckin' mates and get back to fuckin' Pennant Hills before I put me boot right up your arse. All right?'

'Sure m-mister, w-we're on our way. Don't w-w-worry.'

With Norton's help 'Soupbones' managed to get his badly battered mates to their feet and arm-in-arm the walking wounded staggered painfully off down the darkened street for a very sorrowful trip back to Pennant Hills. It would be quite some time before they ever came back to the Cross and anywhere near the Mandrake Room.

'Don't hit me, I'm an asthamatic,' chortled Big Danny to Billy Dunne as he watched them limp off out of sight. 'What about that bloke you hit in the mouth? Christ, I hope his mother's got a sewing machine when he gets home.'

'He wasn't too worried about your ribs, Danny,' replied Billy laconically.

'Fair enough.' Danny paused for a moment then his face broke into a curious grin. 'So what brings you pair of gorillas down to the Drake at this time of the morning. Though I must say I'm sure glad youse did.'

'Hot pants here's after a bit of stray snatch,' said Norton, nodding his head at Billy.

'Ahh, is that right? Wife gone away Billy?'

'Something like that,' answered Billy.

'Well come inside,' smiled Big Danny. 'There's a fair bit of crumpet floating around the joint tonight and I'll shout youse a drink anyway. It's the least I can do for saving my neck.'

'Ahh that's all right,' said Billy. 'We just got paid.'

'Pig's arse it's all right,' growled Norton. 'The ask for the drinks in this dump's enormous. You're shouting, Danny.'

Big Danny grinned and ushered the boys through the haphazard entranceway that leads up to the Mandrake Room and in the door, closing it securely behind them.

Inside, the Mandrake Room was packed, everyone was bopping and through the misty, blue cigarette haze it looked like one riproaring party. Danny walked over to the girl sitting high up behind a reception desk made out of red, wooden louvred-doors surrounded by yellowed, dog-eared rock posters.

'I'm just going to have a drink with Les and Billy. Don't let any more in . . . just let them out. I'll be back over in about ten or 15 minutes. Okay.'

'Righto, Danny,' replied the girl. She smiled a big hello at Norton and Billy, giving Billy an especially big one.

'Come on,' said Danny. 'There's a spot down here out of the crowd.'

They followed Danny through a throng of weirdly dressed late niters into a long, crowded room surrounded by pitch-black walls covered in colourful old movie posters. Scattered around the walls were a number of consumptive looking potted palms which although they did add a touch of greenery to the place were obviously suffering badly from lack of sleep and nicotine poisoning.

Billy winked happily at Les as they threaded their way through more swarming groups of outrageously clothed people of both sexes and some possibly in between. The girls were mainly dressed in multi-coloured, very sexy tank-tops, calf length boots and skin-tight, leopard-skin slacks or tiger-skin mini-skirts. Their hair styles resembled anything from sticks of pink fairy-floss to Roman centurions' helmets. The men mostly had haircuts like US Marines but in a variety of astonishing colours, and wore either coloured overalls or shiny black jump-suits, festooned with zippers and kinky little badges.

'Good thing we wore our tuxedos,' said Billy.

'Yeah. I'd hate to look out of place,' replied Norton sarcastically, as he moved aside for a tall willowy blonde wearing an orange, ocelot-skin jump-suit and a green Robin Hood hat, complete with a long drooping pheasant plume hanging down the back.

Everybody seemed to be having a good time and were getting into the music from an all-girl band, the Party Tarts, who were on stage thumping out a mean brand of rock 'n roll that had the whole joint jumping.

Their lead singer, a huge red-headed amazon with a hairstyle like Orphan Annie, a pair of sunglasses like the Phantom's mask jammed on to her sweating face and wearing a dress made out of what looked like old motor-mechanics grease rags was wailing fiendishly into a cracking version of 'Leader of the Pack'. Behind her a pert little blonde was laying out a riff on a baritone-sax so thick you could almost see the notes coming out of the saxophone and bouncing off the walls — and the crowd were loving it.

'Shit,' said Norton nodding towards the stage. 'What about that sheila singing in the band. Isn't she a horny big thing.'

'Yeah,' replied Danny, 'she looks like you in drag.' He laughed and slapped Les on the back. 'Come on, in here.' Danny turned into an alcove off the main room to the bar. At the end and above the bar was a blackboard with a wine list written on it in chalk. He positioned the boys there and asked them what they wanted to drink.

'I'll have a bourbon and Coke mate,' said Billy, 'and make it a double will you? Plenty of ice.'

'What about you Les?'

'Just a can of beer Danny. Fourex if they've got it. In fact grab a couple will you? It's bloody hot in here.'

Danny turned and caught one of the barmaids' eyes. Although it was six-deep at the bar the girl came straight over when she saw who it was for and in less than a minute the boys all had their drinks.

'Sorry there's no Fourex, Les,' said Danny, raising his can of Carlton Draught. 'But cheers anyway, fellahs, and thanks for the hand outside.'

'No worries mate,' said Norton with a wink. 'Cheers Danny.'

'Yeah, cheers,' said Billy.

They all took a healthy pull on their drinks with Danny and Les finishing their first cans in two great swallows.

'So what's your story, boys?' said Danny, letting go with a resonating belch that was audible even over the band and almost shook the leaves off one of the potted palms standing three metres away. 'Out after a bit of the old summer cabbage are you?'

'Possibly,' replied Billy, peering lecherously around the room.

Big Danny took a decent pull on his second can of beer. 'Well,' he said slowly 'I might just be able to tip you into a little something in that department.'

Billy's ears pricked up immediately. 'Yeah?'

'Yeah. There's a couple of sheilas sittin' over there, they've been here about an hour. I had a bit of a mag to them on the way in, they said they were down from Brisbane for the weekend. One reckons she's down to do a TV commercial or something. Said she's a Meter Maid from Surfers Paradise. Wouldn't surprise me, she's a top little sort.'

'Queensland girls,' said Les happily.

'Yeah. That's the good news. The bad news is only one of them's any good.'

'Whereabouts are they sitting?' asked Billy.

'Just over there,' said Danny, nodding straight across from the bar.

Sitting directly opposite them at the end of a low, narrow wooden table with their backs against a wall made of more wooden louvred doors with soft lights shining through the louvres, were two slightly bored looking blondes in their mid-20s.

One was short and petite with a close-cropped, urchin type hairstyle that suited her pixieish, almost boyish face. She was wearing a tight-fitting, low-cut black dress with a long split up the side and from where he was standing up against the bar Billy could see she had nice tight little tits and a fairly good pair of legs and like Big Danny said, was a pretty good little sort. However, like Big Danny also said that was the good news as her girlfriend was a different kettle of fish altogether.

Where one blonde was petite and quite pretty the other was big and lumpy and wouldn't have looked out of place packing down in a scrum for South Sydney. She had hair like Harpo Marx and so many double chins she probably needed a book-mark to find her collar. The way she was dressed suggested she either lay-byed her clothes off the rack at K-Mart or stole them from the Smith Family. But she had a big, dumb, happy over-made-up face and was doing most of the talking for the two of them, giggling all the time as she'd tap her girlfriend on the arm and enthusiastically point different things out to her all around the room.

'Well. What do you reckon?' said Big Danny, laughing like a hyena with a fish-bone stuck in its throat.

'What do I reckon?' replied Billy with a grin. 'I reckon mine's all right. I don't know about yours, Les.'

'Well I do,' growled Norton, 'and the answer is no. N-fuckin'-O.'

'Come on Les, don't be a nark,' said Billy. 'I'll go for the little one. You grab the big one, she's more your size anyway.'

'Turn it up Billy,' replied Norton. 'I wouldn't be seen dead with that big fat thing.'

'She's not that fat.'

'Not that fat? She looks like some one's been up her arse with a bike-pump. If she ever fell over she'd rock herself to sleep trying to get back up.'

'Now she's not that bad.'

'Not that bad. Have a look at her big fat head. She's got more chins than the Hong Kong phone book. I reckon if there was a peeping-tom in her neighbourhood he'd pull her blind down.'

Big Danny laughed and ordered another round. 'Listen girls,' he said handing the boys their drinks. 'I'll leave it to you to argue about the two lovelies. I've gotta get back on the George Moore, there's a few startin' to come and go now.' He finished the rest of his can in a swallow, wiped the foam heartily from his mouth with the back of his hand and patted Les and Billy on the shoulder. 'I'll see youse after.'

'Righto. See you Danny.' The boys watched silently as Big Danny weaved his way through the crowd and disappeared in the direction of the door. Eventually Billy turned to Les. 'Well, what are we gonna do about these two sheilas?' he said.

'I'm not going to do a great deal at all to tell you the truth,' replied Les.

'Look, mate, just do us a favour,' pleaded Billy looking over at the two girls from Brisbane and then back at Les. 'I'll front the little blonde, if I look like doing all right just give us a back-up and talk to the big one for a while, that's all.'

'I'm not goin' to dance with the horrible big thing and there's no way in the fuckin' world I'm goin' to walk out the door with it.'

'No. Just come over and have a mag to her if I look like doing all right with the other one.'

184

Norton paused for a moment then shook his head and looked at the floor. 'Yeah righto,' he mumbled reluctantly.

With a grin like a kid in an ice-cream shop Billy slapped Norton lightly on the cheek then blew him a kiss. 'Who loves ya, baby,' he said and walked quickly over to the girls' table — the next thing he was leading the smiling little blonde towards the dance floor.

The big one caught Norton's eye and seeing him standing there alone in his tuxedo immediately figured out he was Billy's mate, so she flashed a big dopey smile over at him then sat there with an expression on her face like a big silly dog waiting for its master to throw a stick so it can go and chase it. Norton caught her eye, smiled briefly then turned to the bar and ordered another drink, hoping it would be a long time coming; unfortunately the girl behind the jump knew who Les was and although there were plenty of others waiting he had a fresh beer in front of him in about ten seconds.

He took a pull on the can then slowly turned around — Fatso was still staring over at him. God, how am I going to get out of this? he thought. Norton would have been quite content to just stand there drinking beer and watching all the different types go past, but he'd promised Billy he'd back him up, so taking a good solid pull on his can of beer and feeling more than just a little embarrassed he ambled slowly over to the big blonde's table.

'Hello there,' he said as pleasantly as he could. 'All right if I sit down here for a few minutes.'

'Sure,' replied Fatso, her eyes sparkling. 'My girlfriend's just gone for a dance.' She couldn't believe her luck. A man, well dressed and not half a bad style either, actually walking up to her and asking if he could sit next to her. Australia certainly was the land of opportunity. 'I think that was your friend she just got up to dance with.'

'Yeah it was,' replied Norton. 'I'd ask you for a dance myself but I just had a cartilage operation on my knee and it's still pretty sore.'

'Oh, that's bad luck. Oh well, doesn't matter. We can just sit here and talk.'

'Yeah.' Norton took another pull on his beer, almost draining it.

'How come you're both wearing tuxedos?' asked Fatso. 'Have you just finished work?'

185

'No, we're Masons. We've just finished a late meeting at the lodge.'

'Ooh, you're a Mason?' Fatso's eyes lit up. 'I've never met one before. You've got all those funny little hand signals haven't you? How about showing me some.'

Norton looked at her blankly for a moment. Christ, are you dumb or what? he thought. 'Well I'm not allowed to divulge the secret signs,' he said 'but I can show you one of our IQ tests.'

'Ooh ooh. Show me, show me.'

'Righto. Put your left hand on the table, palm down.' Fatso avidly did as she was told. 'Now watch carefully,' said Les as he placed both his hands, palms down, alongside hers. 'Are you watching?'

'Ooh yes.'

Norton then criss-crossed his hands several times over the top of hers then placed them alongside her hand again.

'Are you watching carefully now?'

'Yes.' Fatso never took her eyes of the table for a second.

Norton criss-crossed his hands over the top of hers again, slowly then quickly, then he placed his hands alongside her hand again and looked her right in the eye.

'Okay,' he said slowly and deliberately. 'Now which is your hand?'

Fatso looked at him for a moment, looked down at her hand without moving it, then looked back at Les. 'The — one in the middle?' she said hesitantly.

Norton felt the nerves in his jaw muscle tic as he tried not to laugh at the serious look on the blonde's fat face. 'You're sure on the ball, love,' he said, reaching over and patting her on the shoulder.

'Ooh, that was an easy one,' she said gleefully. 'Show me another.'

'I'll — ah show you some more later on.'

'You promise?'

'Yes, I promise.'

Norton drained his can and looked around the room for a waitress, catching one's eye about two tables away. 'I'm going to get another beer,' he said pulling some money out of his coat pocket. 'Do you want a drink?'

'Yes please. Gin and Coke with a dash of bitters. Is that all right?'

Norton's stomach turned slightly at the thought. 'Yeah. No worries,' he winced.

Norton ordered the drinks and turned to the dance floor where he could make out Billy's head bobbing up and down among the other dancers. He had a grin from ear to ear and was obviously enjoying himself immensely as he and the little blonde twisted and bumped their way through the sweating, colourfully dressed people packed on to the tiny dance floor. He caught Norton's eye and gave him a wave; Les waved back but more in an upward motion with his middle finger stuck out.

'What's your name, anyway?' asked the fat blonde.

Norton turned and looked at her for a second; I suppose I may as well tell you some of the truth he thought. 'Les. What's yours?'

'Francis. But everyone calls me Fran.'

'Well, I'm pleased to meet you, Francis.'

'Me too, Les.'

The drinks arrived and Norton payed the waitress, who looked at him quizzingly as she wondered why he of all people would be sitting with and buying drinks for what was unmistakably the fattest, ugliest girl in the place. Norton sensed what the waitress was thinking and pushed Fran's drink over to her, gulping down almost half of his beer in one go as he tried to hide his embarrassment.

'What sort of work do you do, Les?'

Norton belched quietly into his hand and looked at Francis for a moment. 'I'm a dental technician,' he said.

'Really? You don't look like a dentist.'

'No. I work out at Manly Aquarium. I make false teeth for gummy sharks.'

'Oh.' Francis paused for a second. 'That'd be a tricky job. I've got an uncle who's a vet,' she said in all seriousness.

'Go on, eh?' Norton looked absently at Francis. Christ, just how dumb are you he thought. I wonder what they nicknamed you back in Brisbane. Probably Fat Francis or Fat Fuck or what about Francis the Talking Fuck. With raised eyebrows he took another large pull on his can. 'And what sort of work do you do, Francis?'

'I'm a hairdresser. My sister and I have a salon in Brisbane.'

'What, just the two of you?'

'No, we've got eight girls and two apprentices working for us.'

'Yeah? You must be doing all right.'

Francis just smiled.

'I thought you might have been a hairdresser,' said Les.

'Oh. Why's that?'

'Because you've got such lovely hair.'

Francis blushed slightly and started to get a big soggy round the crutch as Norton immediately zoomed up the charts to become number one on Fran's Top Forty. After that last remark he was Fran's Paul Newman, Elvis Presley and Bob Hawke all rolled up into one.

'So what brings you down to Sydney, Fran?' Norton took a sip on his beer and belched lightly into his hand again.

'Well. I shouldn't really be telling you this and don't say I told you, but my sister's down here for an operation. She's going to have a cyst removed from her womb.' Francis giggled into her drink. 'We told the big guy on the door she was a Meter Maid from Surfers down here for a TV commercial.'

Norton laughed politely. 'You know, it's a funny thing, Fran,' he said, 'but a mate of mine's wife just had exactly the same operation and they ended up sewing a little window inside her fanny.'

'A window?'

'Yeah. Now she's got a womb with a view.'

Francis looked at Norton for a moment then threw back her head in a deep throaty laugh of bouncing fat tits and rippling double chins. 'Oh Les,' she cried reaching over and slapping him on the arm. 'I think you have me on a bit at times.'

Norton was laughing heartily too and strangely enough, for all the derogatory remarks he'd made about Francis, he found he was taking a bit of a shine to her. She was no doubt as thick as pig shit, definitely as naive as they come and uglier than a hat full of arse-holes, but somehow Norton couldn't help but like her — and after all she was a Queenslander so she couldn't be all that bad.

'I'm from Queensland too, Fran, to tell you the truth,' he said.

'Really. What part?'

'A little place called Dirranbandi.'

'Dirranbandi. Why Les, I was only out there a couple of months ago.'

Norton sat up straight and his eyes started to sparkle. It was the first time since he'd been in Sydney he'd met anyone that had even heard of Dirranbandi let alone been there. 'Fair dinkum?' he almost shouted at her.

'Yes. I've got an uncle's got a property out at Woolerbilla on the Culgoa River.'

'Woolerbilla. Shit, I used to go pig shootin' out there.'

'The last time I was out there we had a picnic about ten kilometres out of Dirranbandi at a little place called Crystal Springs on the Narran River. It's beautiful out there.'

Norton smiled warmly across the table at Francis. 'It sure is,' he said, more than just a little bit sentimentally. 'It sure is. Christ, Francis, let me buy you another drink.'

Norton looked around eagerly for a waitress. The band had stopped playing and he didn't notice Billy and the little blonde standing at the edge of the table — Billy had a very surprised look on his face. He'd expected to come back and find Les with an absolute and complete case of the shits. Instead, he was almost shocked to find him and the fat blonde laughing and chattering away like they'd been friends for years.

'Excuse me, miss,' he said to Francis. 'But is this man annoying you?'

Norton looked up abruptly at the sound of Billy's voice. 'Oh hello,' he said. 'John Travolta's back. How'd you go out there, Trav. Did you get down? Get back up again?'

'We killed 'em mate, don't you worry about that,' said Billy, as he and the little blonde sat down facing each other. The little blonde's eyes were swimming as she looked at Billy and you didn't have to be Albert Einstein to see he'd swept her off her feet.

'Les. This is Colette.'

'Hello Colette. Nice to meet you.'

'Hello Les.'

Up close Colette was even prettier again. Her hair was beautifully styled and apart from some light lipstick and a little eye-liner she wore hardly any make-up. She had high, angled cheek-bones which gave her an almost Slavish appearance, quite unlike her sister, and for such a small girl she had a very deep, very sexy voice which because of it's unusualness absolutely fascinated Les.

189

He introduced Billy to Francis as a waitress appeared and Billy ordered some more drinks — the same again for Les and Francis but a bourbon and Coke and a black russian for him and Colette.

While they were waiting for the drinks Francis said she was going out to powder her nose asking Colette if she'd like to join her. The way she said it, it sounded more like a hint that it might be a good idea if she did.

'Well, what's happening?' asked Les as soon as the girls had moved away from the table.

'Mate, I'm as sweet as a nut with the little blonde,' replied Billy. 'They're only staying round the corner at the Crest. I put it straight on her that we get out of here and go back there for a drink.'

'What'd she say?'

'Sweet. We're going straight back after these drinks.' Billy winked at Les and rubbed his hands together gleefully. 'Mate, I'll have that little blonde's pants off in about five minutes. Colette baby, you little beauty.' Billy laughed wildly and rubbed his hands together again.

'Yeah. She looks like she's got the hots for you all right.'

'Ohh mate, you should have seen it on the dance floor. She was all over me like a cake of soap. It was unbelievable.' Billy paused and smiled slyly at Norton. 'How are you going with the big one anyway. Fran' baby?'

'All right. She's not a bad scout to tell you the truth.'

'Yeah, she's all right. Why don't you whip her Reg Grundys off too when we get back there. Do her a favour.'

'I don't know about that.'

'Go on, give her one. It might be all right once you get under the rolls of fat. She's got a big set. You always reckon you like big tits.'

'Mmmhhh.'

The waitress arrived with the drinks, Norton went for his kick but Billy paid for them, giving the young red-haired waitress one of his big flashy smiles and seeing he was in a jubilant sort of a mood a big tip as well. The young waitress was very impressed and took her time wiping the table, poking a fair bit of cleavage, from where she'd undone the top buttons of her blouse, right under Billy's nose.

While they were sipping on their drinks Norton told Billy what Francis had been telling him about their hair-dressing salon in Brisbane and about the operation her sister was going to have. He didn't want to dampen Billy's enthusiasm but he thought that it might be a good idea to mention it just in case.

'An ovarian-cyst,' chuckled Billy, 'that's nothing. Might even make it better. Give it a whole new twist so to speak.' He took a large gulp of his bourbon and Coke and smacked his lips. 'It'll take more than a lousy bloody cyst to stop me throwing Colette up in the air tonight, I can tell you.'

Norton smiled as he looked across Billy's shoulder. 'Here they come now anyway,' he said quietly.

The girls returned, sat down at the table and took a sip from their drinks. There seemed to be a little bit of tension between them on their return — Colette had a smug sort of a look on her face, whereas Francis seemed a bit concerned about something. It was obvious words had been exchanged in the ladies room.

Norton sensed this but Billy seemed completely oblivious, or if he wasn't he certainly wasn't letting on and got straight to the point.

'Well, what do you reckon girls?' he said, looking directly at Colette. 'We finish these and head back to your place eh? Its starting to get awfully hot and smoky in here.'

'Okay,' said Colette brightly.

'You got anything to drink back there?'

'There's some Bacardi and a bottle of Coke in the fridge,' said Francis. For some reason or other she didn't sound all that enthusiastic.

'That'll do,' said Billy, almost finishing his bourbon and coke in a swallow; it was obvious he was keen to get moving.

'I might just have a quick snakes,' said Norton rising from the table and heading for the gents.

He got back just in time to see Colette finish off her black russian and barely had time to get his backside on the seat when Billy spoke.

'Well, what do you reckon?' he said. 'We get going?'

'Yeah righto,' said Les finishing his can of beer. 'Let's hit the toe.'

The girls picked up their handbags. Billy took Colette by the arm and like a true gentleman ushered her gently through the still-crowded Mandrake Room towards the front door. Francis fell in behind, waiting for Les but he discreetly let a couple of people who were heading in that direction get in between them; you might be a nice friendly Queensland girl, thought Les, but there's no way I'm going to be seen walking through the place with you. I mightn't be Brian Ferry but you're just a bit too ugly.

They got to the entrance where Big Danny was standing just inside the door, patiently opening and closing it for whoever wanted to leave, and although it was late he was doing his best to be pleasant to the patrons as they left. As he saw the four of them approaching, his eyes lit up and a superfluous grin spread across his face.

'Ahh Mr. Dunne. Mr. Norton,' he said warmly. 'So wonderful of you to come. It's always a pleasure. And ladies,' he nodded his head and half bowed towards the girls, 'I trust everything was to your satisfaction. Mr. Dunne. The wine. Service, etcetera?'

'Yeah, it wasn't too bad,' replied Billy.

'Oh I'm so pleased. I really am. And don't even bother to book gentlemen, there's always a table here for you.' Big Danny bowed and scraped a bit more and graciously opened the door for them, letting the girls out first, and giving Billy a knowing wink as Colette unravelled herself off his arm and stepped daintily outside, followed closely by Francis. 'However, there is just one thing I'm afraid I must ask you,' he said, taking Les, who was bringing up the rear, discreetly by the sleeve of his tuxedo. 'Please Mr. Norton. Next time you're in here would you mind not tipping so heavily. It embarrasses the staff. Thank you sir.'

'That's quite all right. I understand.' Norton took 20¢ out of his pocket and pressed it into Danny's palm. 'Here you are, my good man, a little something for you,' he said, checking out the top of Big Danny's head where the crown was starting to thin out. 'Slip down to Sirs and put a deposit on a toupee for yourself.'

'Oh thank you sir. Thank you. Your generosity is exceeded only by your good looks.' Big Danny let Norton out and started to close the door slowly. Just as it had about two inches to go a rather loud raspberry came vibrating through the crack, then it clicked shut leaving the four of them standing on the footpath.

'Do you know that guy?' asked Colette.

'Never seen him before in my life,' replied Billy. 'Seems a decent enough sort of a chap though, I must say. Come on, let's go.'

The short walk from the Mandrake Room to the Crest was fairly uneventful; it was almost 4.30am and the crowd had started to thin out noticeably. Billy and Colette were walking arm in arm as they threaded their way happily through the people along the footpath, but Norton was keeping a circumspect distance between himself and Francis — though he did talk to her and point out a few little things of interest. Before long they were in the foyer of the Crest, Colette had picked up the key and the next thing they were listening to the piped music as they rode the lift up to the girls' room.

'I hope they've given me the right key this time,' said Colette as she slipped the key in the lock and gave it a turn. 'That dill of a desk clerk gave me the wrong one last night.' It was the right key, Colette opened the door and they followed her inside as she turned on the light at a switch near the door.

'Not a bad sort of a joint,' said Norton, casting a quick eye round the tastefully furnished room.

'Hhhmph. It ought to be for the money it's costing,' replied Colette.

The room was fairly spacious, about half as big again as your normal hotel room. As well as a bedroom there was a small lounge room where a brown velvet night-and-day plus a lounge chair faced a tiny curtained-off sun-deck across matching shag-pile carpet. The soft interior lights reflected gently off a glass topped Manilla-cane bar with a built-in fridge; a TV sat next to this and on top of it were the control for the stereo-radio.

'Bacardi and Cokes do you?' said Colette from down behind the bar as she rummaged around for some ice and glasses.

'Yeah. Good as gold,' said Les, settling back on the lounge and crossing his legs. Billy sat on the lounge chair while Francis headed for the bathroom which ran off the bedroom. She got back just as Colette had made the drinks and handed one to Les, sitting herself down clumsily on the lounge next to him. Colette handed Billy his drink and he reached up and pulled her gently down on to his knee.

Norton took a sip of his drink and eased back on to the lounge, trying not to feel too awkward and embarrassed as Francis inched cautiously towards him along the ottoman. She had a dreamy sort of romantic look on her podgy face and any trepidation she might have shown earlier about bringing the boys back to the room appeared to have been forgotten; she was just about frothing at the mouth waiting for Les to grab her on the knee.

'Yeah. Well. What do you reckon Francis?' said Norton, sort of fumbling for the words. 'Not a ah — bad sort of a night eh?' He felt a bit gauche with the other two in the room.

Francis just looked pie-eyed at Les and smiled. 'Mmhh,' she sighed absently. 'It's wonderful.'

'Yeah. Bacardi and Coke's nice.'

'Mmhh.' Francis sighed again and wriggled another inch or two closer.

Norton stole a quick look out of the corner of his eye at Billy and Colette sitting to his right on the lounge chair. Billy was nuzzling the side of her neck and gently caressing the back of her head with one hand — the other hand was half way up her dress rubbing the inside of her thigh. Colette had her eyes closed and was running her fingers lightly through his thick brown hair.

'Yeah. Well, it — certainly is a top night,' repeated Les, turning to face the starry-eyed Francis.

'Mmhh,' she sighed again, 'and you're a top man too, Les.' She wriggled forward another inch or two.

'Yeah.' Norton laughed lightly, feeling slightly embarrassed again at Fran's last remark. A sudden movement caught his eye and he turned around just in time to see Billy leading Colette tenderly into the bedroom. Well, you're sweet son, he thought, as the door clicked shut. Now that just leaves me and Fran. But he did feel a little better with the two of them out of the room.

He took another sip of his Bacardi and Coke and winked at Francis who was sitting on the lounge like a smiling Buddha. Well, what am I going to do with you 'Fat Fuck'? he thought. Will I throw you up in the air or not? You're a beast, there's no two ways about it, but it wouldn't really hurt me I s'pose. He took another sip of his drink. Ah, bugger it. I may as well give you one, it won't kill me. It might even be all right.

Francis, by now, was starting to breathe a bit heavily and being left alone on the lounge next to big Les she was also starting to get very hot and sticky round the violet crumble.

Les reached over to Francis and put his hand lightly on the back of her head. 'You know what I miss most since I left Queensland, Francis?' he said, gently massaging the muscles around her neck.

'Ohh what, Les?' Francis almost moaned. She was a shot duck now.

'Queensland girls, Fran. I can get Queensland beer, I can get Queensland papers. I can even get Queensland food if I want it. But I can't get Queensland girls, Fran, and these NSW chicks don't do a great deal for me.' He smiled and winked at her. 'Give me a nice Queensland girl anytime.'

He placed his drink on the floor, lifted Fran's chin up and kissed her gently on the lips. Fran's eyes spun around like two bubbles in a piss-pot. She gave an audible moan and wrapped her fat arms around Les's neck as her tongue darted hungrily into his mouth. Norton closed his eyes and kissed her avidly in return.

He stroked her throat softly for a moment, then ran his hand carefully over her ample breasts, which although they appeared to be just big and fat, turned out to be quite firm and sexy for their size. He ran his hand over her stomach and up the inside of her dress. Francis spread her huge legs and Norton placed his hand over her by now steaming crutch and started rubbing her ted through the silkiness of her flimsy knickers, giving her clitoris a firm but exciting stroking with his middle finger. Francis, by this time, was starting to cough and backfire like a lawnmower with a dirty spark-plug — she gave another loud moan and started rubbing at Norton's fly.

Whether it was the fuzzy feeling through lack of sleep, the Bacardi or what it was Les didn't know, but suddenly he had a horn that hard you could have hammered horse-shoes on it and where he was a little reluctant to do any business before, now he was raring to go and get on with the job as Francis started to turn into Raquel Welch.

He squashed his tongue into her ear as she started to undo his fly, and giving her crutch another solid rub he hooked his thumb in the side of her knickers to start easing them down over her backside when a shrill scream from the bedroom made him open his eyes and turn in that direction with a start. There was another scream and what sounded like a hefty slap then the noise of something, like a lamp-shade, crashing to the floor followed by another scream, a slap and what sounded like Billy cursing heavily.

'Shit. What was that?' said Norton rising up off the lounge.

'Oh God,' said Francis throwing her hands over her face. 'I knew this would happen. I just knew it.' She pushed herself away from Les and stared in terror at the bedroom door.

'Knew what would happen?' Les was mystified as Francis sat stock still on the lounge, her hands over her nose and mouth, her eyes still staring out in horror over the tops of her fingers towards the bedroom.

Suddenly the bedroom door burst open and out stormed an absolutely ropeable Billy Dunne with a completely terrified Colette gripped savagely by the scruff of the neck. Tears were pouring down her pretty face and she was almost choking as Billy viciously shook her around like a dog with a rat. He still had his tuxedo on but the front of Colette's dress was undone and her bra-strap was down over one shoulder. Billy was totally livid, Norton couldn't even remember seeing him in such a state, his eyes were rolling around in his head and his face was almost black with rage.

'Have a fuckin' go at this,' he hissed vehemently through clenched teeth as he switched on the main light and speared poor little Colette roughly on to the lounge. She burst into more tears and tried frantically to crawl over to Francis for protection but Billy grabbed her brutally by the hair and dragged her back.

'Have a fuckin' go at this!' he roared again as Les stood up to get out of the road. He was dumbfounded but at the same time curiously amused.

'So this is your sister Colette, is it? You fat fuckin' bitch,' he snarled at the ashen faced Francis sitting trembling at one end of the lounge. 'Your sister, eh?'

Wild-eyed, Billy reached down and lifted up Colette's dress. She made a pathetic attempt to stop him but Billy gave her a short back-hander across the top of her head, making her scream and cover her face up with her hands. He pulled her dress up over her chest, then grabbing hold of her skimpy little lace knickers tore them down over her legs and flung them across the room.

'Here Les,' he roared again, spreading Colette's legs wide apart. 'Have a look at this. What's that?' He stabbed his finger in the direction of Colette's crutch.

Feeling a little embarrassed but at the same time slightly bemused, Norton bent down over Colette for a closer inspection of her little brown fanny and find out what Billy was going on about. It was all clean and tidy and trimmed up all right but instead of a nice, neat little ted, sitting there was a tiny little penis, not much bigger than the filter on a King-size cigarette. And dangling loosely beneath it was one, solitary, medium sized testicle.

Norton stood there blinking for a moment. 'Well I'll be buggered,' he said bending down further for a closer look. 'It's a dick.' He gave it a little flick with his index finger. 'And that's a ball.' He gave it a little flick too and looked up at the still fuming Billy Dunne, trying not to smile. 'It's definitely not a drop-kick, mate. Definitely not a snatch.' He stood up and shook his head slowly. Being an old Queensland country boy he'd never encountered anything like this before. 'Well I'll be buggered,' he said again, slowly stroking his chin.

'Yeah. A bloke. A rotten fuckin' drag-queen. But I'll tell you what. It's the last time you'll ever pull this caper, you prick of a thing.' Billy pulled back his fist to punch Colette in the face but Norton grabbed his arm just as Francis screamed.

'Hey come on, turn it up,' he said pushing Billy up against the wall. Norton wasn't turning on his good mate but Colette wasn't much bigger than a jockey and the state Billy was in and with his strength if he'd have hit Colette there was no doubt he'd cause her a serious injury. Possibly kill her. 'Come on mate, settle down. Don't do something you'll only regret.' He stood between Billy and Colette with his hands held up but open and hoping to Christ he wouldn't have to belt one of his closest friends for his own good. Billy's eyes flashed murderously at Norton for a second then over at the two on the lounge then back at Norton. He stood there shaking with rage for a moment then started to settle down a bit, running the back of his hand across his mouth and wiping a few flecks of foam from his lips. He gulped in a few short breaths of air, still glaring fiendishly at Colette but after a few more seconds he calmed down a bit more. 'Come on mate. It's all sweet,' said Norton, slapping him lightly on the shoulder and winking. 'It's all sweet.'

The terrified Colette in the meantime had crawled up to Francis and was cuddled trembling into her ample bosom, noisily crying her eyes out. Francis had her fat arms around her and was softly patting the back of her head. 'There, there, Col. It's all right. No one's going to hurt you. It's all right.' She made a pitiful sight as she looked up at Norton. Her face was all red and flushed and big, glistening tears were streaming down over her fat cheeks, splashing on her double chins. Her eye make-up had run everywhere, leaving black lines all over her face and it looked as if someone had got two prunes and squashed them into the sockets of her eyes. 'Please don't hurt her,' she pleaded up at Norton. 'She didn't really mean any harm. Please Les.' She hugged Colette closer into her and gently patted her head again. 'I'm sorry it happened. I really am, but if you want some money there's some money in my purse. You can have it. But please don't hurt us. Please.'

Norton couldn't help but feel a sense of squeamishness and sympathy at the pathetic sight of poor fat Francis trying desperately to protect her sister, or brother or whatever from the pair of them, big and all as they were, and the pitiful look on her tear-stained face as she offered them her money to try to shield Colette tugged awkwardly at his heart-strings. Though Les was the kind of bloke who wouldn't think twice about kicking some mug's head near off his shoulders in a street fight, the very thought of hurting poor Francis and to think that she might think he would, filled him with compassion and revulsion.

He looked down at her and gave her a bored sort of smile. 'No one's going to hurt you, Francis,' he said, shaking his head slowly. 'And I sure as hell don't want your money. But there's one thing I do want. I wouldn't mind a bloody explanation as to just what is going on here. Even if it's only for Billy's sake.' Norton nodded seriously at Billy, still scowling at them sullenly from against the wall, and turned back to Francis. 'Now I've been pretty fair dinkum with you all night,' he continued, pointing his finger at Francis. 'I even fancied you, being a Queensland girl. I mean I wouldn't have come back here if I didn't would I? So what about levelling with me. What's all this shit you've been feeding me about hair-dressing salons in Brisbane and coming down for your sister's operation. What's the bloody truth?'

Francis produced a crumpled kleenex-tissue from somewhere inside her dress, blew her nose vigorously into it and dabbed at her eyes. 'Well,' she sniffed, 'most of what I told you is true Les. We do own a hair-dressing salon in Brisbane and Colette did come down for an operation. But ... it was a sex-change operation.'

'A sex-change operation?'

'Yes, that's right. A sex-change operation.'

'Yeah?' Norton's curiosity was suddenly aroused. 'What do they do? Cut it off and tuck it in sort of thing.'

'Something like that. Col goes into the Wolvermann Private Hospital in Edgecliff on Monday and she's out on Wednesday. It takes about 14 days to heal and then Col's finally a woman.'

'Just like that?'

'Just like that.'

'Ah well, that explains everything Billy,' said Norton turning to the expressionless Billy Dunne standing against the wall. 'You were just a fortnight too early old son. Another two weeks and you wouldn't have known the difference.' Billy said nothing but muttered something filthy under his breath.

'You don't know what it's been like all these years, Les,' continued Francis, giving her nose another wipe. 'Col's been like that since ... well since the day she was born. Basically she is a woman. But she was just unfortunate to be born with that ... that ... what ever it is.'

'One and a bit I s'pose you'd call it.'

Francis ignored Les's laconic description of her sister's genitalia. 'We've had to hide it in the family through school, work, going to the beach. Col's 22, she's always been good looking but never seems to have a boyfriend. The rest of our relations and other people are always wondering why. It hasn't been easy, Les, I can tell you.'

'Well why didn't you get the bloody thing done in Brisbane years ago?'

Francis laughed scornfully through her tears. 'A sex-change operation in Queensland? Are you kidding, Les. The way Bjelke and the rest of those Bible bashing Right-to-Lifers have got it sewn up up there you just about need a prescription to get a brassiere. Besides, they cost almost $10,000 with your accommodation and air fares. And you don't get any of it back.'

'Yeah. Fair enough I suppose.'

'Col didn't mean any harm. But Billy asked her for a dance and he just swept her off her feet. She told me when we went to the ladies he was the spunkiest guy she'd ever met. She ... she just literally fell in love at first sight. She just couldn't help herself. And I like you too, Les. You know that?'

Up against the wall Billy was still glaring at Colette with hatred and contempt but his ego had just been given a bit of a massage so his temper came down a couple of degrees. He looked at Norton for a moment or two but still didn't say anything. Finally Les spoke.

'Well, what do you reckon mate?' he said, checking his watch and giving Billy a light slap on the shoulder. 'It's gettin' on for five o'clock. We hit the toe?'

Billy didn't say anything for a few moments — he just stared sourly at Colette and Francis. 'Yeah come on. Let's get the fuck out of here.' He turned abruptly and headed for the door without saying another word, leaving Les standing there. 'Come on, are you coming?' he called sharply from the doorway.

'Yeah, righto.' Les smiled down at Francis and moved over to the lounge stroking his chin slowly. 'Well Francis,' he said 'I wouldn't say it's been a good night. But it's certainly been different. If nothing else.'

'Yes, I'm sorry about that, Les,' she sniffed. 'I really am. But you've got the room number, I'm here till Wednesday. If there's no hard feelings call around.'

'Yeah, we'll see what happens.' He put his hand on Fran's shoulder and gave it a bit of a pat. She put her hand softly on his.

'Good night Les.'

'Yeah. I'll see you later Francis.' He stopped for a second and looked at Colette. 'See you ... Col.' Colette glanced up briefly then put her head back on Fran's bosom and continued crying.

'Come on. Are you coming or what?' Billy barked from the door.

Billy was heading rapidly for the lift when Norton joined him in the hallway. Although his temper had cooled down slightly he was still very volatile and extremely bitter about the way things had turned out. It wasn't just the fact that he'd missed out on having sex, his pride along with his manhood had been severely dented. Billy was a man's man and completely heterosexual; the very thought of anything apart from that was complete anathema to him and he was not in the slightest bit amused.

Norton, on the other hand, was laughing fit to bust inside and it was all he could do to keep a straight face as he watched Billy stab viciously at the down button outside the elevator.

'The sooner I'm out of this fuckin' joint the better it suits me,' he said contemptuously.

'Yeah. It's been a funny sort of night all right,' replied Les, his tongue planted firmly in his cheek.

'Funny? I don't know what's so fuckin' funny about it.'

'Yeah I s'pose you're right. Colette really . . . ballsed things up, in her own funny sort of way didn't she?'

'I'd like to go back in there and break it's stinkin' little neck is what I'd like to do.' Billy stabbed savagely at the illuminated arrow pointing down again. 'Come on. What's this fuckin' lift doing?' A second or two later the lift clumped to a stop at their floor, a bell rang and the door hissed open.

'Anyway,' said Norton as they stepped inside. 'I don't know what you're goin' crook about. If anyone's entitled to blow up it's me.'

'What are you talking about?' said Billy, banging the ground floor button with the side of his fist.

'Well, I was going all right with Francis on the lounge. I was just about to get her pants off when you came out puttin' on your drama and stuffed things up. So I missed out on a root. It's enough to give you the shits.'

Billy stared scornfully at Les. 'Are you fair dinkum?' he sneered. 'You're not beefing about missing out on rooting that horrible ugly fat thing are you?'

'Well Billy, she might have been horrible, ugly and fat but she was definitely a sheila. I was having a good feel around there till you blew up and there was definitely no niagras there I can tell you. It might have been a bit like Santa Claus's beard when he's got a cold but it was definitely a snatch, mate. No question about it.'

Billy glared at Norton, then spat bitterly on the floor of the lift. 'Jesus Christ,' he spat again, 'to think I've spent half the night kissing a . . . a fuckin' bloke.'

'Ah, I wouldn't take it too hard if I was you Billy,' replied Norton casually. 'You wouldn't be the only bloke running around Kings Cross tonight kissing other men.'

'What?' Billy almost exploded. 'Listen, I'm no fuckin' poof, pal.'

Norton shrugged his shoulders and put his hands in his pockets. 'That's what you tell me.'

The lift jolted to a stop at the ground floor; the door had scarcely slid open when Billy burst out and stormed across the foyer of the Crest to the main entrance.

The dawn was just starting to break when Norton caught up with him outside. The rain had stopped and a few sickly streaks of musty orange and yellow were starting to blend in with the grey and blue-black of the early morning cloud cover. The sun was doing its best to rise biliously behind the Eastern Suburbs, turning the dirt-caked windows of some of the high-rises around the Cross into shimmering silver mirrors. Although it had cleared up considerably it didn't look like being much of a day and would probably rain again before long.

Norton stopped briefly to get the Sunday papers as Billy strode straight across the pedestrian crossing in Macleay Street. He caught up with him again at the intersection before the tunnel; Billy was walking so fast Norton almost had to jog to keep up as they headed for their cars parked in Royston Street, just up from the fire-station. Abruptly Billy stopped dead in his tracks and turned to Norton very grim faced.

'Listen Les,' he said seriously. 'Let's get something straight before we go any further. What happened tonight is just between you and me. Okay? I don't want you to mention it to another soul. Now I'm fair dinkum about this, Les. Can you get that into your head?'

'Oh of course Billy,' replied Norton folding his two newspapers and putting them under his arm. 'Shit, what do you take me for? Do you think I'm gonna go running around telling everybody that my offsider at the Kelly Club's a dough-nut puncher and hangs around the Mandrake Room till all hours trying to stick it up drag-queens? Turn it up, son.'

'Hey, fuckin' hold on!' Billy's voice almost rose to a shout. 'I don't hang around the Drake trying to tan track drags. What happened tonight was just an accident.'

'Yeah? I don't know. I've been watching you lately Billy and you have changed these last few months.' Norton was like a picador tormenting a bull to get its temper up for the arrival of the matador — and doing a very good job of it. 'Still, I can understand mate,' he went on. 'All these years working at the Cross. It can get to you you know. Environmental work hazards I think they call it.'

'What!' Billy almost exploded. 'Why you dopey big cunt. I ought to ...'

'Now hold on a sec, mate. It's no good gettin' the shits with me just 'cause I'm from Queensland and I'm straight.'

Norton started to realise he'd had enough fun and it might be a good idea to stop baiting Billy; he was extremely agitated, almost in a state of shock and it was time to drop off.

'I can understand your feelings mate,' he said. 'Besides, it's gettin' late and we could both do with a bit of sleep. You'll feel better in the morning.' They strode on in silence to their cars.

'Remember what I said Les,' said Billy as he opened the door of his current model Holden station wagon. 'Not a word to anyone about tonight. As far as we're both concerned it never happened. And I don't want to mention the incident ever again. Ever. You understand?'

'No worries,' said Norton, climbing behind the wheel of his old Ford. 'It's forgotten. It never happened as far as I'm concerned.'

'Good. In fact I'll tell you what,' Billy walked over and stood at the window of Les's car. 'If you hadn't of been there, I'd have choked that fuckin' blonde thing. And probably it's bloody sister too.'

'I could believe that, mate.' Norton started the motor and gave it a bit of a rev.

'So tonight never happened.'

'It never happened, Billy.'

Without saying goodbye, or even another word, Billy got into his car and watched silently as Les pulled out from the kerb; at a set of lights about half a kilometre up the road he drove past Les like he wasn't even there.

But Norton was true to his promise. He kept his word and never mentioned what happened on Saturday night to anyone. Though it would be no exaggeration to say he was absolutely dying to; as far as Les was concerned it was one of the funniest things he'd ever seen in his life. But he never said a word about it to anyone, not even Warren Edwards who shared the house with him.

If Norton thought Saturday night was funny, Billy was the complete opposite. He was still visibly upset when he called for Les to go training on Monday morning and from the moment Les got into Billy's car, all through training and even when they had a drink and Billy dropped him off afterwards not a word was mentioned. It was like it had never happened.

Even apart from his enforced silence on the matter, Norton could still tell Billy was quite rancorous about the affair. When they put the gloves on to spar for a few rounds Billy never pulled a punch and was really working out his hatred and aggression — Norton really had to belt him good and hard a few times just to stop from getting hurt too much himself. But Billy still wouldn't ease up.

A few of the regulars at Gales Baths and some others who had stopped to watch couldn't believe they were the best of friends; especially when Billy hit Les with a left-hook that split his head-gear and sent his mouthguard spinning halfway across the gym. But Norton knew what was going through Billy's mind and copped it sweet.

During a game of handball at the Bondi Icebergs on Tuesday morning and at a drink upstairs in the club afterwards still not a word was mentioned. Nor at training again on Wednesday. Even during the long silent run from Coogee to Bondi and back nothing was said. Coming back through Bronte Cemetery Les was absolutely breaking his neck to say something like 'Jesus you were a bit stiff yourself on Saturday night, Billy' or 'I thought you were a dead set certainty, Billy'. But he buttoned his lip.

Les was also wanting to tell Billy that he'd rung Francis at the Crest and finished up going around there late Tuesday afternoon with a dozen cans of Fourex and a bottle of Great Western and giving Fat Francis three of the best. In the sexual race meetings of life Francis had been scratched quite a few times so at this particular event she made every post a winner. Fit and all as he was, big Les left room 363 about eight o'clock very shaky in the knees but with a big grin on his face. Both he and Francis declared it was an afternoon very well spent. He would have loved to have told Billy this but he never mentioned it.

At work on Wednesday night Billy was still quite sullen, and he was the same on Thursday. The incident with Colette was never mentioned once. As far as they were both concerned it had never happened. Norton had kept his word not to say anything and the whole affair was forgotten. It was like it had never happened.

And it would have stayed that way and everything would have been sweet except who should come ambling round the corner of

Kelly Street about 10.30pm on Thursday night, his hands in his trouser pockets, his shirt collar undone and his bow-tie jammed loosely in the top pocket of his tuxedo but Big Danny McCormack, a few schooners under his belt, on his way to do a late shift at the Mandrake Room. As soon as he spotted Billy and Les his eyes lit up and a grin wider than Sydney Heads spread across his face.

'Well, well, well,' his deep rough voice boomed out loud enough for everyone to hear from Kelly Street down to Garden Island. 'And how are the two lovers tonight. Did old Danny tip youse into a good thing there on Saturday night or what?'

Billy suppressed a groan and nodding his head very po-faced, quickly turned away and tried to dissolve into the brick wall he was leaning against.

'G'day Danny,' said Les with a bit of a smile. 'How y' goin'?'

'Good as gold,' replied Danny, the grin on his face getting bigger, he'd been dying to see the boys all week. Being a laid-back married man with five kids he loved nothing better than a bit of gossip or scandal to tell his mates on the wharves and he thought he was definitely on to a good thing on this occasion. 'So how did youse go on Saturday night? Come on Billy, give us the guts son. What happened with that spunky little blonde?'

'Nothin',' replied Billy shortly, quickly turning away again.

'Nothin'? What do you mean nothin'?'

'You heard. Nothin'. We went back to the hotel, had a cup of coffee in the foyer and pissed off. All right?' Billy half turned his back on Danny and faced the wall again.

Danny stood there for a moment as the grin on his face turned into more of a mystified smile. 'Is he fair dinkum?' he said turning to Les.

'You heard what the man said,' replied Les, shrugging his shoulders as the lightest hint of a devilish smile started to flicker around his eyes.

Danny stood there for a few seconds slightly dumbfounded. 'Well I'll be buggered,' he said, turning back to Billy. 'I thought you would have been a walk-up start with that little blonde. Christ she was all over you like ants at a picnic when you left the Drake.'

Danny shook his big head again. 'Well I'll be stuffed.' He paused for a moment, then smiled at Norton. 'So I suppose you

205

would have missed out on the fat one too, Les. Still, that's understandable. I mean, what self-respecting tart, even if she was a bat, would want to jump in the cot with you?' Danny grinned and gave Norton a bit of a slap on the shoulder then turned back to the still unsmiling Billy.' 'But I can't understand Rock Hudson over here missin' out. I mean, he is half a good sort.'

Billy still didn't say anything, in fact it was almost rude the way he ignored big Danny.

Norton chuckled to himself at Danny's cheeky remark and just stood there with his hands in his pocket idly kicking at a piece of chewing gum encrusted on to the footpath with the toe of his boot.

'That's the way it goes,' he said.

'Ahh. So the big night was a bit of a bummer,' said Danny.

'Yeah, something like that,' replied Les.

'Well that's got me beat. I was expecting youse to have great tales to tell me tonight. Especially you, Billy.' Billy continued his sullen silence, still trying his best to ignore Danny. 'Instead, the night's turned out to be a disaster.'

Norton continued scuffing at the piece of chewing gum on the footpath, then glanced up at Big Danny, a strange smile flickering around his eyes.

'Well Danny. I wouldn't say the night was a complete disaster,' he said evenly, as Billy turned around slowly at the tone of Norton's voice.

'Yeah?' Danny's ears immediately started to prick up. 'Why, what happened?'

'Well,' said Norton. 'Even though I wasn't real keen to go there in the first place. And I got lumbered with an ugly sheila and wasted all my money and didn't get to bed till nearly 6am. I suppose you could say I had a prick of a night. Well, maybe I did. But I know one thing for sure.'

'Yeah. What's that?'

'Billy dead set had a ball ... didn't you mate?'

Fishin' for Red Bream

'Now, what's the story again Les? You want to go training later today because you're going fishing Monday. Is that right?' Billy handed Les a can of Fourex and took a long, refreshing pull on his bourbon and dry. It was about 3.30 on a hot, sticky Sunday morning in summer. Saturday night at the Kelly Club was just over, the last punter had left the club and they were seated in Price's office watching and drinking quietly as Price and George Brennan got the last of the money counted and almost ruptured their spleens trying to stuff it into the safe.

'Yeah, that's right,' replied Les, taking a decent sort of pull on his can of beer, then belched lightly into the back of his hand. 'I'll meet you down at Gales at 12. We'll do two or three hours then go and have a drink. I know for sure I won't feel like training after fishing all Monday morning.'

'How come?' Billy had a bit of a smile on his face as he asked.

''Cause I get seasick. I've never been outside fishin' before and I know for sure I'm gonna get crook.'

'Who are you going fishing with?' Price stood behind Les, dusting his hands together, he'd been half listening to the boys while he put the money in the safe.

'Gary Jackson,' said Les turning around slowly. 'He's got a boat down the boat-sheds at Ben Buckler. He's been after me to come for weeks.'

'You're not going out fishing with Jacko are you?' said Brennan. 'Christ, I hope you've got a decent set of ear plugs. Gary'd talk the leg off an iron pot. You'll end up throwing him overboard.'

'He's not that bad is he?' said Les.

'Not that bad,' laughed Price, as he got everyone another drink. 'You know what his nickname is don't you? The All-Night Night Chemist. Never shuts up.' He turned to George Brennan. 'What'd that bookie from City Tatts say to him down the boatsheds one day. He said Gary if you were a racehorse your breeding would be Haveachat out of Talkalot.'

'That's Gary,' replied George. 'He'd talk under six feet of wet cement.'

'Oh well,' shrugged Norton, finishing his can of beer. 'I don't give a stuff as long as I get a few fish.' He tossed the empty can in a small rubbish bin and started on his fresh one.

No matter what the others said, Les was still looking forward to going fishing on Monday. Being from the country he'd never really been outside in a boat before and it was a bit of a big deal for him and Jackson had been chasing him for ages to come with him one day.

Gary was a member of the Ben Buckler Fishing Club and had an old 14-foot aluminium runabout which he kept in the club house round the rocks at North Bondi. He was a pretty popular bloke around the Eastern Suburbs where he used to own a butcher-shop which he'd sold to get a cleaning run and now that he had more time to himself he spent most of it out fishing. The best way to describe Gary would be a roly-poly version of Jack Lemmon the film star, with shorter hair and a much fatter face. Gary was a red-hot Easts supporter and used to do a fair bit of back-slapping down the Bondi Rex, especially if the team was running well. He also used to back-slap most of the heavies around the area and being the heaviest of them all that's how Les got invited to go fishing. Gary's only fault, if any, was that he did like to talk a lot — especially with about half a dozen middies under his belt, and being an irrepressible gossip Gary was also dying to tell all the team down the Rex how he had Big Les Norton out in his boat.

'So I can expect a big feed of fresh fish up here next week, eh?' said Price. 'Couple of nice snapper would be nice. What about you George, you want to put your order in too?'

'Ohh yeah, why not? Save me going down to Doyles. A nice big flathead'll do me Les. About 5 pound. What about you, Billy?'

'Mmhh, I wouldn't mind a couple of those nice big soup-plate leather jackets. No bones, no scales, they're the grouse. Couple of those'll do me Les.'

'Anything else youse might like while I'm out there?' said Norton sucking lustily on his can of Fourex. 'How-about some king prawns, or maybe a few dozen oysters. Or if you like I can dive over the side and bring up a few pearls. Just name it.'

They sat around for about another half an hour drinking and cracking jokes, though most of the jokes were directed at Les. Then they locked up. Les and Billy saw Price safely to his car where they said their goodbyes and they all drifted home.

It was oppressively hot and humid the next day, but Billy and Les still trained for almost two and a half hours — they were dehydrated when they finished and dryer than two Pommy towels when they got to the Clovelly Hotel about three, where they proceeded to drink enough beer to launch a Polaris submarine — the first six schooners didn't even touch the sides of their throats. When Les got home about 7.30 he was roaring, but when he got down the boat-sheds at six the following morning after a good night's sleep he felt enormous and keen as mustard for a morning's fishing.

There were only two other cars in the parking area at the top of Ramsgate Avenue when Norton drove his battered Ford sedan in there that morning; one he recognised as Gary's spotless Ford station wagon and an old abandoned Holden silently ending its days in a pile of rust and corrosion. The sun had just risen on an absolutely beautiful day, tinting the few tiny white clouds in the turquoise sky with orange and yellow as it bathed the velvety green sea with its warmth. A long black shadow formed by the big rock on the point with its remaining bronze mermaid, and seemed to point like a huge ebony finger towards the beach as he jauntily trotted down the stairs with their dilapidated white wooden railing, to the boat-sheds. A mangy looking one-eyed cat scurried quickly out of Norton's way and ducked under one of several boats arranged neatly in two rows outside the club-house, where it sat blinking at him with its one good eye as he strode past to the open door. Gary had his back to him and was testing an outboard motor in a rusty, 44 gallon drum full of water. He turned it off just as Norton stopped behind him.

'G'day Gary,' said Les waving his fumes aside with his hand. 'How's it goin' mate? Top day.'

'G'day Les,' said Gary enthusiastically as he spun around. 'How y' goin'? Looking forward to the big day's fishing?'

'Bloody oath,' grinned Norton.

Gary was wearing an old faded pair of blue Stubbies, an Easts jumper minus the sleeves and a cap something like Topol wore in 'Fiddler on the Roof'; he hadn't had a shave for at least a week. Norton had on a sweat-shirt, jeans, sneakers and one of those mesh-back baseball-type caps. In his hand was a huge overnight bag.

'Jesus,' said Gary, 'what've you got in the bag, Les? We're only goin' out for a few hours, we're not spendin' a month up the Sepik River.'

Norton held up the massive bag, grinning sheepishly. 'I couldn't find my little one in the dark this morning to tell you the truth so I had to grab this one. I've only got a bit of tucker and something to drink.' He didn't mention the bottles of Quells and Dramamine tablets. 'Besides, I'll need a bag this big for all my fish, won't I?'

Gary winked as he put some more petrol in the outboard motor and loosened the clamps holding it on to the 44 gallon drum.

'What do you reckon we'll get anyway?' asked Les. 'Any jewies? What about snapper?'

'We'll be fishin' for red bream,' replied Gary, with all the sagacious wisdom of an expert. 'There's a ton of reddies on at the moment, me n' Tom the Beach Inspector got 30 the other mornin'.'

'Thirty. Fair dinkum?'

'Yeah, my oath. They're on at the moment. Anyway, give us a hand with this motor, will you?'

With Norton doing most of the lifting they easily manhandled the outboard motor out of the steel drum and over and on to Gary's weather-beaten aluminium runabout, where he clamped it to a wooden plate at the stern with two large wing-nuts. He told Les to throw his bag in the boat while he went into the club-house, returning with a large plastic, box-type container full of fishing lines, bait, knives and other fishing paraphernalia which he carefully placed in the middle of the boat.

'Now, what do I owe you for juice and bait Gary? Ten bucks, is that right?'

'Yeah. That'll do,' replied Gary magnanimously.

Les had agreed previously to weigh in $10 for gas and bait and though Gary's meagre motor would be flat out using 75¢ worth of gas in a day and the bait Gary would have caught beforehand, Les wasn't to know this. Gary always liked to make a little profit on anything he did. If he could take Les fishing for a few hours, get plenty of fish himself and end up $9.25 in front on the day, that was a pretty good result for Gary — not to mention the fact that he sold most of his fish to an Italian mate who had a restaurant in Bondi. When it came to making a dollar stretch further than anyone else Gary ran second to Les in a very tight photo-finish.

'You got change of a rock lobster?' said Norton, pulling a $20 bill out of his jeans.

'No,' said Gary, taking the twenty and pocketing it in the fob pocket of his Stubbies. 'I didn't bring any money with me. I'll have to fix you up when we get back, or through the week. Okay?'

'Yeah all right, I s'pose,' said Les, a little apprehensively.

'Right,' said Gary. 'I'll lock the club up and we'll be on our way.' While he was doing this Les slipped his sneakers off, tossed them in the boat and rolled his jeans up past his shins. Gary returned and with one either side they slid the relatively light boat over some splintery lengths of wood set into the concrete outside the clubhouse, down an old slimy wooden ramp and across some equally slimy weed-covered rocks, where Norton almost went on his arse, to the water's edge where Gary said to wait for a swell. A small wave surged gently around them and they pushed the boat out on to it; Norton flopped clumsily in the front and Gary hopped up on to a seat in the back as adroitly as Ron Quinton jumping up on Gunsynd. In almost the same quick, competent movement he kicked the motor over and they were on their way.

From the moment they left Gary was talking incessantly, but over the roar of the outboard Les could hardly hear him; if he could he wouldn't have taken any notice anyway — this was all new to him and he was more than a little excited. With the salt spray stinging his eyes and splashing over his clothes and the smell of old fish and two-stroke in his nostrils, mixing with the throb of the outboard motor and the screeching of a few seagulls flying overhead, Les felt as if he was setting off on some great adventure. His enthusiasm and adrenalin were surging.

When they got out past the Big Rock on the point and started hitting into a few swells, the enthusiasm and adrenalin inside Les started to turn into a rather shithouse feeling in his stomach. By the time they got another hundred metres out, Norton's face was starting to look like an Italian flag. He rummaged quickly through his bag, found his Dramamine tablets and unscrewing a large bottle of lemonade quickly washed two down.

Looking back at the shoreline it seemed as if they were out 500 kilometres; Bondi seemed to be on the other side of the moon. Norton swallowed and watched some water splashing round on the bottom of the boat and it was then he realised that all that was between him and at least 50,000 metres of water, not to mention monstrous tiger and white pointer sharks plus sting-rays, barracudas and Christ only knows what else was about half an inch of corroded aluminium.

'Hey, how far out do you want to go?' he protested. 'What are you fishin' for? Fuckin' black marlin?'

'I got to find me mark,' yelled Gary over the noisy motor.

'Your what?'

'Me mark.' Gary explained to Les how he lined up with Long Bay Rifle Range and North Bondi Surf Club. That was the mark and that was the reef they fished off.

Gary squinted towards Maroubra, then to North Bondi and cut the motor. 'Here we are now,' he said turning the motor completely off and tossing a kellick over the side. 'Righto, reddies, here comes uncle Gazz.'

Within what seemed like a matter of seconds Gary went deftly through the bait-box in the middle of the boat, Norton had a reel shaped like a large plastic dough-nut thrust in his hands and Gary was baited up and ready to cast over the side.

'Now, you know how to bait a hook and all that, don't you?' said Gary looking slightly suspiciously at Les as he dangled the weighted hook in his hand.

'Yeah, of course I do,' replied Norton gruffly, ripping a piece of half-rotten yellowtail out of a mess of smelly, blood-stained newspapers Gary had spread out in the middle of the boat. 'I have been bloody fishin' before, you know.' Which was true. Les had fished for Murray-cod and perch on the banks of the Narran back at Dirranbandi with quite good results; but that was a lot different to bobbing up and down in a rusty boat out in, what

212

seemed like to Les, the middle of nowhere. He jammed the piece of yellowtail on his hook and dropped it over the side not long after Gary.

Thirty minutes later Gary had six reddies which he quickly unhooked, belted over the head with a lump of wood and tossed in a wet sugar-bag lying near his feet. Another 30 minutes went by and Gary had another five fish. Norton hardly got a bite.

Another hour or so passed by with Gary pulling in a reddie about every five minutes and not one under a pound and a half. Norton still hadn't broke his duck.

'Christ, what's goin' on here?' said Les, starting to get a bit shitty as he baited up again and cast over the side. 'I'm using the same bait, the same hooks and I'm getting fuck all. You're pulling them in like Zane bloody Grey.'

'Just keep goin' mate,' said Gary, pulling in another fish. 'They'll hit you sooner or later.' He was starting to get a bit toey with Les and didn't want to appear to be rubbing it in to him about his not getting any fish — though he wouldn't be able to tell all the team down the Rex about Norton's dismal effort quick enough. Not to mention his seasickness.

Norton had stopped getting the shits, now he was just getting bored and fidgety; the Dramamine tablets had settled his stomach and his sea-sickness had almost disappeared until Gary pulled out his breakfast. Four packets of Smiths chips, two cans of Coca-Cola and a cigarette. Norton started looking around in disgust and boredom. Something in a bag near Gary's feet caught his eye.

'Hey, what's that in there?' he asked. 'Are they binoculars?'

'Yeah,' replied Gary. 'I bring 'em with me just in case there's a bit of fog around and I can't find me mark.'

'Give us a look.' Gary handed Les the binoculars.

Norton wiped the lenses with a dry part of his sweat-shirt, adjusted the dials to suit his eyes and started peering idly towards the horizon. He still wasn't getting any fish so he wound the line around his big toe and let it dangle over the side. There wasn't a great deal to see. He watched a flock of screeching seagulls sitting on top of and diving into a school of surface fish in the early morning mist off to their left. The cliffs at Coogee and Maroubra were too far away and too hazy to make anything out clearly. The same at Bondi. He watched a jumbo-jet go overhead, then swung back to the ocean. A freighter steaming steadily towards their boat seemed to be almost on top of them, 'Christ,' he said out loud, removing the binoculars, but when he did he could see that it was at least seven or eight hundred metres away. As it approached them he started viewing it intently.

'The Shinseing Maru,' he could make out clearly on the side — an Australian flag flew off the stern and a Japanese one was fluttering up near the smoke-stack. It's a dirty looking bloody thing, he thought, studying the rust and chipped paint through the binoculars. The decks were deserted but a sudden movement caught his eye.

A hatchway opened on the deck mid-ship, and out stepped an Asian seaman wearing a bulky, dark-blue, Mao type jacket. He moved cautiously over to the rail, glanced up and down the deserted deck then from under his jacket produced a parcel with a bright orange marker buoy attached, which he threw over the side of the ship. Norton watched it sail down into the ocean where it was momentarily lost in the foaming prop-wash at the ship's stern where it soon reappeared clearly bobbing up and down in the ship's wake. He watched it for a few moments then put the binoculars in his lap. 'Hey Gary,' he said, 'how about we try fishin' somewhere else for a while.'

'You're kiddin' aren't you?' replied Gary, his jaw dropping slightly. 'This is the spot here. This is where they're on.'

'Yeah, maybe for you. All I'm gettin's a wet arse and it's cost me ten bloody bucks. What about just over there a couple a hundred metres near those seagulls. I want to have a go at some surface fish for a while.'

'Ahh shit,' Gary started reeling in his line. He was protesting a bit but he was absolutely terrified of Les, not that Les would have done anything, but he'd also be able to tell the team down the Rex how Norton threatened to job him if he didn't do what he said. It all added to the drama. 'Yeah all right,' he sighed.

'I'll drive,' said Les.

'You don't drive a boat. You steer it.'

'Whatever. Come here and start the thing.'

Gary got the motor started and swapped positions with Les, moving up to the front. Les wrapped his huge, gnarled fist round the tiller and with a very disgruntled Gary facing him steered towards the marker-buoy roughly 300 metres in front of them.

214

Halfway there he slowed down and started pointing excitedly to Gary's right.

'Hey, what was that?' he cried out, half rising from the seat.

'What was what?' said Gary, turning towards where Les was pointing.

'Over there, about 200 metres. The biggest bloody shark I ever seen. Christ.'

'Where?'

'Over there, can't you see it. Here, take the binoculars.' With one eye on Gary and another on the marker buoy bobbing up and down about 100 metres away Les handed Gary the binoculars. 'Now have a bloody good look, Gary, 'cause if it's a shark I'm pissin' off out of here.'

Gary took the binoculars and started scanning the ocean intently, though he was half convinced Les was seeing things. About 50 metres from the marker buoy Les slowed down and swapped sides on the tiller. 'Look there it is again,' he called out, 'keep looking Gary you can't miss it.' With Gary looking the other way through the binoculars Les cut the motor and cruised right up alongside the small orange buoy roughly the same size as a beer bottle. With one sure swift movement he scooped the buoy up, with the parcel attached underneath, into the boat and straight into his huge overnight bag. Still peering through the binoculars Gary didn't see a thing.

'There's nothin' out there,' he said putting down the binoculars and rubbing his eyes.

'Yeah?' said Les. 'Oh well maybe I was seeing things I s'pose. Anyway the seagulls have pissed off so those surface fish are probably gone too. We may as well go back to where we were. Here, you can drive.'

Gary took the tiller, looked at Norton and shook his head. 'Steer Les. Steer.'

'Whatever,' grinned Norton from the front of the boat.

They returned to their original spot, Gary dropped the kellick over the side and they resumed fishing with pretty much the same result as before — Gary pulling in a reddie about every five minutes, Norton scarcely getting a bite. Another 30 minutes or so went by with Les getting more than just bored and a bit restless by now; by now he was starting to get the shits. He could see he wasn't going to get any fish and he was also just about breaking his neck to see what was in the package he'd fished out of the water so he decided to tell Gary it might be a good idea if he took him back to the boat-sheds. He was about to say something when he noticed a large, sleek power-boat come roaring up about 300 metres from where they were fishing, slow down and start systematically criss-crossing the area where Les had picked up the parcel.

The streamlined black boat looked like something straight out of a James Bond movie. It was at least 6 metres long with chrome rails running everywhere, a half cabin was towards the front and at the rear two monstrous Evinrude motors churned the water as they throbbed away in perfect unison. Two men appeared to be on board, one at the controls up front and another at the back searching the water with a pair of binoculars hanging on a strap round his neck.

'Noisy bastards,' said Gary. 'I wish they'd piss off. They're scaring all the fish.'

For about 20 minutes the two men searched the area with Norton watching them intently out the corner of his eye; eventually the boat stopped and they went into a huddle. The binoculars flashed in Norton and Gary's direction then the boat spun around and moved steadily towards them, slowing down about 10 metres away, where it slowly circled them — Norton waved casually, at the same time getting a good look at the two men.

Both of them were very grim faced. The one steering looked to be about 30, with clean-cut blond hair and wide shoulders; a pair of heavy mirrored sunglasses prevented Norton from getting a good look at his face but he noticed he had a rather large, bulbous type of nose. The other was in his late 40s, very stocky with thick, silvery-brown hair; for his age he was quite handsome and looked as if he could have been a sportsman of some type at one stage. Both men wore heavy, Thai-style gold chains round their wrists and neck; two large diamond rings sparkled on the older man's fingers.

'Hey mate,' Garry called out to the man steering the boat. 'Give us a bit of a go willya? You're scarin' all the fish.'

The two men stared at them expressionless, finally the older man jerked his head towards the open sea and the boat moved away. As it did Norton took a mental note of the name and number on the side. DZ983N 'Senorita'.

'Fuckin' gigs in their power-boats,' muttered Gary. 'They give me the shits.'

'Yeah,' replied Norton. 'Anyway, listen Gary. I might get you to ...' Suddenly there was a violent tugging on Norton's line. 'Hey hold on, I got a bloody fish.' Excitedly, Norton started reeling in his line, coming up with a fair sized, speckly brown fish not unlike a groper. 'There y'are, look at that,' he said happily, watching it flopping around the bottom of the boat. 'At least I got a feed.'

Gary started laughing at the back of the boat. 'You can't eat them Les, it's a wirra.'

'A what?'

'A wirra. They're no good. You can't even use 'em for bait.'

Norton was absolutely flabbergasted. 'Are you fair dinkum?'

'Yeah, fair dinkum. You can't eat 'em. They taste like shit.'

'You mean to tell me I've been out here all morning, I finally get a fish and I can't bloody eat it.'

'Sorry mate.'

'Right, well that's fuckin' it.' Norton unhooked the fish, threw it back in the water, wound up his line and tossed it in the plastic box near Gary's feet. 'Take me back to the bloody boat-sheds.'

Gary still couldn't help but laugh but in a way he was relieved Norton was going in; it was getting to be an embarrassment. 'All right Les,' he said, starting up the motor. As they pulled off Norton noticed the black power-boat was still scouring the area.

'Thanks anyway, Gary,' muttered Les as he jumped out of the boat with his bag in one hand and his sneakers in the other.

'That's all right Les, anytime. I'm going back out though while they're still on. I'll see you later.'

'Yeah righto, go for your life.' Gary spun the boat around and headed back out. 'Hey, what about my ten dollars?' yelled Les. Over the noisy outboard motor Gary didn't hear him and just waved back. Great, thought Les. He climbed the stairs outside the boat-shed, got in his car and headed home.

He had a quick clean-up, then over a large mug of coffee he started to examine the parcel he had just appropriated. He removed the orange marker buoy and with a kitchen knife carefully cut through the thick plastic tape binding several layers of heavy, brown tar-paper. Underneath this was a heavy, black plastic bag securely bound with more thick plastic tape. This covered what appeared to be a quantity of white powder in two more clear plastic bags heavily bound with more thick plastic tape. He gently cut through the tape binding the remaining plastic bag, opened it and sprinkled some out on to a piece of plain paper. Also inside the plastic bag was a short note.

'M. Important. Our new phone and address. I will be in touch. T. 650 Plaza Centralos. La Paz. Bolivia. 838.8224.'

He wrote a copy of the note and put the original back in the plastic bag then started to examine the remaining powder on the piece of paper. Not being into drugs Norton wasn't quite sure what he had. If there was a joint going round at a party he'd have a toke on that but pills and powder didn't interest him. If anything they repulsed him, though he had a fair idea what he'd found.

The white, shiny powder wasn't really like a powder, more granulated not unlike a small version of Lux soap-flakes. Under the kitchen light it glistened noticeably and when he ran it between his fingers it had a slimy, silky feel about it. With his little finger he dabbed a bit on the tip of his tongue — it immediately went numb in that area.

'Uh huh,' he said out loud, 'the old Okefenoke.' He looked at it for a few moments rubbing his chin thoughtfully then placed it on a set of kitchen scales. So, I've got myself a kilogram of cocaine he thought. Now what am I gonna do with it?

He wrapped the kilogram of cocaine up exactly as he'd found it and hid it carefully in his bedroom; the amount he'd sprinkled out he folded up in a small piece of Alfoil he tore off a roll in the cupboard. He got a can of Fourex out of the fridge and sat there staring at it intently, thoughtfully stroking his chin the whole time. After about 20 minutes he picked up the phone and dialled a number.

'Hello Price, it's Les. How are you?'

'Les Norton the famous fisherman. How did you go son?'

Without mentioning anything about the cocaine Les told Price briefly what happened. When Price had finished laughing Les spoke.

'Price, have you still got that contact at the Maritime Services Board?'

'Sure. You want something do you?'

'Maybe. All right if I give him a call?'

218

'Sure. It's extension 066, ask for Grahame Keogh. Tell him who you are and tell him I said it's sweet.'

'Okay. Thanks Price.' They chatted for a few minutes then Les hung up and rang the MSB, getting through almost immediately to Keogh.

'Just hold on a minute,' said Grahame, 'while I run that number through the computer. DZ983N, is that right?'

'Yeah.' Les waited patiently on the end of the line.

'You there?'

'Yeah.'

'The boat belongs to a Martin Reynolds. 16 Harbour View Crescent, Rose Bay. His phone number's 307 0552.'

'Thanks a lot, Grahame. I owe you a drink some time.'

'No worries. Say hello to Price for me.'

Norton hung up, thought for a moment then decided to leave it till 4pm before he'd ring Martin Reynolds. He vacuumed the house, made a chicken casserole and did a bit more cleaning up. Then it was 4pm. He opened a can of Fourex and dialled the number Keogh had given him.

'Hello,' said a voice at the other end.

'Yeah, is Martin Reynolds there please?'

There was a pause for a moment. 'I'll see if he's in. Who's calling?'

'Tell him it's a mate of his from South America. I'm sellin' bananas.'

There was another pause, longer this time. 'Just wait there,' said the voice cautiously.

After a while another voice came to the phone, Norton could also hear the click of another phone being picked up. 'Hello this is Martin. Who's this?' a voice said a little brusquely.

'G'day Marty, old son. I'll get straight to the point. Did you lose something this morning?'

There were a few seconds of silence. 'What are you talking about? Who is this?'

'I'm talking about a little brown parcel bound with plastic tape and full of ... well I don't think it's icing sugar.'

There was another silence. 'I don't know what you're talking about. Who the fuck is this anyway?'

'You don't know what I'm talking about, eh? How about T's new phone number and address in Bolivia. Is that any good to you?'

There was silence for a few more seconds. Norton could hear Reynolds's laboured breathing over the phone. 'Who the fuckin' hell are you smart arse? What do you want?'

'You know what I want shitbags. And you know what I've got. I'll ring you back at 9.30 sharp tomorrow morning. I'll sort it out with you then.'

Norton hung up abruptly and laughed to himself. He got another can of beer from the fridge and went out in the backyard to relax on his banana-chair and wait for Warren to come home.

Warren arrived home from the advertising agency about six. After discussing the day's fishing with Les over a couple of beers he had a shower, then tore into the chicken casserole, almost matching Norton plate for plate.

'You sure can put it away for a little bloke, can't you Woz,' said Les, running a slice of Vogels around his empty plate.

'You're not a bad cook for a big hillbilly,' replied Warren. 'I always said there was a bit of old sheila in you. I was expecting fish, though.'

Norton laughed then got up and made some coffee; pouring them a cup each. 'You going out tonight?' he asked, as he sat back down at the table.

'I was, but I might give it a miss. I had a bit of a big one at the Sheaf last night. I got a little chick does a few jobs for Penthouse I can take out though — if I wanted to.'

'Yeah? Oh well, no good going out romancin' if you're not up to it.' Les poured some more coffee and eased himself back from the table. 'Hey Warren, you like a smoke and a snort and that don't you?'

'Ohh yeah,' replied Warren carefully. 'I don't mind the odd drug now and again. Why?'

'You want some coke?'

'Some cocaine?' Warren gave Les a double blink.

'Yeah. You want some? A chick owes me a favour, gave it to me up the Game the other night. I don't use it so here, you can have it if you want.' Norton took the foil package out of the top pocket of his Levi shirt and tossed it across the table to Warren. 'I don't know if it's any good, though.'

'Jeez thanks, Les.' Warren picked up the Alfoil and began to unwrap it. 'It sure looks all right,' he said, squeezing some gently between his fingers. He looked up at Norton and smiled. 'I might have a toot now.'

'Go for your life.'

Warren went to his room, returning with a small shaving mirror and a tiny pocket-knife. He took a healthy scoop of cocaine, placed it on the mirror and began chopping and crushing it up with the heel of the pocket-knife. Norton watched with intrigue.

'So that's how you do it, eh.'

'Yeah, got to crush all the rocks mate.'

'And what would you jet-setting wombats pay for a deal of that?'

Warren stopped crushing the cocaine for a moment and looked at the Alfoil packet. 'There's at least a weight gram there. About $300.'

'Three hundred dollars for that?'

'Oh, shit yeah.'

'So a kilogram of that shit's worth 300 grand.'

'I'm talking street price. A kilo'd probably cost 150 to 200 thousand. But by the time they step on it it'd bring half a million.'

'What do you mean step on it?'

'Cut it with Glucodin and Lactogen.'

Norton shook his head incredulously. 'And they pay 300 bucks for that?' He shook his head again. 'There sure are some nice mugs around. And I've just given you 300 bucks worth. I'm puttin' your rent up next week.'

Warren laughed. 'It's just God's way of telling you you've got too much money.'

Satisfied the cocaine was crushed up finely enough, he formed the glistening powder into two white lines roughly the same length and size as a match-stick. He took a $20 bill from his pocket, rolled it into a tube and stuck it in his right nostril. 'This is called having a toot, Les,' he said, bending his head over the mirror. Holding the tube in one nostril with his right hand and blocking the other with his left he moved the tube slowly along one of the lines, sniffing it all deeply into his right nostril. Then he did the same with his left.

Norton watched carefully as he sat up. Nothing happened at first then Warren's eyes seemed to bulge out like two pink medicine-balls — he jumped up from the table and let out one mighty roar. 'Yaarrrhh!'

'Jesus Christ Les!' he yelled. 'Where did you get that?'

'Is it any good?'

'Any good? It's unbelievable. I feel like I'm 8 feet tall and I'm a genius.'

'I'll soon sort that out,' laughed Norton, getting up from the table.

Warren sprang round in front of him. 'All right you big goose. Out the back now. Come on.' Warren started giggling and throwing punches at Norton; there wasn't a lot of power in them but they seemed to come from everywhere.

'Christ, you are off your head.'

Within a matter of minutes Warren had cleaned up all the mess in the kitchen, made a date with the girl from Penthouse, got changed into his best clobber and was hovering in front of Norton ready to go out. He'd been moving that fast his feet scarcely seemed to touch the ground.

'Well, I'm on my way,' he said, waving his hands around excitedly, his eyes still bulging out all over the place. 'Don't bother waiting up for me, Mum.' He zoomed down the hallway almost leaving a vapour-trail. 'Thanks for that Les,' he called from the front door.

'You're welcome.' The door slammed and the last thing Norton heard was the tyres on Warren's Celica as he lay rubber halfway up Cox Avenue.

Les had a few cans, watched a movie on TV for a while then decided to have an early night. He slept quite soundly, though he did lie there deep in thought for a while at first. The numbers 150 to 200 thousand kept running through his brain.

He rose early the next morning and drove down to Centennial Park for a run, getting back about 8.30 to find Warren stumbling around the kitchen trying to make a cup of coffee. He was in an absolutely appalling state. His eyes were running like a couple of taps and his face looked like something you'd see on a pirate flag. Every few seconds he'd sneeze violently then sit there sniffing and mopping his eyes.

'Have a good time last night?' asked Les.

'Yeah,' croaked Warren feebly, sneezing again.

'You look like a fuckin' shithouse.'

222

'I feel worse.'

'Good stuff that coke, eh?'

'At-choo.'

About an hour later Warren managed to make it out the front door to work. At 9.30 sharp, Norton rang Martin Reynolds.

'Hello Marty. It's your mate from yesterday. You want to talk a bit of business?'

'Talk,' was the brief reply.

'Right. Well you know I've got something of yours and if you're a real good bloke I might just let you have it back. And might I say it's very high quality stuff too. I had it tested last night and I'd say there's around 200 grand there — though by the time you vultures fill it full of powdered-milk and shit you'd be looking at closer to half a million.'

Reynolds didn't say anything but Norton could feel the hatred and venom over the line.

'I'm a reasonable man,' continued Les, 'and seein' as you're not a bad sort of a bloke I'll let you have it back for 75 grand. Fair enough?'

'How about I tell you to stick it in your arse and come looking for you, smarty?'

'Well, you can do that too, but I'll just turn it in to the cops along with your name and address and your mate T's in Bolivia and if that didn't fuck up your little operation I don't know what would. I'd probably get a reward.'

There was a tense silence for a few moments at the other end of the line. 'All right arseole, what do you want to do?'

'You know the old gun emplacement at the top of McKenzies Point Bondi, opposite Marks Field?'

'Yeah.'

'I'll meet you there at 4.30 sharp this afternoon. I'll be wearing a dark blue track-suit. You got that?'

'Yeah. And I'm really looking forward to meeting you.'

'Good. And like the man says on the TV: Bring your money with you.'

Norton hung up and stared thoughtfully at the phone for a few minutes. From the ominous tone of Reynolds' voice when he made that last remark he thought it might be a good idea to make another phone call.

'Hello Price. It's Les. How are you?'

223

'Good Les. What's up?'

'Nothing really. Is Eddie there?'

'Sure. I'll go get him.'

Norton waited patiently on the line while Price Galese went and got his number one hit-man. Eddie Salita.

'Hello Les. What's your trouble, son?'

'Hello Eddie. How's things? Listen, can you give me a hand for about 30 minutes this afternoon?'

'Sure. Why, something wrong?'

'Not really. I just gotta pick up some money off a bloke. There's a bone in it for you.'

'Yeah. Much meat on it?'

'Five grand.'

'Something.'

'Right. Well, be at my place at four this afternoon sharp. Bring a roscoe and I'll tell you all about it then, okay?'

'See you at 4 o'clock Les.'

Norton rang Billy Dunne and arranged to meet him down Gales Baths at 11.30 for a light workout and a swim, and maybe a couple of beers at the 'Bergs afterwards. He didn't mention anything to Billy about the cocaine caper and left about three to go home and wait for Eddie Salita to arrive. Eddie arrived shortly before four.

'Righto Les, what's the story?' he said, as he stepped briskly inside and seated himself comfortably on Norton's ottoman lounge. He was wearing running-shoes, black jeans, a camouflage T-shirt and a loose fitting black wind-cheater. With a green sweat-band wrapped round his head he looked like he'd just stepped off the cover of Soldier of Fortune magazine. As he eased himself back on the lounge, Norton noticed the .38 police special in a holster tucked up under his left arm and the .22 automatic in a smaller ankle holster bulging under his black jeans.

Norton gave Eddie a brief outline on what had happened and what was about to go down, including the amount of $75,000, and how he needed him in case Reynolds brought his mate with him and tried something shifty; if there was any gun-play Eddie could sort it out. He offered him the $5000 and told him there was more there if he wanted it.

Eddie laughed villainously, eased himself back further into the lounge and flexed his arms, stretching every wiry muscle from his shoulders down to his finger tips. 'Five grand's all right for half an hour's workout,' he said with a grin. 'I'd have done it for you for nothing Les, you know that. But I may as well cop the five.'

'Good on you Eddie. Thanks mate.'

'Sounds like a piece of piss anyway if you ask me,' said Eddie rising from the lounge and zipping up his windcheater. 'But if something happens and I do have to knock them we'll just toss them straight over the cliffs, get a boat and pick them up in the morning.' Norton nodded in agreement. Eddie smiled and threw Les an easy wink, but there was 12 months in the jungles of Vietnam in his eyes and business written all over his face. 'Let's go then,' he nodded his head towards the door. 'Your car or mine?'

They went in Eddie's Mercedes; five minutes later they were parked in Kenneth Street facing away from Marks Field.

With the kilogram of cocaine wedged down the front of his track-suit pants and his hands in the pockets of his track-suit top holding it, Norton set off across the windy park in the late afternoon sunshine for his meeting with Reynolds at the old gun emplacement. He was wearing a pair of dark sunglasses and had a small straw hat with the brim turned down squashed on to his head; he wanted to disguise his face from Reynolds as much as possible and at the same time look inconspicuous. He may as well have had a red, neon-sign flashing above him saying 'I am going to do a drug deal, then rob the nearest bank.' Eddie gave him a couple of minutes start, then checking there was no one around resembling Norton's description of Reynolds or his mate, moved off after him keeping to the steep edge of the park well to Norton's left.

A few minutes later an irridescent gold Buick Electra glided gently to a stop in Fletcher Street about 50 metres up from the park. Reynolds and his blond mate sat there quietly for a while before they got out.

'You know exactly what to do?' said a grim faced Reynolds as he locked the car.

'Exactly,' replied the other.

There was an old chipped wooden seat in the ancient gun emplacement; with his hands still in his pockets holding the cocaine Norton eased himself down on to it and spread his legs out comfortably in front of him. A stiff summer nor'easter was gusting across Bondi Bay sending 'the murk' from the sewage outlet underneath the golf links closer into the beach and almost blowing Norton's straw hat off as it whipped across McKenzies Point. Hardly any people were around. Even the late afternoon joggers were very few and far between, preferring to hang on the beach rather than run in the heat which had Norton in a sweat just sitting there as he waited for Reynolds and wondered where Eddie had got to. He'd scarcely had time to think on it when Reynolds and his blond mate appeared at the top of the steep grassy knoll facing the gun emplacement. They spotted Les, then after taking a good look around moved slowly down the grassy decline towards him. Both were wearing sunglasses and expensive Pierre Cardin track-suits. Reynolds was carrying a large brown-paper shopping bag folded in the middle. They looked quite sporty, Les thought as they got closer; Reynolds walked right up to him, the other stood at the entrance to the old gun emplacement.

'G'day Marty,' said Norton pleasantly. 'Nice day. Hello mate,' he called out to Reynolds' associate standing a couple of metres or so behind him. Reynolds' associate didn't say anything, he just stood there expressionless and flexing his muscles, trying his best to look tough. Incredibly enough, he had a small, thin cigar jutting out of the corner of his mouth. It was a pity the nor'easter kept blowing the ash and smoke away otherwise it could have curled up lazily under his eyes just like Clint Eastwood's in a cheap spaghetti western. Norton was terribly impressed.

'So what's doing, Marty?' inquired Les. 'I thought you might've come on your own but you've brought a heavy with you. Or is that just your bum boy? Doesn't really matter.'

'You can cut the shit, smart arse,' said Reynolds. 'You got the dope?' Behind him the other remained stonily silent but the muscles round his jaw were twitching considerably.

'I certainly have,' replied Norton patting the front of his track-suit. 'Is that the money is it?' he pointed to the paper bag in Reynolds' hand. 'I'll just give it a quick count if you don't mind.' Reynolds reluctantly handed him the paper bag, Norton opened it and quickled rifled through the bundles of 20s and 50s; from his observation of the great stacks of money at the Kelly Club, Norton could tell there was $75,000 there.

'Well, that seems in order,' said Les. 'Now, here's your dope.' He handed Reynolds the package of cocaine wrapped up almost exactly as he'd found it. 'That makes us square, Marty, and I must say it's been an absolute pleasure doing business with you. For a shit-pot, greasy dope pusher you're not a bad bloke.'

Reynolds stood there staring at Les then shook his head, a cruel, sardonic smile appeared on his face. 'Are you for real dumby?' he sneered. 'Do you really think I'm going to let a prick like you rip me off for 75 grand and get away with it? I thought you sounded like a hillbilly on the phone. Now I know for sure.'

'Jeez Marty,' protested Norton, a hurt look on his face. 'Don't be like that. I mean, where's your sense of fair play. I've done the right thing. Strewth, I was certain you'd be a man of your word.'

Reynolds still kept staring at Les, a look of disgust on his face. 'You poor simple goose,' he said slowly. 'All right Bradley, he's all yours.'

'It'll be a pleasure,' said Bradley, as he moved in from the entrance to the gun emplacement and stood in front of Norton.

'Ohh shit, you're not going to hurt me are you Brad?' said Les, holding the paper-bag full of money up in front of him in mock terror.

'No, I'm not going to hurt you, arseole. I'm going to shoot you.' Bradley eased a .32 automatic with a small silencer attached out from under his track-suit. 'Once in the knee, once in the pit of your stomach and one right in that big mouth of yours. Then you're going to set a new Australian high-dive record.'

'Jesus Brad, I wouldn't be slinging off at peoples facial appearances if I were you. Especially with that nose of yours. If it was any bigger you could rent it out as a double garage.' Bradley's face grimaced as he levelled the .32 at Les's knee.

'All right Brad,' said Norton, holding up his index-finger. 'If you're gonna shoot me fair enough, but there's just one thing I gotta say before I go. Marty, just take a look behind you will you.'

'Are you for real, hillbilly? That's the oldest trick in the book.' replied Reynolds contemptuously.

'Yeah, maybe it is but have a look anyway. Big bad Brad here can keep an eye on me.'

Reynolds slowly turned around to find himself staring down the barrel of Eddie Salita's .38 police special, held rock steady

227

about half an inch from the end of his nose. While they'd been talking Eddie had climbed up over the edge of the old gun emplacement, making about as much noise as a mouse pissing on a piece of cotton-wool. Standing there holding the .38 his face was an expressionless mask, his eyes cold and harder than two ball-bearings. Reynolds recognised him instantly and his face quickly turned grey as he suddenly found himself a hair's breadth away from being blown to eternity.

'Bradley. Don't make a move,' he cried out in terror. 'You know who this is?'

'Yeah, Brad, you fancy yourself as a gunman?' said Norton, still sitting casually on the old wooden seat with his legs spread out in front of him. 'Well that there's Eddie Salita and you've got about two seconds to drop your gun or your boss's brains get splashed all over the front of your nice Pierre Cardin track-suit, and yours'll get splattered all over these fuckin' rocks.'

'Do as he says for Christ's sake Bradley!' yelled the terrified Reynolds.

Watching Eddie out of the corner of his eye, Bradley's face started to drain of all colour and the cigar still in the corner of his mouth was twitching noticeably as he dropped the gun at Norton's feet. Eddie never moved the .38 a centimetre from Reynolds nose.

'Now, that's much better,' said Norton, picking up the gun at his feet. 'I hate these fuckin' things, they scare me.' He stood up and sent the .32 sailing out into space, and it soon disappeared into the dark green of the ocean.

With everything now firmly under control and not wishing to alarm any passers-by, Eddie lowered the .38 from the side of Reynolds' head and placed it firmly against his ribs, while Norton turned to confront the petrified Bradley. Norton's face looked like it was set in cement and icicles were almost forming round his mouth when he spoke.

'So Brad, you were going to shoot me in the knees and throw me over the cliff, eh?' He took the cigar from Bradley's quivering mouth and puffed on it till the hot tip was glowing brightly. 'That's not a very nice thing to do to somebody you've only just met, is it?' He took another puff on the cigar; sparks and ashes flew off into the wind. 'I suppose you like a bit of a snort yourself now and again, Brad. Yeah, with that big hooter you'd have to. Well try snortin' this.'

Norton jammed the burning cigar up into Bradley's left nostril and crushed it inside his nose; he screeched with pain as Norton forced him to the ground, squashing his oversize nose in a vice-like grip. Bradley made a feeble effort to punch Les in the balls — Norton just belted him several times in the side of the head with his massive fist, mincing his left ear to paste.

As he lay there moaning Les tore the parcel of cocaine from Reynolds' hands and slammed it heavily against the rough sandstone wall of the gun emplacement splitting it open. 'Your nose hurting is it Brad?' he hissed savagely, standing over the top of him. 'Well shove some of this up it.' Norton jerked Bradley's head up and smashed the parcel of cocaine into his bloodied face — it burst all over him like a flour bomb. 'Now get plenty up there Brad,' said Norton, grinding as much of the cocaine as he could up into Bradley's nose and mouth. Bradley coughed and gagged, nearly suffocating on the expensive white powder as what didn't go into his nose and mouth fell all over the ground and was quickly taken away with the afternoon nor'easter; Reynolds silently watched in horror as half a million dollars was suddenly gone with the wind.

When he'd finished with Bradley, Norton stood up and faced Reynolds. 'Take the gun out of his ribs Eddie.' Eddie removed the .38 and placed it back in his shoulder-holster. Norton stared at Reynolds for a couple of seconds then dropped him with a left-hook that shattered his jaw and smashed all his front teeth straight out of his head; he crashed into the sandstone wall of the gun emplacement and lay there out cold.

Norton stood there for a moment glowering over the two prostrate cocaine dealers, then satisfied he'd had his revenge he picked the bag of money up off the old wooden seat and turned to Eddie. 'Come on Eddie, let's hit the toe.'

They scampered up the grassy slope and with the wind at their backs laughed all the way as they jogged across Marks Park back to Eddie's Mercedes.

'That'd have to be the snort of all time, that one you just shouted Brad, Les,' chortled Eddie.

'Yeah. When he wakes up he'll be runnin' three-minute miles for the rest of his life.'

Back in the car Norton threw his hat and track-suit top on the back seat then opened up the paper shopping-bag and took out $10,000. 'There you are, Eddie,' he said, an odd sort of smile on his face, 'ten grand.'

'A nice ten, Les. What's this, a bonus?'

'No. I might have to get you to do a bit of overtime.'

'We haven't got to go and pick up more money have we?'

'My oath. There's a little cunt down the Rex owes me $10.'

A few minutes later they pulled up in Beach Road not far from the hotel. Eddie locked all their money safely in the boot of the car and they headed for the Rex.

'I hope he's in there,' said Les, patting his pocket as they crossed Glenayr Avenue. 'I haven't got a frankfurt on me. All the money's in the boot.'

'Yeah. I haven't got any either,' replied Eddie.

There was a bit of a team drinking in the shade out the front of the hotel, as soon as they saw who was approaching they quickly moved aside to let them through; when they got inside Les and Eddie stood at the doorway for a while, looking for Gary.

It was a scorching day outside and the bar of the Rex was packed with thirsty drinkers going at it hammer and tongs trying to wash away the summer heat. A chook raffle was in progress at one end and in a corner a group of men were laughing and playing darts. Several others were standing around the solitary pool-table listening to a twilight meeting at Randwick on a small transistor radio. As soon as the mob spotted Norton and Eddie standing motionless just inside the door a noticeable hush fell over the bar. It wasn't often Sydney's hardest street-fighter and most notorious gunman walked in the door, not together anyway. One word was on everyone's lips as they watched them looking steely eyed around the room. Trouble.

'There he is over there,' said Les, pointing to a small circle of drinkers standing near the wall between the dart-board and the pool-table.

Gary was in the middle of giving his avid audience an exaggerated description of Monday's fishing trip with Les Norton. Gary was about eight middies up and his jaws were galloping away like Phar Lap.

'Yeah, you should've seen it,' chortled Gary. 'We hadn't even got past the big rock and he starts spewin'. Fair dinkum, his face was green. With his red hair he looked like a Souths football jumper. Then after about six hours and him gettin' no fish the big bludger says "take me in or I'll job you". So I says to him . . .'

'Hey Gary,' cut in one of his croonies. 'Talking about big bludgers gonna job you. Take a look over your shoulder.'

Gary turned around to find a stony-faced Les Norton and an evil-looking Eddie Salita standing right behind him. Norton had just caught the last part of Gary's conversation and Gary's face suddenly turned the colour of bad shit.

'G'day Les. G'day Eddie,' he blurted out. 'How's things? I was just tellin' the boys you were a bit unlucky on Monday.'

'You got a minute, Gary? We'd like to see you about something,' said Norton, his voice dripping with menace.

'Yeah sure,' replied Gary wide-eyed. 'What's the matter?'

'You'll find out,' said Eddie.

Gary followed them over to the bar where several drinkers swiftly moved aside to give them plenty of room. Everyone in the place was wondering why they'd want to shoot or maim poor bloody Gary. He did have a bit of a big mouth but he never meant anyone any harm. It was quite a drama for a Tuesday afternoon.

'Right,' said Les to a very nervous Gary squashed in between them. 'I believe you owe me $10, Gary. Are you going to give it to me or do I hand you over to Eddie?'

Gary looked at Les and blinked. Next thing he whipped out a wallet thick with business cards and money, several of which fell on the floor as he spun a $10 bill out of it so fast Henry Lawson got giddy. 'Fair dinkum, Les I was going to drop it round to your house through the week. I hadn't forgot, honest.'

'That's all right Gary,' replied Norton, 'just as long as I know. Anyway, let me buy you a drink.'

'I'll get 'em. What do you want?'

'Just a middie of new. Eddie, what about you?'

'Middie of new'll do.'

Gary ordered the drinks and tried to make polite conversation while they waited for them — they arrived and he handed them around.

'Well,' said Gary, raising his glass. 'Here's to fishing. Though you didn't have much luck on Monday, did you mate?'

'Ohh, I wouldn't say that,' replied Norton slowly, taking a sip of his beer.

Gary looked at him and frowned. 'What do you mean. You fished all morning, got seasick twice, finished up with a lousy wirra, which you had to throw back, and I got 30 reddies. Jesus, I thought you'd have the shits for sure.'

Norton took another sip of beer, winked at Eddie and patted Gary on the shoulder. 'Well Gary,' he said, 'I might've got seasick and I mightn't have got any reddies, but I know one thing for certain.'

'What's that?'

'I sure finished up with a heap of rock lobsters.'

Robert G. Barrett
The Real Thing

Les Norton is back in town!

It all began in *You Wouldn't Be Dead For Quids* . . . And now there's more of it in *The Real Thing*.

Trouble seems to follow Les Norton like a blue heeler after a mob of sheep.

Maybe it's his job.

Being a bouncer at the infamous and illegal Kelly Club in Kings Cross isn't the stuff a quiet life is made of.

Maybe it's his friends.

Like Price Galese, the urbane and well-connected owner of the Kelly Club, or Eddie Salita who learnt to kill in Vietnam, or Reg Campbell, struggling artist and dope dealer.

But, then again, maybe Les is just unlucky.

Robert G. Barrett's five stories of Les Norton and the Kelly Club provide an entertaining mix of laughter and excitement, and an insight into the Sydney underworld; a world often violent and cynical, but also with its fair share of rough humour and memorable characters.

Peter Corris
A Cliff Hardy Collection

'Like his American mentors – Hammett and Chandler and
Ross MacDonald – Corris has succeeded over a series of
hard boiled novels in creating a recognisable, credible, all but
loveable shamus.'
DON ANDERSON – SYDNEY MORNING HERALD

'The main character in Peter Corris' fiction is not his private
detective but the city in which he lives and works; and his
presentation of Sydney – blowsy, rough, vital and corrupt,
but still sprawling, indolent and beautiful, is one of the most
distinct and satisfying things in his fiction.'
R. S. BRISSENDEN – THE NATIONAL TIMES

'Indigenous thrillers are better than any others, and the best
of all are Peter Corris' accounts of his Sydney private
detective, Cliff Hardy.'
MARK THOMAS – THE CANBERRA TIMES

'The sense of place is meticulous and revealing. It is also
mercifully unobtrusive . . . it's fine, devious, disreputable fun,
with substance, and we have at last an Australian
investigator to rank with Poirot and Wimsey, with Marlowe,
Lew Archer and Sam Spade.
VIRGINIA DUIGAN – THE NATIONAL TIMES

Archie Weller
The Day of the Dog

'I hate your guts, you little mixed-blood misfit . . . If it's the last thing I do I'm putting you back in Freo . . .'

'*The Day of the Dog* is not a pretty story and it does not have a pretty ending . . . Australian literature has gained a much-needed picture of black urban life . . .'
THE NATIONAL TIMES

'Perth is the city of *Day of the Dog* with the despair of Freo (Fremantle Gaol) looming always a few miles away . . . Weller tells his tale stylishly and with compassion, striking imagery and humour.'
AUSTRALIAN BOOK REVIEW

'. . . a fine achievement . . . convincing and straightforward. It comes from Western Australia; from Aborigines, part-Aborigines and poor whites.'
THE BULLETIN

'This is a book on behalf of the underdog . . . and the words behind the words are very angry indeed.'
OVERLAND

Gabrielle Lord
Fortress

'Can you hear me, bitch? We're coming to get you . . .'

It was only a one-teacher school in the little town of Sunny Flat.

It was a quiet morning until the four masked men arrived in the playground.

The nightmare had begun. Sally Jones and her pupils were victims of a kidnap raid that became an ordeal of terror.

As escape became an obsession, they discovered the sadistic brutality hidden behind the kidnappers' masks and the desperate violence that lay within themselves . . .

'This book marks the arrival of a writer of considerable talent.'

THOMAS KENEALLY